THE WARNING

"Some will call it a fluke storm, but old-timers here in Terrel know that the gusts that rocked Terrel's Peak on Halloween were no natural event. For the first time in over twenty years, no body washed up on the beach last week, and the evil that dwells within that twisted growth of rock was angry. Is probably still angry.

"Whatever the reason, the cliff is dangerous.

"And now it's angry.

"Consider this a caution.

"Over the past few years, the cliff has almost always left the townsfolk alone, in favor of luring outsiders to break themselves on the deadly rocks at its feet. But apparently no outsiders offered themselves for the evil to devour this Halloween.

"Someone from Terrel may be called upon to pay the price.

"Don't let it be you.

"Stay away from the cliff these next few days. If you value your life."

JOHN EVERSON

COVENANT

LEISURE BOOKS NEW YORK CITY

For Geri,
who taught me the value of a Covenant.

A LEISURE BOOK®

September 2008

Published by

Dorchester Publishing Co., Inc.
200 Madison Avenue
New York, NY 10016

ISBN 10: 0-8439-6018-3
ISBN 13: 978-0-8439-6018-1

The name "Leisure Books" and the stylized "L" with design are trademarks of Dorchester Publishing Co., Inc.

Printed in the United States of America.

10 9 8 7 6 5 4 3 2 1

ACKNOWLEDGMENTS

Thanks to Shane Ryan Staley, David Barnett and Charlee Jacob for friendship, critique and encouragement, doled out in appropriate measures when I most needed each.

To my dad for letting me turn his Wisconsin cottage into a writer's retreat to work on the final revisions of this manuscript, and to my wife Geri for letting me disappear into the world of *Covenant* for days at a time.

To Edward Lee, Gerard Houarner, Michael Laimo, Jasmine Sailing, Brian Keene, Bill Breedlove, Martin Mundt and Kathy Kubik, who have both inspired me with their visions and supported my own.

To Julie Flanders, Emil Adler and the rest of October Project for countless hours of inspirational listening; this book was produced in scattered periods over the course of several years, but one constant was the sound track of October Project music along with healthy repetitions of discs by Tanya Donelly, This Mortal Coil, Cocteau Twins, Loreena McKennitt, Wild Strawberries, A3, Toad the Wet Sprocket, New Order, the Cure and many more.

And finally, thanks to Cari Laird Jaro, who back in 1994 directly inspired this novel when she pointed out a newspaper clipping about a tavern perched on a cliff that happened to be an incredibly popular spot for suicides. That clipping is long lost, but the idea never left.

COVENANT

PROLOGUE

The cliff.

It called to him.

Touched him with . . . darkness.

Taunted him with a promise made long ago.

So long had he known, so long had he felt its pull that to-day, tonight, was an anticlimax.

A breath of the promise slid over the edge and tickled his nose. James inhaled, savoring its salty tang, its gravestone-cold reminder.

The cliff would kill him.

The pressure was firm at his back. There was no return, no escape. Was there a presence just there, in the wash of black ahead? In the rush of wind that slid naked across the booming surf below and drove hard up the steel gray rock to kiss his salty cheeks?

James cried aloud, his feeling caught, twisted and drained by the yawning night wind.

The vibration of the waves was palpable in the air. It rippled through his body. Its touch was icy, its grip absolute. He'd been born for this, spent nineteen years in preparation, and yet, now that the moment was upon him, he wondered if he could go through with it.

He thought of Cindy.

Put off the present and hug the past close.

She'd been so right for him. So giving. He thought of her pert smile, her upturned nose. Loved the way her hair had lolled loosely across her shoulders. Loved the taste of her eager mouth. Loved the way she'd lectured him against falling for the "traps" his mother set for him.

"Can't you see she needs a fall guy?" Cindy would complain, shaking him by the shoulders. She was so beautiful when she tried to throttle sense into his head. Her hands would grip their hardest—and he almost felt them.

"Wake up and walk out! Come with me to school in the fall."

"I don't have the money to go," he'd answer. "And my grades probably wouldn't get me in if I did."

"You could get in," she insisted. "And if you came with me and worked out on your own for a year, you could declare yourself independent and get financial aid. Please, Jamey. For me. Get away from her. Get out of this town."

But he hadn't left Terrel Heights.

Cindy had.

She wrote now and then, and sometimes he answered. But he couldn't follow her. And he could never have told her why. He couldn't have explained the grip of the cliff.

His destiny.

A shame he couldn't meet it with the moon at his face. Instead, this night was blighted by cloud, shrouded by fog. He shivered at the touch of the night. His toes hung out in damp space. A hundred feet down. Or more.

Against his back the pressure built. It was time.

He thought of those many days in the caves below. Those days of promises, of preparation. The spirit of the cliff was alive, he knew. It needed him. It hungered for him. His sacrifice would keep it from sucking the life from everyone in Terrel Heights. His soul, in exchange for thousands.

This year.

He only hoped Cindy didn't think too badly of him when she heard. She would never understand.

James surrendered. He felt the hands on his back, felt the electric surge of power pushing at him to fly from the edge, felt the hunger of the dark spirit that possessed the prominence. He cried out only once as he tumbled from the steep rock cliff to break his body on the worn stones below.

From high above, a keening voice moaned in reply.

The waves rushed hard against the cliff.

It tasted the offering in darkness.

And accepted the fruit of a covenant.

PART I
Questions

CHAPTER ONE

"Mobile Unit Three, this is Dispatch. Got a report of a jumper at the peak. Looks like we got another one, Bob. Your turn to go out there, I think. . . ."

Joe Kieran looked up at the short, static-filled squirt from the police band radio in the corner. As the new kid on staff, he had landed the unenviable job of night reporter—the guy who sits in the newsroom until the wee hours, pecking away at long-range, nondeadline stories while awaiting any breaking news that might come over the police band. If something did happen in Terrel at one A.M., he was the Johnny-on-the-spot for the *Times.* He would grab his reporter's notepad, hop in his car and speed across town to cover the story, phoning in the crucial details to Randy, his editor, if the paper was about to go to press. So far he remained unconvinced that *anything* happened in Terrel after six P.M. In two months on the job, he'd gotten in the car once, and that had turned out to be a false alarm.

No, being a reporter wasn't a glamorous job in the sleepy town of Terrel. Usually the police radio squawks consisted of noise complaints and domestic disturbances, neither a subject worthy of reporting on in the *Terrel Daily Times.* Then again, most of the articles he was assigned didn't seem worth the cost of the ink used to print them. The Rotary Club was sponsoring a bake sale. The Taft Memorial Library planned to present a showing of nineteenth-century farm ceramics.

Three kids at Shane Grammar School had essays chosen by the county fire department in the "Be a Crier, Stop a Fire" contest.

But now, after two months of catching only police reports about fender benders, domestic plate-smashing episodes and the occasional high-school beer bust, something was actually happening.

"Hey, Randy," Joe called out to the burly night editor across the room. "Did you hear that on the radio? What's he mean about 'another' one at Terrel's Peak?"

Randy looked up from his typing, but didn't say anything for a minute. Then he stared straight at Joe. "Somebody jumped off the cliff again. Don't worry about it. We'll cover it tomorrow when they've got all the details."

"Shouldn't I get out there? Sounds like Page One stuff to me!"

"No. Call the department tomorrow. They'll give you everything we need then."

Joe hadn't covered a breaking story since leaving Chicago, and he wasn't going to give up that easily on the first interesting lead he'd had in weeks. "I'm not working on anything but this library club feature right now, anyway," he said. "So how 'bout I go take a ride?"

"Sit it out, Joe."

There was a strange edge to Randy's voice. Joe opened his mouth to argue, but then stopped. The night editor wasn't going to budge on this one; he could tell. Why, he wasn't clear on. But his reporter's instinct didn't let go of a mystery so easily. And he really did wish for a break in the tediously dull evening—even if it was a broken-body break.

The count of green words on the video display terminal on his desk grew slowly as the rest of the night crawled by. The police band remained quiet after its brief eleven o'clock tease, and Joe silently cursed. There were times he really hated working at a small-town paper. If he'd grown up here, he would know precisely why Randy didn't want to talk about a jumper. And they'd said "another one," as if it was a frequent occurrence. Maybe someone in the editor's family had jumped. Hell, probably everybody in town *but* him knew the cliff's apparently fatal history.

But he *hadn't* grown up here. He'd grown up in Chicago, and, for a little while, had played with the big boys of journalism. He'd covered the twisted saga of the JonBenet Ramsey investigations for Northwestern University's student paper, and the high-profile stories had gotten him a job as a stringer for the *Chicago Tribune* right out of college. He'd typed his share of mundane stories about suburban township meetings and school board crises before the full-time doors opened for him at the *Trib*. But open they had. And he'd luxuriated in his high-flying career. Briefly.

He'd written a series of stories about city-council crime, and had exposed graft and corruption in the very ward where he lived. At the time, he'd felt like a superhero. He soaked up the accolades and continued to develop a network of contacts on the street to help him uncover the ever-deeper layers of white-collar crime that the city seemed to have been built upon. He was the voice of everyman.

Until one of the stories he uncovered hit a little too close to home. His stomach had turned to ice on the day he learned that lies and deceit were not limited to the wardrobes of aldermen and investment bankers.

It was one of the last stories he'd turned in to the city editor at the *Chicago Tribune*. It wasn't many days later that he went home, pulled out a suitcase and began packing. He couldn't stomach the undisputable truth his reporter's instinct had forced him to bite down on. And so he'd thrown his wonder-kid career away to run to the coast and hide in this tiny backwater town near the ocean.

And a cliff.

CHAPTER TWO

The sunlight shifted like water, glinting with fiery brilliance and then hazy shadow through the heavy canopy of oaks, conifers and sugar maples. Moth-chewed leaves and splintered twigs obscured the pavement, which was pocked with an abundance of tire-chewing potholes. Brilliant violet heather poked out of the deep ditches on either side of the narrow asphalt trail. The air tasted sharp this morning, crisp with the promise of a sizzling afternoon to come. Joe drove with one arm crooked out the window, the tape deck chewing ethereally on a Cocteau Twins tape. There were some benefits to living here, he admitted. The Midwest just didn't have mornings like this. Or landscape.

The trees thinned abruptly, and he swung down the visor. It didn't help. Driving east at sunup generally rendered visors about as helpful as a garden spade in the ocean. But Terrel dispatch had said Chief Swartzky would be out here looking over the scene of the jump, and that if Joe wanted answers, he'd have to talk to Harry.

Actually this was a bonus. He could get the full effect of the scene before writing his story instead of relying on a police phone report, like he had at the city desk in Chicago. A jumper in Chicago didn't often set the news trucks out in hot pursuit. Here, it was about the only newsworthy thing that could happen. Which was why Randy's reaction the night before had bothered him so much. He could have gotten the story in this morning's edition if he'd come out here when the police band had first sent an officer to investigate the report of a jump. But Randy had vetoed that proposition.

It just didn't feel right.

The breeze picked up as the car descended a steep decline in the road. The trees had turned to brush, and Joe could feel the weight of the ocean in the air. The water was so close, yet he couldn't see it. One more hill in the way. He stepped on the gas and shot down the rough road, oblivious to the squeaks of his shocks. Through his rear speakers, the Twins' Elizabeth Fraser warbled something unintelligible but evocative, a mystery as rich and tantalizing as the landscape around him. As her voice crescendoed in unknown ecstasy, the car finally broke free from the leafy obstructions and turned with the road to climb the last rise out of the forest. At last he could not only smell and hear, but could *see* the ocean.

Whitecaps broke lazily against the shore, a dangerously dark mess of black and green boulders and pebbles that stretched out before him a hundred feet below. The sound of the surf was intoxicating, a steady rush and swell of noise that crushed the airy music of his tape and left him yearning to pull hard on the wheel, turn off the road and abandon his car to dive into the waves.

But he resisted the impulse and the road began weaving its way down until he was driving just a little higher than the high-tide debris mark. And then he saw it.

The cliff.

It stretched almost straight up from the beach, a jagged, rocky wall that, from the road, looked higher than a skyscraper. One thin prominence stretched out over the choppy inlet like a beckoning finger, a signal of unknown import to the sky. Far beneath the finger's stretch, a police car and a Folter's Ambulance van were parked just off the road, lights off.

At this point, emergency lights were probably unnecessary, he mused. The emergency was long past.

Joe pulled off the road next to the old squad car, grabbed a notebook and walked down to the edge of the water, where the uniforms were gathered. He'd seen three of the four before, but the only name that stuck was Chief Swartzky's. The chief was the oldest of the bunch; his frost-white hair and thick belly stood out in stark contrast to the other men.

The chief nodded slowly at his approach.

"Hey, mornin', Joe," the portly cop said. His voice was iron-hard, yet strangely soft-spoken. It was amazing that he could speak so low and yet be heard over the deafening rush of the ocean.

"You remember Alfie"—he gestured to a young sandy-haired cop—"and this is Mack and Parent from Folter's." The two ambulance drivers looked uncomfortably pale beneath dark manes of hair that caught and twisted across their eyes in the wind. Joe guessed from their hawk noses and blue eyes that they were brothers. And neither on the job long enough to be inured to blood.

"Hi." Joe nodded and shook hands all around.

Looking past the group, he saw why the drivers might have been a bit upset. The body was still here. And it didn't look good.

"What was the name?" he asked diplomatically, unsure of the sex of the body a few yards away.

"James Canady," the chief said. "He was local, nineteen years old. A good kid."

Joe walked past the men to the water's edge. The boy's body, from what he could see, was not going to be a pretty sight when they reeled it in.

Death must have been immediate, he thought. A rocky needle had stopped the boy's fall, but it had been no life preserver. The rock had impaled the boy's naked belly, releasing his guts to the ocean and spiking the body facedown just below the waterline like a tack in a larval bug. Two feet of needle-thin, bony stone rose like a horn from the boy's back. It had saved James Canady from being washed out to sea, but didn't make for a pretty portrait. The boy had been nude when he jumped, and his skin was wrinkled and dead white after hours in the water. Something long and pale stretched from beneath the corpse to curl and twist in the shifting waves like an undulating cobra.

Joe turned away with a shiver. He'd seen plenty of ripped-up bodies after gang shootings. He'd seen the results of domestic fights that got out of hand, leaving dismembered corpses instead of purpling bruises. But unleashed intestines always gave him the willies.

"Why is he still out here?" he asked the chief.

"We got the call that there was a jumper last night—anonymous tip. Came out here to search, but it was high tide and we couldn't get close to these rocks, and couldn't see anything from the road. Didn't know if it was a prank call or not, so we came back to search again a little while ago. Didn't take much searching this morning, as you can see. Low tide just hit."

"Have his relatives been notified yet?"

"He's just got a mother, Rhonda Canady. And yeah, I called her a few minutes ago. She'll be at the morgue to ID him at nine."

The chief turned to the ambulance drivers, who didn't look happy about the idea of going in after the body.

"Get on it, guys. It won't get any easier the longer he floats."

Mack and Parent traded unhappy looks, and then shrugs. At last they trudged their way to the water's edge and waded in.

"Mack went to school with the boy," the chief offered, shaking his head.

"Did he have family problems?"

"Who, Mack?" The chief grinned sourly but Joe didn't laugh. "No. No more so than anyone else, I'd guess. Kind of a quiet kid. Lived with his ma in the old section of town, on the other side of this bay here. Never heard of him causing any trouble in school or town."

"Are you sure it was suicide?"

The chief didn't answer for a beat. Instead he looked up to the top of the cliff overhanging the small bay. When he turned back to Joe, his eyes were gray with weariness.

"No evidence to suggest it wasn't."

Mack and Parent waded into the water, moving to stand on either side of the corpse. Together they grabbed the body at the shoulders and thighs and thrust skyward. It slid up the spike easily, a dark stain dissipating in its wake. They hefted Canady up and off the rock and quickly carried his body to the gravel at the water's edge. Mack ran to get a stretcher from the van; his face looked green as he passed Joe. Scooping someone's guts out of the water is never an easy task. Especially if they're a friend's.

Joe turned back to the chief. Randy had gotten him thinking. There was some kind of history to this spot, and who better to know it than Swartzky?

"Do you get a lot of jumpers out here?"

The chief's steel gray eyes never blinked.

"What makes you think that?"

"Seems like a good spot for suicides, is all."

"There's been some over the years." The chief nodded. He looked up at the rocky finger overhead as he spoke. "But we don't publicize 'em much. You don't know how kids'll take this stuff. Some'll romanticize it, and we'll have a whole class jumping the rocks. Kind of like when one of those rock stars kills themselves, some of their fans'll go do the same damn thing."

Swartzky looked back at him pointedly. "So we keep it low-key."

Joe ignored the hint, smelling a perfect three-part series on the subject of suicide, the cliff's history and how to deal with the topic.

"How could I find out about the others?" Joe asked.

"Let 'em lie quiet," Swartzky said in his quietest rumble, and abruptly walked to the van.

"Mack!" Swartzky yelled, and the ambulance driver poked his head out of the driver's-side window. The two exchanged words that Joe couldn't hear, and then Swartzky stepped back as the van pulled away.

"Joe!" The chief was standing half in, half out of his squad car.

"Yeah?" Joe answered, yelling to be heard across the beach above the wash of the surf.

"People don't want to be reminded about friends and loved ones who killed themselves. Don't go digging that stuff up. Just let 'em know Canady's gone and be done with the business, you hear?"

Joe nodded and began retracing his steps to his own car.

But now he was more curious than ever.

There *was* stuff to dig up.

CHAPTER THREE

"It's almost over, isn't it?"

Karen Sander ran a weary hand through her kinked shoulder-length hair. She'd found gray in it this morning. *Gray*. She'd plucked it, but the twinge of needlepoint pain hadn't blanked the feeling that the hair had given her. She'd deflated. When had it all gotten away from her?

"I don't think it will ever be over," Karen answered. Her voice sounded as worn as she'd felt when looking in the mirror. The reflection had been denigrating enough without its silvering reminder of death.

Black eyes staring cold and empty . . .

"But the only one left is Rachel," the other woman persisted. "If she would just track down Andi, the circle would be closed. We'll all have done it. The contract will be fulfilled. It'll all be over."

Laughter, deep and dark. The voice. "Have you girls ever heard of the Marquis?"

The other woman stared at a wet ring in front of her on the kitchen table. Her index finger traced the perfect O of the ring, round and round and round. Abruptly she dragged the wet finger across the center of the ring to draw a line inside the O.

A thigh straddling hers, smearing the blood. It was warm and sticky. The blood that was not their own, but of their own . . .

"What makes you think it will stop with the children?"

Karen's voice was quiet, tinged with pain. And fear. "All these years, we've focused on the children. I never thought I could do it. Neither did you, right?"

The other woman nodded, her gray eyes hazing over with tears. Karen had another flash of her in a younger time.

Possessed lips swollen with kisses, naked breasts painted with her blood . . . the blood He baptized them in . . .

"But you did. We all did. He made us keep our bargain. And he could certainly make us do more than that. After all, what will he have to do when the last of the children are gone?"

"But there are always others," her friend protested. "There have been lots of them that we had nothing to do with. There always have been. We all kept our contract, except for Rachel, and I think after Andi, he will leave us alone. He will just find others to take, that's all."

A gash on her forehead, blood streaming down her cheeks unnoticed. Black, empty eyes staring at them; black empty eyes laughing at them in a voice not her own . . .

Karen stared blankly a moment, and then shook her head.

"What's a contract to a monster?"

Let's make a little promise, he'd said. *A Covenant . . .*

The other woman began to cry and Karen got up, knocking back her chair with a screech, and embraced the other woman, trying without success to stop her mounting sobs.

She understood the pain—the spiraling pit of despair that dredged ever deeper into the darkness. It was a devilish, secret pain that only five girls who had somehow become graying women could understand.

It was a Covenant they dared not break, though they couldn't be sure that their benefactor would honor his end of the deal. Their contract was more than sacred, especially to a monster.

Their contract was written in blood. And more than their souls were at stake.

Karen hugged the other woman closer, and began to sob. Not for herself, but for the children.

CHAPTER FOUR

". . . and we could have the last part of the series be on the psychological aspects of the problem. I could talk with a psychiatrist I know back at the University of Chicago, giving tips on how to recognize suicidal kids, and how to deal with the loss of loved ones who killed themselves."

Randy looked incredulous.

Stunned.

About as hungry for the idea as a vegetarian for roadkill.

"You're bound and determined to rub salt in this town's wounds, aren't ya?" Randy finally said. "Don't you *get* it? When something like this happens, people need to forget, not be reminded. Leave this alone. I want a six-inch story about James Canady. Straight facts as you've found 'em, and move on. It'll run on page seven. I need a story on the Presthill Theatre renovation for the weekend section, so get on that and quit wasting your time on a simple jumper story."

With that, Randy stalked past Joe and into the paste-up room. Most papers had converted to computer-generated layout and design systems, but not the *Terrel Daily Times*. Here the computers still ran out the stories on long strips of heavy, glossy column-wide paper. Then with an X-acto knife and a pot of wax, the stories were pasted down column by column on long sheets of paper the size of the final morning edition. When the whole newspaper for the following day was "dummied," each page was shot on film using an ancient camera the size of a small car. At this hour of the day there was no one in the paste-up room but Randy. Who was just using the room as an escape.

Now he had to know. It was no longer a story to Joe. It was a mission.

Nobody—*nobody*—told Joe Kieran to back off a story. That simple fact was one of the reasons he had sentenced himself to Podunk Terrel instead of moving up the editor ranks at the *Trib*. There *were* consequences to digging. And Joe didn't have nine lives to sacrifice to his curiosity.

Or nine hearts. He'd lost one of the latter in Chicago.

The newsroom was quiet; this early in the day, you were lucky to find three people in the building at once. Shrugging in resignation, Joe left Randy in paste-up and sauntered down the hall to the junk-food haven. The snack machine was tucked into an alcove near the most important spot in the building for Joe, aside from his computer. The room beyond the vending machine was dimly lit and musty, and crowded with row after row of steel shelves. This was the morgue, the newspaper's library of old editions. Sorting through the stacks of yellowing paper in the morgue was the only way to find old stories. And if you were writing about something new in Terrel, it probably had ties to something old. So in the few weeks he'd lived in Terrel, Joe had spent many hours researching town history here.

Of course, when you were searching the morgue, you not only had to know what you were looking for, but approximately when it happened. The organizational system was simple: every new edition was stacked on top of the last issue. When the pile of old papers grew tall enough that the center of its shelf began to bow, a new pile was formed. Every now and then, someone even bothered to guesstimate the dates each pile represented and write them down on Post-it notes that were then taped to the shelves.

Joe stared into the empty shadows of the morgue and popped two quarters into the vending machine. He punched in the code C4 without even looking at the selection within the glass case. C4 equaled Bugles. And he had a bag every day.

"Why don't you just buy a box?" Randy had asked a week or two after Joe had first started at the paper.

"You just can't depend on the freshness in a box," Joe had answered with a grin. "These here"—he held up the bag and motioned with his other hand—"are fresh-picked. Listen."

He crunched one loud for show.

As he did again now, grinning at the random memory. But the thought of trading jabs with Randy reminded him immediately of the editor's uncharacteristic dourness over the past twenty-four hours. On a whim, he walked down the hall away from the newsroom, and knocked on an unmarked wooden door.

There was no reply for a moment, but Joe waited. Finally, he heard the metallic tumble of a lock clicking open, and the doorknob turned.

"Hey, Joe, whaddya need?"

George Polanski's wrinkled face peered up at him from the shadows of the janitor's back room. The old guy was supposed to be a part-timer, but everybody knew that at some point, George had begun sleeping here. Joe wondered if he still kept a house or an apartment somewhere else for his things. From the number of times and odd hours he'd woken the janitor from napping on the cot in this tiny room, he'd begun to doubt it.

"George, I was wondering something."

"Oh, you were, were you?" The old man chuckled and motioned him inside. They stepped into the jumble of buckets and mops and detergents in the extended janitors' closet and the old man pushed the door shut behind them.

"Have a seat, then."

George pointed out a relatively empty area on the cot, which was currently piled with a litter of magazines, a tin of tobacco, and the remains of an interrupted game of solitaire. Joe obliged, and George pulled up a twenty-gallon barrel of floor wax to sit on. He grunted as he eased himself onto the can and shook his head.

"Back ain't what it used to be, Joe," he said. "Now, what is it you were thinking of? It's been awhile since I've seen you around these parts."

"You've heard that someone committed suicide on Terrel's Peak last night, didn't you?" Joe began.

The old man nodded, painfully slow. "Sad business, that."

"Well, nobody wants to talk about it."

The old man studied Joe, his eyes piercing and blue despite the drooping hoods of age. Almost painful in their intensity. Joe began to wonder if he'd made a mistake in coming here. Would the old guy brush him off too? Then a slight, sad smile took the man's lips and the lines in his face seemed to deepen.

"I'm gonna tell you a story, Joe," he said, raising a finger to shake in Joe's face. "But don't you go taking notes now, you hear? Just listen.

"My best friend was a banker when I was younger, Joe. He dealt with some heavy risks and big money all his life. He had a stomach lined with lead, I always said, 'cuz the stress he was under would've burned a hole in my belly clear through to my back. But he seemed to thrive on it, he did. Early on in his life, the gambles seemed to pay off for him, but later, he saw just as many of his investments go sour. Things turned on him, lead stomach or not. He watched his wife grow mean and spiteful. She divorced him at forty-three. He lived to see his kids move away. He fought with the legislature and lost his business over taxes. He watched his bank go insolvent after the Feds came down and took a closer look at the books. He survived all that and yet he always kept a smile—you know, the kind of smile that says 'I'll buy you a beer but you cross me wrong and I'll cut your liver out.' Still, he told me once in confidence that he broke down and cried when a woman came home with him one night and he didn't work. Impotent, they call it. He wasn't all lead."

George paused, then shook his head slowly.

"I'll tell you another story. I'll tell you about Margaret Kelly. She was a good girl, got good grades, had boyfriends. Lived in a nice house, got along with her family. Her parents are nice—I know 'em. She had a scholarship to a big college, talked a lot of becoming a doctor. Seemed like a happy kid.

"You know what the difference between my friend and Margaret Kelly is, Joe?"

Joe shrugged, a suspicion dawning on where this was going.

"Margaret Kelly turned up on the rocks below that cliff last year, and my friend still lives over on Second Street. He ain't too happy, but he's alive. I'll tell you, if anyone was gonna commit suicide in this town, it'd be my friend, not Margaret Kelly, who had everything still to live for."

The old man seemed lost for a moment, eyes focused on a spot on the wall behind Joe. The reporter snuck a glance in that direction, seeing nothing but the ink-smudged white wall.

"Margaret and James ain't the only kids to've gone over that cliff," George said. His focus returned, and bored hard into Joe's face. "Something's driving these kids over the edge, Joe, and it ain't because they don't have fine lives. Seems to me the majority of the ones that go over are the ones that might have actually had a chance to make something of themselves and gotten the hell out of this hole-in-the-shit-stall town. I don't know's if I'd call it suicide, myself."

"What do you mean, not suicide? You think someone's pushing these people over?" Now, here was an interesting angle, given the responses he'd gotten from officials regarding the cliff. Maybe they were holding a lid on things until the killer could be tracked.

George's brows creased, a salty caterpillar of consideration. Abruptly, he shook his head.

"Don't know what I think. But I do know that it ain't a healthy place to be around."

"Who else has fallen off that cliff, George? Any family of Randy's?"

George was silent; his gaze fell to his feet. Then he stood up and opened the door.

"I got to check the air-conditioning, Joe. It's been leaking over in Jack Romand's office."

Joe took his cue and stepped past George into the hallway.

"You want town history, talk to Angelica Napalona. She's seen it all. And then some."

Joe nodded and turned to go back to the newsroom. But George stopped him.

"And Joe?"

The bags in the old man's cheeks hung low, and he wouldn't look Joe in the eye.

"Stay away from Terrel's Peak. It's evil. Trust an old man on this one."

•

CHAPTER FIVE

There was a feeling you got when driving through the Main Street of Terrel. A feeling of solidity, of history.

Of home.

Joe had felt it the first time he'd driven through the town; it descended silent and complete as an eclipse. One moment it was broad daylight, the next you asked who turned out the sun. One minute you were lost in the country, the next you were cozy and smiling in the middle of a town called Terrel. That womblike feeling of instant security was a big reason Joe had decided to settle here.

Or hide here, his conscience taunted.

The storefronts were drawn with wide, come-on-inside-friendly windows. Every few doorways were embraced by awnings striped in green and gold, scarlet and turquoise. Welcome mats cheered every stoop. Most of the old brick buildings here were rimmed with ornate wood, the curlicues and ridges twisting to the right and left like architectural road maps. Most of the buildings had second- and third-story rooms above the storefronts that housed the shop owners or tenants.

A recent mayor with a romantic eye for history had put in new streetlamps designed to look old-fashioned. Ornate black poles divided each block with arms that stretched inward from the street to hold faux gaslights. And in the center square of Main Street, across from the post office and village hall, the dirty tide of asphalt was dammed by a spread of uneven red cobbles.

It seemed comforting that the street supported a "Fill Your Pipe" shop, even though Joe didn't smoke. He liked it that there was a hobby shop with model trains and large signs beckoning LIONEL in the window, though he never stopped and went inside. And he had actually spent hours browsing, though not buying, in Books and Baubles, where stacks of dusty, beat up novels lay side by side with Donnie Osmond 8-tracks.

Today, however, the uncalculated quaintness of Main Street didn't coax a grin from Joe. The white shutters revealed their peeling paint; the Raggedy Anns in the craft store window had their MADE IN TAIWAN tags clearly showing. All was not what it seemed in Terrel, he'd found.

"This is stupid," he chided himself.

"A kid jumped off a cliff. At the same spot where lots of other people who never thought they'd escape a dead-end Rockwell nightmare also jumped. So what? It doesn't have anything to do with the way the town looks!"

But the problem was, it did. Terrel looked different to Joe today.

Diseased.

Hollow.

In the course of twenty-four hours it had gone from Rockwell cozy to Bosch decay in his eyes. Maybe that was because he had found his first real story to uncover since moving here. *There are hidden things here,* that story cried, just as there were in Chicago. Cozy warm can also mean killing fire.

Nothing was going to hide those answers from him— certainly not a coat of paint or a home-sewn doll.

He'd gone straight for the phone book after his talk with George. Angelica Napalona had an address right here on Main.

2193 Main, to be exact.

Joe followed the numbers as they ascended from the 1001 of the village hall. As he moved farther from the center of town, the red and gray brick buildings diminished, giving way to white frame ranches and worn two-story homes. He began to wonder if he was going to run out of town before he found Angelica Napalona.

And then he was there: 2193 Main. A typical nondescript white frame ranch. At least it had once been white. Dirt and rot had leached any purity from the paint. The front yard had once been landscaped, but now was overrun by evergreens. Their wildly reaching boughs obscured much of the house. Three blue spruces dwarfed the house on one side, making it seem even smaller than it probably was. A stone path led from the gravel driveway to the front door, where a sign hung: READINGS BY ANGELICA.

"This is a joke!" He laughed out loud in the car.

George had sent him to a fortune-teller to find out the town's history? Wasn't that kind of like going to a circus to learn about physics?

He turned the key in the ignition to let the motor die, but still he sat in the car.

Maybe, he considered, she was the best source. After all, if you're going to tell fortunes, it makes sense to know as much as possible about the people you're forecasting for, right?

"A source is a source." He shrugged and stepped out of the car.

As he raised his hand to knock on the wooden storm door, it opened at the hand of an attractive, dark-complexioned woman.

Good show for a psychic. He silently applauded. She must have a motion sensor somewhere on the property.

"Come in, my friend, come in," she urged, opening the door to him. "You are welcome here."

He stepped into a narrow hallway and took a better look at his hostess.

Angelica Napalona took care of herself. She was short and trim, with sexy, strangling ringlets of raven hair bordering her face and eyes, which were too dark to make out their color. She overdid the makeup though, he thought. Her cheeks were violated by scarlet rouge and her eyes were rimmed in a raccoon's shadow of mascara. She draped her shoulders in a long flamboyant cape crazily colored tangerine, gold and purple. But beneath the gaudy trappings of her trade, he could see that Angelica wore very down-to-earth blue jeans and a white cotton T-shirt that hugged what he could see of her figure. At least her Italian name was legitimate, he thought, eyes dallying briefly on her nose.

"Follow me," she beckoned in a musical voice, and led him past a dark dining room into what had been designed to be a back bedroom, but was no longer used for that.

Strands of translucent gold and silver beads hung from the top of the doorframe to the floor. The door itself had been removed, though the hinges remained in place. Angelica pushed aside the beads and took a seat at a small table. Joe followed, noting that the table and its two chairs were the sole furnishings in the room, which had murals of stars and astrological signs covering the walls. The shades were drawn, and Angelica had successfully lit a huge red candle on the table before Joe even entered the room.

"Sit," she said, gesturing at the empty wooden chair. Italian or not, Joe guessed her heavy accent was fake.

"Look, Ms. Napalona," he began, "I haven't—"

"Call me Angelica, I insisst," she purred.

"Angelica, then. I haven't come for a reading."

"You vant to play cards then? Here, I'll deal you your life." With that, she produced a deck and began laying out a series of cards facedown on the table. The backs were covered with mystical runes and figures. She turned one over and beamed. "Ah, ze Jack of Good Fortune." She set the card to one side. "A good friend to have on your side. Now you pick. Which card will you choose?"

"I'm serious, ma'am. I'd just like to talk with you for a few minutes."

"Time iss money, my friend." She settled into her chair until the twin steeples on either side of the backrest were far above her head. She looked like a little girl playing in her mother's clothes.

Joe had the feeling that this was a losing proposition all the way around, but, having gotten this far, he felt obliged to continue. He retrieved his wallet and pulled out a five-dollar bill.

"Will this be enough?"

"Enough for hiring the services of a professional hamburger flipper, perhaps," she taunted. "Enough for renting a copy of *Gone with ze Wind*, if you like. Even enough to buy a paperback novel. But enough to compensate a seer, who vill look into your life's deepest tangles and help you to unweave them . . . ?"

Joe rose to leave, chalking up this whole fiasco as a waste of time. But Angelica's hand darted out to hold his own.

"As it happens, I have no pressing business right now, and I am curious about your reasons for seeking me."

The five dollars somehow left his hand with hers.

"I will speak with you for five minutes. After that time, you may decide whether you wish to know more. And at what price."

Angelica relaxed again in her chair, folding thin, braceleted arms across her chest. Joe smiled at her posture in spite of himself. Had she any idea how foolish she looked and sounded?

"I want to talk to you about Terrel's Peak," he began, watching her reaction closely.

Her face remained blank, but did her arms tighten?

"Go on," she intoned.

"I'd like to know about who has committed suicide there, and when."

The five-dollar bill suddenly appeared back on the table before him.

"I will not take your money for speaking of zat," she hissed, and abruptly stood.

"Who sent you to taunt me like this? Was it Karen? Melody?"

As her voice rose, her accent slipped away. For a second, Joe saw through the getup and glimpsed a middle-aged small-town housewife wearing a loud robe over her daytime clothes. And then Angelica the Reader returned, eyes still flaring slightly, but otherwise in control.

"You can leaf now, sir," she said, still standing.

"Please," he began, suddenly sure that George had sent him to the right place. "I wrote a story for the newspaper today about the Canady kid's death—he jumped last night— and I just wanted to find out more about the cliff. Nobody will tell me anything about it, but someone said you might know. So I looked you up."

"Who zent you?" Angelica asked in a calmer, richly colored Gypsy voice.

"I don't think I should tell you," Joe replied, staring her down. "But it wasn't one of those women you mentioned. Actually, it was an older gentlemen who said you knew town history."

"Of that, he vas surely correct," she said. The seer put a finger to her lips and stared hard at Joe. Pacing the room, she trailed that same finger across a tawdry collection of crystals, baubles and beads. She lingered a moment at a dull bronze key, hung from a nail on the wall near a collage of old photos.

"Listen closely, and I vill tell you what I know."

Angelica straightened her cape with a hand, recrossed the room and eased back into her chair.

Her eyes were brown. A deep, forest brown that hid behind lashes too-black. They stared at him intently over the top of steepled fingers. Fingers each ornamented by a ring.

"There is an evil spirit in the cliff, my young reporter friend," she began. She leaned across the table, so close he could feel her breath upon his face.

"It feeds not on the bodies, but on the souls of men."

"The name's Joe," he offered.

Her gaze did not falter at his interruption and she continued to speak, soft and low. He was starting to see why people could be sucked in by her. When she spoke, her eyes flickered with an inner spark and her lips parted in some secret glee. He was sure she could be convincing.

"I have not felt where this spirit came from, or how long it has been here," she murmured. "Perhaps it iss the haunt of Indians long dead. An earthen spirit that still yearns for sacrifice and in this age of unbelief finds only murder left to fill its belly. Or perhaps it is a demon chained for all eternity in ze bowels of that dark rock. Its history isn't of importance, but its hunger is. Every year, that spirit drags at least one person off of ze cliff to crush them on ze cruel rocks below. Its hunger is great. And growing. Most of those who die are strangers to Terrel. Drifters. Businessmen from out of town."

She leaned forward to whisper. "Walk carefully, Joe," she warned, and turned away. When she looked back, her eyes were glossy with moisture.

"Every year, at least one of those unlucky enough to visit the rocks at the bottom of that cursed hill are stolen from this town. And we who live here mourn them quietly, and in fear. For we never know when it will be ourselves that the cliff calls."

This seemed to be going nowhere fast, Joe thought. He should have known better than to expect anything but fairy tales from an astrologist.

"What can you tell me about the last few people who jumped?" he prodded.

"That they have met their destiny."

Angelica stared him down at that, her hands no longer crossed, but palm-down on the table. She looked ready to either jump up or throw the table at him; he wasn't sure which.

"So I suspected," he countered. "But who were they? When did they jump?"

"Why do you vant to know these things?" she whispered. Her face was now as white as her hands, which were pressed hard against the table.

"Because I do, is all," he snapped, and slapped himself inwardly for his irritated tone. "I saw them take the Canady boy out of the water. The police chief didn't want to talk about it. Hell, my own boss didn't want me to write much about it. I want to know why these people are jumping. And don't tell me it's because of some hocus-pocus monster locked up in a cave!"

"Your five minutes is up, Joe. And I'm afraid I have better paying clients scheduled for the rest of ze afternoon. We'll have to do this another time."

She nearly ran from the room, the beads exploding behind her as they clinked and tangled together.

"I guess I'm letting myself out?" he asked the room with a slight grin. He started to leave, but then paused in the doorway to look back at the table.

The five-dollar bill had apparently flown from the room as well.

CHAPTER SIX

"Sometimes you just don't know when to give up," Joe said to himself as he scanned the crowd. "*Why* are you here?"

The cemetery was crowded with people trying to keep out of the midmorning sun and under the green and white canopy. A minister stood at the front of the crowd next to a brilliantly glossed oak casket. Joe caught a "dust to dust" passage before his eyes lit on a familiar face. He sidled through the people slowly, making his way toward the front of those gathered to the left of the casket. An older woman glared at him as he stepped in front of her, but he excused himself and kept moving. Until he stood beside her.

"Angelica?"

Her eyes widened as she recognized him.

"What are you doing here?" she spat.

"I don't really know," he whispered back with a half grin. "It just seemed right, me having been at the scene of the crime and all."

She stared at him a moment more, as if searching his face for another reason. Then she faced front again and ignored him.

Joe shrugged and crossed his arms. He'd talk to her some more after the ceremony.

A portly woman cried openly in the first row. He assumed this was the mother, Rhonda Canady. She wore a gray skirt and jacket, suitable for mourning, he supposed. When the minister walked over and leaned in to have a private word,

Joe knew for sure it was her. Another woman, this one tall and thin, held Rhonda's arm through it all, patting her on the shoulder when the minister returned to the casket. He gave a signal, and two men began to lower the wooden box into the earth.

"Who's that with Mrs. Canady?" Joe whispered to Angelica. She stared darkly at him through slitted eyes and hissed, "That's Karen Sander. We went to school with Rhonda."

We, she'd said. Without much of an accent. Which would make sense if she went to school here. How could you grow up with a thick Gypsy accent in Terrel?

Joe glanced at her surreptitiously. She hadn't mentioned anything the other day about knowing the Canadys. But maybe that's why George had sent him to Angelica. If she was friends with the dead kid's mom, maybe she knew more than she had let on. Maybe the old janitor hadn't steered him sour after all.

"Did you know James well?" he whispered.

"No," she answered quickly. "Rhonda and I have not been friends for some time. Excuse me now."

She pushed her way past him and strode quickly away from the gathering as, in the front of the crowd, Rhonda Canady tossed a handful of dirt into the hole where her son's casket lay.

Joe waited until the crowd began to disperse and Mrs. Canady was busy speaking with the minister. Then he strolled toward the grave.

"Mrs. Sander?" he said, reaching out to gently tap the woman's arm.

She turned to him slowly, as if moving through tar. Her eyes were red with tears, and the stress of the situation was highlighting the crow's-feet just beginning to wear at their corners. But the freckles on her nose and cheeks, and the wave of her dark hair still held some flash of youth. Joe figured her in her late thirties, early forties. *A little old, but not bad,* he found himself thinking, then shook the thought from his head.

"Mrs. Sander, I work for the *Terrel Daily Times,* and I wrote James' obituary for yesterday's paper. I didn't want to bother Mrs. Canady, but I was hoping you might be able to tell me more about James."

"What do you want to know?" she asked. Her voice was heavy, and her eyes refused to leave the six-foot hole in the earth a short distance away.

"Well, I've heard that Terrel's Peak has claimed a lot of lives. I was just wondering if James ever talked about being suicidal before this happened. Or, do you know if he happened to be friends with any of the kids who have jumped from the peak in the past?"

"Was he a copycat? That's what you want to know?"

She turned at last to give him her full attention. Her eyes flared from empty pits to fiery black holes.

"No, ma'am, not exactly. I just want to know what kind of—"

"What kind of kid jumps off a cliff, Mr. . . . ?"

"Kieran, ma'am."

"The kind of kid that jumps off a cliff, Mr. Kieran, was my son, William. The kind of kid that jumps off a cliff is"—she pointed at a slim blonde woman talking with Rhonda— "Monica Kelly's daughter, Margaret. There is no *kind* of kid that jumps off a cliff. There are only dead kids who've done it. I'm sorry, Mr. Kieran, but I just really don't want to talk about this right now."

Amazing, Joe thought as Karen Sander abruptly walked away to join Rhonda and Monica at the edge of the grave. Within five minutes he had managed to drive two women away from him—at a funeral, where people were supposed to be open armed and comforting. Was it him, or were people in this town really touchy about this cliff?

And it was damned strange that all three of those women had had kids go cliff-diving without a hang glider. What were the odds? And they all knew Angelica. Maybe he'd have to pay the palm reader another visit. But this time, he needed to have a little more information before he tried to pump her. He needed a handle to prime the pump. The *Times'* morgue would take days to weed through to find what he was looking for. But with some names to scan for, he could use the library's microfilm collection of the *Terrel Daily Times*. He ought to be able to sift through papers fast enough to get the dates and circumstances of the deaths of Margaret Kelly and William Sander. He doubted their obituaries would say much, but it never hurt to check.

So absorbed was he in following his train of thought, that he didn't even realize that for the first time in weeks, he was truly, utterly happy. As Joe Kieran walked away from the funeral and unlocked his car door, he was whistling.

CHAPTER SEVEN

Cindy Marshfield waited to cry until she was home from the funeral. And then it all came out like a June rainstorm. She left her mom downstairs and hid in her room with the door closed. It seemed like someone else's room now, she thought, lying back on the bed to stare at the ceiling. She'd been away for months, and coming back to her old high school room was like visiting a friend's home—familiar, comfortable, but not hers. Her eyes filled with tears as she traced the spider-web patterns in the paint on the ceiling and relived the past couple days.

The call had come while she was at class. Her roommate, Brenda, had actually picked up the phone and talked to Cindy's mom. It was two hours later before she could relay the news to Cindy.

"I've got some pretty bad news," Brenda had begun just after Cindy walked into their cramped dorm room. She'd looked curiously over at Brenda, waiting for the punch line that was sure to follow such a pronouncement from her usually giddy friend. But Brenda's face hadn't lifted.

Cindy crossed the room and put her hands on Brenda's shoulders.

"What is it? Did Bill cancel on you for tomorrow night?"

"It's not about me," Brenda had stammered. "It's about . . . James."

Cindy's face stretched as her eyes widened. "What about him?"

"He—Your mom called earlier."

Brenda gently pushed Cindy down onto her bed.

"What's the matter with him? Tell me!"

Brenda's face turned funny. Her lips pursed and opened, but then closed without uttering a word. And then they blurted it out: "Cindy, James jumped off a cliff last night."

"Oh, God. Oh, my God."

Cindy didn't wait for the impact of the news to be felt. She jumped up and ran to her closet. Her suitcase was in the back, and she pulled it out and threw it on the bed.

"What are you doing?" Brenda asked. "Why don't you call your mom before you go packing up?"

"I have to get home. I have to be there. I should have been there."

Cindy sank down to the cold tile of the floor.

"I should never have left him. I should have known this would happen."

"How could you know?" Brenda had asked, and then recoiled from the black look in her friend's eyes.

"I knew if he stayed in Terrel he'd be doomed, just like all the others."

Those words echoed in her head again and again all week. She heard them as she hugged Mrs. Canady at the wake, and then again as she knelt before her old boyfriend's casket.

"Why wouldn't you come with me?" she whispered at the still, white face before her. But he didn't answer.

The wake had been bad, but it got worse.

When the funeral procession stopped at the open hole in the ground at the cemetery, a cold stone dropped in her stomach.

I will never see his face again, she thought as the casket was carried across the green to the grave. *Never.*

Then the preacher talked about God and taking lambs back to heaven and a bunch of other crap.

God had nothing to do with this! she wanted to scream.

But she hadn't.

She'd watched as they threw dirt on the casket, as Mrs. Canady and Mrs. Kelly and Mrs. Sander stood around the grave. She saw Mrs. Sander talk to and then angrily walk away from a young man with a notebook. And she saw the crazy lady, Angelica Napalona, bolt from the cemetery before anyone else.

Then she had come home and cried.

His face kept coming back to haunt her. His picture stared at her from her old white bureau. The trinkets from their high school dances still hung from her mirror across the room. She could even hear his voice, telling her that he couldn't go away to school. That he couldn't leave Terrel.

She cupped her hands over her ears, willing that voice to go out of her head and instead become flesh before her. Willing James to be alive again. To be with her.

But the room remained silent except for the uneven gasps of her breath.

CHAPTER EIGHT

Despite the hawkeyed glares bestowed on whisperers by old Mrs. Malone the library wasn't nearly as quiet as Cindy Marshfield's bedroom. Joe could hear the quiet chatter of schoolkids gossiping in the aisles of bookshelves around him, and the microfilm machine spoke in its own rhythm, squealing of unoiled cogs and humming in complaint at power long denied.

Joe scrolled through screen after screen of old headlines, reading of school board elections and weather predictions, the zoning grant that allowed the construction of the warehouselike Wal-Mart and the fence permit for Mrs. Ola Levinthal of Elm Street. The obituaries were slim but steady over the months of newspapers he searched; mostly older folks who had passed on from heart attacks and "natural causes." A couple drownings, roadside accidents and even a domestic homicide.

Mrs. Malone had been no help at all to him.

"What is it you're looking for, young man?" she'd asked, crone eyes boring into his own with uncanny brilliance.

"I'm trying to find the obituaries of Margaret Kelly and William Sander," he'd answered. "They were a couple kids who jumped off Terrel's Peak a year or two ago."

"Yeah. I remember 'em," she said. "Real bookworm, that Margaret was. It's a shame she had to go do a thing like that. But I can't help you on when it was they went. I think it was in the fall, both of 'em. Why don't you just ask their families? They still live here in town."

"I don't want to bother them," he lied.

Mrs. Malone unlocked the door to a room near the study carrels. She pointed to a row of small cardboard boxes, not much bigger than packs of cigarettes, stacked behind the microfilm reader. "Well, here's the stacks of *Terrel Daily Times* film. I don't think you'll find much though. They don't write much about kids who go and do stuff like kill themselves. Best not to talk of such things."

With that, the old lady took her silver hair and eagle eyes from the room and left Joe to figure out the workings of the microfilm reader.

It didn't take too long before he was scrolling speedily through issue after issue of the *Times*. He started with the film from last December and worked backward, not relying on a cranky old woman's memory for much.

His heart jumped when his eyes picked out the words "Terrel's Peak" from a death notice in the November 2 issue. But then his eyes saw the deceased was a Parker Matthews, age thirty-four, a salesman from out of town who had apparently parked his car to watch the sun set from the edge of the cliff and then dived after it.

If he caught up with the sun, it wasn't in this dimension.

Joe kept scrolling backward, and was beginning to despair of ever finding a death notice for people he'd heard of when he saw it.

Margaret Kelly, 18, died on May 22. The wake will be held tonight at Folter's Funeral Home. Services will be held tomorrow at St. Patrick's Church at 11 A.M. The family has requested in lieu of flowers, that donations be made in Margaret's name to the Troubled Children's Fund, 535 Argathe Way, New Brunswick, NJ 08901.

Well, he had a date now, if no other information. Just over a year ago. On a hunch, he scrolled back a year to the previous May, and began looking through the obituaries.

And found one for William Sander.

Who died on May 22.

Joe felt the hair on the back of his neck begin to rise. Today was May 26. His obituary for James Canady had run two days ago, the day after the body had been taken out of the ocean. Which meant that James Canady had jumped off Terrel's Peak on May 22. What were the chances that three teens would each jump from the same place on the same anniversary?

Three years in a row?

What the hell was going on here?

Joe grabbed another box of film from the wall. And searched for the *Terrel Daily Times* of May 23, 2001. His heart raced faster than the scrolling film as he advanced to the section of the paper that held obituaries.

There were none.

He continued through the film of the May 24 and May 25 editions, and found nothing. Nobody died the whole last week of May 2001 in Terrel or the surrounding suburbs.

He slumped back in his seat.

OK. So the chain wasn't very long. But it couldn't be just a coincidence that three kids had all jumped from the same cliff on the same day, one year apart each.

Why?

What was so special about May 22?

He picked up the rolls of film that were scattered around the viewer and began reinserting them into their boxes. And then stopped.

What if the chain had only skipped a year? And what about that death in October?

He pulled the film for 2003 back out and rethreaded it through the reader. The gears protested with an increasingly high-pitched whine as he advanced to the end of October. Nothing for May 30 or 31. Then he found it. November 2. But the date of the actual death was earlier, naturally.

October 31, 2003.

A shiver ran through Joe's spine.

Why didn't he believe that the out-of-town salesman who took a dive off that cliff last year had been suicidal?

He rewound the film and put on the roll for the fall of 2002. He advanced to November 1, and then 2. But there was no report of any Halloween deaths.

There was a story about the town's centennial that caught his eye.

TERREL TURNS 100! boasted the front-page headline.

He skimmed through the puff copy. God, there were times he detested backwoods journalism! It read as if it were written by old women who thought journalism was just a creative step sideways from putting down their thoughts late at night in their farm journals after cleaning the supper dishes.

It was a century of change. The telephone, the radio, television, the motorcar. Through it all, the citizens and town of Terrel have remained nestled near the prominent outline of Terrel's Peak.

"The river of time has rushed through Terrel and left us changed, and yet, somehow, still the same," said Mayor Pierce Harden during the centennial ceremonies held Saturday in Memorial Park.

Founded by Broderick Terrel in 1893, the town grew from a lonely watchtower to a small, thriving community by the turn of the century and was granted township in 1902. Terrel's lighthouse on the peak provided safety not only to ships navigating the dark and foggy coasts, but to the people who began to build a community at the peak's base.

While Terrel never became a haven for large shipping commerce due to the treacherous currents of its shallow, rocky bay, for a time it was a well-used port for small crafts stopping down from Port Haven, fifty miles north.

After the sudden death of Broderick Terrel, however, the lighthouse fell into disrepair, and ships began to avoid chancy stops at the town's tiny seaport. The lighthouse, both a landmark and memorial to the town's founder, was destroyed in 1951 during a storm that also leveled several homes in town. It was never rebuilt.

More than he needed to know, Joe thought, scrolling past the end of the story. Terrel was a backward little town near the sea that didn't actually get anything out of the nearby ocean but the view. And apparently even the view wasn't safe to enjoy.

The obituary ran on November 4.

The body hadn't been found for a couple days and was badly mangled and snagged on some rocks when a couple kids on a boat ran across it at the base of the cliff. The coroner's report indicated that the woman had apparently died sometime between October 31 and November 1. The cause of death was a broken neck, presumably from hitting the rocks on the beach below the promontory. The brief obituary said the woman had been traveling through Terrel on her way to visit a relative in Virginia.

Go for three? Joe asked himself, and rewound the film. He didn't really believe it could be that easy, that he could just scroll to the same week in year after year of the *Times* and find an obit for a suicide. But his heart started pounding faster as the 2001 microfilm spooled noisily through the machine. He wanted to find out that he wasn't crazy. That something or someone was killing people every Halloween and every May 22 on the cliff, the shadow of which blanketed this town every morning and evening. And then again, he didn't want to find that out. Because what was he going to do with the information? He couldn't publish it. That had been made quite clear. And the police were apparently not interested in following up on it either.

November 1, 2001 was clean. No death notices.

November 2, 2001 was not.

Richard Chambers, 45, of New York City, was found dead on the rocks below Terrel's Peak yesterday morning. Mr. Chambers suffered massive head and back injuries due to a fall from the cliff. The coroner's report said Mr. Chambers died twenty-four to twenty-eight hours prior to the discovery of his body. Mr. Chambers was a computer salesman for Elek-Tek, en route to a convention in Sara Clair. The police have located his next of kin, who will hold services for Mr. Chambers in his hometown of Queens.

On October 31, 2000, it was an auto dealer from Georgia. And on May 22, 2000, it was a local kid named Bob O'Grady. Eighteen years old.

On October 31, 1999, it was a transient man from California. A John Doe.

But the death toll for May 22, 1999 was again zero.

Three more Halloweens were followed by obituaries, but the Mays were clean. Apparently Bob O'Grady had signaled the start of the May killings.

Joe could think of them now only as killings. This wasn't a case of copycat kids toying with suicide, or the occasional lonely wanderer dropping off the edge into the blessed, churning peace of the ocean.

But now another question nagged at Joe's mind.

If the May murders had started just five years ago, how long had the Halloween killings gone on?

He ran out of microfilm in 1985, and hadn't missed a Halloween death yet. Joe packed up all the film and closed his notebook. Maybe there was another room with older film. He went to find Mrs. Malone.

"Oh, no, I'm sorry, young man. The library started putting things on fiche back in 1985. That's when we got the grant to get the machine, you know. We never got around to putting all the old stuff on it, but we haven't missed an issue of the paper since."

"So there's no way to find older copies of the *Terrel Daily Times* than 1985?"

"Sure there is." Mrs. Malone laughed out loud at his discomfiture, and then abruptly silenced herself, looking around to make sure she hadn't disturbed any of the patrons. "We have some bound copies of the paper in a back room. We don't leave them out, because the kids get too rough on them. We have copies of the paper dating back almost as old as the town itself. Although I don't know that you'll be able to read many of those papers. The older issues pretty much crumble apart if you do much more than look at 'em. But if you're careful, I'll let you see what you can see."

"I'd sure appreciate it," he mumbled, but Mrs. Malone was already motioning him to follow her behind the librarian's desk.

She opened a door and turned the corner, and suddenly they were in a different building.

Gone were the white foam ceilings and bright cream walls of the main library. They walked down echoing cement steps to a gloomy room lit by two bare bulbs. The walls were bare brick, the air chilled.

"It ain't much of a study carrel, but we've only got so much space upstairs." Mrs. Malone shrugged, gesturing toward a lonely spot in the corner. "Here's what you're looking for."

She motioned to a rack against the far wall. It was filled with twenty-inch-tall binders. Joe scanned the dates, marked in pen on the spines. *Terrel Daily Times* 1984, read the closest one. His eyes slid down the row, noting 1980 . . . 1974 . . . 1958 . . . 1930.

"You can use that desk over there to read, if you like," Mrs. Malone said. "Or, if you know what year you're looking for, you can just bring the book upstairs."

"Actually, I'd like to skim through a bunch of years, if I may," he answered. "So I guess I'll stay here for a while."

"Suit yourself," she said, crossing her arms and shivering

slightly. "Please be careful handling them, and put them back in order. When you're finished, just come on back upstairs."

Her steps *click-clack*ed quickly up the stairs and Joe was left alone in the library basement.

Pulling out a sampling of years, he walked over to the desk the librarian had indicated. It was old and wooden, and its legs wobbled when he set the stack down. He pulled up the chair and began to read.

And the death toll mounted.

In 1980, an apparent gang execution had taken place. One Ricardo Hijuana, twenty-two, of Key West, was found wedged among the rocks at the base of Terrel's Peak. His wrists were tied together behind his back. Twine bound his ankles together and stretched from his feet up his spine to connect to the gag that was lodged in Hijuana's mouth. It was a very ruthless Halloween trick.

In 1976, another interesting Halloween snuff: After a child uncovered a dismembered hand while building a sand castle, the rest of an unidentified Caucasian male was discovered floating in various parts of the bay. Police reports indicated that a stick of dynamite had been tied to the boy's midsection and lit just before he was pushed over the edge of the cliff. A gruesome bicentennial bit of fireworks.

In 1954, the half-eaten body of a baby girl was discovered washed up on the beach on November 5. She'd been dead nearly a week, the obituary estimated. In subsequent reports, Joe found that police were unable to discover the child's parentage.

In 1948, the grisly remains of a black woman were discovered by two grade school children playing by the beach. Joe had to laugh at the paper's instant discriminatory supposition.

> Police officials have been unable to establish the identity of the woman, however they theorize that she may have been on the run.

"A lot of these kinds of people steal the silverware

and other valuables in the night and then head up the coast, looking for someone who will agree to turn their stolen bounty into greenbacks," said Police Chief Billy Bob Grunson. "Why else would somebody from out of town have been up there after dark? She may have been so weighed down by whatever she was carrying that she fell right over the side of the cliff in the dark."

Case closed. Joe smirked.

In 1935, the *Times* reported the death of a local man. But this account was not as abbreviated as those in following years.

Arnold Harver, 54, passed on after venturing too close to the deadly edge of Terrel's Peak on October 31. Harver was among the earliest inhabitants of Terrel, having come here with his father, Arthur Harver, in 1910. Harver often visited the old lighthouse on his nightly walks. He had said that his strolls near the lighthouse brought him closer to the spirits of the past. Unfortunately, as many who failed to heed the warnings about the cliff have learned, those spirits have too often felt and slaked their desire for blood.

Joe shut the old newspaper binder with a thud. Bits of musty yellow newspaper fluttered to the floor. He didn't know what to think. At first he had assumed there was some kind of serial killer at work here, something that the Terrel cops just didn't know how to handle, and didn't want to talk about with a relative stranger.

But if he believed what he was reading here, this was not about serial killing. Not unless the entire town was in on it.

This was something much more deadly than some guy with some rope and a thirst for hearing screams from flailing people on the way down.

This was about cults . . . or ghosts.

Terrel's Peak, Joe decided, was haunted.

Except Joe didn't believe in ghosts.

He reminded himself of this fact and stilled a shiver. He suddenly felt as if the shadows of the damp room were moving behind him.

After looking around at the piles of books and newspapers in the room, Joe began to hurriedly stuff the binders back on the shelves in the empty holes he'd left for them.

The lighting in this basement was not helping his nerves any.

There was a cold sweat starting beneath his arms, and gooseflesh rippling on top of them. Grabbing his notebook, now rife with the names of long-dead people, both strangers and natives of Terrel, he vaulted up the stairs.

He had done enough studying for one day.

CHAPTER NINE

Her breath was coming in heaving gasps by the time Cindy reached the top of the cliff. It was a long climb from town without a car. The sweat rolled down her back, but a brisk wind from the bay kept her from overheating.

"You would have thought all the walking to classes at school would have put me in shape for this," she said to the wind.

She picked her way through brambles and tangles of ketch vine and spiny grass to the hard rocky face of the peak. Here, very little vegetation survived the harsh sun and scouring winds and rain. But the view was worth the effort.

Spread out before her was a picture postcard. She could never describe this to her friends in college. And pictures couldn't begin to capture the beauty she'd been brought up to accept as mundane. Straight down, the ocean broke in foamy kisses against the boulder-strewn beach. Sea green beyond the rocks, the water stretched to the horizon, which was already bruising purple with the coming night. Behind her, she could follow the winding road down the slope. It disappeared into a maze of trees, but slithered out the other side and reappeared entering the town proper of Terrel.

From the top of the cliff she could see the bell tower of St. Matthews, the rust-tiled roof of the Anderson Hotel, and the grassy knoll to the west of town where she and James used to picnic. All around, poking through the canopy of forest were a collage of black and green roofs of the surrounding homes.

The steady intake and exhalation of the ocean filled the air, but in the distance she could hear the call of gulls. They'd be heading home now, to wherever it is seabirds shelter for the night.

Cindy walked closer to the edge.

She could see a spot where the gray rock extended out over the ocean just a few feet farther than the rest of the plateau. He'd jumped there, she decided. They all jumped from there, didn't they?

She approached the spot slowly, hesitantly. As if to a shrine.

Why? What could have possessed him to do it?

The word "possessed" took root and echoed in her brain.

She sank to her knees then, and the tears snuck through the dike she'd built against them these past couple hours of walking and thinking.

Even though James refused to leave Terrel for college, she'd still thought they would be together this summer. And maybe then she could have convinced him to reconsider. She pounded a fist into the denim of her thigh.

He hadn't even waited to see her! One more week and she would have been with him. They would have had three more months, if not forever. And maybe those months would have led to the beginning of forever, if things had gone the way she'd hoped. Hadn't they been in love? Hadn't she pulled him to her chest under the blanket of night and met his whispered promises with secret words of her own?

Her heart ached with conflicting emotions. She wanted to hit him for leaving her, and at the same time kiss him and beg him to come back.

She rocked with sobs on the edge of the cliff, unable to do either.

CHAPTER TEN

Joe hit c4 and watched the Bugles drop with a gentle *thunk* to the bottom. He pulled out the bag and was munching contentedly until he got back to his desk.

Randy was there waiting for him.

"Where've you been?" the night editor demanded. "We've got a paper to put out here. I need to get your story on the library renovation—and the fire safety piece—by six o'clock!"

Shit.

"I'm sorry, Randy. I was down at the library doing some research. The time got away from me. I'm almost through with both of those anyway. Give me another hour."

"Well, get on 'em."

Tom Hicks, the slot editor, looked up from the copydesk and winked at him. Then he wrinkled up his face and exaggerated the editor's tantrum through painful facial grimaces.

It was all Joe could do to keep from laughing in his boss's face. Randy turned to go back to his desk, but then stopped.

"Oh, and I almost forgot. A woman called while you were gone. Italian. Angelina? No, Angelica. That fortune-teller lady from the south end of town. Angelica Napalona. She said you had her number. Why you'd have her number, I don't want to know. But if you're thinking about using her as a source for anything that doesn't involve mental illness, you can pick up your pen and pad and head back to Chicago."

"Don't worry, I just had a question about my palm," Joe

quipped, but inside he was jumping. Why was she calling him? Had his presence at the funeral changed her mind?

He sat down at his computer and tried to concentrate on putting the final touches on his stories for tomorrow's paper, but he kept hearing a fake Gypsy accent.

As he fixed up his quotes from Mrs. Malone to sound intelligent, he kept feeling Randy's eyes on him. The guy hadn't let up all week. And the more he dicked around with lame stories like this, the more he missed Chicago. The boonies were good for a vacation, but there was something to be said for a newsroom that buzzed and thrummed with action and constantly ringing phones. God, what he wouldn't give for a good murder trial or a city councilman exposed on a bribe charge.

But isn't that exactly why you left? a voice chided him. A life spent nailing people to pulp paper wasn't healthy. For the soul or the body.

But was writing about the new paintings in the Terrel library any better?

He finished up his stories for the day by six thirty and ducked out without hanging around to argue with Randy about his edits. He didn't really give a shit what the copy editor did with either of the stories he'd turned in. He had a bigger story to chase right now, and he couldn't even write about it.

Yet.

The scents of spaghetti and barbecued pork were fighting it out in the air outside his apartment building as he climbed from the car.

Hmmm, he thought, tasting the air and envying whomever was cooking. "That smells very nice," he joked aloud, "but I think we'll be having something better tonight. Some truly haute cuisine. Say, Hungry Man Yankee pot roast?"

The key rattled nervously in the lock as he twisted the knob and entered his apartment.

And stepped over a piece of paper that had been slipped under the door. He bent down to retrieve it.

It was just a scrap of yellow legal paper, folded over twice. Inside was a single sentence:

Death usually finds those who look for it.

What the hell did that mean?

The writing looked feminine to him, its message delivered in big showy loops, but he couldn't be sure. He read it over again and again. Then he stuffed it into his pocket and looked sharply around the apartment, thoroughly spooked now. He flipped on the kitchen light and then slipped his hand around the neck of the living room's lamp to find its switch. The apartment was silent except for the occasional *thump* from the kids in the unit upstairs.

He strained his ears, trying to hear if there was any motion in the far reaches of his rooms. The hallway to the bedroom was dark. The chickenshit side of his brain whispered that surely no one was here. The note had been slipped under the door, right? There was no real reason to go looking around in the bedroom, was there?

Biting his tongue and stifling his yellow half, Joe marched down the hallway, expecting someone to jump out of the shadows from his bedroom or bathroom at any second.

He reached into the bedroom and slid his hand along the wall, searching for the light switch. Someone could still be in his room, his mind cautioned. They could hack off his hand with an axe, and while Joe was screaming and staring at the bloody stump, the killer could step out and finish him off.

The ceiling light clicked on above his bed, casting aside the dark. He breathed a sigh of relief, but barely believed his eyes. The only thing out of place was a pair of rumpled socks on the floor, where he'd kicked them off the previous night.

Even so, he went back to the living room and sat in the chair that put his back to the wall. He wanted to keep the rest of the apartment in view.

He was a good reporter.

He was not ready for death threats.

Flipping open the phone book, he flipped as fast as he could to the Ns. He knew a certain Gypsy who hadn't been completely straight with him. It was about time he got some answers instead of questions.

Angelica's house was dark when he pulled into the driveway, but as he switched off the ignition, a light flickered on in the front room. Joe killed the lights and walked through the tangle of shadowed shrubs to the front door.

She'd been strange on the phone, almost afraid.

I vant to apologize for being so short vith you ze other day, she'd said.

It's okay, he'd assured her, and then asked if he could come by to talk some more.

Now? Her voice had raised an octave.

Is this a bad time?

She cleared her throat.

No. I . . . just . . . No. Now iss fine.

The door opened as he set foot on the front step.

"Come in, come in," she urged, and with her hand on his back nearly shoved him through the entryway into the living room.

Tonight, Angelica wore a royal blue robe of silk—or some imitation—with aqueous purple and pink creatures darting around its hems. Her hair looked damp and hung in ringlets on her shoulders. She didn't seem to be wearing anything beneath the robe, he noticed as it shifted to reveal a dark shadow of tantalizing cleavage.

"Please, sit." She nodded toward an old yellow stuffed chair in the corner of the room.

He accepted the offer, and she sank back onto a loveseat across from him. A maroon painted hurricane lamp between them provided the only light in the room, which left most of the house in shadow. The lavender scent of burning candles or incense permeated the room, though he saw nothing currently burning.

This was like talking to someone across a campfire, Joe thought, as he noted how the low light played across Angelica's olive skin. She looked deeply tanned, and, he noted with some discomfort as she crossed a bare leg across her knee, much younger than she had at the funeral.

"Did I get you out of the shower?" he ventured, feeling awkward. "I could have come later, or tomorrow."

She smiled and shook her head.

"No. I always take a shower at night, and then it just zeems foolish to get all the way dressed again. Do you mind?"

"Uh, no. Not at all."

"May I zee your hands?" she asked.

He extended his palms across the lamp table to her.

"I didn't come for a reading, Angelica."

She ignored him, leaning forward to take his palms in hers.

He couldn't help but stare at the gentle swells of her breasts as her robe parted slightly. They hung heavy and lush as she bent across the table, the dark line of her cleavage looming dangerously close as her forefinger traced the life line on his right palm. Her hair brushed his forearm. It was damp and cool, raising goose bumps from his biceps to his fingers. He felt himself growing excited to be in the room with her and stifled the urge to reach out and take her shoulders in his hands. He was here to find out answers, not seduce a bad palm reader.

"I am zeeing much danger for you, my friend," she cooed, her voice a languorous snake. "You vill be wise to keep your head down, your eyes on the ground. . . ."

She smiled demurely as Joe pulled back his hand. She began to speak but he motioned for her to stop.

"Angelica, I said I didn't come here for a reading. And I don't need to hear the phony accent. You grew up here, and Terrel is not known for its large indigenous Gypsy population."

Her eyes flashed briefly, but the smile never left her face. Quite.

"What is it you want then from me, Mr. Kieran?" The accent was gone. "I am a fortune-teller."

She stood up and stepped around the table to get closer to him.

Her hands flattened the robe against her midriff.

"This is what I do, Mr. Kieran. Why else would anyone be interested in talking to me? I put on pretty robes and zen I talk like zhis and I tell people what I think is going to happen to them."

She bent closer to him, her lips only inches from his own. Her voice dropped to a whisper.

"And you know what? Since I was eighteen, I've hardly ever been wrong."

"Well, I'm not interested in the voodoo crap, Angelica. What I *am* interested in is Terrel's Peak. More specifically, why is it that people in this town seem to have the uncanny knack for jumping off that cliff every year on the same day?"

Angelica knelt then, the blue silk sliding along the seam of Joe's jeans with a gentle swish. She rested her arms on his thighs, and he could feel her chest molding itself to his legs. What was she trying to do here?

"Well, I could tell you all about that, Joe Kieran. But I don't think you'd believe me. I think you'd call it a bunch of hocus-pocus 'voodoo crap.' Wouldn't you rather talk about something else, Joe?"

She slid her hands over his T-shirt to wrap around the back of his neck. Her tongue tickled the creases of his ear and she whispered to him. "Wouldn't you rather talk about what's under this robe, Mr. Kieran?"

In spite of himself, Joe again felt a stirring in his jeans, which grew more uncomfortable as she suddenly drew herself up to kneel on his lap. Her robe slid from her shoulders to fully reveal her breasts, perfectly formed caramel cream mounds tipped with areolas like thick, dark bruises. She wrapped her arms around his head, pushing his mouth into her bosom and crying out as she did.

"Yes, yes. Oh, kiss me."

Joe collected his wits then and pushed her back.

"No."

God, what was he doing? How could he say no to the only good time he had had in months? Angelica continued kneeling on his thighs, but her hands gripped the arms of the chair. Her robe had fallen completely open, exposing a very well-toned body for a woman probably ten years Joe's senior. Between her breasts a silver pendant hung from a leather thong—an astrological symbol, he guessed. Even as she crouched, her belly held itself beautifully taut, and the dark triangle below was clearly carefully groomed. As she leaned in to try to kiss him again, he turned his head.

"No," he repeated. "I didn't come here for this. If you're still offering later, I might accept. But first I want to know what's going on."

"Well, later just may be too late," she snapped, and slid off his lap to straighten her robe.

"According to this, I may not have long anyway," Joe answered, and handed her the yellow slip of paper from his pocket.

Angelica's face paled as she read the subtle threat.

Death usually finds those who look for it.

She handed the note back to him without a word and then stood up and crossed to the curtained front windows. She moved the drapery aside and looked outside for several minutes. Joe sat quietly, watching to see what she would do next.

"Wait here," she said suddenly, pulling the drapes closed and then disappearing into the back of the house.

Joe stood and straightened his pants and shirt, undoing the damage Angelica had done in her bizarre and uninvited attempt to seduce him. He walked to the window. From up close, he saw the draperies were the same shade of royal blue that the palm reader wore tonight. But they were of a far heavier, less revealing material than Angelica's robe. He smiled to himself and pushed them aside to glance outside. The moon was out and lit the yard in a harsh spotlight. He saw the branches of the honeysuckles sway slightly, their motion exaggerated by the long shadows they cast writhing on the ground. While she lived just seconds from the main drag of Terrel, Angelica had apparently encouraged nature to shield her from the town. The yard was a forest of trees and bushes. Only a short stretch of the street was visible from this window.

He let the drapes close and checked out the room. It looked much larger than it was because of the mirrors mounted on three of the four walls. Angelica had put in small shelves between them, and long tentacles of ivies and vines stretched to reach the light wood of the floor. The center of the floor was covered by an Oriental rug, which Joe assumed was an imitation piece bought at the local Wal-Mart. But it looked fancy, and the intricate array of designs fit in perfectly with Angelica's profession.

How many customers can she really get in this backward town, though? he wondered.

"You won't believe me anyway, but maybe this will help," she said, breezing back into the room like a silk-clad princess. In her hands she held a red leather-bound scrapbook. She set the book on the table and leafed through it until she found the page she wanted.

Then, drawing her robe modestly around her, she sat back on the loveseat.

"Read it."

Joe leaned forward to see what she'd brought. It was a yellowed clip from the *Terrel Daily Times*. The date read November 6, 1951.

CURSED CLIFF, read the headline.

It had run on the op ed page.

Joe quickly skimmed the opening of the article.

Some will call it a fluke storm, but old-timers here in Terrel know that the gusts that rocked Terrel's Peak on Halloween were no natural event. For the first time in over twenty years, no body washed up on the beach last week, and the evil that dwells within that twisted growth of rock was angry. Is probably still angry.

Nobody knows what spirit dwells in that cliff. But whether it's a lesser demon or the devil himself, there's nobody who's lived in Terrel for any amount of time who doesn't own up to the fact that Terrel's Peak is a deadly place where bad things happen. I've done my share of searching, and the deaths have occurred here since the first years of Terrel's settlement. Perhaps our founder made some deal with the devil that offered our lives as payment for some service we'll never know about. Or perhaps the peak is simply the gateway for the souls of hell that are released every year on All Hallow's Eve.

Whatever the reason, the cliff is dangerous.

And now, it's angry.

Consider this a caution.

Over the past years, the cliff has almost always left townsfolk alone, in favor of luring outsiders to break themselves on the deadly rocks at its feet. But apparently no outsiders offered themselves for the evil to devour this Halloween.

Someone from Terrel may be called upon to pay the price.

Don't let it be you.

Stay away from the cliff these next few days. If you value your life.

—Jarvid Hardin.

Joe looked up from the story to stare at Angelica. "Is this really what everyone in town thinks? That as long as some stranger dies on Halloween, they'll be safe for another year?"

Angelica nodded. Her eyes were hooded and dark.

"It's not always true. Turn the page."

He did and found another newspaper clip.

This one was much more recent. The date was May 23, 1981.

LOCAL GIRL DROWNS IN BAY

Bernadette O'Brien, 19, of Terrel, drowned while swimming with five of her school friends yesterday in the bay.

While an accomplished swimmer, O'Brien was apparently pulled under by a strong current, and trapped for a time underwater by seaweed or other debris.

"We swam out into the bay and were lying out on the rocks below Terrel's Peak, just sunbathing," said Karen Sander, one of the last girls who saw Bernadette O'Brien alive.

"Bernadette dove into the water and started swimming back toward the shore by the cliff to cool off. We didn't think anything about it, but then Margaret [Kelly] noticed that she couldn't see Bernadette anywhere. We started calling her name, and when she didn't answer, we all dove in and started trying to follow her path back to the shore."

When the girls reached the shore and still hadn't found any sign of their friend, Sander went to call the police while the other girls continued searching. The body of O'Brien was found at about seven P.M., lodged between two of the boulders beneath the peak. Services will be held at Folter's Funeral Home tomorrow from three to nine P.M.

"May twenty-second," he murmured before looking up to meet her gaze.

"You were there, weren't you?" he asked quietly.

Angelica nodded.

"And Mrs. Canady?"

"Starting to see a pattern?"

"So six girls went swimming one spring day and one of them didn't come back. What does that have to do with the deaths of the survivors' children twenty years later? On the same day?"

Angelica stared at a spot on the wall behind his shoulder.

"That's one I don't have an answer for, Mr. Kieran. But I can tell you that that day changed all of our lives. There is a presence in that cliff. We all felt it. It has been a shadow over my life ever since."

"So do you suppose it was a 'presence' who sent me this little note?" Joe asked, waving the yellow paper in the air. "I don't buy it."

"You don't have to buy anything. I don't know who left you that note, but I can tell you that they were right. You want to know about things that are best left alone. There is a reason that it's almost never people from Terrel who die on Halloween. It's because we leave well enough alone. Very few people are stupid enough to spend much time swimming in the bay. You just never know when it might get hungry."

"I'll offer you a different reason," Joe interrupted. "I'd say that there's some weird little sect of people in Terrel who like to have little Halloween sacrifices every year. What do you think of that?"

"I think you're wrong, but I told you that you would not believe my story."

Angelica reached forward and shut the scrapbook. But she didn't sit back.

"There's a devil that lives in Terrel's Peak, Joe. And if you look hard enough, you're going to attract its attention. You don't want it to turn its sights on you."

"Sounds a bit like a threat."

She sighed. "I'm trying to help you."

Angelica stood and stepped around the table to stand in front of his chair once again. Her eyes didn't waver from his as her hand undid the ocean blue sash, allowing the robe to slip from her body to pool on the floor. She straddled his left knee and kissed him full and hard on the lips. "Now, are you going to help me?"

This time, Joe didn't push her away.

CHAPTER ELEVEN

His apartment seemed cold and sterile in the light of morning after a night in the wanton whimsy of Angelica's bedroom. Joe couldn't quite remove the smile plastered across his face as he kept revisiting the moves of the night before. Angelica had practically dragged him to her bed, and she was not a woman who should have needed to drag anyone. She certainly knew what she was doing once she got there, that was for sure. The muscles in his belly and thighs ached with the memory of her expertise! She was flexible and inventive.

But he doubted her motives. While she seemed aroused to the point of savagery when they tangled in her sheets, he somehow doubted that it had anything to do with his own rugged good looks. Because he didn't really have any, he thought as he stared into the bathroom mirror. He pulled the razor across his cheek and tried to still the voice within him that kept asking why.

But his questions kept being obscured by the memory of her golden skin folding and moving around him, the feeling of his hands moving over the softness of her perfect breasts, and of her tongue in his mouth eagerly seeking his core.

He still didn't buy the evil spirit explanation. Angelica was hiding something about the cliff from him, and incredible sex or not, he intended to track down exactly what it was. Maybe it was time to give the other ladies of this apparent circle a visit.

Starting, he decided, with Karen Sander.

Joe left his apartment intending to set up a meeting after work with the Sander woman, but the day didn't go quite as he planned. There'd been a burglary overnight at the 7-Eleven on the west end of town, and he ended up spending the bulk of the afternoon tracking down the police chief and the witness, a slow-speaking high school kid, for comments. Which backed up his other stories. Which meant that when he got home it was ten P.M. and it was too late even for Hungry Man dinners. He collapsed into bed without thinking about deadly peaks or palm readers. And with Randy off on vacation to Florida for two weeks, he didn't have time to think about them again for a while.

But it never quite left his mind. He carried the yellow slip of paper around with him everywhere, and he had sketched out a tree chart of the May 22 killings, starting with the swimming accident of 1981. He'd met four of the five survivors of that event so far. Fuck, he had slept with one of them! The only one who hadn't lost a child to the pull of the cliff. As far as he knew.

Two weeks after sleeping with Angelica, he finally called and set up an appointment with Karen Sander. She didn't sound happy to hear from him, but she gave him directions to her house anyway.

"I don't know what I can do for you, Mr. Kieran," she said. "But I'll tell you what I know."

Somehow he doubted that, but he climbed into his car after work and aimed it in the direction of her place anyway.

He was interested to hear if she would tell the same story as Angelica.

Somehow he doubted that she would.

And he was right.

The radio was blasting "Should I Stay or Should I Go" as Joe pulled his car into the gravel driveway at 154 Waveland Lane, Karen Sander's house. His stomach was tight, but in a good way. Joe smiled to himself, remembering.

This was how being a reporter felt. On edge. You never knew what that next interview was going to turn up, but you barreled in anyway. Usually, it was an empty casket. Every now and then, if you didn't slip up and rattle the source, you found not only the bones, but also the closet they were hidden in.

Joe smelled bones as he stepped out into the cool dusk of an early summer night in Terrel. And that musty smell made him smile.

"Mrs. Sander?" he said in his warmest voice when the middle-aged woman opened the front door. She nodded. The corners of her eyes crinkled up as she took him in.

"I'm Joe Kieran. We met at James Canady's funeral. I called you the other day from the newspaper?"

"Yes Joe, I remember. Come on in."

She ushered him into a sterile front room. The carpet was white; the walls, cream; the furniture a mix of deep woods and dull corn yellows.

"Have a seat. Would you like a glass of iced tea?"

"That'd be great, thanks."

She dipped her head in acknowledgement and disappeared through an entryway into the kitchen. Joe sat, staring at the cool disassociation of the room. A picture window took up most of the east wall of the house. A large Magnavox TV, jet-black, dominated the floor space before the windows. Two earth tone couches, a couple of small end tables, and a picture on the wall. That was the one thing he realized that really didn't go here. The rest of the room was bright, if empty of spark. But dominating the front room's main wall was a huge painting of the ocean. In contrast to the whites and yellows of the room, the painting showed a dead gray expanse of steely sea shuddering against a rocky coastline. Far from shore, hidden in a plume of fog, he could just make out the jut of a mountain or steep hill. The whole painting seemed designed to exude frost.

"I call it *The Covenant*."

Joe jumped at Karen's voice. She was standing directly behind him; he hadn't noticed her reenter the room.

"Here's your tea," she said, setting the glass on a wooden coaster on the table beside him.

Karen Sander was a woman who'd thought a lot about life, Joe decided as he took her in. Her face was broad and easy, her nose dipped up just enough to give her the appearance of blue-blood heritage, but her eyes looked worn and warm in their depths. And the lines running from their corners told him that Karen Sander had done a lot of living and dying in her forty years. He'd figured out on his murder tree that if the girls who were swimming in the bay on May 22, 1981 were all classmates, then they were all about 18 at the time of the drowning. That put them all just over forty now. Angelica looked—and felt—younger than her age, but Karen Sander was starting to suffer from its effects. Silver darted like schools of tuna through her once-black hair, and she groaned as she eased back into the sofa across from him.

"What can I help you with?" she said in a soft voice.

Here it was. Joe either hooked her here or left without learning a thing. "A source either trusts you in your first few words or they never will," one of his editors used to caution. So far, he'd found the advice fairly accurate. And you didn't generally gain people's trust by lying to them. At least *he* hadn't found a good way.

"Ma'am, I'm the guy who wrote the obituary for the Canady boy's death last month. For the *Terrel Daily Times*. Now, I'm fairly new here in town, so I didn't know what to think when nobody wanted to talk about a boy jumping from a cliff at such a young age. I thought that especially odd when the boy seemed to have so much to live for. That got me looking around a bit, and pretty soon I found that James was not the first kid in this town to jump off that cliff, not by a long shot. I found out that you lost a boy, and Margaret Kelly lost her daughter. And then there was the boy before her."

Karen's eyes didn't look away from his at all as he gave his litany. She almost looked ready to smile.

"Now, I still wouldn't have thought too much of this—kids in Chicago, where I'm from, knock themselves and each other off all the time. Not a big deal. What got me about this, though, was not that some kids here in Terrel were copycat jumpers; what got me was that they all jumped on *exactly the same date*."

Karen didn't look shocked at his bomb. He hadn't really expected her to. Instead she gave a sad grin and shrugged.

"And you want me to tell you what, Mr. Kieran? That there was a calendar in my son's room that said 'May twenty-second, the day of atonement'? What are you asking me?"

"I'm asking you if you have any idea why four kids over the course of five years decided to jump off the same cliff in the same town on the same day. Don't you think that's a bit odd?"

She stood up, smoothing the loose-fitting fabric of her blouse to her waist.

"Odd, Mr. Kieran? No."

She crossed the room to stare at her painting.

"Sad. Heartbreaking. Maddening, even. But not odd. We all deal with grief in our own ways, and the kids were all very close. If you'd been here long enough, you'd know—and maybe you've found this out already from your 'investigations'—but all of us mothers have been friends for a long time. So the kids were always around one another."

"I'm sorry, Mrs. Sander. I didn't . . . I shouldn't have said *odd*. But I'm trying to understand what's been going on in this town. And nobody seems to want to talk about it. It's as if they're all afraid to speak, as if they're protecting someone. I'm inclined to think that these kids didn't jump off that cliff of their own accord, and I was hoping you could steer me in the right direction."

"Do you see this picture, Mr. Kieran?"

Karen pointed at the gloomy sea painting in front of her.

"Yes."

"I told you I call it *The Covenant*."

"Yes. You painted it yourself?"

"I did. Almost twenty years ago. It was the first time I held a brush."

"That's incredible," Joe said, wide-eyed. He looked harder at the painting, with a critical eye. It gave one a chill—its melancholic depiction of the sea looked almost real. The detail in the piece was intricate, even for a seasoned artist.

"Have you ever done a gallery showing?" he asked. "If this was your first, I'd love to see what you're painting these days!"

"I've never painted again," she said.

Karen turned and took Joe by the shoulders. Her eyes were lit with an inner fire as she spoke.

"The Covenant, Mr. Kieran, is that in Terrel, we live off the sea, but ultimately, the sea will take us all. What we take from it, we merely borrow. It will drown us and choke us and pull us under. It will dash us on the rocks and spit at us when salvation looms just ahead. The Covenant we keep is death. My child kept his part of the bargain, and I'm betting I'll get mine before long. And you'll get it too. Sooner rather than later, if you keep asking people about their dead kids."

She took her hands from his shoulders and stepped back, covering her mouth. Then she brushed her eye and stuttered, "I'm s-sorry. I . . . I still miss my boy."

Karen pulled a tissue from her pocket to wipe her eyes, and Joe sensed it was his moment. He could push and lose it all, or try to soothe her, and still find out nothing.

"Mrs. Sander, I wouldn't ask you any of this if I thought there was the chance that your son's death was something normal—some statistic that all parents have to grow old dreading. But I think your son is a special case. As are Margaret Kelly and James Canady."

Karen looked up with reddened eyes at him.

"What do you mean?"

The moment.

"Mrs. Sander, has anybody ever noticed that the date that Margaret and James and William and Bob died, May twenty-second, is the same date that Bernadette O'Brien died while swimming with five of her friends in 1981? Those same five friends who have, one by one, been losing children off that cliff for the past five years?"

Karen sunk back into the sofa and just looked at Joe. Her eyes were surprised, yet seemed relieved.

"If you had grown up around here, that wouldn't seem like such a strange thing, Mr. Kieran."

"Why's that?"

"Because everybody knows that Terrel's Peak is the home of the devil," she whispered.

Joe did his best to keep from smiling. Karen leaned forward. Her face grew thin.

"You think I'm kidding. And coming from a town of thieves and murders like you have, you probably can't think of anything but that when someone dies, there must be a knife holder. Well, you've found the cradle of hell, Joe Kieran. And the knife is invisible. But the chopping block is not."

She pointed to the hint of a cliff poking through the swirling mists of the painting. "It's there. It's Terrel's Peak. If you want to understand, go up there after sundown tonight and listen to the wind. But don't presume that you'll come back to talk about it."

With that, Karen Sander turned and walked from the room.

Over her shoulder she called, "Please finish your tea, Mr. Kieran. And then let yourself out. There is nothing more I can tell you."

CHAPTER TWELVE

Joe shook his head and smiled as he backed out of Karen Sander's driveway. He tasted a story here. A big story. The kind that gets the Press Guild to send you to a podium in the fall. The kind that brings in the county police scratching their heads and saying, "We don't know how this could have gotten past us, but we're certain that we'll catch it if it ever happens again!"

He could see Chief Swartzky's face as the TV cameras blinded him with the lighthouse strobes. Swartzky would swear he'd never had an inkling and no one had ever brought the issue before him.

"There'll be a department overhaul starting next week," he'd promise. "I'm embarrassed that no one ever put a pattern to those kids' deaths. But I've known Karen Sander and Rhonda Canady since they were kids, and they never were anything but the sweetest women. Who could have suspected them of killing their own kids?"

Oh, when he pulled together some more evidence, he'd offer it to Chief Harry Swartzky. He had no doubt that Terrel's police chief would find a reason to ignore or bury it.

And he'd offer the story that he was already writing in his head to the *Terrel Daily Times*, but he doubted that it would be published there. But there were bigger towns in this county. Maybe he'd take it up north to the *Port Haven Dispatch*. If he found evidence for what he suspected, he'd have no trouble selling the story to a larger paper. And Terrel would be crawling with state and county cops for a week afterward.

Maybe longer, if he didn't find the source of the Halloween murders. They'd have to start searching for that mystery's solution if he handed them this one. Maybe they were connected. But he doubted it, for some reason. The May 22 Murders, as he'd begun to headline them, smelled like copycat killing to him.

One thing was certain: he didn't believe that there had been a bogeyman hiding out in the mountain pushing people off one day a year for the past century. But there was also no way all these deaths were the offspring of a single psycho serial killer. This kind of regularity took organization.

As for the recent May 22 murders, well, it really all pointed back to five women, didn't it? Or at least four. Rhonda Canady, Karen Sander, Melody O'Grady and Monica Kelly were all present over two decades ago when Bernadette O'Brien mysteriously drowned. And then twenty years later their own kids, one by one, were suddenly disappearing just as each of them turned eighteen. Was it some kind of sacrificial rite they'd sworn to as girls?

It was wicked. Twisted.

Unfathomable.

But it didn't make any sense that the killer was outside the circle. Why the hell would a murderer wait twenty years to strike back at the girls who escaped death the first time?

And then strike back only indirectly, through their kids?

No, Joe felt that at least one of the five had played a part in the kids' murders. They sure hadn't been suicides. That was the one point he was completely sure of now.

The easiest person to point a finger at, of course, would be Angelica. She had no kids, and so was the only one who had not yet been hurt by the deaths.

Could *she* have drowned Bernadette when they were kids, and now, for some reason, was getting back at her friends for something?

Or, perhaps more likely, what if the other four girls had been responsible for Bernadette's death? Maybe Angelica had been Bernadette's best friend, and had been plotting revenge on the other four ever since. They would be blackmailed into not turning Angelica in as she played angel of death to their kids, because she could bring them down for their own ancient crime.

Could it be her? He tried to picture Angelica smuggling her friends' kids off to the cliff on May 22, the year they each turned eighteen. Could she really be the one who took their lives at the same spot where their mothers had killed so long ago?

No. He couldn't believe it. There were few mothers who wouldn't give their own lives to protect their children. It was unlikely that all four of them were so cowardly as to allow Angelica to snuff out their babies, just to protect themselves. This had to be something that they couldn't stop.

And as twisted as Angelica's little magic act was, he couldn't see those hands pushing kids off cliffs every spring. He was prejudiced in her favor, sure. A fiery night of sex after months of nobody but Lefty could sway anybody's thinking.

But then again, were the other options any better?

Four mothers who each had killed their children as part of some weird pact from their pasts . . .

A killer who had waited for two decades for a group of women to birth and raise kids that could then—and only on a certain day—be shoved off a cliff . . .

Or how about the apparent town favorite: a devil who lured people to walk his plank and fall to their deaths on the blackened rocks and powerful surf hundreds of feet below?

They were all pretty unpalatable. But whatever the answer was, he had an idea it lay hidden in the hearts of one or more of the five. He had some more visits to make.

But first he would take a ride out to the instrument of this little Kevorkian festival. He could still hear the vinegar in Karen Sander's voice.

If you want to understand, go up there after sundown tonight and listen to the wind.

Okay, he thought to himself. *I can do that.* It wouldn't hurt to have a look around the diving board before jumping into the pool.

He'd skipped dinner in order to meet with Karen Sander right after work, and his stomach was growling angrily. But instead of turning off Main Street to head back to his apartment, Joe followed the road straight out of town.

It looked to be a good night for a little ocean gazing anyway. The cicadas were buzzing as he drove through the already darkening canopy of trees at the edge of Terrel and began the steady climb toward Terrel's Peak. The sun would be down in twenty or thirty minutes, and then maybe he'd see some stars before heading back to the four walls and bed he hid in every night.

The road only allowed you to climb so high in your car, but the hike up the last stretch of hill to the peak would do him good.

If he didn't decide to jump, he ribbed himself.

But somehow, it didn't seem very funny.

He kept hearing the other thing the Sander woman had said: *Don't presume that you'll come back to talk about it.*

PART II
Discovery

CHAPTER ONE

The climb for her had become a pilgrimage.

Every night by seven o'clock she was here. And every night she found herself staring over the edge.

Listening.

She'd never bought into all the stories about Terrel's Peak that she'd heard all her life. There were dozens of stories about ghosts and demons and haunts that lived inside its deadly face. The most popular was of a single demon that lies in wait for the unwary after dark, ready to feed on the souls of the unwary after breaking their bodies on the rocks below.

Old women used the cliff as a prop to scold their grandkids. She'd been behind an old crone in the park just a few days ago who had had her hands full babysitting three preschoolers. The oldest of the three, a ruddy-faced boy with a shock of blond hair, a face full of freckles and jeans whose stains declared him "a handful," was trying to push one of the smaller kids off the jungle gym. The smaller child was screaming, and finally the old woman got up from her park bench to mediate. Cindy had been sitting on a bench nearby, and shook her head when the old woman grabbed the bully by the ear and pointed toward the ocean. You could just see the top of Terrel's Peak from the park.

"You keep pushing people around like that, and He'll come for you, just like He's come for all the others. You want Him to push you?"

The boy had shaken his head in terror, and ran away from her and the other kids to play by himself on the swing set.

Devils and ghosts and evil, people in town claimed of the peak. But Cindy had always smiled sadly and raised an eye at such things. The peak was not a playground for ghouls, she believed. She didn't believe in ghosts at all. Even when James had told her earnestly about its deathly lure.

There's a presence in the cliff that waits for all of us, he'd say.

It's a piece of rock, she'd laugh.

But not anymore. She knew now that it *was* alive. Or something in it was.

She knew because it spoke to her.

The first night Cindy had heard the voice, she'd been afraid. She had climbed up to the peak still freshly wounded from James' funeral, looking for a reason behind his death.

She'd found it. But it wasn't something that anyone outside of Terrel would believe.

On the night of James' funeral, the tears had rained from her eyes onto the rock beneath her like the tides hitting the shore below. Her nose began to run and she was so glad she could just let it all out at last, with nobody around for miles to see or hear her blubber. She'd cried in great gasping bouts, then slowed, and then, just as she had caught her breath, she'd started bawling afresh. There on the edge of the cliff, probably in the same spot where James had jumped, she'd exorcised her grief, howled out loud to the ocean, the sky, to God if he was listening.

"Why did you take him?" she'd screamed. What she'd never expected was an answer.

But it came.

Because of a Covenant.

She wiped a sleeve across her face to clear her eyes and turned her head quickly, right and left and then right again, searching for the source of the words.

"Who's there?" she whispered. It had grown dark since she'd come up here. The sky was mostly covered by clouds, and here and there, where they could break through, shone the dots of stars. The wild ocean rushed below with the steady, unstoppable sound of an angry gale. The ground near her was barely blacker than the rest of her surroundings. If someone was going to mug her, this would be the best time and place they'd ever get.

"Who's there?" she repeated, slowly creeping back from the edge.

I won't hurt you.

"How do I know that?" she asked the wind.

Because of a Covenant.

She realized then that the voice wasn't coming from around her. She could hear the wind, and the voice wasn't broken by the wind. It was still and clear. It was in her head. *Oh God,* she thought. *It's all true—everything they've ever said.* She wanted to scream; she wanted to jump to her feet and run away; but instead, she stayed rooted to the ground. She needed to know more.

"You took James?" she asked it.

Yes.

She had known the answer before she asked the question, but still, its impact fell like a rock in her stomach.

"But why? He never hurt anybody. I needed him. I still need him!"

There was no answer.

Cindy curled her fingers into fists, and beat the ground in anger. Then she brought one hand to her mouth to bite. The pain almost stopped the tears from starting again.

"I loved him."

But the voice said nothing more that night.

Since that night, she'd walked the long path up the cliff almost every evening. No one saw her come here; given its reputation, Terrel's Peak was not exactly a popular spot for after-dark visiting. Too many people ended up not coming back when they did visit. But Cindy went there every day after dinner. Her parents said nothing about her long walks, but she saw them glance at each other. They were worried. They would have been more worried if they'd known where she was walking to.

Mom tried to help her in the only way she knew how: mothering. Over the past month, she'd cooked Cindy's favorite dishes a dozen times. She suggested shopping trips and pointed out how handsome the Miller boy was getting to be. None of which Cindy had much stomach for. But she smiled thinly and humored her mom, who was, after all, only trying to help.

The one thing that did seem to help was walking. It took her a good forty-five minutes to get to the top of the peak, and once there, she could sit on the edge of the rock face, feet dangling one hundred feet over the deadly ocean below, and think.

She would remember all the little things she'd loved about James. The way he'd tried to grow a mustache last summer, and ended up with a dirty line of thin fuzz. About when he kissed her the first time behind the old oak tree in the park. And about the other things they'd done, later that year, in the same spot.

Sometimes she thought about college and Becky. It was amazing how small Terrel felt to her after having been away at school for barely a year. For eighteen years this town had been the world to her. Then she went to a university that enrolled more students in its undergrad program than there were people in her entire town. And yet she'd had to leave Terrel and then return in order to believe one of the truisms she had rejected through most of her childhood: Terrel's Peak was more than just dangerous. Something evil hid behind its stony face, waiting to steal the souls of those who foolishly trod there after dark.

But for some reason, she wasn't afraid.

Because the voice continued to speak to her.

Not every night, but when she needed to hear a voice, it was there. Reassuring her. It told her that James had been sacrificed as part of a sacred covenant. It wouldn't tell her what that covenant was, but it assured her that James' death had not been for naught. The voice said that James' sacrifice, his soul, helped keep the rest of the people in Terrel safe.

For some reason, when it spoke to her, the grief went away, at least for a time. The voice warmed her in a way that the fancy dinners her mother was cooking couldn't.

And so she returned to the peak, night after night.

Tonight the voice was silent. Cindy stared hard into the narrow band of purple that marked the last gasp of day on the edge of the horizon. It was almost time to head back home. She sighed heavily. The favorite part of her days now was her time spent here, staring out at the water and sky. Petty things like death and grades and careers didn't impact the elements. She envied them their stability.

Cindy stood and turned away from the edge to start back toward town.

Where a shape moved against the sky.

Someone was walking in her direction!

There was no place for her to go, to hide. She didn't know why, but she had an overwhelming urge not to be found here. She crept along the edge to the north, hoping that whoever it was would keep going past, without stepping out to the very edge of the peak.

"Hey," the figure called. It was a man's voice. "Who's over there?"

She'd been spotted. And there was certainly no place to run. He blocked the road back to town and she wasn't of the mind to take the other route. Defeated, she turned toward him.

"I'm Cindy," she called, and walked slowly back in his direction.

"Joe Kieran," he said, gasping a bit for breath as he got close to her. She took his extended hand and shook it.

He was older than her, she saw, but not much. His dark hair blew in the breeze from the sea, and his eyes seemed brighter than the dusk light. He had a strong chin and a firm grip, she observed.

"I've seen you somewhere . . ." She hesitated.

"I'm a reporter for the *Times*," he offered. "I'm around town a lot."

"Well, this isn't town. What brings you all the way up here?" she asked. "There's no news going on."

"Not now," he agreed, looking pointedly at her. "But I could ask you the same question. What's a nice girl like you doing up on a godforsaken cliff after dark?"

He laughed before she could answer, and pointed toward the ocean.

"It is something to look at though, isn't it?"

"Yeah."

"Seems like a lot of people around this town look at it a little too closely though."

She looked away, her forehead creasing.

"What's the matter?"

"My boyfriend was one of those people."

"James Canady?"

"Yes. He jumped from here just last month. Just a week before I was coming home from school."

"Oh, God, I'm sorry," Joe said, patting a hand on her shoulder. "I know about James; I wrote his obituary for the paper."

Cindy looked up at him in the gathering darkness. "Now I know why you looked familiar. You were at the funeral, weren't you?"

"Yeah."

"You were arguing with Mrs. Sander there, right?"

"Yeah," he said sheepishly. His eyes dropped to the ground. "Not good form for a funeral, I know. I'm sorry if I caused a scene."

"No," she laughed. "You didn't, really. But any enemy of Mrs. Sander is a friend of mine. You wanna sit down for a minute?"

She gestured to her recently vacated seat overlooking the bay.

"I'd love to."

Joe sat down Indian style at the edge of the cliff. Cindy let her legs dangle over the edge, something that made Joe just a little nervous.

"Do you come up here a lot?" he asked.

"Almost every night since James died. It's peaceful here. I don't know, I feel somehow closer to him when I'm here."

"How long had you guys gone out?"

"Two and a half years. It would have been three this fall. I was hoping this summer I could convince him to go away to school with me. But he didn't give me much of a chance."

"He didn't want to go?"

"Oh, he did. I know in his heart he did. But he wouldn't even try. He'd say his grades weren't good enough, or that he didn't have enough money. Different day, different excuse. But the real reason he wouldn't go was because of his mother."

"Why?"

"She just had this . . . this hold on him. I don't know—it's tough to explain. James was a really nice guy when we were away from his house. He was a lot of fun, told a lot of jokes, but real natural-like, not obnoxious, you know? But when we'd get to his house, all the fun in him just seemed to leak away. He'd get real quiet and serious, and whenever his mom said to do something, he'd just do it. That was it. I mean, I don't give my mom a lot of shit or anything, but I don't act like her slave, either!"

"So you think she kept him from applying to college?"

"Oh, I know she did. I heard her tell him once. When I was getting ready to go away last fall she took him aside when she didn't think I was listening and told him, 'Now, don't think you're going to follow her, James. You've got a job to do here.'"

"A job?" Joe asked.

"Just a peon job. He worked at the department store. But he helped his mom pay for things around the house. I told him if he went to school, he could get a real job and send money back to her."

"Sounds like the best thing that could have happened to him would have been to have gotten away from her."

"That's what I told him, but he'd just shrug and change the subject."

Cindy shivered as the wind from the bay picked up. It carried the cool of nightfall in its wake.

Joe wondered where to take the conversation now. She was thoroughly bummed out, staring at the promontory where her boyfriend had abruptly become her ex. It just didn't seem to be the time to dredge any deeper. A change in subject seemed in order. And perhaps a change in scenery.

"Hey, do you want a ride back to town? I didn't see a car up here when I parked."

"I walk it, usually. But sure, if you're offering. It's getting late and I should probably get home."

"Well, whaddya say we hit the road, then?"

Joe settled behind the wheel of the Hyundai and tried to still his excitement. This was the break he'd been looking for—someone who was close to one of the jumpers and would talk to him about things in Terrel, not kick him out. And it didn't hurt that she was cute!

Cindy settled in beside him, a wisp of lilac accompanying her. She flipped a spray of blonde hair back from her eyes and then pulled a seat belt over her T-shirt. He couldn't help but notice the swell of her chest against the fabric as she tightened the belt.

"Where to?" he asked.

"You know where Parkside is?"

"Sure."

He put the car into drive and spun around to face the town. In moments they were on the slope leading down to Terrel, tree branches grabbing at the car from the sides of the narrow road like leafy arms. Down in the valley the air was moist and still warm from the heat of the day, and Joe inhaled deeply. They didn't have air like this in Chicago. Or girls like this, he thought, glancing at his buxom passenger.

"Lived here long?" he asked, looking for a new conversation starter.

"Long enough," she grinned. "All my life till college. I used to think it was a small town—and then I went away and found out just how small it was!" She laughed, a cool but rich chime that Joe found irresistible. "What brings you out to a tiny place like this?"

Joe's face clouded briefly. "You want the real answer, or the one I tell my parents?"

"Can't a country girl git both?" she teased, tossing her head to one side and watching him expectantly.

"Sure." He grinned. "But neither one is very exciting. Which first?"

"Gimme the lie," she said. "I like to hear a good one now and then!"

"Okay. I came to Terrel because I realized that I couldn't stand the hustle of the city desk at the *Chicago Tribune*. It was too impersonal, too harsh. I wanted to grow into a family business in a smaller town with a better climate."

"Doesn't sound too false to me. What's the lie?"

"Well, actually, I love the hustle of the city desk, and I miss it quite a bit. I don't miss the climate."

Joe ruffled his hair and settled back into the driver's seat. They hit the first sign of Terrel, an old abandoned barn, and turned onto the rim road that would take them into Parkside, the newer area of the city.

"The truth of it is, I came here to escape. And I have to say, the first time I've felt like a reporter in the months I've been here has been the last couple weeks as I've looked into the history behind that cliff up there."

"What do you mean?" Cindy stared closer at Joe, her interest raised. He noticed her eyes were blue. Sky-on-a-fine-picnic-day blue.

"Well, what do you know about the cliff?" He threw the question back at her.

Cindy stared out the window a second.

"I know that everyone in this town is afraid of it. I know I never believed in it until this summer."

"Believed in what?"

"You'll think I'm silly."

"No, I won't. Really."

Cindy shifted uneasily.

"People say the cliff is evil. That it's dangerous. I used to think they were ghost stories and that the people were stupid for buying them."

Joe pulled into the main entrance of the Parkside subdivision, two white pillars with ornate placards marking its beginning.

"Which way?" he asked.

"Right, up two more blocks on Ewing."

Cindy stared out the window and was silent.

"I don't know about the cliff being evil," Joe hazarded. "But I do believe it's convenient. A very easy spot for someone to get rid of people he or she doesn't like."

Cindy snapped at the insinuation.

"Everybody liked James! He didn't have enemies. Except maybe his mother. But she wouldn't *kill* him. She's a bossy bitch, but she's not psycho. But neither was James. He would never have jumped on his own. You have to believe that. If you had known him . . ."

She pointed suddenly at a slat-sided house on the right side of the street.

"There. That's my house. Could you stop here? My parents would freak if they saw me pull up with a stranger."

Joe hit the brakes and pulled over to the curb. Shifting into park, he turned to look closely at the girl next to him. She looked agitated now, after talking about the cliff. Much more so than when he'd first seen her dangling her feet off it.

"Would you mind meeting me sometime to talk about it more?" he asked.

She looked at his face and considered. Then decided.

"Sure. I guess that'd be okay. Are you doing a story or

something about it? I don't think the paper has ever really run any articles about it. Mostly, everyone just talks."

"Call it a story I'm doing for myself," he said. "I don't know if anyone will ever publish it, but I need to write it."

She nodded as if she really understood.

"How about meeting on the beach at the foot of Terrel's Peak this Saturday? I've been wanting to head down by the water since I've been home, but I keep climbing up instead of down!"

"Around noon?"

She nodded again. "Yeah. See ya there!" She opened the car door and got out. But before the door shut, her head popped back into the cab.

"You're going to think I'm nuts, but for the record? All the rumors about that cliff are true. Seriously true."

With that, she backed up and slammed the car door shut, blonde hair swishing as she pulled herself away from the car.

Her too? Joe groaned inside. It had looked as if he'd found a good source for background on the cliff, but if she was another demon believer . . .

Cindy walked two houses down the street and then turned into a drive. Joe let the car creep forward until she disappeared into the gray house. Then he pulled away from the curb and turned at the end of the block toward home. For good or bad, he had a date on Saturday, anyway.

Now to set up some time with a couple others. And maybe it was time to call on Angelica again.

CHAPTER TWO

That night, sleep came slowly for Joe. The sheets stuck in humid tangles to his legs; the pillows lumped at every twist. The blue light of the clock radio silently ticked away the night: 10:45, 11:18, 12:23. He couldn't stop thinking about Cindy. And the answer to her question. Why was he here? And could he really escape for the rest of his life?

When he did finally get to sleep, his dreams were troubled.

In one, he stood dressed all in black at the outermost point of the cliff, staring over the water. It lapped blackly against the shore, each wave crashing like a white noise explosion, the whitecaps glinting like teeth with the light of the moon. Cindy hung on his outstretched arm, only it wasn't Cindy, not really. It was Ann, the reason he'd left Chicago.

"You couldn't just keep it quiet, could you?" she cried at him above the rush of the waves. Tears were streaming down her cheeks, their trails glimmering in the moonlight.

"Don't you know you ruined my life?" she accused. "Why couldn't you mind your own business?"

"I was just doing my job," he answered.

"I hate you," she screamed, and beat at his chest with her fists.

"I loved you," he answered, and planted both hands on her shoulders. With a shove, he pushed Cindy/Ann over the edge of the cliff and into the black night air. Her scream was deafening at first, but quickly grew faint before disappearing altogether.

He didn't even look over the edge. Instead, he turned away from the water and walked back to his car. He was smiling.

Joe woke up in a cold sweat. "Shit," he cried. "*Shit,* shit!" The clock radio read 3:19. Bunching the pillow over his face, he tried to blot the images from his mind, but instead kept seeing Cindy/Ann's face as she accused him.

You couldn't just keep it quiet, could you? he heard over and over again in his head.

"Not my job," he mumbled.   •

Angelica hadn't called him since the night he slept over, and the two messages Joe had left on her machine had remained unanswered. But he pulled into her driveway anyway.

He didn't expect her to come to the door, but she did.

Promptly. She was, again, in full costume: purple silken robe, this time covered with stars. Beneath it he caught a glimpse of a tight-fitting black shirt. Her legs were bare tonight, and he felt a surge of lust at their smooth curves.

"C'mon in, Joe," she said, looking none to happy to see him. "I don't know what I can get you; I haven't been to the store in over a week."

"Don't need anything," Joe answered. He sat down on the small couch where their last session had begun.

"Then what can I do for you?" she asked, her lips pulled tight. She gave off none of the friendliness or eros of the Angelica he'd seen last.

"Well, you can start by telling me why you haven't answered my calls," he offered.

The room was silent.

"I've called you a couple times," he said.

"I've been . . . busy," she answered with a shrug.

This was going nowhere quickly. So he switched subjects. "I met James' girlfriend the other night up on the cliff."

"And how is she?"

Angelica settled on the arm of the couch, obviously not ready to sit for a long talk. Joe decided that small talk was out.

"She's dealing with it." Then he blurted, "Hey, I've been wondering. How come you never had kids?" It was the kind of personal question that he always hated springing on people. But they usually flushed out some leads too.

Angelica arched a dark eyebrow. "Who said I never did?"

Now there was one he hadn't expected. He waited a beat before continuing. "I've just been thinking over the last couple weeks that it's strange that out of the group of five who were there when Bernadette O'Brien was killed, you were the only one who didn't have a child. I guess I assumed you hadn't had one since I didn't see one when I was here last, and, well, not to be rude, but I haven't heard of any Napalona's who have gone over the side of the cliff."

She didn't smile.

"I was too young when I got pregnant, Joe. I did have a child. But I gave her up for adoption as soon as she was born. I haven't seen her since. Who knows? Maybe she has been one of the people who have been killed. Or maybe my giving her up saved her from the curse. I hope so."

"You've never tried to find her?"

"It doesn't seem like a very wise move, does it, given what's happened to all the kids of my friends?"

Angelica stood and paced the room, her violet robe dragging slightly on the floor behind her. She peered out the front room window, and then turned back to Joe.

"I think it's over now, Joe. Whatever it was, it's done. Something in that cliff wanted a piece of all of us kids that day, and it took Bernadette completely. Now it's stripped our kids from us. What do you suppose is more important to a mother? Her life, or her children? It took the most painful part. After that, death would be easy. So I think it will let us live now. Story's over Joe, so let it lie. It'll just wake up and bite you if you don't—trust me."

She held her hand out to him.

"I'm expecting someone for a reading tonight. Thanks for what you did for me last time. I appreciate it."

He didn't hear a wealth of gratitude in her words, despite their meaning.

She led him back to the front door.

"Some things are better left in their graves, Joe," she said. "Leave this one buried deep."

The door shut behind him, and Joe realized he'd been expertly evicted. And he was more puzzled now than when he'd gone inside.

As Joe pulled away from the READINGS BY ANGELICA sign, he identified the odd pit in his stomach. He'd been used. Angelica had taken him last month, used him like a vibrator, and thrown him away like a wet condom. She didn't even want to speak to him now.

A moment of recrimination briefly pricked at his conscience. Was this what his sources felt like when he was done pumping them for information? No, he told himself. He had better manners.

CHAPTER THREE

Saturday dawned with a promising glare of gold through Joe's bedroom window. He stretched and rolled over, then forced himself to lift a bleary eye to the clock radio—10:14. He dimly recalled reading a Grisham novel until well past three A.M. Coffee would be a necessity if he was to be beach-ready in an hour and a half.

The shower steamed around him and brought with it a rush of questions, harbored since his midweek meeting with Cindy and his unproductive quest at Angelica's.

He wanted to find out from her what the average person in town *really* thought of the cliff and of the murders. He wanted to know more about the five mothers. And the Halloween deaths. During the week, he'd hatched the mad idea that Terrel harbored a pagan sect of murderous Druids. That could explain how the annual Halloween string of death reached backward for a century, but he hadn't had a chance to poke around much looking for the fringe element of Terrel. Maybe Cindy would be tapped in, or at least have friends who were.

By the time he got out of the shower and toweled off, Joe's mind was back on track, churning ahead at full speed.

A strong pot of java still wouldn't hurt, he thought, and after pulling on black bermudas and a Cure concert T-shirt, he plodded into the kitchen to grind some beans.

As the caffeine soup brewed, he pulled out the weekend

entertainment section from the *Times* and skimmed the local offerings. The theater was playing a Hitchcock revival this week: *The Birds* and *Stranger on a Train* tonight, *Rope* and *Psycho* tomorrow.

Did people in this town really need to see *Psycho*? Or to look at it another way, had the theater perhaps shown *one too many* Hitchcock murders to the locals?

The Columbian Coffeehouse was hosting a folk singer this weekend. And Lower Space, the town's one rock club (hidden on the outskirts of Terrel, near a cheap hotel) boasted Charleston's punk saviors Toxic Gas. He grinned at that. Now *there* might be the perfect place to look for Terrel's fringe element.

After retrieving a cup of coffee from the still-hissing machine, he brought a pair of scissors back to the table and clipped the ad. Maybe Cindy had been to Lower Space. He wanted to remember to ask her.

Joe stomped often on the brakes to keep his Hyundai below fifty on the curving path the local department of transportation defined as a road. The car shifted and bumped, complaining with multiple squeaks as he plummeted down its winding descent to the waterfront. The day had turned out splendidly—the sun was hot and high, the sky achingly blue. He'd thrown some chips and cookies in a bag with his suntan lotion and an obnoxiously orange towel. His shades were on.

Now if Cindy only showed up.

The thought brought a pang of fear to his belly, which surprised him. He really was looking forward to this! He'd known the girl less than half an hour, but he realized that he was going to be bummed out big time if she blew off this "date."

The car rounded the last curve and suddenly the trees and brush disappeared, leaving him staring straight out into the blue-green waves breaking against a jumble of dark rocks. The cliff was less than a mile ahead.

He followed gravel-filled ruts that skated along the edge of the waterfront the rest of the way. Driving this close to the ocean, it was hard to resist the temptation to watch the waves instead of the road. Then the gravel ran out and Joe kicked up sand with his tires as he pulled away from the beach onto a grassy stretch of earth. Despite the perfect weather, the sand was empty for as far as he could see, except for one figure just a few yards ahead lounging on a beach towel. Someone that looked tantalizingly female.

He grabbed his bag and kicked the car door shut.

"Hey," the sunbather yelled out against the roar of the surf. "No reporters allowed. There's no news here!"

Joe grinned and quickened his pace as Cindy mockingly shooed him away.

"Excuse me, ma'am," he answered when he got closer. "I'd like to get a statement from you."

"What about?"

"Well, let's see . . . Did you know that wearing a swimsuit like that is dangerous to the mental health of all males within a thirty-yard radius?"

Cindy made a face and gestured at the electric pink and yellow triangles that just barely covered her chest and the private patch of real estate below her belly button. "What, this lil' old thing?"

"Exactly!"

She bent and picked up her beach towel, wrapping it tightly around her shoulders.

"Well, I wouldn't want to be responsible for you gettin' hurt!"

"No, don't worry about me." Joe laughed. "I've been specially trained to deal with these types of suits."

"Oh, really? And tell me, how does one get that sort of training in . . . where was it? Um, Chicago?"

Cindy tossed a wisp of blonde hair out of her eyes. "Do they have these kinds of suits in Chicago? I wouldn't think they'd be very comfortable to wear in the snow, ya know."

"Oh, it gets above thirty-two degrees there now and then," he quipped, playing along. "Heck, there're even a few beaches—with real sand!"

"Yeah, but isn't the water usually iced solid or slushy?"

"Solid, no. Slushy? Depends which way the currents from the Indiana refineries are moving—and what sort of waste they're carrying!"

She laughed and let the towel slide off her shoulders, revealing a dark but not heavily tanned complexion. Cindy looked like the type who could tan easily, Joe thought, but she'd said that she hadn't been out in the sun too much yet this year for all her cliff-walking.

"Well, you're welcome to share a towel," she offered, holding two corners and letting the wind spread it out in the air like a magic carpet above the sand. "If you think it's safe."

"I'll take the chance." He grinned and dropped his bag to the beach.

They sat cross-legged on the towel and Cindy nodded to the foamy water a few feet away.

"Doesn't look so horrible from here, does it?"

Joe shrugged. "It's all perspective, I suppose. Things seem a lot different depending on where you stand. Kinda like how people look at that cliff up there." He leaned back to stare at the rock face that jutted out over the bay. "Some people think all those people are just depressed suicides. Others think there's some monster in the cliff that draws people to their deaths. And then others, like me, think there are some people behind this whole death spree. All depends on how you look at it, I guess."

Cindy's eyes took on a faraway look as she followed his gaze. But she remained silent. *Shit,* he thought. *Diving in too fast. Let the girl warm up to you a minute before dunking her!*

"Um, hey, I'm sorry. I didn't mean to bring that stuff up right away like that," he apologized.

She shook her head and looked puzzled for a second.

"Oh . . . no, Joe, it wasn't that. Don't worry about it. Believe me, I know about things looking different from where you stand. A couple years ago I came out here and thought I knew everything about this town, this beach. And then I went away to school, and everything here just kinda shrunk, ya know? Like it wasn't important at all anymore, like it never was? But then James . . . you know."

She bit her lip and Joe stifled the urge to reach out and hug her. He hardly knew the girl, after all. But the way she always seemed to put that little question mark at the end of her sentences . . . well, he could just die for that!

But before he decided whether to reach out and pat her shoulder, she started talking again.

"Well, now I see that I didn't know everything there was to know about Terrel. And I can't look at it as just a sleepy small town anymore, either. I know you've heard some of the rumors about this cliff, and you probably think everyone's stupid for believing them. I know I did until this summer. I thought people were crazy as cornflakes for thinking some evil spirit or whatnot lived in that rock. But now I know better."

"Maybe that's where I need to start," Joe interrupted. "Tell me what the rumors actually say about the cliff. All I've heard is that I should stay away from it. You know, someone actually stuck a note under my door warning me if I didn't leave the place alone, 'death would find me.'"

Cindy's eyes widened for a moment, and she looked up at the top of the cliff again, as if expecting an answer.

"That's silly," she said slowly, not really sounding like she believed it. "There's a Covenant. . . ."

Joe's eyebrow lifted. "A Covenant?"

"Um . . . yeah. I don't know. One story goes that old man Terrel, when he used to run his lighthouse up there on the cliff, well, he got lonely. So he used to read to himself a lot. Thing is, the guy had some pretty weird tastes in reading, which only got stranger the longer he sat up there on the hill. They say the ships that docked here used to bring him in books from all over the world, magic and occult kinds of books. Supposedly, he used these books to summon up a demon to keep him company through the long nights."

She looked at Joe and grinned. "Some company, huh?"

"Yeah, I think I would have worked on conjuring up a woman, myself," Joe said, feeling his face redden slightly at admitting such a thing to a relative stranger. And he couldn't help but see *her* as the woman he'd conjure, which didn't help his conscience. She only laughed, a delicate, easy sound that put Joe at ease once more.

"Well, supposedly, once old man Terrel died—and there's one story that says the demon killed him during an argument—once old Terrel died, the demon was stuck here and *it* got lonely stalking around the lighthouse every night. The city council tried hiring other lighthouse keepers to take Terrel's place, but none of them would stay in the lighthouse for more than a couple weeks. They'd complain about noises in the night, and weird lights in the hallways. Some didn't last more than a night. So pretty soon, the lighthouse just sat empty. But they say during storms, even though nobody was up on that cliff, people could see the lamps lit up and beaming out into the bay. That's when it was most important for a lighthouse to run, ya know. To save the ships from crashing into the shore when the visibility got bad during the choppy seas and rain. The people said the demon had made a pact with old Terrel; they called it a Covenant, to protect the town. You know, when people started jumping off the cliff, it was never anyone actually from the town of Terrel. People got pretty superstitious about that, figuring that the demon took sacrifices in exchange for guarding the town. They figured, well, if they kept their mouths shut, then the thing would just take outsiders and leave them alone."

Joe shook his head and grimaced.

"But that was, like, fifty years ago," he said. "Are you saying everyone in this town still thinks that there's a demon in that cliff that's watching over them and sacrificing the lives of outsiders once a year?"

"Pretty much!" she chirped. "Crazy, ain't it?"

"Pretty much," he agreed. "And everyone in town knows these stories?" he asked.

"Oh, geez, you hear 'em from the time you're a toddler," she said. "There's all kinds of stories about the 'ghost' of Terrel's Peak."

"Like what?" Joe asked.

Cindy leaned back on her elbows, giving him a good view of her body. He found himself longing to kiss the thin pucker of her bellybutton, and imagining the heaven that was only barely hidden beneath her suit. He crossed his legs, not wanting to give her a good view of what her stretch had just done for him.

"Well," she said, face staring into the blue of the sky as she thought. "There's one that supposedly happened to a kid named John Ryan. I first heard it on a camping trip with the Girl Scouts. It's one of those stories that you have to tell around a campfire."

"Can we just pretend we're by a campfire?" Joe asked. He wiped a bead of sweat from his forehead. "It's starting to feel like we're sitting by a fire out here."

She laughed, and then sat back up, tucking her legs to her chest and wrapping her arms around.

"You can see that Terrel's Peak is this town's haunted house," she explained. "I mean, look at this beach. Any other beach like this in summer would be packed! But people do still go up to the peak sometimes. Usually on a dare. In other towns, kids dare each other to go inside abandoned houses. Here, we dare each other to climb the peak. So, the story goes that this kid, John Ryan, went with a group of high school seniors up the cliff to where the road ends up there to have an early graduation party. They sat around drinking and smoking and making out, right? So, after draining a couple of six-packs, it gets late, and someone dares John Ryan, who's like, the wimp of the bunch, to take a flashlight and climb to the top of the peak. He says no way, but they don't let up. 'Afraid of the bogeyman?' they say, and they keep taunting him. This goes on for a while, and at last, humiliated and a little drunk, the kid grabs the flashlight away from one of the girls and starts up the trail.

"'Flash the light when you reach the top so we know you went all the way,' one of the gang shouts as John Ryan marches up the path that goes to the very top of the peak, where the old lighthouse used to stand.

"'Flash it three times if you see the ghost,' another of the kids says.

"They watch him walk up the cliff and out of sight, and everything gets real quiet. Nobody really wants to talk now, because they know that they wouldn't have gone up that trail, and they all feel a little guilty for riding him that way.

"It was a moonless night, and the waves were loud against the rocks. When you looked over the edge, you could see the whitecaps, but just barely. And when you looked up, you could just make out the tip of Terrel's Peak.

"So the kids all just stand there and watch, and the minutes tick by with no light and no sign of John Ryan. They start to get real nervous, watching the top of the cliff and then looking down below.

"'He probably turned and ran right past us back to town,' one of the football jocks said.

"'Maybe someone should have gone with him,' the flashlight girl suggested, feeling guilty.

"'We didn't say he couldn't use the flashlight *before* he got to the top so he could see his way,' another nervous kid reasoned.

"Then, at the top of Terrel's Peak, an orange glow flickered on.

"'There he is,' someone cried, and pointed at the glow.

"But the light snapped off just as fast as it had come on. And then they heard a screech, an awful, horrible ear-piercing scream.

"'What was that?' one of the girls said, just as a light winked on again, only this time, it seemed to come from the open sky just below the cliff's edge.

"'Look!' They pointed, and the light went off. 'What was that?'

"The light came back on again for the third time, just for a split second, down on the beach below Terrel's Peak. One of the girls saw it and screamed. The kids all got into their cars then and sped back to town, promising not to tell anybody, because then they'd have to say what they'd been doing up there at night. But one of the girls broke down to her parents, and they called the police.

"The next day, a search party found the flashlight, shattered and broken on the rocks below the peak."

Cindy's eyes grew wide and she leaned toward Joe, pausing dramatically before whispering, "But John Ryan's body was never found."

Cindy pulled back and laughed, rocking back and forth on the towel. "Spooky, huh?"

"Yeah," Joe agreed, "but who's to say the kid didn't just fall off the edge because he was drunk and his body got sucked out with the tide?"

"That's exactly what I used to say," she agreed, and then leapt to her feet.

"Wanna get wet?"

Cindy ran toward the surf and Joe followed, after shucking his shirt and kicking off his shoes. By the time he tiptoed through the pebbles and shells and sunk his toes into the cool, sandy mud of the bank, Cindy was already twenty yards out. With a twist and an arch, her pink and yellow butt came up out of the water, and then her whole body disappeared beneath the waves. Joe launched himself into the breakers and began paddling hard to catch up to her.

"C'mon, already," she yelled, head popping up even farther ahead. "Don't they teach you Chicago kids how to swim?"

"Sure," he called back. "But if we go too fast we run out of water!"

The waves felt a lot stronger than they looked, Joe thought, as he redoubled his efforts to catch her. It felt good though, to swim without worrying about bumping into one of a thousand other people crowding and fouling the water. A handful of people had taken up spots here and there down the stretch of sand since they'd first arrived, but the beach still looked empty. Actually, the fact that this beach wasn't mobbed with people on such a perfect day was nice, but also kind of creepy. It was also proof, he supposed, of the superstition that gripped the town.

The ocean was cool, but not icy-cold like Lake Michigan, which didn't even warm up much in the middle of summer. Fish zipped past him in mini schools, sometimes brushing with tickling fins at his thighs and calves. Dunking his head underwater, he opened his eyes to see a murky green bottom, with fronds of God-knows-what growing between rocks covered with fuzzy muck and plant life. Small mountains thrust up here and there from the ocean floor, rising to spires and plateaus just above the waves. A few feet away, he watched a green and gold fish dart away from his path. Coming back up for air he saw that he'd never catch Cindy—she had a good head start and was used to plowing through these kinds of waves, while he kept getting mouthfuls of salt water.

Just as he was beginning to question whether he'd have enough stamina to swim back, she pulled herself up on one of the outermost boulders that dotted the inner reaches of the bay and waited. He was out of breath when he reached her, his legs aching with the effort of kicking his body forward. She lay on her belly on the rock and offered him a hand.

"C'mon up, landlubber!"

He was grateful for the boost, and collapsed in a heap next to her on the rock. It was just big enough for both of them to lie side by side, feet hanging off the end.

"I love swimming out here," she said, her voice just barely audible above the rush of the ocean. "It's so calming."

She pointed a finger out to the open sea.

"Out there it's so vast, so huge. It's like outer space, in a way. You could never explore it all. And back there"—she pointed toward the spires of the Methodist church, one of the only visible markers of the town of Terrel from this distance—"it's, like, claustrophobic sometimes. So this is the perfect middle ground. We're right between zero and infinity."

She laughed then, a nervous but light sound that Joe found intoxicating. "That sounds really dopey, doesn't it?"

"No," he answered, still gasping a little for breath. His chest felt as though it were on fire. "I think it's probably pretty sharp. The thing is, you can't really live very long right here, in the middle. You have to pick a side. What do you want to be? Explorer or small-town housewife? Do you want to live in the comfort of zero, or the chaos of infinity?"

Cindy turned away from the beach and looked out at the waves. The sky seemed to meld in an arc of blue right into the farthest point of the ocean the eye could see. A perfect kiss of air and sea.

"I used to know," she said finally. "But now I'm not so sure."

She flipped back, resting her head on her hand, her elbow on the rock. He couldn't help but notice the way the suit clung tight to her body, every yellow and hot pink–painted curve pressing toward him. Her nipples were erect with the cool kiss of the ocean still dripping off her. The water pooled in her bellybutton, dripping down her gleaming skin to disappear in the pores of the rock beneath them. He had to keep telling himself that he was not here to seduce, but to get information. But as her eyes met his and he saw the way they glinted in the early-afternoon sun, he found his original purpose more and more obscure.

"What about you?" she asked. "What do you want to be?"

"I thought we went over this the other night."

"We started to, but you kinda copped out. I want to know

why you're here in Terrel. You seem like the explorer type to me. I think you're a real reporter. And Terrel doesn't really need a *real* reporter!"

"You're telling me."

"So, why here? Are you here to stay, or just passing through? Or"—her smile deepened, revealing just a few too many teeth—"are you on a big, secret undercover story?"

"The story of my life."

"Yeah?"

"It all started when I was a boy . . ."

"Stop it! C'mon. Give!"

"Maybe later. After a couple of beers. You can drink, can't you?"

"Depends who's buying."

"Me, if you can beat me back to shore."

"Don't consider taking up gambling, huh?"

With that she slid off the rock into the water, and in an instant was slicing through the waves back to the beach.

Joe followed, but this time, he didn't bother to try to catch her.

CHAPTER FOUR

"Have you heard Him call?"

"Yes," Karen answered, clutching her glass tightly enough to whiten her knuckles. "And we're going to have to answer soon."

"I hear Him over and over again in my dreams. I can't get any sleep anymore. And when I do fall asleep, my dreams are . . ."

Bloody arms holding and stroking and caressing . . .

Karen ran a trembling hand through her hair. "I know, I know. I told you it wouldn't end with James. I've even felt that . . . that tingling He gives. Like I need to be with someone again. It's been years since I had that feeling, that compulsion, other than on *the day*. I've even felt like painting again. But I refuse to pick up the brush. I just won't give in to that."

The other woman nodded. "I've been playing the piano for hours at a time this week. It's like someone else is using my hands; I can't stop. But I still say Rachel is the key. If we find out what she's done with the child, the Covenant will be fulfilled. And then we'll be left alone."

"Not if that reporter keeps bugging us." Karen sighed. "What if he finds out the full story? You know He will never let us leave, but if the story comes out, the people in town will kill us if we stay."

"Have you talked to the others about it?"

"No. But I'm thinking it may be time for a meeting."
Karen nodded, as if in saying it she had made up her mind to
call one. "But not at the water."

"We have to go there soon. I'll go crazy if I don't."

"When we go—*if* we go—we'll go as a group," Karen
cautioned. "Remember that."

"Then call it soon. Please."

CHAPTER FIVE

The Lower Space was a lot cleaner than Joe expected, but exactly as dark. The walls were painted black, and the floor was tiled in dark squares. A scuffed but impressive hardwood bar that might have once graced an ornate theater jutted from one wall. At the back of the club, an entire wall was devoted to nothing but posters and free handouts. There were magazines on the floor for the taking, and the walls were plastered with black marker–scrawled signs advertising civic club meetings and screaming "Looking for Roommate." In between were posters for bands coming to town soon and other similar debris. A shelf held a variety of colored paper handouts. He'd been right to mark this as the place to come to find out about the underside of Terrel's culture.

Cindy had raved about the place when he'd brought it up earlier at the beach.

The Space? She brightened. *Yeah. Lots of cool bands play there. I go there sometimes—they don't card much.*

He told her that he was looking for a place that might clue him in to finding cults or weird groups that were active in Terrel.

She rolled her eyes at him. "You're not going to find your cliff-sacrificing Druids in Terrel," she warned. "If there were any, you'd probably find them at the Space, but I'm telling you, there aren't any. That's not what's behind this."

She had promised to meet him at the club tonight anyway.

While he waited, he leafed through the assorted photocopies in the back of the club.

His eye was quickly drawn to a stack of purple paper that proclaimed, *Readings by Angelica. See me, and see your future.*

He shook his head and pulled another ad, this one for the Renaissance Revival Group, which met in the circle to "dissemble and play" on Wednesday nights at seven P.M.

There were other ads for locally produced comic books, bands looking for guitarists, and even a tantalizing massage offer. *I come to you when your muscles are hard,* it said, *and leave you limp with relaxation.*

And then he found one that looked like pay dirt. It was printed on yellow paper, bordered by a frame of twined snakes.

CLIFF COMBERS
is looking for new members.
Come worship the spirit of the earth with us.
Learn about the force that can swallow us all.
Learn about what dwells below Terrel's Peak.
Explore the mystery with us.
Contact Ken Brownsell at (880) 555-3556.

Joe pocketed the announcement with a smile. Now, here he might find some interesting wackos to interview.

Someone tapped him on the shoulder.

"Excuse me sir, but didn't I see you earlier today, indecently exposed in a pair of swim trunks?"

He smiled and turned to see Cindy grinning up at him. She was dressed casually mod in a loose gray top and tight black pants. Her hair was pulled back tight; the effect of that and her makeup made her easily look twenty-five. Tiny silver skull earrings dangled from her lobes.

"Yes, well, didn't I see you flaunting yourself pretty indecently in a teeny bikini earlier?"

"Maybe. Got a problem with that?"

"Not at all."

"C'mon and grab a seat. Another half hour and it'll be standing room only."

They worked their way through a maze of round tables and huddles of laughing, talking people until Cindy pointed at an apparently vacant table near the stage.

"Here, this one's open. We might get pushed back by moshers later, but . . ."

Joe shrugged and pulled out a chair. Which Cindy passed by to take one of her own.

"I can get my own seat," she pronounced. "But you can get me a beer. Miller—Genuine . . . please."

He sat down himself and grinned. Cindy had a way of making him do that, he was finding. She was like some kind of human butterfly, flitting from place to place without ever quite settling still long enough to be caught. But he was enjoying the chase, and the humor she drew from him as easily as juice from a ripe orange.

The waitress was hovering over them before Joe had even glanced around. He ordered two MGDs, and with a nod she was gone to the next table, piling empty bottles onto her tray as she took new orders. She wrote nothing down, and how she could possibly remember who got what, he couldn't imagine.

"So, have you seen these guys play before?" he asked.

"Toxic Gas? No." She shook her head. "But I know a guy in the opening band 'cuz they're from here. Anglicide. You'll get a kick out of them. Last Halloween they did their whole show with an upside-down cross hanging behind the drum kit. Then at the end of the set, they dropped the cross into a flaming bucket. They're really theatrical."

"I didn't wear enough black, did I?" Joe asked, looking around and noting the dominant color. Black lipstick, black pants, black nylons . . .

"Doesn't matter," she said, scooting closer to put her arm around his shoulders. "They get all kinds of people in here;

tonight's just more of a punk night. If I was really into it, I would have put on some ripped nylons and maybe a black low-cut top with some chain around my waist. And I'd probably tease my hair out some. And maybe get a double or triple pierce . . ."

"Okay, okay." He laughed. "You're scaring me. So, is your friend's band any good?"

"They're kinda like the Cult, but gloomier."

The waitress returned with the bottles, and Joe handed her a ten.

"How long till they start?" he asked as the waitress left—without ever carding, as Cindy had promised.

"Oh, probably twenty or thirty minutes. They always advertise the start time like an hour earlier than it really is."

She took a swig of the Miller and nodded at his.

"Drink fast."

"Why?"

"You owe me a life story, but you said it had to be after a couple beers. So drink fast."

He lifted the bottle obligingly. "What do you want to know?"

"How about . . . how old are you?"

"Worried I'm too ancient to be seen with?"

"No. Just curious. If I guess right, you can buy me another beer?"

"Sure."

She leaned forward and stared hard at his face.

"Hmmm. No obvious wrinkles or liver spots, yet . . ."

He batted her hand away from his hairline. "Call it," he demanded.

"Twenty-four."

"Not bad. The girl gets points for under-guessing. Twenty-five."

Her lips fell into a mock pout. "No beer?"

"Oh, never fear. Flattery gets you drunk," he said. "Do your parents know you're out with an older man?"

"Don't they say a guy should be like four or five years older than a girl anyway?" she asked, flipping her hair over her shoulder. "Men don't mature like us girls!"

"Please. Answer the question."

"Actually, they do know. I told them I met a nice young reporter who was taking me to see a fine, artistic, musically challenging group."

"Is that musically challenging, or musically challenged?"

"You decide. I think they're about to start."

She nodded at the stage, where a group of twentysomething guys were filing onto the stage. The singer slunk his way to the mike, lips glossy red against an obviously accentuated pale complexion. A faded picture of Robert Smith pouted on his chest.

"Wannabe," Joe said.

Cindy's gloomy Cult description turned out to be fairly accurate, Joe soon decided. As the bass pounded through the club, he was reminded of college nights spent hanging out in the dark caverns of Chicago's Cabaret Metro, catching shows by Stabbing Westward and Black Tape for a Blue Girl and other punky, gothic-oriented bands. Anglicide, however, was definitely more of an homage act than an original gestalt. Joe could hear ripped-off riffs and see affected "attitude" before they were through with three songs. But they had energy. And hair. And a certain knack for theater, as Cindy had pointed out. The singer raised his hands with every lyric, praying and spinning at the mike, as the mournful guitars twined.

Three rounds and a Joy Division cover later, and Anglicide turned the stage over to Toxic Gas. They brought a completely different air to the club, with their shaved heads and cutoff shorts and overdriven guitars. Joe quickly decided that this band believed in truth in advertising. They did nothing if not live up to their name. Cindy nodded with a pained frown when he asked if she wanted to go before the band had gotten halfway through its set.

"Oh, God," she complained when they stepped out of the smoky club and into the fresh air of the street. "I felt like they were going to reach into my ears and pull out my brain!"

"Pretty noisy," Joe agreed, trying to shake the buzzing out of his head.

Walking back to the car, she put her hand in his.

He grasped it like a lifeline.

"So do you want to go home, or try someplace else," he asked, once they were in the car. "It's still early."

"I don't feel like going home yet," she said. "Would you mind?"

"Name the place."

She thought a moment, and then brightened.

"How about Memorial Park?"

"Done."

Ten minutes later they were walking across a clearing in the densely forested hillside on the west side of town. In the middle was a statue of a proud military figure astride a horse. A Civil War hero, Joe guessed. But he didn't get close enough to see. Cindy led them to a giant white gazebo on the far side of the park.

"C'mon," she urged, almost running.

She pulled him by the hand up the stairs, and then they were standing together on the main floor of the structure. It was obviously meant for small concerts and such, Joe thought, noting the benches that were built into the walls, leaving at least a fifteen-foot stretch of central flooring clear for bands, speakers, podiums—whatever.

They knelt side by side on one of the cool wooden benches and leaned over the rail to stare out at the lights of the town below. The park nestled high on a hill that looked down on the town. If you looked closely, you could see the tip of Terrel's Peak through the cover of trees that rose above the valley on the other side of town. The whisper of the ocean drifted on the air, even here.

Joe cupped his palm over hers, and she looked up into his

eyes. He thought she looked sad, the fire dimmed in those blue orbs that normally didn't seem to slow from their pinball-bouncing course through life.

"Thanks for bringing me here," she murmured.

He shrugged. "Not a problem."

She gripped his hand tighter.

"I used to come up here a lot with James at night," she said, staring back out at the twinkling lights of the town.

"We would sit right here and look at the stars, and the lights from the houses. It was like we were the only two people in the world sometimes. I haven't been up here . . . since . . ."

Joe wrapped an arm around her shoulders.

"It's okay."

She bowed her head a moment, leaning back into his chest. And then he felt her take a deep breath. And sit forward.

"Do you know any constellations?" she asked. Her tenor was bright, an abrupt shift, but he thought there was still the faintest tremor in her voice.

"No. I think the sky looks a lot different here than back home. I used to be able to find the Big Dipper sometimes, but out here, there's so many stars, I don't know how you can find anything!"

She laughed a little. "They are pretty. Have you ever seen a falling star?"

"No. I don't think so."

"Watch, then."

She pointed toward the ocean.

"If you're patient, you can almost always find one. And then you get to make a wish."

"Wishing on a falling star, eh? That's a little Disney, isn't it?"

She didn't answer.

Joe stared out into the sprinkle of stars against the velvet black night and waited. The wind whispered in the trees. The chirp of crickets sang through the night and locusts hummed in the trees around them. But otherwise, the town was silent. It was as if they'd left all of humanity behind. It made his eyes grow fuzzy to just wander across the heavens. Like there was nothing to do in the world but stare into space. He wasn't used to this kind of kicking back. And he wasn't one to be patient.

He remembered the constant barrage of voices and noises and smells of the big city and marveled. In gaining the cosmopolitan, one loses so much of where he comes from. And in leaving Chicago, he had lost so much of what he'd once been. Sometimes he missed it; sometimes he missed *her*. But not now. He looked at the silent girl next to him, face limned by the summer moon.

"I can't think of what I would wish for," he said quietly. "I think I have everything I want right now."

The corner of her mouth drew up and she squeezed his hand.

"This is nice," she said, but didn't meet his gaze. Her eyes seemed far away.

"What would you wish for?" he asked.

She shook her head. "If you want it to come true, it has to be possible. And I don't think it's possible for James to come back."

Joe fell silent, and watched the heavens for a chance to cast his wish. He didn't want anything for himself now.

"There's one," she said, pointing low on the horizon, just above the dark pines.

He saw the faintest trail, like a scratch on film, and made his wish.

"I wish for you to be happy," he whispered.

She kissed his cheek and met his eyes at last. Her cheeks glistened with quiet tears.

"They say wishes don't come true if you say them out loud, silly."

"Well then, we'll just have to wait here until another star falls," he said. "And this time I'll keep my mouth shut."

She drew closer to him, pressing the warmth of her chest

against his. She hugged him tightly and kissed him again, this time on the lips. Her arms were dotted with goose bumps from the night air, but to Joe, she felt as hot as flame.

"You don't need to wish for me," she said. "You've already made me happy."

Joe leaned in to kiss her again, but as her tongue met his in a delicate flutter, he looked past the halo of her hair to the sky, watching for another flaming stone to drop from the realm of angels.

He didn't like to take chances.

CHAPTER SIX

It took a long time for Joe to fall asleep. He kept closing his eyes and remembering flashes of Cindy from their "double" date. He'd seen her both in Day-Glo frolic and night-club vision, and she'd been radiant both times. He felt her fingers slipping between his, and her cool shoulder pressing back into his own. Again and again, he relived her quick, warm kiss, just before she slid out of his car at the end of the night. He saw glimpses of her running like a kid across the pebbly sand of the beach in the afternoon. Of her golden hair tossed back across her shoulder at the bar. Of her eyes sparkling with mischief, and a hint of something else. Of promise?

But then he thought back to her words from the beach. Something she'd said had troubled him, nagged at him all day. When she'd talked about the founder of Terrel, she'd talked about a covenant.

Just like the title of Mrs. Sander's painting. Could there be something here after all?

He pushed those thoughts away. He didn't want to think about cliffs and suicides and murder. He wanted to concentrate on seeing Cindy's face again, a wide-mouthed smile beaming at him from mere inches away. He wanted to slip into dreams with her kiss lingering on his lips like a prayer.

And eventually he did.

But Sunday when he woke up, he lay in bed staring at the

ceiling feeling foolish. Here he was, having erotic day and night dreams about a pretty girl who was only a college kid, for chrissakes. What would she ever want with him? He was no Chippendale. Her hugs and handholding and soft kisses last night had probably just been the reaching out of a girl who needed a friend. Some nonthreatening dalliance that would blot out the horror of losing her true love. She'd told him what a difficult time this was for her, and how her parents couldn't really help her.

He gave himself a mental shake. Enough already!

Time to get back to his pet case. Though he was starting to wonder why he bothered. If the whole town believed in a genie in a rock bottle, well, hell, why should he try to convince them different?

But he pulled out his jeans from the night before and fished around in the pocket.

The yellow snake-bordered paper was still there, folded and creased. He unfolded it and considered. Was there really any point to this? Would a group of cultists really advertise themselves through flyers on the wall of a club?

Learn about what dwells below Terrel's Peak.

He read that line again and again. He wanted to learn exactly that.

What can it hurt, he thought finally, and took the paper over to the phone to dial Ken Brownsell.

On the sixth ring, a groggy voice picked up.

"Sorry to wake you," Joe apologized after introducing himself. "I was wondering when I could get together with you to talk about your Cliff Combers group."

"No problem, I had to get up anyway," the voice gurgled. "We're having a meeting this afternoon if you want to join us. On the north face of Terrel's Peak. You wanna meet up with us there?"

"Sure. I'd love to," Joe answered. "How do I get there?"

He copied down the directions, thanked Ken, and hung up.

Once again, a date at the cliff. But this time, he'd be a couple miles away from the murder sites. In an area he'd never visited.

He found it easily enough. Instead of taking the high fork of Main Street up to the top of Terrel's Peak, he swung the Hyundai onto a gravel road that dug deep into the forest and wound the long way around the rocky crag. The meeting site was hard to miss, since the road dead-ended into it.

A handful of cars were parked along the side of the road, and he pulled up behind a sky blue VW Bug. Why and how so many of those things were still on the road, he had no idea, though he often wondered. And there seemed to be a lot of them here on the coast. He considered the motley collection of beat-up, rusty autos, and the lanky long-haired kids collected just beyond the impromptu parking lot and shook his head. This should prove . . . interesting.

The group was sitting in a rough circle on the ground and on boulders, and as a group they looked up at Joe's approach. Measuring him.

"You must be Joe," a dark-haired, long-nosed, lanky guy in khakis said as he approached the group.

"Ken?"

"The same. Glad you could make it. We hold our meetings here, usually, unless it's raining. Then we go into a little cave down the ravine there."

He pointed down a short slope of brush.

"There are caves in this hill?" Joe asked.

"Yeah! That's the whole point. I formed the Cliff Combers a couple months ago to explore the caves. I couldn't do it on my own. That's the first rule of spelunking, you know. But have a seat with the others, and we'll get things started."

"Your ad said something about discovering the dark things that could swallow the town and worshipping a spirit or something. . . ."

Ken laughed and slapped Joe on the shoulder.

"Yeah, I was trying to find some way to make caving sound mythic. Brought you out, didn't it?"

Ken moved away and Joe took a seat on the ground. From the bohemian looks of the other club members, he was getting the idea that this was a wrong turn. But he felt stupid turning around and walking away, so he tucked his knees in and kept his mouth shut.

Ken stepped up on a pink and gray granite boulder in front of the small group and bowed with a flourish.

"Greetings, fellow Combers and recruits. Welcome to our fifth meeting. Today, there is something . . . special . . . that I have to show you. So I won't waste time standing here talking. We won't be going deep today, but our rules still apply: check your flashes now, check your rope, and get a partner. I don't ever want to have to call old Chief Swartzky to pull in a search party after any of us."

The caving guide rubbed his long fingers together as the group began milling about, checking equipment and pairing up.

This was not what he had been hoping for. A bunch of hippies playing tag in some muddy caves was not what he'd looked to find. There wasn't a whisper of the occult about this band of losers. Joe decided now might be a good time to escape. Looking around to see if anyone was sizing him up for partnership, he found no one. But before he could begin heading back up the path to the car, a hand slapped him on the back.

"You probably didn't bring any equipment with you this time, huh?"

It was Ken, who, Joe now noticed with distaste, had extremely yellow teeth.

"No. Maybe I can catch up with you guys on another meeting."

"Nonsense," Ken boomed. His voice was as long and tapered as his figure. "I've got some extra rope and a flash, and no partner. You can come with me. It's a great introduction for you to our group. I was down here a few days ago, and discovered something really exciting. Come on."

Ken marched him over to a large black hiking backpack, and proceeded to clip a bundle of rope to his belt. He also fitted what looked like a miner's helmet onto his head, and flipped on the flash on its front.

"Let's move in!" he yelled, and the party moved down a dirt path into a gully that ran parallel to the road. In seconds, they were lost in a maze of shrubs and grass and trees. The back end of Terrel's Peak rose up slowly ahead of them, and suddenly Joe saw where they were headed. A black hole between a stand of thin, scraggly evergreens led straight into the ground. It wasn't large, maybe three feet or so wide, but the trampled dirt path led straight to it.

"Hope you don't mind getting your jeans muddied up," Ken said, clapping Joe on the shoulder *again*.

One more and I'll punch him, Joe thought.

"Duck down and go slow through the entry—it drops off pretty quickly," Ken warned, before climbing through himself.

Joe followed, and was forced to take it slow because he couldn't see where the hell he was going. The air changed from summer heat to autumn cool as soon as he passed the lip of the entrance, and his skin grew goose bumps instantly. He rubbed his arms and waited for his eyes to adjust to the surreal mix of pitch darkness and the piercing glares of the helmet lights. Someone grabbed his belt from behind and something went *click*.

"There, Joe. Now you're tethered to me," Ken explained, stepping around him. "If anything goes wrong, I'll be right around the corner." The guide grinned his dentist's nightmare again. It seemed well-suited to the underground. Like a badger, Joe thought.

"Okay, people," Ken yelled, his voice disappearing and then echoing through the cavern in a strange play of acoustics. "We're going to take the left fork that we explored last week, but when we reach the third room, we'll be starting a new route. Hank, would you be our back tether?"

A portly behemoth of about nineteen nodded, rippling his rosy jowls and sandy hair, and moved to clip a rope to a piton previously hammered into the entryway.

"All right," Ken grinned. "Let's go!"

The next hour was, as near as Joe could figure, hell on earth. Somebody was trying to punish him. Maybe it was the cliff itself. He slogged through damp, dripping, muddy passages and crawled across slimy floors where the ceiling was only a foot above his head. He'd never been claustrophobic, but as they wriggled their way between open caverns, his stomach began to tie itself up in knots as he considered the weight of the mountain bearing down over his head.

Behind him, the grunts and groans of the rest of the group echoed. He wondered how Hank was sliding through the narrow chimney he'd just squirmed through. The worst part about it all was that he knew he had to go through it again just to get out.

Ken kept pushing farther, turning around every few minutes to whisper, "You still with me, Joe?"

The desire to unclip his rope before Ken turned around the next time was almost undeniable.

But at the end of the hardest crawl, they emerged into a large cavern. How large, it was impossible to tell, since the helmet beams stopped short of connecting with any rock but the floor. The temperature here seemed to have dropped another ten degrees. Ken stopped pulling Joe forward.

"All right, Cliff Combers! You all still with me?" A chorus of enthusiastic assent followed. Joe mouthed a hesitant "Yes."

"This is it. Last time we went forward and hit a dead end. That really bothered me for a few days, so this week, I came back with Charles Donahue. I was sure that with this large of a main cavern, that a tributary chain had to extend off of it somewhere. Charles and I tried this way." He pointed to the right. "And we were lucky. Follow me. And listen closely."

Listen for what? Joe wondered. *Bats? Avalanches?*

The quiet reverberations of the cave chambers were starting to give him the creeps. There were the coughs and footsteps of the group, but now and then, it seemed as if something moved ahead of them. As if a bat or a snake had shot forward, desperate to evade them. Joe fervently hoped if there were animals in the cave ahead of them that they succeeded in avoiding them. And he was feeling cold and damp. Where were all the beautiful stalagmites and stalactites he'd always heard were the big payoff of caving? All he'd seen so far were gray walls and muddy floors. He felt as though he were crawling naked through a rabbit's burrow searching for a pot of gold. The reward was unlikely, at best.

A tug came on his rope and he reluctantly forced his legs into motion again, following Ken into the darkness. Their lights bobbed off a wall to the right and reflected off the floor when he looked down, but ahead lay only a veil of dark mystery.

"What are we looking for?" he finally ventured, only to receive a stern "Shhh. Listen."

Joe rolled his eyes and trudged on, noticing that the walls were at last starting to close in again. When he looked to the left, his light trailed across a smooth gray sheen of moist rock. Something skittered across the path of his light and he turned away from it to stare again at Ken's broad back. He didn't need to know what it had been. He'd caught a glimpse of something that had a lot of legs and some kind of tail. And eyes. If he ignored it, maybe it would ignore him, he reasoned.

Are we almost there yet? a voice nagged in his head.

"God, I hope so," he told himself. He was really starting to feel thirsty. The low trickle of water somewhere up ahead wasn't helping.

Trickle of water?

Up ahead?

That was what Ken must be so smug about! He must have discovered the remains of the channel that cut these caves out.

Joe was so proud of figuring out Ken's surprise that he almost walked right into the lead caver.

"Hold up!" Ken called out. The group slowly collected. Joe paced over to the left and squinted into the distance. He could just make out the walls on the far side of this chamber, but the floor began to get rougher and descend just ahead of where Ken had stopped. The faraway trickle had grown in volume to a dull rush somewhere below. He moved tentatively, one cautious step at a time, toward the black void that ate the floor just a few feet ahead.

"This is what we've been looking for over the past month, everybody," Ken was saying. "The creator of this cave system. The 'dark force' that eats the very rock out from beneath us."

"The only dark force in this cliff that I've ever heard of doesn't seem too interested in eating rock," someone joked.

Joe edged his way closer, trying to catch a reflection of the water that roiled somewhere below. It sounded close, but everything in these caves sounded close. It could be a couple hundred feet down, for all he knew. Or the passage below might be dry and the river working another level below it.

"Now we know it's still active," Ken continued. He sounded extraordinarily smug in this announcement. "More caves are being cut in this mountain every day. What we have to do now is find the route the water has carved to lead us to the heart of the hillside. Step carefully here; when we find that route, the drop could be a big one."

Joe stepped away from Ken, threading his way down a slight slide of stone to peer out into the void. Somewhere down there, black water was rushing with the force of a mighty river, carving its name into the slick rock of the mountain.

Joe jumped back from the edge abruptly. There was some

kind of reflection bouncing back from below, but whether it was water or rock, he couldn't tell. They were closer to the bottom than he'd thought. He grabbed a slippery spike of limestone and heaved his weight up the slight slope to the main floor, where the rest of the group was gathered. But his weight was too much; the limestone gave way with a sharp and sudden crack and Joe felt his weight shift.

"Oh shit," was all he got out, and then his balance was gone, his feet sliding upward as his back went down. His head struck the stone, and the cave was suddenly a lot brighter—the air exploded, lit with brilliant stars of pain. Joe scrabbled with his hands to gain another handhold, but his fingernails only scratched stone that might have been coated in Teflon.

His head was already in space when it occurred to Joe that he was really going down. Maybe all the way.

He was free-falling, yelling at the top of his lungs and praying that it was water he had seen in the inky blackness below.

CHAPTER SEVEN

It lasted forever and yet it took no time at all. His body slipped in a timeless flight through the pitch-black hole in the earth. Joe felt the bone-chilling, damp air rush past him like the breeze from a bird's wings, and then he hit the bottom with a shocking crack.

He noticed the cold first, the icy hand that slapped him in the face and punched him in the groin. And then he realized that unless he tried to move, he would be carried into an even worse predicament than this one. Because he had survived the fall and in doing so, he now had firsthand knowledge of the river Ken had been looking for. But the current was fast and he was already several yards from where he'd hit the water. Forcing frozen arms and legs into motion, he made a tentative turtle swish, and then began scissoring his legs in earnest to reach the top. His lungs were burning with heat while his skin was on fire with cold. The fall had knocked the wind from him, and so far, he'd managed not to suck in a chestful of water. But he needed air now.

Everything was black. *This must be how a sensory deprivation tank feels,* he thought. There was a faint lessening of the darkness above him, and he forced himself to swim up toward it. The current urged him backward and down, but he fought it, breaking the surface just as he finally inhaled, gasping and sputtering.

Great, he thought, looking around the cavern he'd dropped

into. It extended into inky infinity as he looked upstream, and it dropped off suddenly not too far downstream from where he was now. But the worst part was, the walls seemed to be of polished limestone. Alternately gray or green depending on how his light hit them, they looked as smooth as polished glass.

How the hell was he going to get back up?

"Maybe you should stick around," answered a thick voice.

It seemed to come from all around him, and at the same time, boomed inside of him. He could feel its vibrations in his heart. His blood chilled even further, and he began to shiver uncontrollably.

"Huh?" he called out. "Who said that?"

Something tugged at his waist, and he panicked for a second, wondering what was grabbing him to drag him down.

He slapped at the water to free himself, and his hand hit something thin and rough in the dark. Running his hand along it, he realized it was his guide rope. And it extended in a taut arc from his belt to the surface of the water and up into the air above the underground river.

"Wouldn't you like to stay here with James and I? Wouldn't you like to swim down, down, down into the blackness with us?"

Joe screamed.

Then the ghostly conversation was interrupted. Someone was calling him.

"Joe? Joe?" a voice echoed from far away.

The line pulled sharply taut again, and his progress downriver stopped. He felt like a rock jacked up in the midst of a stream of rapids. The water shattered and poured around him on its way into a deeper blackness. On its way to hell.

"I'm all right," he coughed back, his head swiveling back and forth like a pendulum to watch for anything that might be moving in the darkness. Ducking his head back underwater, he strained to swim against the current to close the distance between him and the other cavers.

"Been looking for me, I hear. What can I do for you? Suck on your bones?"

The voice slid through his head and played a merciless beat on his heart. It tickled his toes and kissed him on the lips. Joe shook himself from its hypnotic grip and shrieked aloud again.

"No!" he cried. "Let me go."

"No, Joe, hang on!" Ken called from above, not understanding. "We'll get you. Try to get near shore, if you can."

Guessing that he wanted to be on the right, Joe angled that way, his headlamp bobbing like a spastic searchlight off glistening, sheer rises of rock. But as he got close to the rock on the right, he banged his toe painfully into something, and recoiled.

"Shit," he complained, but then his whole foot touched bottom. He kicked off the rock floor with both feet toward the shore and pulled like an oarsman with his arms.

At the base of the wall, he was able to stand up. The current still tried to pull him back in, but he could withstand it while wading waist deep in the water. There was no way to get completely out of the river; it was as if he stood in a half-full tube of rushing water. But he pushed his way back, following the tug of the rope toward the point where it angled upward. The point where he'd fallen in.

"Joe, can you hear me?" Ken's voice echoed strangely in the dark cavern, but he sounded a little closer.

"Yeah, Ken. I'm here."

"Are you okay? Anything broken? We heard you yell."

"No. Just cold. The river broke my fall. But there's no stairway to climb back the way I came!"

There was some muffled conversation from above, and then Ken's voiced called back down.

"Are you familiar with rappelling?"

"In theory."

"We're going to try to pull you up. If you can kick off the rocks in between our pulls, it might help."

"I'm all for it."

The rope suddenly tightened painfully around Joe's waist. His feet left the bottom of the river and he began, inch by inch, to rise along the sheer rock face.

"I feel like a poor man's Peter Pan," he called up.

"Well, start waving your arms and helping us out," came a muffled reply.

"Doing my best," he cried out weakly.

He couldn't stop looking below him, waiting for something to jump out of the murky water to bite down on his legs and drag him back into the river's depths. The rope began to swing a little, and soon his body was arcing in toward the rock wall. He pushed off with his feet, as Ken had suggested, and felt himself jerked upward as soon as he left the wall.

He hit again, and once more kicked off, but this time, there was a yelp from above him.

"Hold on, Joe!"

And he was falling again.

The water kissed him with a slash of icy steel, and he gasped in pain, floundering for a second to get his bearings again before kicking himself to the surface once more. His body was shaking with fear and cold and shock now. The thought that he might not actually make it out of this hole finally whispered its dismal message across his mind.

"Decided to stay after all?"

The voice shot through his bones like an electric current. He felt his kidneys give way at last.

"Who are you!" he shouted.

There was no reply. Just the rush of water sluicing over a fall somewhere downriver.

"Sorry, Joe! Are you okay?"

"Maybe," he called back.

"Our anchor rock gave way. Let's give it another shot."

"I'm everything you ever wanted. . . ." came a belated answer in his mind. A shimmer of heat flowed through his belly at those words, as he thought of Cindy and Chicago. The things he wanted.

The rope ripped against his gut again, and with a series of short, sharp tugs, he was airborne again.

"And everything you didn't," the voice continued, freezing his bowels.

"Hurry up!" Joe yelled, kicking wildly at the air. He started trying to climb the rope hand over hand. He had to escape the thing that was in his head. Now.

"You can run, but we'll meet again," it promised.

Joe's feet pulled free of the current once more, his heart beating thunderously above the rush of the water.

"Please, God, let them pull me up this time. Please!" he murmured.

He kicked viciously at the rock wall when it came near, willing himself higher. He could hear the grunts of the cavers above as they pulled him inch by inch, foot by foot, back up the steep drop.

"Almost there," Ken called, his voice a raspy wheeze of exertion. "Hold tight."

The top came suddenly, a blinding glare of headlamps lancing into Joe's face as his head cleared the top.

Ken was at the front of the line of rope pullers; they had strung themselves out evenly around a large boulder and were using the rock as a pulley.

Hands reached out to grab his own, and then Joe was lying flat on the cave floor, his breath coming in gasps of relief, his body shivering with the cold and fear. Hands pulled off his shirt and pants and shoes, but he couldn't focus on what they were doing to him. The air was swimming around his eyes, and all he could think of was the voice, telling him it knew of him, was waiting for him.

And promising that it would speak with him again.

He was staggering with his arms propped around the shoulders of two of the others in the group before the fog finally cleared from his head.

"C'mon, man. You've got to crawl through here, remember?"

He stared blankly at the narrow tube before him and shuddered at the thought of climbing that close to the earth again. Now that he knew something was here . . .

"We'll be right behind you."

"Let him be, guys." Ken's voice came from behind them. "Go on ahead. Take the rest of the group out first and we'll follow."

One by one, the cavers filed to the opening, stooped down to the crack in the wall and shimmied their way inside the earth like worms groveling their way back into the mud.

"Not exactly the best introduction to the mountain, huh?" Ken said, putting a hand on Joe's shoulder. Someone had donated a blue-checked, long-sleeved shirt and a pair of too-large jeans to replace Joe's sodden clothes. The jeans owner's shorts and bare legs were now sticking out of the dark crevasse ahead of them, sliding out of sight like a snake.

"No," Joe mumbled, shaking his head and turning to look at the caving group leader.

"We shouldn't have taken you in so fast," Ken said, looking dejected. "It's my fault. You should do some preliminary crawls and stuff to get ready for this. Caves can be dangerous—that's why we always go in twos. And that's why we always have the guide ropes. Although"—he cringed slightly—"if you had fallen much farther, you would have dragged me over the edge with you! Our rope was just about out."

"I'm sorry," Joe said, his voice still shaking. "I went too close to the edge. It was my fault. I'm sorry I ruined your outing."

"No, no!" Ken said, shaking his head vigorously. "I'm sorry it had to happen, but everything worked out fine. The group saw the river, and also saw how dangerous it can be down here. A victory and a lesson all in one. It will make us all a little more careful. Will you come with us the next time?"

"I don't think so."

"Don't let this put you off. We've been coming down here for weeks and never had an accident like this."

"It's not that."

"Then what?"

Joe took a deep breath and, looking around, realized that they were alone. The rest of the group had slithered through the vent and were probably almost outside by now.

"Have you ever heard the rumors about this cliff?" Joe asked.

"You mean the bogey monster that keeps making people think they can fly?"

Joe nodded.

"What about it? You don't buy that crap, do you?"

"Until today, no," Joe said. "I came to see you because your ad sounded like you were into the occult and focused on this cliff or something. I've been following up on all the suicides from the peak, and wondered what was behind them. I figured, there's no way that it's natural for one person to jump off the cliff every Halloween. There must be a group that's behind it."

"So you thought the Cliff Combers might be some kind of killer Cliff Cult?"

Ken laughed out loud, his voice echoing far behind them into the depths of the earth. Joe stared at his yellowed teeth and shivered hard.

"Not us," Ken said finally. "And I wouldn't be down here if I thought there was someone else waiting to meet us. That's kid stuff, man. People jump off that cliff on Halloween because it's Halloween. Creepy night. The time for all the weirdos to want to join the undead and all that. This is the biggest peak for a hundred miles, and all the crazies just naturally seek this place out. And it's kind of legendary for that, so they just keep coming."

"That's not good enough for me," Joe said. "I don't buy it."

Ken shrugged. "What can I tell you? We could sit around

down here and creep each other out with weird stories and shit, but I'm saying this is just a cave, like any other. And I want to find out where that river runs to. Whether it hits the ocean or keeps going deep underground, beneath the ocean floor. It was freshwater, wasn't it?"

Joe nodded.

"Figured. It's too big and too high to be an ocean runoff channel."

They sat and looked at each other in silence for a moment. Then Ken wrinkled his forehead and asked, "When I asked if you bought that bogeyman stuff, you said not until today. What did you mean by that?"

"Just what I said," Joe answered. "Until today, I thought there were people behind all the suicides."

"And what changed your mind?"

Joe looked at the other man and smiled sadly. "If I tell you, you'll think I'm nuts."

"If you don't, I might anyway. So what?"

"When I was in the water down there, I heard a voice."

"Yeah. That was us. We were calling down to you."

"No. This was a different voice. I could hear it in my brain and in the water and feel it vibrating right through my bones."

Ken gave him a sideways "yeah, sure" look. "What did it say?"

"That it was everything I ever wanted, and didn't want, and that it had been waiting for me."

. "So maybe you heard God and we pulled you back from the brink of death. Or maybe the devil's waiting for your soul." Ken grinned as he punched Joe in the shoulder.

"Cold water does strange things to a man's head," he offered, and then stood up. "We should catch up."

"It said one more thing," Joe said as Ken motioned him into the tunnel.

"What's that?"

"It said we'd meet again."

Ken looked at Joe and then looked behind them into the whispering, damp blackness that extended as far as the eye could see.

"Let's get up top, huh?" he said.

Joe nodded and gritted his teeth as he forced himself into the tight channel of rock. He imagined the earth pulsing all around him, a giant gullet waiting to crush the human meal inside. With panicked breath and desperate arms, Joe pulled himself forward. He could hear the panting of his partner behind him.

"Just a little farther," Ken called.

The ribs of the earth seemed to constrict then, until Joe's shoulders were scraping earth on both sides.

"Are you sure . . . this . . . is the . . . right way?" he asked.

He could feel the dank blackness closing in around him like a cape. He was smothering in night, choking on fear. What if the owner of the voice was here, at the end of the tunnel, just waiting to snatch him up and toss him over the cliff?

The end came suddenly.

Sweat was pouring down Joe's face and he couldn't control the tremors in his arms and legs. And then somebody grabbed his shoulders.

He reacted instantly, slapping the help away and shrieking.

And then he saw it was only one of the other cavers.

"Whoa, dude, take it easy," the shorts-clad man cautioned. "I was only trying to give you a hand."

Joe grinned sheepishly as he saw the concern on the man's face.

"I'm sorry," he said. "Just got a little spooked in there."

He shook away more offers of help, and climbed up on his own power into the open cavern. Ken followed quickly, and the group moved without pause toward the cave entrance.

When they stepped outside, Joe couldn't help but look back the way they'd come. He felt pursued, hunted. But whatever grim reminder of his ordeal he'd expected, he saw nothing. Only blackness. And felt a whisper of cool, damp air.

Like the breath of a grave, he thought, and hurried into the dying heat of the afternoon sun.

CHAPTER EIGHT

"It spoke to you, didn't it?" Joe grabbed Angelica by the shoulders and shook her. "Didn't it?"

Her eyes widened, but she didn't answer.

He let go of her then, and pushed his way past the fortune-teller to enter her house. Angelica stared after him with her mouth open.

"How dare you barge in here and, and . . ." she began, finally gathering her wits and following him into the sitting room. Joe planted himself on the couch, clearly not going anywhere soon.

"Level with me now, Angelica. The cliff spoke inside your head when you and the other girls went swimming that day, twenty years ago, didn't it? And one of you didn't talk back sweetly enough."

"Joe . . ." Angelica knelt before him, resting her elbows on his knees. Her mouth opened in surprise and fear. "Did you hear it, then? The voice at the cliff?" Her voice grew more agitated, and now it was her shaking him. "Tell me, what did it say?"

Joe resisted the urge to say, "I asked you first." Instead, he leaned back and drew a deep breath before relating his experience in the cave in quick, clipped sentences.

When he finished, Angelica looked at him with something resembling pity.

"You've got to go, Joe," she whispered. "If it's seen you, if it knows you . . . you have to leave Terrel before it's too late. It's already too late for the rest of us."

"What do you mean, too late? What's stopping you from getting in a car and driving out of Terrel anytime you want?" Joe asked, making a face.

"He won't let us." Her voice grew tremulous. "I've tried to leave Terrel so many times, I can't count. But every time I get near the road out, I hear him calling. And if I ignore it . . ."

"What?" he asked. "What can it do?"

Angelica stood up and looked out the window at the street. Her body was a dark shadow against the orange haze of the streetlight outside. The sun had fallen fast after Joe had arrived, and its leaving dragged behind it the anticipatory taste of dusk.

She moved away from the window and eased into a love seat across the room.

"What can he do? I'll tell you. He can kill you. He can laugh at you. And worst of all, He can let you live. As He has let all of us live. But it's a life knowing that we've tasted Him. Been used by Him. Been lived in by Him. Because the one thing He wants is our flesh, Joe. He can't ever fully possess us, not completely. So He plays with us instead. It's worse than death. Let me tell you about the last time I tried to leave Terrel.

"It was right after Bob O'Grady died. Back in 2000. He was the first of the kids to be taken, and I couldn't handle it. Neither could Melody, his mom. For years we had lived with the fear of that day, always there, in the back of our minds, but I don't think any of us really believed it would ever happen. I don't think we could have lived all those years after Bernadette drowned if we'd really believed that He would take our children. That we would let Him. That we would help Him.

"The night that Bob died, I didn't just cry. I was a maniac. I screamed for hours. I tore up this house in anger. Literally.

I threw dishes against the walls, pulled the bookshelf down in my reading room—I even put one of the kitchen chairs through a window. And then the next day, I packed up a few things and got in the car. I couldn't stay here anymore. I remember thinking that I was lucky. That I would never have to surrender my daughter to the monster in the cliff. And that He would never touch me with another's hand again.

"I'll never forget that night. I really thought that night that I was going to make it . . ."

Her eyes took on a faraway look as Angelica began to tell the story of the night she tried to run. . . .

Angelica pulled out of the driveway and headed down Main Street and out of town. Her heart was beating a mile a minute. Could she really do it? Could she really be free of the nightmare at last?

She thought of Bob, remembering his quiet humor, his easygoing attitude. She hoped that the devil was satisfied with the taste of his soul tonight. Maybe with Bob to entertain him, the demon of Terrel's Peak would be preoccupied. Not paying any attention to her flight. That was what she hoped, anyway.

She was wrong.

The touches were tentative at first, and she brushed them off. But then a pain lanced through her head like a knife. Angelica cursed and the car veered off the road, which, through waves of white-hot pain, seemed to shimmer and shake. Everything grew fuzzy and Angelica could just make out that the yellow lines were moving farther away to the left, the car bouncing more and more violently along the gravel shoulder, headed toward the bay. A grove of trees loomed just ahead, and she tried to swerve back toward the road, but instead, to her horror, her right foot stomped on the gas as her arms locked the wheel straight ahead. The car leapt forward and Angelica shrieked.

In her head she heard a low, horrible chuckle, and then a

scream. The former was the laugh of a demon playing with one of his favorite toys. The latter was Angelica herself, as the car crumpled head-on into the trunk of an oak. The hood crunched and folded with the ear-piercing sound of grating metal. The air filled with the shimmer of splintering glass and cracking wood. Angelica's forehead bounced off the windshield, and everything disappeared for a while.

Angelica woke in darkness, the sound of summer insects buzzing all around. She shook her head to clear away the cobwebs and gasped; the pain was crippling. But this was real pain, not a prod of His. She gingerly touched her forehead with a finger and traced a circle around a thick, hot bump that swelled across her head right below the hairline. It hurt like hell, but didn't seem to be hemorrhaging. There was a sticky scab right in the center of the bump, but there didn't appear to be a big cut. She prayed that it was only a minor concussion.

The stars were twinkling overhead, and Angelica suddenly realized that she was not lying against the cushions of her car. She was flat on her back in a patch of tall weeds just beyond the tree she'd barreled into. Even in the moonlight, she could see that the car wasn't going anyplace under its own power again. It looked as if its engine were sucking on the tree trunk like a lollipop. The hood was buckled back to the windshield, which had spiderwebbed and partially fallen in, but luckily, hadn't shattered completely.

Angelica stood up slowly, running her hands over her body in search of cuts or broken bones. Finding no serious damage, she began to walk toward the road, hoping that she could still flag somebody down. There weren't many cars that cut through Terrel after dark. Her head pounded with every step, but the road wasn't that far off.

And then He came back.

Angelica's hands rose from her side of their own accord, and began to slowly, deliberately unbutton her blouse. Tears slipped down her cheeks and she silently cried, *No* and concentrated on regaining control of her betraying fingers, but it only made her head throb worse with pain. She stopped walking for a moment, but then even her feet turned traitors, and she began to march in the other direction. She was helpless!

Angelica's fingers jerked and twitched and thrust, and despite her efforts, one by one, they clumsily opened each button. Like a poorly dominated marionette, Angelica shrugged off the blouse as she jerkily approached the road, and then her arms reached behind her to unclasp her bra. When that too fell to the weeds, her hands busily went to work on her jeans, unbuttoning them and then unzipping her fly. Her errant feet stopped marching then, just for a moment, as first one and then the other kicked off its shoe, allowing her body to shimmy clumsily out of the pants. One thumb hooked into the front of her pink panties and toyed with the fuzzy cleft beneath. Then, with a hard thrust, it yanked downward, carrying the soft cotton down her thighs. Angelica stumbled and fell to the gravel, crying out as her shoulder was gashed and gouged by sharp stones. And then the invisible strings pulled her erect again and she started walking, stark naked, toward the road.

She shook with anger and fear, but was powerless to stop herself. It wasn't enough that He had stopped her from leaving town, wrecking her car in the process. Now He was going to get His revenge in some horrible, humiliating way. She knew that He had something more than stripping her naked in store.

Tears streamed down her cheeks as Angelica walked, zombielike, to the edge of the asphalt. Her head felt as if spikes had been driven in behind her eyes, and her feet were gouged and sliced by rocks, shards of broken glass and sharp grasses with every step. In her head, she prayed that nobody would come, that she would stand there at the edge of the road with her thumb out for the rest of the hellish night. Eventually, if nobody pulled up to see the bloody, bedraggled nude girl on the side of the road, she thought maybe He would get bored and leave her for more interesting prey. And then, before His attention shifted back to her, she could somehow collect her clothes and lost dignity in a broken bundle and escape back to her house. To hide.

But tonight, He had left nothing to chance.

Angelica stood on the side of the road, legs spread, one hand crooked on her side, the other launching a thumb into the air. Presently, she saw headlights.

Her headache had lessened some, but now her joints were screaming with the forced posture. With the glimmer of light in the distance, she poured all her will into moving, first trying to lift a foot. She could feel the tendons shiver with exertion, but His lock on her refused to ease. Next she tried throwing back a shoulder or her head . . . anything just to topple her body off balance. She didn't care what hit the ground, so long as the oncoming car couldn't see her exposed there in the darkness.

But nothing worked. He held her with an iron grip in the same position the whole time, as little by little, the lights in the distance grew brighter, stronger, wider.

Her left thumb pointed outward, in the hitcher's universal symbol, as her right hand slid from her pale ribs to tangle in the hair at the nape of her neck. He forced her back to arch so that the cones of her breasts jutted out. He kept her right leg bent, knee toward the yellow line, a universal symbol for "come hither." She looked like a hitching stripper, posing for a pickup. And He had chosen the suitor.

The headlights caught Angelica in their glare with a blinding intensity that ripped through the already-shredded nerves of her skull. Tears wet her face again as blood stained the stones cutting the soles of her feet.

She realized from the height and noise level that the oncoming lights belonged to a truck. In seconds it had slowed down, then, just a few feet away, eased off the road to stop with the complaint of old brakes. The lights dimmed to parking yellow, and then she could see the rusted wreck that had "come to her rescue." It was a '72 Ford pickup, painted school-bus yellow and idling at a choking scream.

Angelica knew that truck. And when recognition dawned, she started crying harder.

The man who stepped out of the driver's door was the reason for her tears, and her insides quivered in revolt. She pushed and strained to make her feet move until the sky ran red behind her eyes, but He wouldn't let her run. Her feet stayed planted. This was His ultimate punishment. And pleasure.

Angelica groaned as her hitching arm slowly dropped to her side, and the hand behind her head came down to massage and exhibit her chest for the creep walking toward her.

The creep was Harold Palmer, local mechanic for hire. The bane of her existence since junior high. For years he had hounded Angelica for dates, cornering her at her locker in school, and later, turning up at her house for readings . . . and an attempt at a cheap feel. She had always—though sometimes only narrowly—avoided his advances. And now she was feeling herself up for him in a cheap, vulgar display of faux lust in the middle of nowhere. This time, Angelica knew, there would be no escape from Harold Palmer. Her stomach begged to be sick as she pinched the heavy bead of a nipple, offering it to the grease monkey moving toward her.

Harold knew that this time, he was going to get lucky with his little Eye-tal-yan girl. She'd given him a good race, but her hard-to-get days were over. From the look of it, she was dying to deep throat him. He almost wanted to make her beg for it . . . but he didn't know if he should push his lu~~

As he strutted over, fingers looped in the belt loops of his pants, he was licking his lips.

"Well now, Angie," he said, drawing his words out into a drawl that sounded obscene in itself. "Lookin' reeaaal good tonight."

In answer, her tongue traced the outline of her lips as a

slim, teasing fingernail traced the boundaries of an areola. Inside her head, Angelica began to wail. She felt like a girl trapped in glass, pounding on a surface that she could see through but couldn't break, no matter how hard she tried.

He was on her in a heartbeat. Angelica screamed inside as his beefy, sweaty paws groped at her chest and cupped her ass. She could feel the slime of engine grease smeared wherever his fingers roamed. His breath was sour with rancid meat, and his stubble left raw flesh behind wherever he moved his lips. And he moved them everywhere.

Her body acted as if he were Romeo, responding to him as if he were the man it had been yearning for all night. She could feel her nipples harden, and the crease between her thighs grow thick and damp. Her hands fumbled at his buttons, helping him undress, and her stomach again tried to heave as his tongue entered her mouth. But instead of puking, her tongue grew fevered, trading him lick for lick, kiss for kiss. They slicked each other in spit until each backed off, short of breath. And then Angelica heard a voice that wasn't hers coo from inside her. It stole her tongue and lauded the mechanic, begging with a stolen voice, "Oh, Harold, I've wanted you for *sooo* long. Do me from behind. Do me now!" And as she gagged on that, her hips swiveled and her body bent over, grasping the hood of the truck and mooning the object of her hatred of so many years. Drool was dripping from the corners of her mouth, but the grease monkey didn't notice.

Harold had barely gotten himself between her cheeks before he'd cum, but he pumped himself into her anyway and knocked off another load before he was done. He'd been waiting for this for a decade and had saved up enough spunk to nail her five times in a night, if she'd let him.

Of course, the real Harold wouldn't have had the stamina, but the Harold that grasped at Angelica's tits and slapped his thighs to her ass was not the real Harold. Well, he was Harold, but with a bit of augmentation. The real Harold would have cum, cried and run away in shame. But it was no accident that it was Harold who had driven the road out of town in the middle of the night. He'd been called, whether he knew it or not.

Flashes of knee-melting pleasure mixed with pangs of rage and humiliation as Angelica accepted his dick inside her—even encouraged him to ride her harder. Her mind was raging near insanity inside, alternately crying and yelling with Harold's weak but penetrating thrusts. But nothing came out of her mouth. Only the thin drool of the lunatic. She willed hands that would not respond to beat on the stinking flesh that rutted with hers, that raped hers . . . but it was no good. Her hands only stroked his sweaty face like a true lover and toyed with the slick tool between his legs. She was his slut and nothing she could do would stop it. This humiliation would have been bad enough to break hers, or anyone's, spirit.

But of course, it got worse.

Just making her fuck the most disgusting man she knew wasn't enough for Him. He knew how to twist the knife. After they'd rolled around on a dirty blanket Harold had dragged from the bed of his truck, after he'd done his thing with her three times, until the stench of his B.O. was skunk-sprayed inside her head and she felt as if she'd bathed in his filth, they lay back from each other. Damp and naked to the night, they stared up at the stars. But they were thinking very different thoughts.

"I've dreamed of you," he whispered, "for so long, Angie. Why'd you make it so hard?"

Angelica wasn't sharing his reverie. As Harold reveled in the fulfillment of a lifelong dream, her hands were busy. She struggled to understand what He planned next. It wouldn't have mattered if she'd guessed. She couldn't have stopped what He planned. She was His instrument tonight. And He was using her body to hurt her where it hurt the most.

"You're everything I've ever wanted," Harold said to her then, and as she raised herself up on an elbow, she could see the tears running down his fat, stubbled face. He was an ugly man, far less desirable even than the nerdy kid he'd once been—the geek who'd chased her a dozen years before into high school hallway cul-de-sacs. She couldn't help but to feel something when he said those words, charged with the longing and heartache and loneliness that two decades of obsession had fertilized.

He was gross.

He was ugly.

He smelled bad.

But all he had ever wanted was her. Angelica's heart turned over at the pathos of it all. A spark of something between pity and compassion took root in her heart.

That was when He struck.

Angelica felt her hands raise the belt they had carefully snaked out of the mechanic's discarded pants, and slipped it around his neck so quickly, Harold's first thought was that she was coming down on him to kiss him full force. Then he realized that his wind had been cut off and he tried to push the object of his desires away. But it was too late. As soon as he lifted his head from the blanket, Angelica rolled over behind him, allowing Him to tighten the belt without Harold having a clear grab at his tormentor.

Angelica's mind screamed so hard, she felt something in her neck snap. She'd thought fucking him was horror, but killing him was worse than having his cum inside her, worse than tasting him when He had forced her to put her mouth on his fat, grotesque dick.

Harold bucked his legs and back against her as though he were a rodeo steer as she cinched the belt tighter and tighter. Her arms held on snugger than any cowboy. She strangled the life from him with a borrowed strength that pulsed through her biceps as the leather gagged the fat man beneath her.

His voice was gargling out past his spit to beg for his life.

That was the worst part.

"Please, Angie," he croaked. "I love you."

"I love you."

Tears coursed down her face as she heard him pledge his love. The hatred she'd felt for him for so long had died, but now she could do nothing to save him, only watch as her arms betrayed them both. In the sterile glow of the moon she could see his face turn prune purple, his eyes flashing and bugging wildly. His arms flopped from side to side. She felt one clammy paw slap her in the belly. Another sent a jolt of pain through her chest as he hooked a finger on her right nipple and pulled hard.

But soon his struggles degenerated into wet, weak slaps against her thigh. Through it all, Angelica's grip never loosened on the belt.

Eventually his choking and struggling slowed down, and she lay with her full body weight on top of his, tightening the strap even more than before.

"I . . . lu . . . ve . . . d . . . you," was the last thing he gasped.

For the first time all night, He spoke to her.

"That was sweet," He mocked. *"Give him another kiss, why doncha. Love shouldn't go unrequited."*

"No," Angelica blubbered. "Please."

She begged Him to let her go, but it didn't do any good. His control of her didn't lessen. He forced her to watch as her hand toyed with Harold's dead wood, and then her foot lifted over his thigh, positioning her cunt to straddle him. Angelica's head twisted and locked, forcing her to see what she was doing, to stare into Harold's dead eyes. They were wide-open, like he was looking at a ghost. Only they were already glazed.

Gone.

Empty.

His face was a dark color, his mouth wet with foamy spit. But she bent down, touched her lips to his, and . . .

. . . slid her tongue into the stinking abyss of his already cooling mouth.

Her chest gasping with sobs, she slid herself up and down his dead body, tasting the salt of his semen, licking his ears, prodding her tongue between his rubbery lips. For an hour she crouched over him, forcing him within her until her insides were raw. She could feel herself lubricating his cock with blood, finally, and then . . . for a long time she was gone.

She couldn't watch anymore.

She couldn't feel anymore.

Despite His hold on her, Angelica turned off.

Later, she would dimly remember dragging Harold away from the road. She would shred her fingers prying up rocks and piling them over his body in a rough, thorny spot near the shore. Mosquitoes buzzed and flies stung. The sound of the surf gave her a rhythm: lift, move, drop. Lift, move, drop. Soon she couldn't see the pale, hairy flesh bubbling out from between the rocks. The wide clay features of his face were all that was left.

And then, the biggest rock she'd been able to lift dropped down on that face and crushed that clay to the ground. Tears wet the sand between the stones as she scooped and threw, scooped and threw. Then more rocks. Lift, move, drop. Lift, move, drop.

Scoop and throw. Scoop and throw.

Angelica worked for hours, until her back and legs and arms were a maze of mosquito welts and her thighs and ribs were streaked with sweat and sand.

When even He could squeeze no more strength from her muscles, she staggered up the bank, climbed into Harold's truck, and drove it to the other side of town. At dawn she was walking stark naked through the center of Terrel, oblivious to everything.

She walked all the way home.

CHAPTER NINE

Angelica stared down into her lap, refusing to meet Joe's eyes.

"I don't know how many people saw me walk through town that night, or what they thought. But nobody ever said anything to me. And nobody ever found Harold's body.

"It was a long time before I was right in the head after that. What He made me do that night . . . it was worse than dying. But it was effective too. I've never tried leaving Terrel again since: He made His point."

Angelica finally looked up, black mascara streaked down her cheeks. "Is that what you wanted to hear? Is that a good enough story for you? I don't think the paper will publish it in Terrel."

"Did you ever go back to"—Joe cleared his throat—"look for the body?"

She laughed.

"Are you kidding? At first I didn't really want to find it, but eventually, I had to. I had to know. I was sick to my stomach for weeks—both from thinking about what I'd done, and from worrying about what the police would do to me when they found him. I took a lot of walks over that stretch of land. And every time, I felt like someone was staring at the back of my neck. I always went in the daytime, but it was like He was watching me, laughing at me. I never did see anything that looked familiar. I remember building a mound of rocks on top of him—you'd think that would be easy to spot. But, the end of that night is kind of a blur in my mind. I'm sure some of that's deliberate. I don't think He wants me to remember some of those details . . . and anyway, who *would* want to remember what I did?"

A suspicion suddenly dawned on Joe—one that made him nauseous just to consider.

"Angelica," he said. His voice was low. "When you called me over here that night, and you were only wearing a robe . . ." he began.

She looked up at him, eyes filled with pain. And tears.

She nodded.

There was a sinking feeling in Joe's stomach. He knew in some way he'd been used that night, but he'd never suspected this! She hadn't really wanted him, had she? Maybe she was even grossed out by him, like she was the mechanic. Maybe the thing in the cliff had chosen a man she found repulsive and rubbed her nose in him. Literally. The images of that night came to him like the fast-cut trailer to an adult film. Her eyes wild and wanton. Her hands moving over him velvet smooth and then digging in, claws of pleasure.

What did she really think of him? He suddenly felt like he had to know. Did she see images of that night in her mind and have to stifle the urge to vomit? Could he ever hope to know?

Angelica stood up then and walked over to the front window again, pushing the curtains aside slightly with the back of her hand.

"Who are you watching for?" Joe asked. "Every time I've been here you've done that."

"I don't want them to come and catch you here," she said.

"Who's them?"

"The other girls. Rhonda, Karen, Monica. If He's aware of you, He might send them for you."

"Angelica . . ." he began.

She turned and crossed quickly to the couch.

"Joe, I wasn't kidding earlier when I told you to leave town. He won't let any of us do it. We've all tried. And sometimes He uses the rest of us to stop someone who's trying to escape. If He's already set his sights on you, it's probably already too late. But if you can, Joe, you should go. Fast."

"Was it hard for you, the night we . . ."

She smiled a little, lips twisted in a troubled attempt at good humor. Then she bent forward and kissed him softly, on the forehead.

"Not like you think."

Then she pulled him from the couch. He marveled at the strength in those slender arms.

"I'm serious, now," she said. Her face bled desperation. "If you've heard Him . . . you have to go."

Just then, a piercing light flooded the living room. A car pulled up in the driveway. Angelica panicked.

"Shit, shit, shit." She started toward the door, then stopped, motioning wildly down the hallway.

"Quick," she cried. "My bedroom. Go. No one should see you here."

He stood to go and she turned about and grabbed his elbow, shoving him down the hall, to the left of the bead-curtained reading room. Grudgingly, he went. The door slammed closed behind him, and then he heard the knock on the front door.

There were voices, female from the pitch. But he couldn't quite make out what they were saying. He could hear the growing sense of upset in Angelica's voice, though. It grew louder and sharper against the lulling murmurs of the other women. He sat down at the doorframe and rested his head to the crack. It did no good. He couldn't make out what was going on down the hall. After a few minutes, he gave up and looked around. The last time he'd been here, he hadn't had time to take in the sights. He'd been a bit preoccupied with its owner.

It was a small room, or at least it seemed so with the dark

oaken furniture that was crammed into it. A grandmother's bedroom, he thought, noting the decorative carving work that had gone into the legs and edging of the heavy antique bureau that rested to the right of the four-poster bed. A bed that absorbed you into its bosom as if you were a little kid, he recalled with a smile. Then he frowned as he remembered why he knew that. After the revelation that she had been possessed, coerced into sleeping with him, it was not the kind of conquest he wanted to remember.

Did she enjoy it at all? he wondered again. *Not like you think,* she'd said when he asked if it had been hard for her to accept him. What did that mean?

That she did find him attractive and the demon hiding out in Terrel's Peak had only helped her fulfill a hidden desire? Or that when it took over her mind, she could pretty much fuck a troll and manage to get a kick out of it?

Joe shook his head, trying to knock these thoughts away. Best not to think about it. Chewing on something without asking questions never brought answers, he'd found. However, chewing on something and searching for answers . . .

This was a perfect opportunity for a little investigative reporting, he realized. Joe stood up and walked to the dresser. It was an old, narrow piece, probably handed down from someone's grandmother. If it hadn't had so many nicks and scratches across its face, it probably would have qualified as a valuable antique. The surface was strewn with the usual litter of feminine jewelry and trinkets. Angelica's pieces were more gaudy than most, he noted, staring at the mess of rhinestone-studded bracelets and twinkling beads of iridescent plastic that hung from a hook on a small wooden jewelry box at one corner. He supposed her profession demanded a certain lack of conventional taste when it came to accessorizing.

A statuette of the Virgin Mary peeked out from behind a stack of what looked to be bills. He thumbed through the stack. She owed the electric company $67.52. She bought underwear from the Victoria's Secret catalogue. He grinned. He had yet to see evidence that she *wore* underwear. She owed Visa $453.

At the back of the stack was a yellow bit of legal paper, folded in half and then folded again. He glanced over his shoulder at the door, and then opened it.

Bernadette was scrawled in the center of the paper in blue felt-tip marker. *June 28th, 8 p.m.* was written below it. And then, at the bottom of the sheet, two words: *No excuses.*

Joe glanced at his watch. It was eight fifteen. And today was the twenty-eighth.

She'd known they were coming. That's why she'd looked out the window repeatedly. But what did they want?

He suddenly knew who the voices belonged to. The letter had said *Bernadette.* There was only one Bernadette who he'd ever heard of, besides the saint. And she had lived and drowned in Terrel two decades before. In the company of Angelica. And four other women: Rhonda Canady, Karen Sander, Monica Kelly and Melody O'Grady. He'd bet a Buick that this was the roster of the group in the living room right now. The only one missing would be, of course, Bernadette.

Joe refolded the paper, replaced it at the back of the pile of bills. He wanted to take a walk into the living room now more than ever. Stroll through casually, nod his head at the assemblage and say, "Hi, ladies. Any word from our pal in the cliff lately?"

What if they said yes?

He shook the thought away and tried the dresser drawers.

She *did* actually wear underwear. At least that's what he took the silky, lacy panties in the top left drawer to mean. On a hunch, he pulled at the waistband of the black and electric blue pair on top. A Victoria's Secret tag was woven into the elastic.

So . . . one bill accounted for. Sum easily paid. But what price did the Bernadette bill carry?

In another drawer, he found the garish costume blouses

and robes of her profession. And in another, blue jeans. It was in the center cabinet that he found what he hadn't realized he'd been looking for. The door allowed access to three tightly set drawers. Stacked in the top one were rows of small bottles and vials—more tricks of the woman's trade—a pile of perfumes and cosmetics. But in the center drawer was a book. A leather scrapbook that he'd seen before. The book which held the newspaper clippings she'd shown him the night she'd seduced him.

At that moment, it occurred to him that it might not have been Angelica at all who had decided to let him read the clippings in the scrapbook. The monster that had apparently possessed her had volunteered that information. It had given him a piece of the puzzle, lured him deeper into its mystery.

Why?

Shouldn't it have instead tried to protect its history? Or did it want him to know more?

The thought made him shiver. How did he fit into its plan? It had used him once, unbeknownst to him at the time. And it had spoken to him in the depths of the mountain, promising a future meeting. Suddenly Angelica's plan for him to leave town sounded like a good, not lunatic idea.

He set the book on the deep blue bedspread and opened the cover. He paged through the opening pages, which were a collage of diary entries, photos of the cliff from various vantage points, and newspaper clippings. On the first page, in loopy, blue ballpoint handwriting that reminded Joe of notes passed in first-period algebra class, Angelica had begun a diary of sorts. The girlish script read:

June 30, 1981: I don't know what will happen to this book, but I feel like I should write something. It's been over a month since Bernadette died, and I wish I could say that the memory is fading. But it's not. Every night I hear His voice in my head. Every night I feel that heat in my belly, that special feeling He gave us in the cavern. Sometimes I cry and it goes away. And sometimes, it makes me sick to admit . . . sometimes, I love it.

Just then, the author of the diary screamed from the other end of the house.

"Nooooooo," Angelica yelled.

Joe slammed the book shut and stood up. He hesitated at the door, waiting for a sign. The cry had sounded desperate, but should he go? What if she was just yelling at the other women and he barged out and ruined things for her? His presence could conceivably damage her standing with the group. None of the other women had given him, the newspaper snoop, any real information. If he burst out of Angelica's bedroom to surprise the meeting . . .

He leaned into the door, listening for any clue as to the state of things in the living room. The talk had dropped again to a murmur, and then he heard the front screen door slam. He ran to the bedroom window, slowly lifting the shade just in time to see the back door of a van close. Two dark figures opened the driver and passenger doors, respectively, and climbed in. Then the vehicle roared to life and peeled out of the driveway.

Joe dropped the shade and ran back to the bedroom door. He eased it open quietly.

He crept down the short hallway, careful not to disturb a creaking board to alert anyone left behind to his presence. But when he peeked around the corner of the living room, he saw that the room was empty.

And Angelica was gone.

Shit. He should have moved faster. Her cry *was* one of danger. And she'd paid for his caution.

Now what?

Joe surveyed the room while he thought. There was no sign that anyone had been here. A steel pole lamp gave off a yellow glow between the two cushioned chairs on one side of the room. A copy of *TV Guide* lay open on one. Angelica may have just stepped into the other room for a beer, by the looks of things. But Joe knew better.

They already had too much of a lead for him to catch up, unless he knew where they were headed. He hesitated, looking at the front door. Should he try to follow? He knew what direction they'd gone, at least.

No.

Now was an opportunity for uninterrupted research. He could look at source material here that Angelica might not ever volunteer. *If* he was able to find her. He walked back to the bedroom. Worry for her nagged at his gut, but he was not going to run off after her half-cocked. He might find more answers here that would help him in his search.

Instinct kicked in and stilled the gnawing ache in his belly; he continued his search of her dresser where he'd left off. But the rest of her drawers offered nothing more than old underwear and T-shirts.

Her jewelry case did offer one item of interest—the necklace she'd been wearing the night he'd spent with her in this very room. He wouldn't easily forget it; it was the only thing she'd had on most of the night, and the erotic twining of the two horned figures that made up its pendant had bounced against his chin and chest—sometimes painfully so—as she'd ridden him. Twin silver figures, joined at the hips and sprouting wicked grins and antlers. Or devil's horns. He lifted the pendant on its leather thong and slipped it into his pants pocket.

Then he picked up the leather scrapbook and decided it was time to make his own exit before the women decided to return.

CHAPTER TEN

Angelica had prayed that this day would never come. But as she hustled Joe into her bedroom and slammed the door shut behind him, she knew she was shutting that door on him, and on the rest of her life—forever.

He was calling the circle together again.

He wanted her daughter. The last of the children.

And she couldn't deliver.

When she'd given the child up for adoption, she knew that someday her own life might stand ransom for that of the child's. But she didn't care. She wasn't weak like the others. She didn't cling to life and pleasure so strongly that she would give up her firstborn to the vampiric demon of the mountain.

They pounded on the door.

She couldn't even try to run. Where would she go? There was only one way out of town, and she'd tried that before. She would only end up naked and rutting with God knows what by the end. No, this time she had to face them. Face the anger of their betrayal. She had negated the bargain and He was calling for payment due.

"Open up," echoed the shrill voice of her childhood friend, Rhonda. A friend no more.

Angelica walked slowly to the door, every step a point of no return. Her heart pounded in desperate fear. *Don't open it!*

But she really had no choice. She felt Him grinning in the

back of her brain. He'd let the women do His dirty work, but if they failed, He was ready. She'd rather suffer their punishment than His.

She turned the knob, and a bloated, piggish face greeted her with a steely smile of success. Rhonda Canady pushed her way into the room, and Karen and Monica followed. The circle was as complete as it could be. Melody O'Grady wouldn't be joining them.

Couldn't.

After her son Bob's death, after carrying out her part in the bargain, Melody had begun to paint on the walls of her house. Some thought the resulting mural was genius. There had been photographers and psychiatrists and art critics all at once stepping back and forth across the floor of the O'Grady living room. She'd made the national magazines.

But the fame came after they'd committed Melody. After they'd given her transfusions to replace the blood she'd used as pigment.

Her husband had come home to find the garishly realistic bloody shades of hell tattooed on the wall behind his television set. Melody's demons, all teeth and decay, looked deadly. The fires they danced in, scorching. And on each and every one of the disemboweled children she had depicted the finely etched nose and features of Bob. His open lips screamed silent, bloody accusation from every corner of the room where Melody lost her mind.

"Are you ready?" Rhonda spit out, once the three were inside. "I know you got my note. It's time for you to keep your part. We've waited for years. We've been patient. But He won't let us leave you alone anymore. Where is your daughter? Where have you hidden Andi?"

Angelica stepped back from the other women, retreating into the living room. She'd spent twenty-plus years hiding from this day. And she still wasn't ready to face it.

"No," she said simply, and sat down on the couch, her back to her former friends.

"We have all kept our part of the promise," Karen's voice reminded her. She was quiet, but undeniably firm. "You've used your gift more than any of us. And paid nothing."

"I won't keep a promise with the devil," Angelica insisted.

This time it was Monica who answered. Her voice cut the air like a telephone ring. "You won't have much choice."

She began to laugh. "Actually, I have a lot of choice," Angelica said. "I don't know where she is. I can't turn her over to you because I have absolutely no fucking idea where she is. So get the hell out of my house and leave me alone."

She screamed the last, but her anger met deaf ears. Rhonda, Monica and Karen stood stock-still in the middle of the room, staring at her blankly. As if they were listening to something else.

"Did you hear that, you fucking monster?" Angelica screamed at the women, though she wasn't actually talking to them. *"I don't know where she is. So leave me alone."*

Karen Sander's eyes suddenly focused. A slight, pained smile crossed her lips. "How could a mother not know where her child has gone?"

"Because when I gave her up for adoption, I *gave her up*. I never inquired about where she was taken. I didn't *want* to know, for just this reason."

"A mother could find a way to know," Karen said slowly, as if the idea took time to brew. Her face twisted into a devilish show of teeth. "Could trace her. Very simply. Go to the adoption agency. Give your name. Give hers. They'll find her. I've seen it on *Geraldo*."

Her teeth gleamed wide in triumph.

"Could," Angelica said. "But won't."

"Rachel," Monica squeaked, and then came around to sit by her old friend.

Angelica shook her head. "My name is Angelica now. I gave all of this up. I changed my name, gave away my daughter . . . I want nothing to do with any of this. I started a new life."

"You can call yourself whatever you like," Karen said,

pushing a stubborn wisp of gray from her cheek. "But it won't make any difference. Whatever you call yourself, He knows where you are, and He made a bargain with you. Your second sight, your fortune-telling, for the life of your firstborn."

Monica put her arm around Angelica's shoulders. "Do you think we *wanted* to do this? Do you think He let us have a choice? Our choice has been gone since the day Bernadette died. Your choice was gone long before you gave up your old self and became 'Angelica.' You sealed the bargain when you used the gift He gave you. But we could finally end this thing. Once you turn over Andi, the bargain is complete. The promise is over. We can all, finally, rest."

"Her name isn't Andi," Angelica said. "There was no name on her birth certificate. I wouldn't give her one. I only told you that name to make you feel safer—I knew you might try to find her someday. And we'll never *rest,*" Angelica murmured. "That much I can tell you for certain. My gift, you know. Seeing."

"Don't make us do this," Karen said, again, soft. And cold.

"I won't find her for you."

"Then you'll stand in her place."

Hands gripped Angelica's arms and feet, and she let out one long *"Nooooo"* before a towel was stuffed into her mouth. She shook and kicked, but the women's fingers only dug deeper into her flesh. They carried her out of the front door and down the dark driveway to Rhonda's van.

As they dropped her on the floor of the backseat, a familiar caress moved down the back of her neck beneath the skin. The soft fingers of a lover.

"It will be so nice to see you again, my dear. I'm looking forward to it."

And then, deep inside her mind, He laughed.

CHAPTER ELEVEN

Cindy felt Him touching her thoughts and smiled. It was a light feather on her brain, a stroking that tickled her teeth and warmed her from collar to crotch. She shivered in pleasure.

He'd become so much a part of her these last few weeks that she didn't know what she'd done in the past, when her head had only held her own tired thoughts. His soothing touch had smoothed away her sadness over James; in fact, in a way, His touch *was* James' touch because James was a part of Him now. In that sense, she was closer to her late boyfriend than she'd ever been before. Maybe Joe's wish for her that night on the gazebo had come true! Sometimes at night, as she sat on the cliff staring over the edge at the rock-strewn surf below, she could close her eyes and feel James stroking her hair, touching her inside and out. It made her consider joining him. Jumping . . . to freedom.

But in her mind, a voice always convinced her to stay earthbound for now.

"Not yet," He would tell her. *"I may need you on the side of the living soon."*

She would edge back from the drop-off when He said things like that, and lie back on the wind- and rain-polished rock to stare up at the stars. The ocean breeze massaged her like a lover, and it occurred to her that she'd never felt so happy to be alive. Not only did she have a secret protector, a soul friend in her head, but she had an older man who showed undeniable interest in her. Not that she hadn't inspired a glance or two from men in the past, but this one was just so . . . so cuddly-cute. She smiled as she thought of his reaction to her French bikini. It was nothing she would ever have dared wear at a normal public beach. But she'd known that Joe would likely be the only one to see her in it on the beach near Terrel's Peak. Almost nobody ever swam there, despite a good stretch of clean sand. History spoke too loudly.

In the past, she'd always scoffed at the fear that kept people away. Now she knew they were right to be afraid. But she also knew that the source of their fear wouldn't hurt her. Hell, the fuckin' monster of Terrel's Peak was currently her *boyfriend*.

Beat that, *Jill Cheerleader.* She smiled and rolled away from the edge of the deadly drop. It was almost time to go home.

Joe tossed Angelica's diary/scrapbook into the backseat of his car, and pulled away from the house. His headlights skimmed the dilapidated front of the house and then rested on the READINGS BY ANGELICA sign as he backed out.

He was torn.

Should he try to find where Angelica had been taken, or head home to read her book before she returned—*if she did*—and realized he'd stolen it? Could he even hope to find where they'd gone? And could he learn something by finding them? He could go house to house looking for a van, listening at windows, hoping to find out why Bernadette's name was resurrected here, now. Why it still held power after twenty-five years. Why Angelica had screamed *Nooooo* and left without a good-bye. Had they tied her up to take her away, or had she, in the end, gone willingly?

When he reached the turnoff for Highway 31 he made a left without even thinking. The lights of Main Street disappeared almost immediately as the trees grew thick and still around him. The shelter of the forest was the quiet embrace of night's tomb. He was heading toward the cliff.

Where else would they go?

PART III
Captured

CHAPTER ONE

Ken Brownsell was a cautious caver.

Normally.

He'd been fascinated with the underground since he was a kid. If he'd bothered to trace his obsession with tunnels carefully, he would have admitted that it all began with volcanoes. When he was five years old, WBNX-TV used to play old episodes of the Japanese live-action kids show *The Space Giants* in the afternoons. Goldar and his family, the *original* Transformers, lived in a volcano, and turned into rocket ships when the need arose to fight evil. When the call came, they became metallic, majestic superheroes and shot out of the depths of that volcano, human jets of power and might. Ken hadn't cared as much about what they did aboveground. When he had watched *The Space Giants*, he had wanted to escape down into the caverns with them. Live near the glowing fires of liquid rock. *Magma*. He'd been so proud to learn that word as a kid. Rock turned to boiling magma deep in the earth, where diamonds were forged and strange-colored creatures without eyes crawled. There was mystery there, and Ken wanted to be the one to solve it.

Now Ken rarely thought of Goldar, or even of venturing into the depths of an active volcano. But he still got a rush of excitement every time he pushed through a tiny, grimy opening in the earth to discover another hidden chamber on the other side. The dreams of lava and diamonds had turned to ones of mud and basalt. But the childlike thrill was the same.

Ken had joined the Spelunkers of America Club in high school, and during college had taken trips to Kentucky and California and Arizona to burrow underground with others who shared his interest. But his main object of exploration had always been closest to home. The cliffs of Terrel offered hundreds of entryways into the earth. The carvings of salt and spume from a millennium ago. Most proved to be dead ends in short order. But Ken had spent months of weekly expeditions charting some caverns before they petered out into blank, rocky walls.

He'd almost always used the buddy system. You never knew when an apparently solid floor would give way under your weight and cast you into a pit. Dying alone underground wasn't one of his preferred caving fantasies. He did, however, often fantasize about the "big find." Emerging from a slick narrow shaft into a cavern of Mammoth Cave proportions. Of blundering into a hall of natural splendor as beautiful and breathtaking as leading an expedition into the heart of a cathedral-size geode.

And when the masses streamed in to pay their ten dollars in order to walk the path he had forged, it would bear his name.

COME TO TERREL'S PEAK AND SEE THE WONDER OF BROWNSELL CAVERN, the billboards along Highway 31 would read.

The thought always made him glow.

Today he was hoping to make that dream come true.

The entry point he'd been mapping with the help of the Cliff Combers these past weeks was perfectly positioned for tourists. Relatively easy access. And so far the interior hadn't been rough going. Oh, there were points that would have to be blasted wider if a public walking tour was ever to be inaugurated, but that was easily doable. But the best part was, it was still active. They had found the access path of the river. The cave was *alive*. Water was still carving its bowels clean. Somewhere, in a sheltered burrow, Brownsell Cavern might exist. Just before that freak show had taken a dive into the river on the last Comber outing, Ken had seen a likely entry-way into a side room. He'd heard the call of the cave too. And it kept him awake at night with visions of stalagmites and stalactites.

Ken was in love with the earth, and it was doing a strip-tease for him that he couldn't ignore.

Come on in, the water's fine, it said. *Want to see my 'tites?*

He almost called Jeff Avery to partner him, but then the cave showed him another vision:

COME TO TERREL'S PEAK AND SEE THE WONDER OF AVERY-BROWNSELL CAVERN, the billboard said.

"Uh-uh," he murmured to himself. Ken packed the VW bug for a party of one.

He was sharing this discovery with no one.

The day was bright with hope as Ken unloaded the trunk in front of the cave mouth. The sun beat hot on his shoulders, and sweat ran rivers down his armpits before he was ready to go below. He was dressed for the damp, fifty-degree chill of the underground, not the sunbathing eighties of the beach-front. Shrugging the pack onto his shoulders and strapping on his Nevada miner's helmet (one of his souvenirs from spe-lunking in the Rockies), he strode confidently toward the dark, weed-covered mouth in the hillside. He could smell the earthy breath of the underground as soon as he ducked his head to step inside its shade. The fetid aroma of mold and worms was sweet musk to him. With a smile, he flicked on his lamp, and began the now-familiar path toward the heart of Terrel's Peak.

Through the narrow passage that he'd had to coax the freak show through—Joe, his name had been.

"Won't be seeing him again anytime soon," Ken laughed out loud.

"Don't be too sure," a voice in his head answered.

Ken stopped suddenly. Had he just thought that? Or had

somebody spoken to him? He shone his light around to the gray lime walls. Shook his head. The underground did strange things to you sometimes. Especially when you went in alone.

"A stupid thing to be doing," he mumbled to himself, but instead of turning back and calling for a partner, he pulled a strong, thin nylon rope from his belt dispenser and attached its anchor clip to a pinion the Combers had hammered into the rock face nearby. He was entering the last stretch of familiar territory, and it was time to assure some guidance for his return. Ahead he could hear the soft murmur of the underground river. He could only hope that the walkway he'd been treading continued to parallel the water, instead of being absorbed in its path.

Now he was next to the point where Joe had tumbled down, and knew the water was only yards away. The sweat had dried to his flesh, and Ken shivered slightly as he peered over the embankment. The cone of light from his helmet disappeared into the inky blackness below without revealing a thing. The crack in the rock face seemed to continue downward forever, a fissure into hell. The narrow tunnel's far wall remained blank, offering no clues as to the geography below or ahead. Ken stepped back from the edge, then began to move forward again into the black mystery of the mountain.

CHAPTER TWO

Something had to be done about the reporter.

Chief Harry Swartzky sucked in an angry breath and closed his teeth on the well-weathered stem of his pipe as he listened to the woman in front of his desk.

"He's been by to see me and Rhonda," Karen was complaining. "And he has been out to Angelica's a couple times that I know of. He won't let this go," she complained. Her eyes beseeched him to put a stop to the *Terrel Daily Times* investigation. And why shouldn't he? This was a suicide, clear and obvious.

"He made us feel like we were responsible for Jim and Bill's deaths. It was awful; *he* was awful. What if he goes to Monica's? She'll lose it. You've got to *do* something about him, Dad. Make him stop."

"I'll do what I can," the chief promised his eldest daughter. She'd once been Daddy's little girl. And then that business with Bernadette had happened. Something had changed in his little girl that day; she hadn't been the same since. Oh, after the stories died down and time moved on, she'd gotten on with her life, gotten married for a while, had a child. But she never had quite the same open exuberance about life again. She had remained always a little distant. Removed. A wall had gone up between him and his baby that horrible day and he'd never managed to bring it down. It had only gotten taller when the water claimed her only son. But he still tried. And when she needed something, really *needed* it . . . he was there.

"I can't promise anything," he told her, keeping his tone low and gentle. Fatherly. "He's not doing anything illegal. You know, you don't have to let him in when he drops by. Just call me—I'll send Rod or Billy over. And if he won't leave you alone, we can issue a restraining order on him. But one or two visits isn't really enough for that."

The chief fingered the warm bowl of his pipe for a moment. Karen recognized the signs that her father's wheels were turning and remained silent. Finally, he looked up at her again and nodded.

"I'll give Randy over at the *Times* a call to see if he won't rein in his dog. He owes me a bark or two."

She smiled then, one of the few rays of happiness Harry had seen on his eldest daughter's face since Bill had jumped from that cursed cliff four years before. Karen gave him a quick peck on the cheek, and then was gone.

Fragrant fumes of blue-white vanilla-spiced tobacco drifted upward to the ceiling as he considered her complaint some more. He opened the bottom drawer of his desk and pulled out an old Matchbox car. A yellow 'Vette. Its paint was pocked and the front windshield was missing. As Swartzky nudged it along the top of his desk, it wobbled to the left.

Anyone entering the police chief's office at that moment would have thought the head of Terrel's law and order had gone daft. Smoke trickled lazily from his nose to the ceiling and his eyes stared far away, hands resting idly on a broken kid's toy. The chief was lost in a long-gone world. A world where William (*never Billy*) Sander was still alive and eight years old. A world where a sandbox waited in Grandpa's back yard for that charged-up 'Vette. Roads aplenty.

"Grandpa, wanna drive to London?" William would ask, and imitating the sound of a racing engine, he'd disappear with a squeal around the corner of the kitchen, through the living room and out into the yard. He'd need to be hosed down tonight or sand would be everywhere.

Harry picked up the phone to dial the *Times*. He cursed the paper under his breath. Why couldn't those damn reporters stick to informing people about the dates of the church socials and the plans for construction of a new civic center? There was enough heartache in the world without grave robbing to find old pain, picking at the gristle clinging to its bones to make it worse.

The night editor of the *Times* picked up the phone.

"Hello, Randy," the chief began. "How's the wife? Yeah? Those peaches were fine. Please give her my thanks again. Listen, Randy, I need to talk to you about one of your reporters. . . ."

CHAPTER THREE

"I need your help, Cindy. Will you help me?"

Cindy raised her hand from between her legs. She'd been lying on the edge of the cliff, swimming in the languorous pleasure of His touches for what seemed like hours. It was funny how good He was to her, and she couldn't even see Him. But every night He made love to her now, here on the edge of the world. An invisible boyfriend. Not exactly the kind you could take home to meet mom and dad. She had to laugh at the thought of *that*.

"Mom, I really love Him," she'd say.

"Has he touched you?" Dad would growl, interrupting their mother-daughter chat from the other room.

"Yes," she'd answer. "Every night since I've been home from school. He takes me passionately right on the cliff."

The newspaper would hit the floor and heavy steps would pound into the kitchen.

"Where is this asshole?" Dad would bark, his face turning a beefy shade of crimson. "I have a few things I'd like to say to him."

"Why, He's right here," Cindy would answer, and point at the air beside her. "And there," she'd counter, pointing at Dad's recently abandoned chair. "Say whatever you want; He's everywhere."

Cindy grinned openly at the vision, and pushed the damp hair from her eyes. The stars winked brightly above like glittering shells on a dark beach. The moon was rising like a wounded orange to the southeast. It was a beautiful night.

"What did you have in mind?" she whispered to the empty air. In her mind, He began to explain.

The Hyundai spun rocks into the night air as it slid around a graveled corner and began the ascent to Terrel's Peak. Joe knew they were up there somewhere. They had to be. Where else would a meeting about Bernadette take place? The trees slipped by in a shadowy blur and soon the sound of surf rushed through his window. Normally he found its rhythmic noise soothing, but not tonight. Now it sounded like the siren song of death. A song of swan dives from sixteen stories high.

The car's headlights picked out weeds and boulders on the side of the road, and a faded, single yellow line cracked down its middle. The darkness was fading as Joe left the forest behind and climbed to the peak he'd grown to know so well over the past few weeks. He could almost taste the scent of death in the air. It stank of the bloody tang of brine and betrayal.

He didn't feel right about this at all. His inner ear was tremulous, listening for a voice to come out of the darkness and speak inside his soul. Praying the surf would remain the sole sound he heard from the cliff, Joe pulled over to the side and switched off the ignition. Then he stepped out of the car and into the sighing wind and gentle refrain of crickets.

It was a short walk up the rocky rise. The stars and moon gave Joe plenty of light to walk by as he made his way to the only place he could think to go to look for Angelica. But even as he moved toward the edge of the cliff, he knew that it wasn't right. There had been no van, no other cars alongside the road near here. And there was no place for them to have ditched the vehicle. What purpose could they have for bringing her here anyway? Unless they planned to push her off the edge. And his sense wasn't that Angelica's death was the aim of their meeting. No. The summit of Terrel's Peak wasn't the right place.

His feet faltered and he considered turning back to the car. This involved the cliff, and the devil inside it. Somehow, somewhere . . .

"Joe?" a familiar voice called. He started, then peered ahead. A figure stepped around a stony outcrop. A figure in a sun yellow tank top and faded jean shorts.

"Cindy?" he answered, and smiled. It had been days since he'd heard from her, and he hadn't realized how much he missed her until now. "What are you doing up here?"

Her face grew clearer as she moved close, and he could see that she'd been crying. Wet streaks marred her brown cheeks, and her lips looked heavy and sad.

She didn't answer, and he hurried his steps, wrapping his arms around her slim form when he finally reached her.

"What's the matter, baby?" he whispered, pushing her face into his chest as he said it. His heart ached for her.

Cindy looked up at him then, eyes wide with a mixture of pain and relief.

"I've missed you," she said, and he felt his chest flutter.

"I'm sorry," he said. "I've been working overtime this week. This cliff thing has—" He stopped short, realizing that the reason for her tears was likely part of his "cliff thing."

"It's okay," she said, shaking her head. Then she strained upward and kissed him softly on the lips.

"Just hold me, okay?"

He did, and felt her body cave into his own. Her hair smelled of surf and flowers, and her warmth made him tingle with feeling.

"Why are you up here?" she asked after a moment. "Were you looking for me?"

"No," he answered. "Actually, I was—" He stopped, realizing how what he was about to say would sound to the girl.

"What?" she persisted, and then took his hand and led him up to the edge. They sat there on the roof of the world, the waves breaking frothy white in the darkness so far below them. The light from the moon lit an eerie trail from the horizon to the inky line of the shore.

"Tell me," she pressed and he found he couldn't lie.

"I was at Angelica Napalona's tonight," he said. "The fortune-teller?"

Cindy nodded.

"She believes all the local legends about a demon living in this cliff."

Cindy looked nonplussed.

"She says that it has some kind of hold over her and the women who have lost their children here, like Mrs. Sander and Mrs. Canady. She said that it can possess people, and that it has taken the children of her friends."

Again, Cindy nodded. She didn't seem to find his brief sketch at all preposterous.

"The really weird thing about it is that when Angelica and Mrs. Sander and Mrs. Canady and a couple other girls were kids, they used to swim down here, probably right where you and I were that day. One day when they were out there, a girl named Bernadette drowned. The rest of them were okay, but now, each one of those women who survived has lost a child. Except for Angelica, because she doesn't have any kids. Anyway, the point is, tonight I was at her house, asking her about some of this stuff, when the other women showed up. She hid me in her bedroom, and went to meet them. While I was waiting, I found a note from someone that said tonight was a meeting about Bernadette, the girl who drowned all those years ago. And then I heard Angelica scream. I didn't know what to do. She didn't want the other women to know I was there, so I looked out the window, and saw them all getting into a van. I came out of the bedroom then, and Angelica was gone. They kidnapped her. But why, I have no idea. I came up here, thinking that this might have been where they took her. Crazy, huh?"

Cindy shook her head. Then her face went slack. Joe waited

for her to say something, but she seemed a million miles away, her gaze locked on the empty sky over his shoulder. Puzzled, he looked behind him and then leaned forward to pass a hand in front of her eyes.

"You okay?" he asked.

Her eyes locked back on his, and she spoke slowly, carefully.

"You know . . ." she began, her voice barely a whisper, "Angelica *did* have a child."

"Yeah," he said. "She told me that she'd given a baby up for adoption once."

Cindy continued, her tone slow and deliberate. "And her name isn't Angelica."

"Huh?"

Cindy didn't blink, just stared at him with eyes wide and still. "She wasn't always called Angelica. Her name used to be Rachel. She changed it when she started being a fortune-teller. I guess she thought it sounded more Gypsy to be Angelica. Or maybe she wanted to forget about being Rachel."

Joe said nothing. He thought back to the newspaper accounts of Bernadette's drowning. How could he have not picked up on the name thing? Of course, as he thought about his sources, most of what he'd learned about Bernadette's drowning had come from Angelica and Karen. The newspaper hadn't even listed the girls who had been with her when the girl had drowned.

"What do you know about the baby?" he asked finally.

Cindy closed her eyes a moment. Her lips pursed briefly, and she looked as if she were gathering herself to recite a memorized speech. When her eyes opened again, they were staring over Joe's shoulder. But she began to speak.

"Once Rachel—Angelica—had a lover. Nobody in town knows who he was. Maybe he was one of her clients. Maybe he was an out-of-towner who just passed through and got a little something extra while he was here. But Terrel saw the evidence. Her belly grew big and she delivered in the hospital. She never brought it home, though. She gave up her baby for adoption as soon as it was born. Most people around here have probably forgotten the whole thing, since she never had the child in her home and has never married. Hell, it apparently happened back when I was a kid, or maybe even before I was born. But for a little while, Angelica was all the gossip there was here. Our fortune-teller was our town scandal."

Joe looked out at the ocean, too stunned to speak. He thought of Angelica's story of rape and murder. When she had been younger, Angelica had hidden away her child so the demon could never find it—the spirit had taken revenge on her for hiding her baby by staging the rape, and the murder of Harold, Joe bet. But what had become of the child?

A tremor shook Cindy and she shrugged her shoulders. When she opened her eyes again, they were bright and alert, as if she'd just successfully shaken off a nap.

"Out of all the women who were there when that girl drowned, Angelica is the only one who hasn't had a child jump from the cliff, isn't she Joe?"

It was his turn to nod now, and suddenly everything was clear to him. It was Angelica's turn. Her child must die. She'd tried to hide it from Him, from the other women. And so they'd taken her, no doubt at His direction. They would probably torture her until she told them how to find the kid. And then they would kill it.

"You were a reporter in Chicago, right?" she asked, and put a hand on his arm. "Did you know anyone there that could help? Maybe someone who could help you find her child and warn it?" Her face held a look of deep concern.

Joe thought about his contacts back in Chicago with the child welfare department. He might still be able to pull a string or two.

"*Rachel* Napalona, huh?" he said, and Cindy nodded. "All the other kids died when they were eighteen. How much you wanna bet this kid's just about eighteen years old?"

Cindy looked sad, and with a tired smile shook her head affirmatively. "It's a good bet," she said.

"I'll try to find something out tomorrow," he said. "I might be able to track the kid down."

"What are you going to do now?" she said, a quaver in her voice.

Joe looked at her, saw the heaviness of tears in her eyes, but the desire for something else there as well. He needed to keep looking for Angelica. Who knew what they would do to her? But how was he going to find her, if she wasn't up here on the cliff? His heart was torn, thinking of Angelica being tortured somewhere. Beaten and bled for information that would ultimately lead to the death of her only child. But here in front of him was another woman who needed his help. He didn't know where he was going to go to look for Angelica, but he knew that he could comfort Cindy and see her safely home.

"I guess that depends on you," he said finally. "What would you like to do? Can I drive you home?"

In answer, Cindy leaned into his neck and kissed his ear with a tremulous whisper. "Would you stay here with me a while longer?"

Visions of Angelica, tied to a chair in a white room, weeping mascara over bruised and bleeding lips danced through his mind. But where *was* that room? In front of him, with no question of where she was, Cindy's smooth, perfect face pleaded for his attention.

Shit.

He slid a hand around her back and she melted in closer. Gently he stroked her hair and spine, and then, hardly believing that he was doing it himself, he moved his fingers up beneath her loose tank top and rubbed the silky smooth flesh of her back. She slipped sideways and demonstrated to him that she wasn't wearing a bra.

Presently, she wasn't wearing a tank top either.

CHAPTER FOUR

Caves were funny things. Just when a tunnel looked as if it were opening up to some enormous cavern, instead it narrowed down to a fissure the width of a dime.

Ken Brownsell shone the headlamp on the smooth gray face before him and shook his head. There had to be a branch-off that he'd missed. There was no way it could just peter out like this. He had gotten barely one hundred yards from where the freak show had taken a dive into the river. Just around a couple bends and then, pow—a solid rock face. And it didn't narrow down to nothing, like most false tunnels. It ended in a wall. As if someone had cemented up the way to keep intruders out.

He took out his piton hammer and began to test the depth of the rock before him. Was it only a pile-in that had closed off the path? Was there an empty chamber of breathtaking beauty just a foot or two away?

He put an ear to the wall and tapped with the hammer. Slowly. Listened for a telltale hollow note. One careful inch at a time, he worked, sounding the cave out. Praying that this run was not over.

His face was cold with perspiration. And fear. He couldn't bear to think that this was it. No. He *wouldn't* believe it. The way had been too wide up to now. Too promising. Brownsell Cavern too close.

He pounded, over and over again, pausing each time to listen, to evaluate the ring of the hammer on the rock.

Wait.

Was that a hollow knock? He punched the hammer harder, shoved his ear flat against the cool lime. Banged again.

And again.

And then . . . an answer. There was a slow, steady groan echoing through the passage. The earth seemed to be moaning, like some mythic ice giant struggling to turn over in its bed. The seamless rock face before him creaked.

Cracked.

"Shit."

The floor beneath Ken began to shiver, and before he could get to his feet, the wall in front of him was gone. He had been leaning on it as he pounded, and as it fell forward, so did he. But there was no ground to fall onto. Ken was launched into space, his hand still clutching a piece of cool stone from the wall. It had fractured beneath his hammer like glass.

"Fucckkkkk!" he yelled, and then struck something hard. A red-hot pain sliced through his shoulder as he bounced off an outcropping on the cave wall, and Ken was again airborne, but only for an instant. Then the fire in his shoulder was doused in icy cold as he hit the river. The same river that Joe Kieran had swam in just days before. Only this time, there was no one waiting above to pull the tumbler out.

"I was wondering how long it would take you to end up down here," a voice in Ken's head said with flytrap-happy menace.

Then the current sucked him under, ice-cold water seeping up his nose and then into his lungs as he opened his mouth to gasp. Everything went black.

CHAPTER FIVE

Joe's mind was a million miles from writing about city councils and bake sales as he slipped in the side door to the newspaper offices, passing the morgue on his way to the newsroom. He almost ran right into George, who was mopping the hall.

"Whoa there, son," the janitor laughed, raising a hand to shield himself from a collision. "You don't watch where you're going, you'll never get there!"

Joe laughed and clapped the old janitor's shoulder. "I'm sorry," he said. "Just a lot of things on my mind right now."

George squinted one eye and looked Joe over critically. Glancing behind himself, and then over Joe's shoulder, he finally said quietly, "You been staying away from that business we talked about, have you?"

Joe shook his head. "I couldn't, and now . . ."

"Come here," the janitor instructed, and pulled Joe by the elbow toward his office.

Once inside, George shut the door and turned back to Joe, motioning him to sit on the cot, as he had before. Again George pulled up a large plastic canister to sit on.

"Alright then, what've you gotten yourself into?"

"I just wanted to do a real story on the suicides," Joe said. "I took your advice, and went and visited Angelica, but she didn't really help—not at first, anyway."

He told George about receiving the threatening letter, and then about meeting Cindy. When he described the urban legend she'd told him about the disappearance of John Ryan, the janitor just nodded, as if he'd heard it all before.

"I didn't buy any of that," he said, "until I went with a group to explore the caves at the foot of Terrel's Peak."

George's eyebrows raised, but still he said nothing.

"Everything was fine, until I lost my footing and fell off the trail into an underground river. That was when I heard Him."

George's eyes widened. "Him?"

"The devil, the spirit, whatever it is that's inside that cliff. There is something there, George. I know it now."

The janitor stood then and walked to the door. When he turned around, Joe saw that his left hand was shaking. The older man steadied it by reaching out to hold onto a shelf of cleaning materials.

"It's spoken to you," he said, shaking his head.

"And that's not all," Joe continued, quickly outlining what had happened at Angelica's the night before.

George sighed as Joe fell silent.

"I warned you to stay clear of this business," he said.

"Too late." Joe shrugged. "But now I need to find out more about this thing. I've got to help Angelica. But I don't know where to go. How did it come to be here in Terrel? How can I fight it, if it comes to that?"

The old man seemed to shrink in on himself, then stepped closer.

"You can't fight it," he whispered. "All ya can do is hope to stay out of its sight, and ya haven't done a very good job of that."

"No," the younger man agreed.

"There's nobody I know of in town who could give you any more than you've gotten from Angelica," George said. He rubbed a hand on his chin. "Like I told ya before, it's sometimes better not to know about some things. I know that's not what you wanna hear, being a reporter and all."

"But I have to find out more about this thing," Joe insisted. "Angelica is in danger, and I won't just abandon her."

George nodded slowly, and then walked past Joe to the shadowed recesses of the long janitor's room. He reached up and pulled down a shoebox from the top of an old steel newspaper shelf that had bowed so much in the middle that it could no longer hold much of anything. Removing the lid of the box, George pulled out a small book and brought it to Joe.

"You're not the only one in this town who's worried about those kids," he said. "A couple years ago, when those kids started jumping, and not on Halloween, I did a little reading on the subject myself."

Joe took the thin volume and read the small white letters on the nondescript brown spine. *Witchcraft, Demonology, and Possession.* No author was listed.

"It's not about Terrel, or the problems we have here," George said, "but it does have some interesting theories about demons and the like. I don't know what you can do with that knowledge, but you're free to borrow it, if you like."

Joe nodded, leafing through the pages. It was a short book, but the print was small and there appeared to be no diagrams or pictures.

"Thanks," he said. "I'll take a look."

He stood up. "I better get to my desk. Randy's going to have a cow, I'm so late."

George nodded, but the look of concern didn't leave his weathered face.

"Joe," he said as the reporter opened the door to leave. "I can't tell you to stay out of it. But be careful."

Joe turned the book over and over in his hands as he hurried to his desk. He still felt funny admitting that this was real. Part of him still denied hearing the voice inside the cliff. But the other part already longed to crack open this volume. He needed information, any information, about what sort of being could be behind all of this. He needed to know how to avoid being turned into a demon's marionette, as Angelica had once been.

He stashed the book in his backpack and sat down to start on the day's stories. But he'd barely begun to type, when he heard his name.

"Joe," Randy called from across the newsroom. "Come into my office a minute?"

That didn't sound good. Randy never called anyone into his office unless he had a beef. Everything else was open newsroom game. Hell, there were rarely more than three people in the newsroom at any one time as it was.

Joe steeled his shoulders and followed his boss to the broom closet the editor used as an office. What had he screwed up now?

The stupid library story was done, the village board meeting story had been a no-brainer, as they usually were. It wasn't like the village board had a whole hell of a lot of business to take care of in a sleepy burg like Terrel. It certainly wasn't as if they spent any time talking about people who periodically plummeted from the town's favorite natural landmark.

"What's up, Randy?" he asked nonchalantly as he strode between the stacks of yellowed newspaper that bordered the doorway. The burly editor didn't smile.

"Shut the door."

Joe clenched his jaw and did as he was told. This was definitely not shaping up to be a good talk.

Randy walked behind his steel desk and pulled out a battered leather chair with a screech of unoiled ball bearings. He sat heavily, and stared for a moment at his only full-time reporter as though he were a prison guard looking at the inmate who's just incited a food fight. It was not a look of pride.

"I told you to lay off the suicide story, Joe."

He nodded.

"You haven't."

"I haven't written anything more about it," Joe sidestepped, wondering how the editor knew he was still investigating the subject. Had he been eavesdropping outside the janitor's closet? Surely George wouldn't have warned the editor about him.

"Maybe not," Randy continued. "But you have been going around and asking people a lot of questions. Questions that hurt people. Questions that bring up painful memories of the dead for no reason. You're giving the *Terrel Daily Times* a bad reputation, Joe. This isn't the *National Enquirer*. We don't pick at scabs again and again to keep them bleeding. The Canady kid's dead. So's the Sander kid. And the O'Grady kid. Now listen to me, Joe, because I'm not having this conversation with you again."

The editor leaned forward and looked hard at Joe.

"Leave them to rest in peace."

The twin caterpillars above Randy's eyes rose in question.

"Got it?"

Joe nodded.

"Good. Now go get me a story I can actually *use* in tomorrow's edition."

Randy broke eye contact then, and turned away from Joe to stare at his computer monitor. Within seconds, he was typing as if Joe had already left the room.

He took the hint.

On his way back to his desk, Joe tried to figure out who had ratted on him. He didn't dare ask Randy. Who had called the paper to complain? Rhonda? Karen?

Angelica . . . or should he say, Rachel? He smiled at the new/old name. It was very biblical. Despite Cindy's theory that it hadn't been Gypsy enough, it seemed to Joe as if it could have been used for a fortune-teller name.

Or maybe Angelica had just wanted to escape from the person Rachel had been. She hadn't escaped the consequences, though.

Whoever the complainer had been had just made his job harder. Because now he needed to dig more than ever. He needed to find Angelica's child before the women did. He didn't know where to turn to begin to search for Angelica, but he could at least put some wheels in motion to help protect her kid. Which meant some long distance phone calls. And a trip to the county registrar's office. He needed a date of birth and a hospital before he called Chicago. He looked up the number and address in the phone book and jotted it down on a notepad, then stuffed it into his pants pocket. Then he picked up the phone and dialed another number.

Angelica's.

Not surprisingly, she didn't pick up.

He hung up the phone and settled into his chair. He had some business to take care of before he could spend any more time on his pet project, or else he'd be out of a job. Randy's angry scowl flashed in his memory.

But as he stared at the dusty screen of the old VDT, he kept thinking of last night. Of a yellow piece of paper with *Bernadette* written on it in the same hand, he thought, as the yellow paper that had warned him to quit looking for death. And of the warm lips and tender arms of Cindy, who had clung to him so passionately in the night ocean air of the cliff.

She had wrapped herself around him like a vine, squeezing her smooth flesh to his own with a need that he wasn't sure he could fulfill. She seemed so hungry. Her eyes flashed with the light of the stars as he kissed her neck, her chest, her chin.

"I love you," he had said eventually.

"Yes . . ." She sighed and rolled on top of him.

Joe shook the daydream away. He had found someone special on Terrel's Peak last night, but it wasn't who he'd gone there looking for. And *that* woman might be in great danger now. He had driven by Angelica's house on the way to work, and she hadn't returned home. Her phone remained unanswered. Where had they taken her? What were they doing to her?

And what would they do if they found her child before he did?

Steeling himself to run through his checklist of today's stories as quickly as possible, Joe opened a blank Word file and began to type. He wanted to get over to the registrar's office before five.

CHAPTER SIX

Angelica's back bounced painfully against the steel floor of the van as the vehicle turned off Main Street to head out of town. She knew where they were going, and there was nothing she could do about it. Rhonda and Monica had bound her hands as soon as they got in the van. She had struggled against them, but she was no match for Rhonda's weight—and pure-bitch mean streak. The woman had always had a bitter fire in her that was best left alone. Beefy hands had gripped her shoulders like pincers, and Angelica had thrust a shoulder at Rhonda's face and connected with a satisfying "oooff" coming from the target. Teeth closed on the shoulder then, and Angelica had screamed. Rhonda had let go and laughed.

Had the bitch drawn blood?

Angelica couldn't see out the back windows, but she knew where they were going. She could feel Him getting closer with every mile.

The van lurched suddenly, and then tilted off balance, hood facing forward. The back end bounced unsteadily with a heart-skipping lurch, but then, just as quickly, the vehicle evened out again. They had reached the beach, she knew in an instant.

After a few minutes of listening to the engine whine and moan as the tires spun their way through gullies of sand, the van finally came to a sliding stop and Karen killed the lights and motor. The side door slid open and two hands reached in to help Angelica out of the van.

"Let's go," Rhonda growled, and pushed Angelica up from the seat. With her hands behind her, it was difficult to step down from the van, but Monica and Karen held her arms and half pushed, half dragged her down to the sand.

They herded Angelica through the dark, eerily swaying tall grass near a scattering of heavy boulders, and then down along the water. She recognized the spot instantly. It was the cove beneath the cliff, where six girls had once come on a hot sunny day in 1981 to swim.

And then there were five.

The tiny mountain loomed above them here. Its shadow blotted out much of the sky, but there was still enough light to pick their way through the rocky shore. They were headed toward a cave that was only accessible at low tide.

They had all been there once before.

A car passed on the road, growing higher and farther above them, and Angelica watched the pale nimbus of its headlights ascend to the top of the cliff. But instead of passing on, it stopped just before the peak and waited. Then the lights went out.

Somebody was parked up there. Probably some high school kids making out in the backseat, she thought as they trudged along the beach below. It was the perfect necking spot, if you could ignore the history. If she could just break away long enough to get on the path to the top . . .

Rhonda pounded at her back to shove her forward, and Angelica took the opportunity. She exaggerated the effect of the blow and fell into the backs of Karen and Monica. Karen lost her balance and had to catch herself on hands and knees on the sand. They both turned to rail on Rhonda.

"Take it easy, Rhon," Monica squealed.

"I'm only giving her a taste."

Attention momentarily diverted, Angelica ducked from beneath Rhonda's guiding hand and leapt from her crouch to run back toward the van. The path was easy to see beyond it; the grass of the road broke where the gravel curved down to lead to the beach.

She had had the advantage of surprise, but was hampered by not having the use of her arms. Her feet slipped and sunk in the loose sand, and it felt as if she would lose her balance and fall forward to eat the beach at any moment. But she ran hard, determined to make it to the road, where she could scream for help from whoever had stopped up at the cliff. She had to get closer though. Nobody would ever hear her cry here above the crash and wash of the surf.

Angelica passed the van, her strides lengthening as she grew more accustomed to running without elbows pumping at her sides. She was going to make it!

She set one foot on the slippery incline, then another. Her head topped the rise and she was on the road that led either back into Terrel or up to the top of the cliff.

And then something heavy slammed into the back of her head, and she did, indeed, taste the ground.

The floor was cold and damp beneath her hands.

From somewhere far away she could hear voices. They were talking about her. The quiet one said, "Jesus, Rhonda, did you have to hit her so hard?"

"Yeah," a high-pitched one added. "What do we do if she doesn't wake up?"

"She'll wake up," a third voice answered, and suddenly something cool and salty splashed across her face.

It ran down her nose and into the back of her throat and Angelica coughed. Her eyes fluttered open as she struggled to breathe, choking out blood and salt and the grit of sand from her mouth.

"Told you." Rhonda grinned. The chunky woman was kneeling above Angelica, a flannel shirt twisted up in her hands. She wrung a few more drops of water onto Angelica's face.

The fortune-teller shook her head, and rolled away from

Rhonda to find herself staring at the knees of Karen and Monica.

"Anything more you'd like to tell us about Andi?" Karen said. She sounded sad, somehow. Angelica could see in her eyes that she didn't want to do this. Rhonda, on the other hand . . .

"I told you, I couldn't do anything if I wanted to."

"All right then." The other woman sounded resigned. "We'll be back tomorrow."

"Yeah, we'd love to stay and chat about the old days"— Rhonda smirked—"but the tide's coming in. Pretty soon this cave will be closed off by the ocean. A perfect cage for our little Rachel. You understand. But you won't be totally alone. You'll have Him to keep you company."

Karen cut the other woman off.

"Come on, let's get out of here. We've done enough."

And with that, the three women rose and walked, single file, out of the rocky room and into the passage that led back to the ocean.

"Does the water fill up that room during the day?" Angelica heard Monica ask as they hurried out of the cave.

"I don't know," Karen's voice echoed back. "For her sake, I hope it does."

She sounded beaten.

Angelica writhed and twisted, but succeeded only in grinding loose dirt down beneath her belt and into her underpants. That just added to her discomfort.

They had brought her back here, after all these years. To the sanctuary.

To the site where they had forged their "Covenant."

Across the room, tucked into a crevice in the rock, a candle burned. Its flame guttered wildly as she watched, throwing eerie shadows up the wall to scrabble and scratch long fingers of light across the ceiling. She could almost see the silhouette of Him coming to claim her. If He'd been human, she knew just what He would do before He killed her. Unconsciously, she locked her knees together. But *that* wasn't what she had to worry about at the moment. He wasn't human, and He couldn't have his way with her physically.

No.

The way He fucked you was much worse. He fucked with your mind. Made you want things. Do things. Made you sign away your future . . .

She was eighteen again and her name was Rachel.

"Rhonda, come over to the rock!" Rachel called, pushing a wave from in front of her with interlaced fingers. She loved to watch the water break against her hands, rolling around them and splattering her with salt water. Mom warned her against swallowing the sea foam. "You'll catch God knows what sort of germs or slimies if you go swallowing that dirty water." But Rachel never paid the warnings much mind. She licked the spray from her lips and smiled. The taste stuck to her tongue, a near-oily residue of life. Well-salted life. Tears in a cup. Sweat in an ocean. The water was her place, her womb. And she dragged her friends here whenever she could.

"I really should get back soon," Rhonda complained in that familiar "let's wrap this up" tone. If the ocean was Rachel's life documentary, it was just a short sitcom for the rest. Jump in, have a few laughs and get out without getting anything wet deep down. Soul deep. Rachel came out here to play, but the gang never seemed to totally understand that there was more. When you sat on the rocks out in the middle of the bay, you could stare into someplace beyond. Some days, she thought the whole town was really more like a pier. Just a place where you could dive off into the water, if you were brave enough. If you wanted to see what was beneath the dark, rushing waves. That was where reality was, she thought. That was where life began.

Rachel thought maybe she had skimmed the surface of those secret primordial depths, if not dove in. Her friends showed no interest in doing more than strolling out along the pier . . . and then turning back.

"It is getting late," Karen chimed in. Her freckles stood out more in the dying light. She never seemed to tan in the sun, only grow paler around the freckles. Her hair hung in a long hemplike braid, its natural orange fire dulled to a sodden brown. Karen followed Rhonda in everything. And Melody, Monica and Bernadette were usually not too far behind. The bigger girl had a way of getting what she wanted.

"One more lap?"

Rhonda rolled her eyes.

"C'mon, it won't take too long," Bernadette offered, taking Rachel's side for once. Rachel flashed her a smile and dove into the deep green-blue water, heading over toward the foot of the cliff. There were more shells to find there, where the rocks jutted like pylons from the water, and held on to the refuse that the tides dragged in from the depths of the ocean.

The splashing behind her increased as her friends followed. They had already piled a stash of sea treasure on the bank, but one more run wouldn't hurt. Who knows, maybe they'd find something cool from a ship. They'd brought in a long fiberglass shard earlier today that Rachel was sure had belonged to some kind of boat.

"Maybe the pilot's body is wedged between one of these rocks," Rhonda had suggested drolly. "Maybe the next time we go down, we'll find his skull."

Karen had splashed her in the face and the whole group had struck back to shore for a while. But sunset wasn't far off now. It *was* time to head home. Missing dinner was a capital offense. But Rachel really hated to go home. Any excuse that she could think of to stave off that torture . . .

"By tomorrow, if there is anything else left of this boat, it will all have been pulled back out to sea," she called over her shoulder. The other girls didn't need much prodding, however. They all had dreams of sunken treasure chests and long-lost strings of pearls in their heads.

Rachel reached the spot where they'd found the long piece of fiberglass and turned to the others. "Let's start here. Anything you find, pile up here on the rock, okay?"

The others nodded, and split off to the surrounding boulders, taking deep breaths and then plunging their heads beneath the surface to scan the murky ground beneath.

The treasure hunt was on.

It was Bernadette who found the cave. She'd gotten quite close to shore, beyond where the rest of the group was trawling for broken clues from a broken boat. Chances are, the boat hadn't even sunk near here, but had been washed up by the tide from miles away. All sorts of strange debris had piled into Terrel Bay over the years. Its deadly currents were legend on this coast.

"Hey, you guys! Over there." She pointed at the base of the cliff, just a few steps of sand up from the rock-strewn water. "Is that an opening?"

"Could be," Melody said, nodding. "Let's check it out!"

The girls trudged out of the water to convene on the beach once more, and shaking and squeezing the water from their hair as they went, walked over to the small opening in the mountain. It was only three feet wide, but that was plenty of room for Rachel to stick her head inside.

She whistled, and the sound echoed for what seemed like miles.

"It gets bigger and bigger," she said, pulling her head out. "It looks like a huge cave in there."

"How come we never saw it before?" Bernadette asked, her naturally sloe eyes squinted even tighter in wonder.

"It's probably underwater most of the time," Karen said. "Look at how close the tide is to it now."

"Can we look inside?" Bernadette pressed.

Rachel knew that if she had asked, Rhonda would have

said no. Absolutely not. Time to go. But instead, the bigger girl turned and ran down the beach.

"I've got a light on my bike," she called over her shoulder in explanation.

Ten minutes later the six bikinied Terrel High seniors were tiptoeing beneath the cap of Terrel's Peak. A smooth rock path wound up and away from the ocean into the bowels of the mountain.

"We should follow this for only a few yards or we could get lost," Rachel warned.

Rhonda shushed her. "Just watch out that you don't step on any creatures from the black lagoon. We go straight in, we go straight out. It'll be fine."

They stepped, single file, up a slow, smooth incline. And then the path opened into a room.

Without warning, Bernadette screamed.

The other girls reached out for her, but the girl was already in motion, running across the width of the cavern into the dark.

"Bernadette, wait," Rachel called, and the girls began to run forward after her.

Rhonda shone her light around the room, revealing glistening gray walls, but no sign of Bernadette.

"Bernadette, what the fuck?" she growled, and then her light found the girl, huddled up in a ball against the farthest wall of the cave. Her face bobbed back and forth, as if looking for something. In the light of the flash, her narrow eyes seemed to have bulged to twice their normal size.

"Did you hear him?" she whispered as the rest of the girls gathered around her.

"Hear who?" Rhonda asked.

"He said . . . He said he'd been waiting for us."

"Quit screwing around, Bernie," Rhonda barked. She always called the younger girl Bernie when she was annoyed. "We should probably get home."

"I heard a man," Bernadette insisted, but the rest of the girls ignored her.

"Probably just the ghost of a pirate." Rhonda laughed. "Trying to keep us from getting at his gold. Maybe it was the guy from the boat."

"Hey, what's this?" Rachel called. "Shine the light here."

She was just a few feet away, and something sparkled at her feet in the yellow light from Rhonda's bike light. Rhonda moved closer with the light, and then they all saw it. It glinted like treasure in the light.

A box just a little bigger than a cigar box. Bits of its lid glittered silver in the light of the flash, though most of it had corroded and darkened to turn black and green from the salt air.

"Open it," Monica squealed.

"No!" Bernadette cried.

But Rachel did. There was no lock on the fastener. Ignoring Bernadette's warning, she tried to pry the simple metal clasp off its peg. The lid wouldn't budge at first, but then it did, lifting off with a pop that put Rachel off balance. She fell backward to land unceremoniously on her butt, and the contents of the box spilled out onto the ground.

It was a strange collection to have hidden away in a box.

There was an artist's thin paintbrush, its wooden handle stained a variety of dark shades. And there was a jagged charcoal sketch pencil. A small leather-bound book. A necklace, with two horned, coupling figures. And the broken, yellowed key to a piano.

The girls all squealed with delight. They'd found it. After years of getting goose bumps and blue skin from diving and fruitlessly pulling up muck around the rocky beach, they'd found buried treasure at last! Well, a treasure chest with old junk, anyway.

"Look at this," Rachel said, opening the pages of the book. "Whose do you suppose it was?"

"What does it say?" Melody asked. "Is it a diary?"

As they each grabbed and passed around the box's bits of refuse, they all heard the voice that had sent Bernadette stumbling.

"So glad you could come," it said.

This time, Bernadette didn't scream. But the girls all looked at one another, eyes wide as if to say, "Did you hear that too?"

"It's been so long since I've had the pleasant company of young women!" the voice enthused. *"Please, don't be afraid. Take what you want from the box. Each piece will bring you something special."*

It was Bernadette who'd voiced what they all were thinking.

"Are you . . . a . . . genie?" she'd whispered, her voice trembling as she looked around and around at the blank gray walls. Nobody else was in the room. Nothing moved.

"In a manner of speaking," He'd replied. *"But I don't give wishes away for free."*

Rachel absently hung the erotic necklace around her throat, fingering the horns on its figures' heads. Karen toyed with the paintbrush, swishing long curved lines in the sand. Each of the girls found their hands drawn to one of the pieces from the box.

The voice began to laugh. *"Yes,"* he said. *"It has been a long time."*

Rachel felt warmth spread through her body, a tingling sensation that made the world seem fine, fine, fine. It was like being drunk. At first it felt good, after the hours they'd been in the water. But then it grew uncomfortably sunburn warm. Hot, sweating, but in a weird way. She felt excited. Dirty. She looked at the figures of the pendant at her chest and licked her lips in thirst. But not a thirst for water.

God. The head had slipped from her chest to her belly and then lower, and she reached down to scratch the skin along the laces of her bikini and suddenly knew what the heat really was. She wanted to *fuck!*

"What . . . ?" she began to say, and then, through blurred eyes, she could see that the others felt it too. They were all behaving strangely, their faces glazed as their hands knotted into fists and then sneaked across their bodies to scratch themselves, sneakily at first, and then without care for propriety. Rhonda's tongue was licking her upper lip as her left hand disappeared into her bikini top, and Karen had sat down with her back to the wall, allowing her fingers to gouge red trails on the white flesh of her inner thighs.

Then Rhonda's hand pulled away from her breasts, allowing one tit to hang free obscenely as she stepped out of her bikini bottoms to expose the curly black hair of her cunt. Quiet, shy Monica had even slipped her hand inside her bikini bottoms. Rachel watched as the girl's fingers bunched and relaxed rhythmically against the taut material of her suit. She didn't seem to care that her friends could clearly see her masturbating. They had always been close friends . . . but not *that* close.

"It's been a long time since I've seen women in action," the voice said. *"Show me what you've got, girls."*

Rhonda moved like a zombie toward Bernadette, one hand lodged in the exposed thatch of dark hair between her legs, the other hand supporting her young but already heavy, fleshy left breast, fingers pinching an erect brown nipple. She moaned as she moved with obvious intent toward her friend. The smaller girl had backed against the wall and was looking wide-eyed at the rest as if they were aliens. She alone seemed unaffected by the strange erotic heat that had stolen the wills of her friends. She alone was not touching herself in some obscene way.

"No!" she screamed as Rhonda's lips pressed to her own.

"No, no, *no!*" she cried, and threw herself from the room.

"I didn't say you could leave," the voice said smoothly. They all heard him. But Bernadette continued to run down the path leading to the ocean.

In a moment, there was a short scream from outside the

cave, but the girls barely heard it. All of them were engrossed in the honey-sweet sensation that had blurred their minds. The sexy heat was coating their limbs, throbbing in their thighs, pouring like hot honey down their throats. They were swimming, drowning, engulfed in its musk. They abandoned themselves to it, lapping it up like mother's milk. They felt starved for it, couldn't get enough of it, couldn't taste it fast enough. They touched themselves and longed to touch their friends. Their suits dropped in a jumble of colorful triangles on the cave floor and the five girls quickly stepped toward one another, eyes glazed and tongues searching. The cave floor soon became a tumble of sucking, rubbing flesh. There was no hesitation or shyness as they rolled around with one another, arms and legs outstretched. They kissed in blind abandon, mouth seeking mouth, hand slipping down and inside as one through the mud.

They didn't even stir when Bernadette returned from her frantic escape to stand in their midst. She was naked, her small breasts pale and beaded with seawater. A puddle of cold water formed around her feet as drops perspired down her slender thighs, beaded in the wiry tangle of her pubic hair and splattered to the rock floor, drip by drip by drip. The girls formed a circle, twining and moaning around her feet, a humid sultry breeze of sex pounding against the cool breeze of the surf that slid from Bernadette's body. None of the girls seemed to care that Bernadette was also bleeding heavily from a deep gash that ran from her left eye to cross her forehead and disappear into the wet coils of her hair.

Rachel would later remember sucking on that cut as Bernadette's strangely unfocused eyes rolled in her head and deep laughter sprang from her girlish belly. Seawater sprayed from her mouth as she laughed, cooling the girls who moaned and writhed closer to Bernadette, thirsting for more of her cool wetness to assuage their strange heat, the ocean soothing the red blush on their skins and then burning away as the fire within their bones burned hotter again. Their thirst was unquenchable, and Rhonda licked the drops from Melody's breasts, and then tickled Bernadette's underarms, drawing a deeper, longer laugh, and a thicker, messier spray from the girl's mouth. They didn't care—Bernadette was their fountain. Sex was their sun.

Mostly what Rachel remembered of that afternoon was bliss. A tangle of hair and arms and breasts and musky, thirsty, unquenchable sex. A dirty, evil, wonderful hour of touching and sucking and playing lover and loved with one another. They were mindless. There were no boundaries. It was ecstasy.

And then, as quickly as it had begun, the strange, distorted orgy was over.

The honey taste dripped away from their lips to leave a bitter residue of iron and salt. Their vision cleared.

Rachel lifted her mouth from the hard nipples of Monica's firm eighteen-year-old chest and met her friend's look of horror with equal disgust.

Karen rolled from between Melody and Rhonda and spit the taste of their orgasms from her lips, grabbing and holding her discarded suit ineptly across her well-explored privates. Her eyes looked wild with fright and incomprehension at what had just happened.

And Bernadette stood in the middle of them and smiled crazily, congealed blood smeared across her breasts and the tiny pit of her belly button and the light, short hair of her pubes. The same blood that coated all of the girls' bodies.

Melody wiped a hand across her face and stared at the blood that came away on her fingers for many seconds before her lips began to tremble. A low, horrible, frightened sound came from her lips.

"That was fun," Bernadette said.

But it wasn't Bernadette's voice that said it. It sounded deeper, littered with razors and gravel. And her eyes looked wrong. Vacant. Like shiny black marbles rolling back in her skull.

"We'll have to do that again sometime."

Karen was frantically shimmying her bony legs into her suit bottoms. But she stopped and screamed when she saw the smears of blood on her calves, staining the edge of her suit. She started to push the suit bottoms back off, and saw the blood speckled on her feet. With a moan, she slid to the floor, suit bunched at her knees, eyes filled with tears and paralyzing fear.

"Right now," the Bernadette voice continued, "I'm sure you all want to go home."

Somebody else started to cry. Rachel thought it was Rhonda.

"But first I'll tell you about your gifts."

Bernadette's hand pointed at Karen. Its fish-white fingers were streaked with blood.

"The paintbrush will allow you to paint the most realistic artworks you can imagine. That brush has kissed the lips of saints and copulated with the diseased cunts of hell. Once it belonged to a man who brought the light of heaven to the walls and ceilings of churches. His name was celebrated throughout the halls of Europe, and written of by priests and artists alike in honor and awe. He was a saint on earth, until he found a succubus mistress who turned his praises to lust. The sacrilege of her breasts and thighs, used by men and women alike, became the new worship of his art, rather than the sterile purity of angels. His paintings were banned, and he fled with his mistress to a forgotten isle, where they painted each other's bodies in piss and blood and slept with the bones of savages. I knew him well, and before he died, smothered in the decay of her flesh, he gave me this brush. Use it well."

Bernadette next pointed at Rachel. "Long ago, I received this necklace from an Etruscan prostitute. Night after night, she begged for the means to leave this world, but her master kept her bound and helpless until a customer was at the ready. One night, as she writhed and cried beneath the robes of a dealer in antiquities, one of her steady customers, the man was touched by pity for the woman. He asked what was the matter, and she told him. Now this dealer had just come into a huge treasure, stolen from the tomb of an ancient king. He was feeling generous, and reached into a satchel at his waist to pull free this necklace, placing it around her neck. 'Use this well,' he warned, and stood to take his leave of her. 'It is said that it once adorned the neck of the most powerful high priestess in Egypt. Legend says it will show you whatever you wish to see. You may stare into the future to see your death, if you so wish, or use it to see your way to a new life.' The prostitute did not understand his words at first, and he probably did not understand the power that he had bestowed. But eventually, the prostitute realized that she did not want to die. She used the sight of these gems to help plot her escape from her master, and eventually used it to become one of the most celebrated fortune-tellers in Italy. She died very rich. You may do the same. Touch someone's hand with it around your neck and you will see their future. An easy talent. But let them inside you, and its vision deepens. You may tell them of the dark secrets their offspring will hold in the heaviest pits of their hearts."

Bernadette raised her voice like a carnival barker. "Amaze your friends and family. Seduce them, lie in your incestuous bed and whisper in their guilty ears of the whores their children will take. Kiss them and slip your tongue in their ears as you speak in whispers of when and how they will die." She laughed grotesquely. "Your bed could be an addiction, an affliction!"

Monica was staring in fear at the broken charcoal pencil. She held it away from her lap, yet couldn't seem to drop it to the ground.

Bernadette stooped to stroke her outstretched hand. When Monica pulled the pencil and hand away, her wrist was sticky.

"That pencil once belonged to a mistress of the Marquis de

Sade," Bernadette said. "Do any of you girls know of the Marquis?" Bernadette's empty gaze slid over the girls, stopping to stare and smile at Rhonda's big breasts. The girl had covered her most private bits with an arm, but Bernadette stepped closer, slid her hand beneath Rhonda's forearm and held the nipple hidden there between cold fingers. Rhonda shivered.

"No, I don't suppose any of you ladies have been bad enough to learn about the loves and lusts of the Marquis just yet. Remember the name—he would have loved the game we played here today."

Bernadette pinched harder until Rhonda screamed out loud. The creature who was once their friend only laughed harder, grabbed a lock of Rhonda's hair and forced her face to look upward. Then Bernadette's free hand came down to slap Rhonda's cheek with a force that made all the girls shudder.

"We have played a little game today," Bernadette said. "Just a taste of what we could enjoy together. And you each enjoyed it, did you not?"

She stepped back to Monica.

"The Marquis' mistress could not get enough of these sorts of games. She licked and sucked whatever he would entreat her to. And when she went home, bruised and sore and bleeding in all of her hidden places, she would draw the most ghastly visions. Beautiful bits of hell. I give you her gift. Her spirit still moves in this pencil, and it will help you see the depths to which we could plumb together."

Bernadette nodded back at Rhonda, who held the piano key.

"Yours is a simpler gift. Play whatever instrument you wish, and people will listen. You will hold them in your sway. You will be the Pied Piper of Terrel. They will do as you bid. And if you play for me, I will come to you and dance in your bed all night and all day. We will take your lovers apart, bone by bone. We will cover ourselves in their blood to complete our own sweet love. For I do love you girls, do you know that?"

Bernadette's body leaned in to kiss Rhonda on the lips, and left bloody mouth prints on each of the other girls in turn.

"These are gifts from me, your genie, your devil." Bernadette laughed. "Enjoy their fruits. Use them well, for you will pay me for them with your lives. I loan your lives back to you. But I warn you: Ignore my gifts, ignore me, and I will suck your shells as dry as I did this one. Ahh, she was sweet while she lasted."

With that, Bernadette's body crumpled to the floor.

"Let's make a little Covenant," the voice continued, without a mouth once again.

And moments later, the fate of five women was sealed.

Angelica shook tears from her face as she remembered the last time she'd been trapped in this room. When the Covenant had been struck. She'd never meant to keep it. And she knew the others hadn't either. They'd thought as soon as they'd gotten clear of the cliff that it would all fade away.

But He'd never let them go.

"The interest on your loan is due," a voice chuckled deep inside her head.

Angelica let the tears flow fast and free.

CHAPTER SEVEN

One benefit of working for a big-city daily is that you make contacts. In lots of strange places. And Joe happened to have a couple friends in the adoption industry.

And it was an industry. There was money exchanged in unconscious irony beneath strip-joint tables, and a black market of babies traveling along a pipeline paved with both good intentions and greed. He'd done a whole series on the issue for the *Tribune*, and had managed to make a couple friends in the process, along with the predictable enemies.

The friends were actually an unusual benefit to this particular story. The enemies were natural enough. Nobody liked to be exposed for graft.

That thought brought to mind Ann, his former girlfriend. Or girl*fiend*, as one particular smartass at the paper had dubbed her.

She'd been well intentioned, if totally unethical in her little graft connection to the alderman who held a lucrative waste management contract over several people's heads. In trying to take the alderman down, Joe had sent his own lover over the waterfall as well.

The resulting sick feeling hadn't gone away in an hour or a day or even a week. The scenario had played over and over in his head when he'd been forced to break the story. As it had on almost every day since. But there was some iron within him that didn't bend. He did not regret his decision to run the story. To expose her in the tale of corruption. She had made her bed. But he still awoke on his own sometimes to the sound of her accusing cries.

"Joe, they're going to send me to prison! To prison, Joe!"

She'd looked at him incredulously after reading the page-three story in that day's *Tribune*. The worst part about it was that she hadn't come flying at him with fists raised, voice screaming. Instead, she'd simply deflated, as if the article that connected her and the alderman and a handful of other city officials with the graft scam was a giant pin, and she a balloon. She had sunk to the wooden floor of her apartment, legs crossed over each other, head hanging almost low enough to kiss her own toes.

Joe had left her that way, crying in her oversize Chicago Cubs nightshirt, not knowing how to answer for his honesty. Not knowing how to face the fact that his job's habit—no, duty—of exposing people's darker activities had finally come home to roost. It had swooped down on his private life in a way that didn't allow him to maintain his distance from the subjects of his story. This time, he'd fucked up his own life while exposing corruption that was ruining the lives of others.

He hadn't tried to fix it. That would have made him as corrupt as those he'd exposed. He tried to go back to the newsroom, to take joy in an exposé over the Illinois Tollway Authority. But it felt hollow then. The "story" had ceased to matter to him. In losing the independent spirit of Ann to the truth of the story, he'd killed a part of himself. After a few weeks of staring at his reflection in the newsroom VDT monitors and seeing only empty, half-felt words take shape on their screens, he'd finally walked away. He didn't even clean out his desk. He'd simply run.

All the way to Terrel.

And now the thirst and drive of "the story," the thing that had driven him to journalism in the first place, had returned. He'd come out of hibernation, come out of the mind-numbing morass of library renovation and summer festival "coverage" to find himself thirsting after the truth again. And in doing so, he found himself, again, screwing up the lives of others who had secrets they wished to keep. In his latest story, he was messing with the lives of five women. They would be hurt by his research. But he couldn't stop. That was why he was waiting for Angie Harkenride to take his call. That was why he was putting up with ten minutes of Kenny G on-hold music on a long distance call. Ultimately, he had always believed in the importance of being a reporter, even if he'd shrunk inside himself and hidden for a while from its consequence.

Kenny G suddenly was replaced by a click and a warm, feminine "Hello, Joe?" that instantly heated his blood. There were some things . . . and some people, that he missed in Chicago.

"Angie," he said. "I need you to talk to Brett. I need a little favor."

As soon as he hung up the phone, Joe found himself wondering how long it would take Angie to get in touch with Brett, and for him to actually search through the records. He hated having to trust his research to someone else's schedule. He paced the apartment a couple times, knowing that it would probably take hours—or a couple days—before he'd hear back from Brett. Then he realized that there *was* some research that he could be doing himself.

In the rat race of the day, and his rush to get to the registrar's office to try to narrow down the date of Angelica's child's birth and adoption, Joe had almost forgotten his conversation with George in the morning.

He retrieved his backpack from where he'd dropped it by the front door, and pulled out the copy of *Witchcraft, Demonology, and Possession*, setting it on the table next to his recliner. After fixing himself a Jack and Coke, he sat back in the comfortable chair and pulled the lever to raise his feet.

The copyright in the book read 1956, but he'd never heard of the publisher, Necrorium Press. The contents listed a dozen topics of occult interest, from "Keeping Familiars" and "Calling a Demon" to "Possession" and "Sacrifice."

He flipped ahead to the chapter on callings, and began to read.

5. *Calling A Demon*

There are as many schools of thought on performing a calling as there are types of demons to be called. Some ancient Wiccan rites demand the use of a pentagram and advise that the area of the calling be bordered with trails of salt, human blood, blessed candles and other esoteric paraphernalia—including by one report, the excrement of a virgin—to ensure that the demon cannot escape the circle unbound into the world before a covenant of service is established.

Most modern experts claim that there is no way to restrain a demon using minerals or religious artifacts. They are, after all, ethereal creatures. The key is not keeping the spirit contained, but rather in keeping it bound to this realm. Because our earth is not the natural realm of demons, such beings may not remain here for more than a few moments unless bound in service to something corporeal. The covenant is the key, and if the demon has an interest in remaining in this realm—and many do, at any cost—then a highly beneficial covenant can usually be forged between the caller and the demon. At the moment of calling, such a demon will be interested in hearing the terms of the proposed covenant, rather than escaping into the world for a few minutes only to be pulled back from whence it came.

One of the key tenets of demonology is the power inherent in names. It can be highly dangerous to attempt a calling without addressing a specific being and having some understanding of the nature of that being. A demon cannot be bound in covenant completely to an earthly master unless its true name is spoken in the invocation. Justorius wrote in A.D. 654 of an incident in which a calling was conducted without a name being specified. A Borlock demon of extreme maliciousness answered the call and decimated half a village before losing its grip on this realm and disappearing. This incident also gives credence to the uselessness of salt and candle boundaries. The witch who attempted the calling had, in fact, used a salt barrier to restrain the being prior to performing her inexact invocation.

This, naturally, begs the question, "How does one find the name of the demon one wishes to call?" There certainly is no phone book of the other realm, with listings by specialty of demons interested in assisting the earthbound with issues of fertility, protection, healing, wealth accumulation and the like. However, there are several occult volumes that have been published over the past centuries that have listed a number of demons that have been successfully called and utilized for service by those established in the dark arts. Demarck's excellent *Devils and Delirium*, first published in 1798, includes an appendix that lists several dozen key spirits. . . .

The phone rang, and Joe marked his place in the book and set it aside for later. He hoped it was Brett, though he couldn't believe that they'd have results this fast.

"Hello," he said after rattling the receiver out of its cradle on the third ring.

"Joe?" It wasn't the voice he expected, but his face brightened anyway.

"Hey, Cindy," he said. "What's up?"

"Well, you know tomorrow's Friday already," she said, letting the sentence dangle provocatively.

"You want to do something?"

"Is that an offer?"

"Dinner, a movie?" he said.

"I accept," she chirped.

By the time he hung up the phone, Joe had forgotten all about demon calling, and went to the kitchen. After a quick survey of the anemic contents of his refrigerator, he pulled out a paper and pen and started a shopping list.

It was going to be a long one.

CHAPTER EIGHT

Ken's unconscious form sped through the black veins beneath Terrel's Peak without protest. His lungs filled with water as his body temperature dropped at a rate that would have alarmed the paramedics from Folter's Ambulance service, had they been present to measure it.

But they weren't.

The water swept Ken along like a fallen leaf down its well-worn path, a watery road that led to the warm and salty womb of the ocean.

But the ocean wasn't to be his final destination.

"This will do nicely," a voice offhandedly announced inside the empty, uncomprehending confines of Ken's brain. In a slow but deliberate motion, one of the spelunker's arms lifted and then slapped its weight against the water. The other joined it, and presently, in a strange, spasmodic motion, Ken's body propelled itself to the invisible shore, a zombie swimmer of the underground.

His face scraped up against the rocky edge of the riverbed, and both arms slapped upward to grasp at the shore, but not before the current had dragged him face-first into a rocky projection. The collision of flesh with limestone was audible throughout the chamber, but it didn't bother the body's animator.

"Good as any other anchor," the disembodied voice observed.

Ken's arms slid across the gray rock to wrap around the L-shaped overhang at the banks of the river. At the same time, Ken's right knee bent, and with an uncoordinated thrust, his right leg threw itself up onto the bank, out of the water. With a final push against the stone, Ken rolled away from the water, finally moving his entire body out of the cold river. He came to rest on his side, still unconscious and now bleeding from half a dozen gashes, one of which sliced his cheek from eye to chin. He was going to have a hell of a headache when he woke up.

If he woke up.

CHAPTER NINE

Joe had never been much of a cook. But there was good reason to have Cindy at his apartment for dinner rather than taking her out to a local restaurant.

People would talk.

Most particularly, people would talk about that big-city newspaper fellow getting his dirty fingers wet in the panties of a young girl.

Wasn't proper. Wasn't seemly.

Wasn't what Joe—or Cindy—wanted at the moment. There might be talk if they turned up at a club together, but mostly, the kids drinking and listening there couldn't care less if a twentysomething guy turned up with a younger girl. The local eatery waitresses and patrons, however, were a different story.

Hence Joe's current dilemma.

The aisles of Carter's Grocery had never seemed so foreign, so full of possible pitfalls as tonight. He'd thrown a head of green lettuce into the cart (seemed crisp, but not too hard) followed by a couple tomatoes (hothouse pale, probably tasteless, but what're you going to do?), a green pepper, a cucumber and a bag of green onions. He then pulled the onions out and tossed them back on the now-misting shelf. Didn't want to chew up a bad breath salad now, did they?

He walked two steps and then backpedaled.

COVENANT   207

What was a salad without green onions? Every restaurant he'd ever eaten in put onions in their salads.

He picked up the now-sodden bag of onions and tossed them back to the bottom of the cart.

Then came the salad dressing. He didn't trust the bottle of Italian he vaguely remembered being half full on his fridge door, so he grabbed a new bottle. Then he considered the fact that she might not like Italian.

He hadn't asked Cindy about dressings when he'd made sure that salad and steak for dinner were acceptable. So he grabbed French, Thousand Island and a bottle of Bleu Cheese for good measure. They clinked together merrily, toasting the coming evening, in the growing pile at the bottom of his cart.

The steak, he thought he knew how to choose. He only prayed he wouldn't burn it to a crisp when he slapped it on the grill. He really was hit and miss with his meat preparation, but when it was only yourself that you were feeding, the occasional tough brown shoe for dinner wasn't a problem.

Tonight he couldn't afford to serve shoe leather.

He pawed through half a dozen cuts, looking for one with a minimum of fat but still laced with enough white to sizzle up good.

When he'd finally grabbed one, picked up some fresh sour cream for the potatoes and pushed his cart to the checkout, there was (naturally) a line that was six carts long.

Fabulous.

He scanned the tabloid headlines as he waited, amused with their obvious chicanery. Sometimes they annoyed him; their tall tales and outright lies gave his whole profession a bad name. But mostly, he was amused. People really would believe whatever they chose to, he thought. It all just had to do with what source they chose to sip from. Did the font espouse ascensions and virgin births and resurrections? Future messiahs, past lives, eons of karma? Palm reading, séances

and tarot? Bigfoot, Loch Ness Monster or UFOs? A living
Elvis? Poltergeists? A cliff inhabited by a malevolent spirit?

But the last wild story, Joe was beginning to believe himself. It was, quite possibly, the only bit of otherworldly nonsense that he'd ever come close to swallowing as truth. And
apparently, bizarre as it appeared, it had never made headlines, locally or otherwise.

That, in itself, somehow lent it more credence.

Shaking his head away from headlines of spirits and two-
headed babies, he scanned the women's magazines. *What
Men Won't Tell You!* screamed one two-inch tall headline.
Wow Him Back To Bed teased another. *Fifty-six Tips for Better Sex: the Results of Our Reader's Poll* bragged still another.
Joe smiled. If you couldn't hook 'em with magic and reli-
gion, snare 'em with sex. He'd glanced through some of
the articles on tips and sex secrets in the women's magazines and couldn't believe that anyone would come back
more than once to seek sensual wisdom from those sources.
He'd had deeper thoughts about sexual experience when
he was fifteen years old and looking at bra ads in the Sears
catalogue than the adult scribes at *Cosmo* and *Woman's Day*
offered.

At last, he approached the black treadmill of the checkout
counter. Joe grabbed a plastic grocery divider, placed it on
the belt ahead of his items and shook his head when he noticed a Kool cigarette ad plastered to it. *Is there no place safe
from advertising?* he thought. *I mean, seriously, a grocery divider?*
After separating his groceries from those of the dumpy forty-
ish woman ahead of him, he began loading his fourteen
items onto the conveyer. He noted with annoyance that the
woman ahead of him had brought twenty-three items into
the fifteen-items-or-less aisle.

Not only did people read stupid, obviously shallow or false
newspapers and magazines, but they *didn't* read and follow
signs, he thought. You see only what you want to see. He

sighed. Mentally he added up his items once more and nodded with satisfaction.

Fourteen.

Joe squirted lighter fluid onto the charcoal and dropped a match. The flame sprang up hungrily, and he went back to the apartment as it fed on itself. Armed with a butcher knife and a wide, deep wooden bowl, he diced and sliced a salad, which he tossed into the fridge, and set the steaks on a platter. Then, cold Miller Genuine Draft in hand, he retreated to the couch to wait for the knock of his young date. He could hear the prying voice of his mother now: *Yes, Joe, she seems very nice. But she's just a kid. What do her folks think? Shouldn't you try to date someone a little closer to your own age? What do you have to talk about? What do you have in common?*

She'd smile that slightly crinkled, all-knowing smirk of hers, and he'd wither an inch or two before crawling off to his bedroom to feel stupid and guilty in the comfort of loneliness.

"Not this time, Ma," he said out loud.

The room didn't answer. Not that he'd expected it to.

Had he?

But he felt funny having spoken out loud to the dead. He got up and went outside to check the grill. A cool breeze was blowing in, and the sun was a bloody blur on the horizon. It was going to be a chilly night.

The coals were well-seasoned; white on the outside with fiery pits of orange in between, when Cindy arrived at the door. She held out a bottle of red wine, which he accepted along with her hand and a quick peck on the lips before she stepped inside.

"Do I want to know where an underage girl like you got that bottle?" he asked.

She winked, and shook her head.

"You look great," he said, noting that her dandelion yellow

stretch-cotton top clung closely to her chest and midriff and her blue jeans revealed rather than concealed just about every conceivable curve of flesh below that. Her lips glowed with life; her eyes sparkled, even in the dim light of his living room.

"Thanks," she said, blushing just a little. "I like this outfit. It's comfortable, and I know some guys seem to enjoy it."

With that, she winked again and stepped past him.

"I'd be careful about what guys you wear it around," he countered, and joined her on the couch.

"Are you dangerous?" she asked, eyes wide with feigned innocence.

"Maybe. Hope you're hungry," he said, sidestepping her jibe.

"Hope you can cook!"

"That remains to be seen." He laughed. "That's why I hope you're hungry. That way, if this doesn't work out, you'll eat it anyway!"

"You hope."

Joe picked up the TV remote and tossed it to the couch. "Well, if you want food, I'm going to need to get these things on the grill. How do you like your meat?"

"Throbbing?" Her face remained inscrutably blank. But after a second, she couldn't hold back a giggle.

"I can offer you a fine cut that throbs later," Joe said, not missing a beat. "But the steaks are quite dead, I assure you. No movement, or throbs, at all. How's medium rare?"

"Long as it's not bloody," she said.

"Done."

He took the platter and a long fork to the patio and laid the steaks with a sizzle on the grill. As he looked through the grating to judge the intensity of the fires below, a hand slipped around his middle. He saw the delicate tanned fingers creep like a spider across his belt line, descending with a slow but obvious intent.

She's just a kid, a voice inside screamed.

Doesn't act like one, his conscious mind retorted.

"So, have ya missed me?" she said, interrupting his private argument.

"Yeah," he grunted, and, ignoring her attentions, flipped the bubbling meat with a fork.

"You?"

"Nope, haven't missed me at all," she said.

When he turned around, she was smiling. "I don't have to go home tonight," she announced.

"Won't your parents worry?"

"They think I'm off with a friend from school. I said I probably wouldn't come back tonight."

Joe's groin jumped at that thought. The night they'd spent a couple of hours in the backseat of his car had been heaven. But it wouldn't compare to the luxury of a bed. And that was obviously a luxury she intended to make use of tonight.

He sure hoped he didn't burn dinner.

He didn't.

Joe set the small kitchen table with two plates and bowls, put the salad in the center and set out all of the dressings he'd bought. A tried and trusty corkscrew relieved the wine of its cork, and he filled two long-stemmed glasses with its tart, dark vintage. Then he retrieved the steaks from the grill, which, even though it was outside, had filled the house with the mouthwatering scent of charring beef. His stomach growled and Cindy laughed.

"You keeping a wild animal in there?"

"You just never know," he said.

He set the meat on the table using the only china he had; luckily he wasn't hosting a dinner party, since the blue flowered set had only three remaining plates (the claim of *unbreakable* had been suitably disputed, he thought).

She cut her steak as delicately as a princess, he thought, watching her wooden-handled steak knife slice slowly, gently, firmly through the juicy slab of beef on her plate. She looked up at him with a small smile—a look of thanks and acknowledgement and hunger, all in one small glance. Hers was a face of expression, a mouth that pursed one way to show laughter, the other to spit derision. One wrinkle on her forehead could mean a chapter, and Joe was starting to hope that he was allowed to read the whole book.

"Steak sauce, ketchup?" he asked.

"If it's any good, it doesn't need dressing up," she said, and with exaggerated temerity, brought a fork of steaming pink meat to her mouth.

She chewed a moment, as Joe watched. His eyes waited for the slightest hint of dissatisfaction.

"Well?" he asked after she'd swallowed a piece.

"You can cook for me anytime." Her teeth shone white as she popped another forkful between them.

He laughed.

What the hell was he getting into?

Bed, as it turned out.

Dinner led to collapse on the couch, and more wine.

They talked some, her about college and roommates and growing up in backwoods Terrel; he about college and roommates and living in a big city. The TV buzzed through old episodes of *The Dick Van Dyke Show* and *Star Trek*, and they scanned past VH-1 and MTV. Finally they settled on a Discovery Channel program about disappearing breeds of penguins and long-armed monkeys. Cindy's head moved from upright, to leaning against his shoulder, to lying in his lap.

He worried with the latter position that she could feel what was going on in his pants as he looked down on her sweet, slightly flushed face. He longed to bend over and take her tongue into his mouth. He wanted to scoop her snuggling body up in his arms and carry her back to his bedroom. But she was, in his eyes, still a minor. And despite their activities in his car and on the cliff, he felt funny doing anything that might be construed as "forcing" himself on her.

Flirtations aside, if she wanted to go to bed with him, she would have to make the first move.

Ultimately, she made the first, second and third moves.

"I really like you, Joe," Cindy said out of nowhere. She rose from Joe's lap to kiss his lips.

"I don't know what I would have done if I hadn't had you these past few weeks. I mean, when you first saw me, I was so broken up about . . . you know. And it still hurts—it does. My family's been great, but they can't fill that place, you know? Having you here, though, well, I don't feel so empty inside."

Her eyes filled with liquid and Joe just nodded, not sure what to say next.

"And please don't think I'm just using you to . . . I don't know, tide me over till the next guy comes along."

"Well, I *am* a little old for you," Joe whispered, not wanting to say it out loud, but somehow feeling that he had to.

"No you're not." She shook her head violently. "You're perfect. You know what you want; you've been around a little bit, but not too much. I really like being with you, Joe. I want you to know that, no matter what. I *want* to be with you."

She kissed him again, deeply, closing her eyes and drawing him tight to her. Then she pushed him down on the couch and began to unbutton his shirt. He didn't protest, but he didn't help either. Though when her hands began fumbling with his belt, he felt it was time to intervene.

Pushing her back, he sat up, shrugged off the loosened shirt and scooped her up in his arms as though she were a child. As he stood from the couch, he found that she had done well with the belt. And the zipper. His pants slid to his ankles and he kicked them off as he shifted her weight in his arms. She kissed him again and wrapped her hands around his neck as he maneuvered her carefully around the doorway and into his bedroom.

It had been years since he'd lived with anyone else, but for some reason, he felt the need to kick the door shut behind them. Had there been any other tenants in the small flat, that flimsy wood wouldn't have hidden the sound of their lovemaking, regardless. Cindy shed her skintight jeans with a speed and assurance that left Joe marveling.

And the equally quick loss of her top left him marveling more, with less intellectual backing this time. When she slipped two long-nailed fingers in and coaxed down his gray Jockeys, Joe stopped marveling at the maturity of her lusts and began to help her meet them. With hands they guided each other, and with lips kissed appreciation.

And other things.

CHAPTER TEN

He was running down a long white hallway. A hospital. But one bereft of patients. Maybe it was the morgue. Cool white doors interrupted the flow of the otherwise expressionless wall on either side, but they were all closed. And he didn't slow to try them, only ran on and on and on. Toward a window. At the end of the hall.

A window with the shadowy limbs of a tree slapping it softly: *shlphat, shlphat*.

He had to reach the window or Cindy would die. He knew that. But the faster he ran, the farther away the window seemed to get.

A door ahead of him opened, and there was Mrs. Canady, her bovine body a human roadblock of grinning mass and malevolence. One of her eyes glowed bloodred in the sulphuric light of the hall, a lighthouse of warning. *Do not come this close.*

But he did. Her arms wrapped around him like crab claws, but Joe didn't slow. Without thinking, he kneed her in the belly and slipped from her grasp, leaving her grunting and moaning on the floor.

He ran farther, and the other mothers stepped out from doors on both sides of the hall. They had baseball bats, and swung them with quiet menace back and forth, back and forth.

He did what any good little league graduate would.

He ran straight at them with all the bluff and bluster he

could, and then, at the last second as they swung for his head, he dropped to the ground and slid between their legs as the women swished empty air above.

"Strike one," he called, and leapt to his feet again.

And then there was Angelica.

She wore only a gaudy silk robe, and it was not belted. Her sex was invitingly exposed as she stood, legs far apart, in the center of the hall, arms open to clutch him to her breasts. Which, even through the sheen of the robe, appeared eager to receive him.

As he prepared to do a slide between her legs as well, a scabbing, pus-covered green arm slid out from her vagina, its blackened fingernails sharp and pointed and snatching at the air in his direction.

Gulping with fear and disgust, Joe threw himself to the left and smashed against the hard concrete wall as he jumped over her bare left foot and then staggered back to the center of the hallway.

He could hear them now, behind him. The clicks of heels in flight, the slap of bare flesh on tile. The window seemed a little closer now, and through it, he could make out something near the tree—hanging from it? Something yellow. Something with blonde hair.

Cindy?

Joe threw himself forward, his stomach burning hot, his thighs screaming in unexercised complaint.

A nail scratched his thigh, and he willed himself not to turn around to see who was right on his ass. One turn and she'd have him, whoever it was.

But he had a suspicion that it was a decayed fetal arm. A baby still hidden in Angelica's womb that would grip his testicles and wrench with glee until they came off.

A bell rang then. An alarm. Or a "class is out" warning. He wasn't sure.

And then a hand did sink its fingers into his shoulder, and

as it shook him hard once, twice and then a third horrible time, he gave in to all of his fears and screamed. . . .

Screamed out loud.

In his bed.

With Cindy's wide eyes staring into his own in concern.

"The phone, Joe. The phone is ringing! Do you want me to get it?"

He shrugged away the shreds of dream and then shook his head.

"No, no, I got it."

He slid out of bed and walked naked across the room to grab the ringing phone, only realizing his nudity and feeling a twinge of embarrassment once he put the phone to his ear and turned toward Cindy as he said, "Hello."

A dangling feeling and Cindy's own hand holding a sheet across her breast conspired to make Joe turn sideways. *Why do people who have just fucked like rabbits feel modesty the morning after?* he wondered, and then lost the thought as he listened to the voice on the other end of the line.

It was Brett, his friend from the Chicago welfare department. A simple hello and Joe had placed that gruff 'n' gravel voice immediately.

"I think I tracked her down last night, Joe," Brett growled on the other end of the line. "Sorry it took me a couple days, but I had to wait till things were quiet around here to look this one up."

"Yeah? What've you got?"

"Well, unlike whatcha said about her sending that kid far away, it doesn't look like she went far at all. In fact, I almost ignored the listing, 'cuz you said she'd be outta state," Brett said. He had a tendency to ramble on before getting to the point. That trait was especially noticeable after a couple bottles of Guinness.

"You did say the mother asked that she be adopted out of state, right?"

"Yeah, that's what she said," Joe agreed.

"Well, I found here an unnamed baby girl, belonging to a Rachel Napalona, given up to the adoption ward nineteen years ago. Doesn't look as if they sent the baby out of state though."

"Well, where did she go, Brett?"

"Looks as if she never left that little town you're in." Brett laughed. "The agency'll do that sometimes, especially given a request like that. Contrary people, those adoption administrators can be."

"Where'd she end up?"

"A family called Marshfield. Since the baby hadn't been named ahead of time, the records on my end show the Marshfields named her right off. Cynthia, they called her."

There was an icicle in Joe's belly. He struggled to keep from doubling over.

"Thanks, Brett. I owe ya."

"Case a' Guinness next time you're in town?"

"You got it. Later, man."

Joe hung up the phone, trying to shield the shocked expression on his face. How many surprises could there be in a town the size of Terrel?

He looked across the room at Cindy Marshfield.

Cynthia Marshfield. Missing daughter of Rachel/Angelica Napalona. Predestined cliff diver. Daughter of the woman who had fucked him while possessed by the devil of Terrel's Peak. The young, energetic woman who he'd fucked on his own last night. The missing person in his bed let the sheet drop a bit as she freed her hand.

"Anything wrong, Joe?" she asked, stifling a yawn with one lithe, tanned arm. The bed sheet slipped some more, revealing the soft rosebud of a nipple as she stretched.

"No, nothing wrong. Just a friend from home."

He padded back across the room, slid beneath the covers and took Cindy protectively into his arms. She was in deadly danger, and she didn't know it.

And if the being in the cliff really could read people's thoughts, she was now in the most peril from him.

Not for the first time in his romantic life, Joe realized how dangerous a little knowledge could be to a relationship.

Only this time the danger wasn't trial or jail. This time it was life and death.

Cindy's life.

And death.

CHAPTER ELEVEN

Ken woke up with a pounding headache. His jaw felt like a bag of loose rocks. And there were various other not-so-fresh feelings here and there across his frame.

But as luck would have it, he'd somehow managed to avoid getting washed into a sinkhole or out to sea. As he carefully, slowly swiveled his eyes and neck to take in his surroundings, he saw that he'd come to rest on the bank of the river, rescued by the arm of the low-hanging rock in front of him, he guessed.

Gingerly, he pressed a hand to his face. It came away wet and sticky.

"Okay," he murmured. "Systems check. Right leg?"

He kicked his leg without any shooting pains. Tried the left with similar success. He'd already tested his right arm by touching his face. "Left arm?"

Nothing happened.

Fuck.

Ken rolled to his back and felt his left arm from shoulder to wrist. Dimly, he could feel the pressure of his fingers kneading the flesh, but it was far away, as if he were experiencing it from a distance.

But he hadn't felt any broken bones. Nor was there any—

And then the heat came. Pins and needles and fire-hot pokers shot through his flesh like skewers.

"Shit!" he cried, and sitting up, began to shake the arm, which responded by sending even more confused signals to his brain. For a second, he wondered if a broken bone could have been more painful. But at last the sleeping arm woke up, and Ken counted himself as lucky. Fully operational, and damn, damn lucky not to be drowned or completely incapacitated. Even his helmet light still worked, which meant he couldn't have been unconscious for too long; the batteries wouldn't have lasted more than a few hours.

He groaned his way to his feet and took note of his surroundings. The river ran to his left; the ceiling was only a foot or so above him, and tapered to near water level on the far side of the underground river. To his right, a broken shale path led into the darkness in both directions. Judging that the easiest course would be to follow the river to the ocean, he opted to follow the path in the direction of the water's current.

He'd either get out that way or starve to death.

He had every intention of getting out.

"Then you'd better not go this way," a voice spoke in his head.

Ken jerked around.

"You can't see me, Ken, so don't bother looking."

Ken shook his head, trying to clear it. He must have really hit the bottom hard. Now he was truly hearing voices.

"You're head is fine, Ken. But it wouldn't be if I hadn't helped you back there. I got you out of the river. You should be thanking me."

The spelunker finally began to get scared. This didn't feel like going crazy. This felt real. He remembered the guy who'd fallen into the river just a few days ago, and what he'd said when they pulled him out. That something down there had spoken to him.

"That was me," the voice acknowledged. *"Everything you've ever heard about this place is true."*

"Oh, shit," Ken muttered, backing against the wall of the corridor.

"Don't worry, Ken, I'm not going to make you jump off the cliff. I'm here to help you get what you've always wanted. And you can help me too. How about we make a Covenant, just you and me . . . ?"

CHAPTER TWELVE

"What if the tide fills that room when it comes in?" Monica whined, her voice like nails on a chalkboard to Karen.

Why were we ever friends? Karen wondered, not for the first time. A vision of her friend naked, licking, covered in Bernadette's blood passed before her eyes.

Since the Covenant had been made, they'd been tied together, whether they liked each other or not. And whether they'd ever indulged or admitted it, they all wanted each other in that way again. He had mainlined them cocaine, and they would never be free of its attraction.

"What if Rachel drowns and it's all our fault?" Monica kept it up from the backseat.

"Then that's it, I guess," Rhonda barked, not looking away from the wheel, but never one to miss an opportunity for brusqueness.

And why did I ever listen to her? Karen thought, looking at their de facto chauffeur, and seeing through the matronly blouse to the thick fall of her breasts beneath. She peered into the backseat with a sad smile, taking in both her friends. The haunted look on Monica's emaciated old-lady frame. The thrill of sadism in Rhonda's beady near-black eyes.

What has become of us? Karen thought. *What has He done to us? What might our lives have been if we had thrown those gifts in the ocean? If we had found the strength to run from the caves, instead of dropping our swimsuits on the cold rock floor? He killed Bernadette for that, but . . . if we had all done it . . . could He, would He, have killed us all?*

But she had *what if*ed too many times. She shook the thoughts away. They were *here*, it was *now*, and they had left the bargain shirker in the place she belonged. This was a private little battle, an all-or-nothing pact, and nobody outside the circle would ever understand the stakes, the winners or the losers.

"Just forget about it for now," Karen's weary voice told the other two. "Let's just go home. Tomorrow night we'll come back, and we'll see if this thing can finally be over."

In her heart, she had the feeling that it wouldn't be over though. No matter what Rachel decided. He had always wanted more from them. When He had spoken with Bernadette's voice, He had tried to steer them to the debauchery of de Sade. To the sick promises of group pleasure—and pain. He had begged them as He'd handed out His evil gifts to invite Him, in some fashion, to their beds. He'd suckled them with honey on a carrion finger, and expected them to come back for more. In the night, He had come to each of them after that evil day and plied them with visions of their pleasure in the cave, of the erotic ecstasy they had achieved with one another, under His command.

He had offered them the vision over and over again. They had all whispered of it to one another, if they were too shy to talk of its details or to admit that they secretly wondered if they could recapture that rapture in the privacy of their bedrooms with one another. They were all seduced by, if resistant, to its promise.

At nineteen, at twenty, at twenty-one and beyond, lying in her nightshirt—and sometimes not—in the bedroom above her parents, Karen had been visited by Him in the darkest, heaviest humidity of summer. He begged her to shed her inhibitions and dance naked and sweating in the road with Him. In the brilliant white light of morning in the winter, He had invoked her to stoke the fire and suckle the sagging organs of her parents. "Bring them the love you can," He whispered. "You are young. You can make them so happy."

His visions were alternately despicable and enticing in her ear, and again and again He had shown her the tight, naked bodies of her friends, coupling at eighteen. At first she was repulsed. *Lesbian!* her mind had spit. *Never!* But He would remind her body with the spasms of orgasm she had known at the fingers and tongues of her friends in the cave and then cut off the sensations as He laughed at her.

"*Lesbian?*" He would say. "*Don't spit with such enmity on what you have enjoyed so well.*"

He had interrupted her private finger play in the quiet hours (she couldn't help it, she had to have *something*) with visions of Rhonda's thick red lips sucking leechlike on her tits. He had teased her with the sight of Melody's blue-painted fingernails stroking her moistest and neediest places as Rachel leaned in, copper breasts swaying over Karen's forehead to kiss her wetly on the lips.

Years later, in bed lying next to her husband, fallen asleep sweat-slicked and snoring after Karen had fulfilled his pedestrian lusts, He had entered her mind and shown her tricks and twists. He had teased her with twisted secrets of the flesh that would make her man come even harder, after staying harder, longer. She had refused to act on most of that knowledge, knowing that her husband would wonder at the degradations she had enacted. Wondering where she had learned such defilement. Would think her a whore as he moaned and enjoyed the orgasm, regardless. These visions made her legs drip with need and her hands clench with helplessness. And He had also shown her the tangled skeins that could be woven with her friends astride her man, and herself, the lot of them sharing and fucking in one twisted, sweat-stained bed. He had shown her all this, and more, and no doubt had shown her friends the same things, perhaps indulging Rhonda's sadistic side with visions of whips and corsets and humiliated men, and Melody with rows of effeminate but attentive men who would take her in every hole and leave her with flowers rimmed around her dehydrated body.

Karen shook away the erotic thoughts that she had steeled herself from indulging in all her life. Rhonda was a fool if she believed that this game with Rachel/Angelica was going to close the book. He relished the games He played with them. He relished the way He could make their nipples hard with visions. He laughed at the need He awakened in their cunts.

In her heart, Karen had the feeling that the book was not nearly over, that they had all just begun a brand-new chapter.

CHAPTER THIRTEEN

Cindy kissed Joe good-bye with the perky energy of a true morning person. Joe was still in his sweatpants, hair tousled and sandpaper stubble on his face. He had let her shower first, but now he was looking to be late to work for the deal. He'd pulled Saturday duty this week.

He looked longingly into the dark kitchen for a moment and then shook his head wearily. No coffee this morning.

He plodded to the bathroom and decided without conviction that a five-minute suds job was in order. It turned into fifteen, but who was counting?

A clean blue shirt and pair of Dockers later and Joe was on his way, but the scare that had rocked his belly an hour earlier was still seated there, like a burrito that doesn't know when to digest.

He was scared for Cindy. Scared for himself.

She'd begged him to meet her up on the peak tonight. The last place he wanted to go now. But she hadn't relented.

"If you don't show, I'll just walk home," she'd smiled with a nonchalant toss of her blonde hair. She knew he wouldn't let her walk home from there after dark if he had the choice.

And so did he.

And yet it might be safer for her if he did. She'd been going there safely on her own for weeks now. But what if the thing could read his mind? It had been in his head once when he'd been inside the peak. What if it reached him on the summit?

What if it discovered her true lineage, thanks to him? Maybe it would use *him* to push her from the cliff right then!

He needed more information. Somehow he had to find out more about this thing. What was it? How long had it really been there?

How could he get rid of it?

The answer . . . or at least the start of it, came to him at lunchtime. He'd stopped in at his favorite kill-some-time haunt, Books and Baubles. On a whim, he scanned the occult section of the store's bookshelves, which yielded virtually nothing. He skimmed the pages of a book on poltergeists, but it offered very little advice on getting rid of the supernatural pests other than one: move.

He needed to finish the book George had given him, he thought. He hadn't gotten far the other night, but there could be some help there. He was curious to see what it said on the subject of possession.

Next to the occult shelf was a book on Dizzy Gillespie. And near that, a volume about and by Bill Cosby. They were new mass market biographies, but interspersed with them were older volumes. Red leather classics about famous people. And not-so-famous people. One of them, he pulled from the shelf for its ornate gold lettering. *The Journal of Arthur Godwyn*, read the spine. He had no idea who Arthur Godwyn was.

But the title gave him an idea.

The Journal of . . .

It rang a bell for him.

The newspaper reports he'd read of the early days of Terrel spoke of the lighthouse that had once been at the top of the cliff. The earliest stories of cliff divers stretched back to the days of the lighthouse's operation. But the destruction of the lighthouse hadn't resulted in the destruction of the entity, which seemed anchored to that location. If the being had "haunted" the lighthouse, wouldn't it have disappeared with the structure?

When Joe was a kid, he had vacationed in New England with his parents. One of the places they'd gone was a light-house on the top of a rocky promontory overlooking the Atlantic. He remembered the dank stone steps leading up to the room where the giant warning light was lit. He also remembered the steps leading down, belowground. A storm shelter for the lighthouse keeper to retreat to, if the winds got too dangerous to risk staying aboveground.

Could Terrel's lighthouse have been built along the same lines?

What if the lighthouse had not only guarded ships from hitting the shoreline, but guarded people from finding the entrance to the lair of the cliff's prime evil? What if the storm cellar of Terrel's lighthouse had been the entrance to the de-mon's underground lair?

And why Terrel? Had it been called here by a lighthouse keeper? Could there be notes or books still buried beneath the remains of the lighthouse that could shed more light on the nature of this particular demon?

It was a long shot, but Joe thought that if there were any-thing left of the story of the cliff's demon, it was hidden belowground. Maybe he had been on the right track with the Cliff Combers. Just in the wrong location.

Tonight, he vowed, before he met with Cindy, he was go-ing to have a closer look around up on the top of the world.

And with any luck, he'd rediscover the stairway to hell.

CHAPTER FOURTEEN

The rush of the river gradually receded from an overpowering roar to a distant fuzz of white noise as Ken made his way down the haphazardly carved path toward what he hoped was an ocean exit. What he would do if the trail ended in a pit of black water that gave no indication of the closeness of the ocean, he wasn't sure. But he was betting against it. The cavern seemed wide enough to indicate that it had once been a major waterway. As such, he expected it ran straight out of the cliff and across the beach. There were many such inlets from the ocean shore.

One stony outcropping looked much like another, especially in the dark.

"Why didn't I bring someone to buddy me?" Ken berated himself again and again. But it was too late now. Now he was lost underground with no one to call on. No rope to pull him back to safety.

Images of himself lying alone in the deep shadowed dark slid through his mind like a private perverse slide-show.

Ways to Die in a Cave, #42 read the caption of one slide. In it, Ken's foot was missing, vanished into a hole in the rock floor. He couldn't get it back because the shattered bone of his femur extended like a white icicle from the bloody hole it had pierced in his jeans. Ken lay on the cave floor staring at the broken splinters of bone with a soundless scream frozen on his slide-show mouth.

Ways to Die in a Cave, #54 was even better. This was one of his subconscious' favorites. Here, an emaciated, eye-bulging Ken staggered down an endless corridor of slimy gray-green rock, banging his head and shoulders against the sharp edges without caring. Behind him, a small herd of beady eyes glowed hungrily. The eyes chased him through the darkness, and every now and then, one got close enough so that he could see the matted brown fur and long pink tail. And the teeth. Two of them, yellowed and pointed. The pack made a low, shuffling, scuffing sound as they chased and chased and chased him through the dark labyrinth. A labyrinth that never ended.

Ken slapped himself in the face.

"Stop it," he cried out loud. "Enough."

There will be an exit, he repeated silently. *I will find my way out of here.*

And maybe I'll even find a cavern that will be worth all this, a quieter portion of his brain tossed out.

He forged on.

CHAPTER FIFTEEN

The hours seemed like days to Angelica. She had long since ceased to struggle against her bonds; her arms had gone numb and then come back to life half a dozen times as she twisted and strained against the ropes. You could say one thing about Rhonda—she knew how to tie a good knot.

Angelica had worried for a while that the tide would sweep into this room and drown her, but she had heard it come and go without ever feeling its damp probing. Which made sense, she supposed. If the tide did reach this room, the "gifts" she and the other girls had found here so many years ago would never have remained in the room. Still, it was a relief when she realized that the sound of the surf, which had gotten louder after Karen, Rhonda and Monica had left, had receded once again. Which meant that it was daytime. She had spent the night tied up in the cave where she had once buried her mouth in the naked, forbidden places of her friends. At the urging of a demon who had never let her forget.

She had slept in his bed once before. What would the consequences be this time?

A sound came from beyond the room. A voice.

Angelica lifted her head to listen harder. Had the girls come back? Would they torture her some more, or realize that she really couldn't help them and at last set her free?

". . . sell caverns, yes," she caught. More of a mumble than a conversation. And it didn't sound like Karen or Rhonda. Or Monica.

"Who's there?" she called out, and felt instantly foolish. But could things really get worse for her?

The noise from beyond the cavern stopped. She listened through the silence, only the distant sound of waves lapping at the rocks on the shore slipping through the absolute black absence of noise. And then, a trickle of rock noise. As if a shelf of loose limestone had tumbled to the ground only a few feet away.

"Yes," the voice said, as if in answer to something.

Angelica drew her body up into a tight ball, trying to disappear into the wall. And then a blinding light flashed through the cave and caught her in the face.

"Who're you?" It was a man, his voice deep and raspy out of the painful glare of white and yellow light.

"Turn out the light," she begged.

"Oh, yeah, sorry."

With a twist, the light suddenly shone on the far side of the room, and she could see, through the rain of red and green dots in her eyes, a stubbled, youngish face. He was tall, lanky. His dirty brown hair hung in tangled ropes past his shoulders. Angelica instantly pegged him as a college student. Maybe a philosophy major, she guessed. Probably a Deadhead. His jeans and blue flannel shirt were stained with dark splotches. He'd been down here a while, she guessed.

"Who are you?" he asked again.

"My name's Angelica," she said. "Some friends of mine were playing a little prank and tied me up here. Could you help me out?"

"I'm Ken."

He didn't answer the rest of her question. Instead, he came and sat down next to her. The rank odor of sweat mixed with seaweed came with him. She noticed his face was smeared with something dark. Mud? Or blood?

"Ken Brownsell," he added, and grinned in a way that made Angelica go cold.

"I was hoping I'd discover a good cavern while I was here." He reached out a dirty hand and stroked the hair from her forehead. His eyes traveled down the shadow of her cleavage.

"This one looks like a beaut."

"Yeah," Angelica answered. "It's, um, very nice. Would you mind untying my arms?"

His eyes met hers for a full minute. Black, empty marbles of eyes. Eyes that didn't show a soul or a feeling that she could understand.

Angelica had seen those eyes before. She'd seen them in the face of a rapist she had killed. And before that, she'd seen them in the head of her friend Bernadette, right before the girl had collapsed to the ground for the last time.

"I don't think so," his mouth said. But his eyes didn't say a thing.

Angelica realized that things *had* just managed to get worse. A lot worse.

CHAPTER SIXTEEN

Joe pulled into the now-familiar parking pit at the top of Terrel's Peak. The car slid into the gravelly offshoot of the highway with a satisfying lurch, and Joe quickly yanked out the keys, slammed the door shut with a hollow bang and stepped up the path toward the edge of the promontory.

It was near sunset, and he didn't have too much time before Cindy would probably be heading up here herself. He wanted to be done with his explorations before she arrived. And then he wanted to get her the hell away from this cliff. Chicago suddenly didn't even seem far enough away.

A gull shrieked overhead, its shrill call sending a ripple down Joe's spine. It was a mournful sound, and not one that he really wanted to think about right now. He forced his attention to the ground, searching for any evidence of a filled-in hole in the earth. There were rocks everywhere, ranging from pebbles to car-size boulders, and he weaved in and out of the tumbled piles.

Scrub grass poked weakly out from the cracks and crevices in the rock. You had to be tough to survive up here, he mused, drawing the collar of his jacket closer to his neck. The wind whistled past in a nonstop, bone-chilling rush, and out beyond the edge of the cliff, where the blue of the ocean stretched out to the gray of the horizon, a handful of gulls hung lazily on the current, not flapping or moving, it seemed. They hung suspended in the sky, surfing the wash of air that screamed past Joe to suspend itself above the cliff and out over the edge of the world. This was a gull's world, he decided, and, in his musing, almost tripped over the broken bricks that marked the edge of the remains of the old lighthouse foundation.

He stopped and knelt, examining the perimeter. A wavy line of dull red cobbles ran in a circle as wide as a house. At five-foot intervals, heavy white pillars stuck out from the earthlike splints. Each of these was fractured off within three feet of the foundation's base. In between, a spray of rubble covered the earth. Splintered beams that looked like petrified fossils were jumbled in five piles and mortared with broken brick and stone. Most of the lighthouse had crashed out into the ocean, but here were the pieces too heavy to be blown away by any storm.

Joe walked through the circle slowly, stepping gingerly around the boulders and broken beams. Treading quietly, as if in a cemetery.

And wasn't this a memorial, of sorts, for dozens of the dead?

A preliminary walk around the decaying foundation yielded nothing. There was a lot of rock and rubble here, nothing more. Scrub grass crept up the sides of the rocks, forming a barrier of green and shadow over spots of the otherwise barren promontory.

He began to look past the former walls of the lighthouse. Could there have been another structure here? Another entrance to a storm cellar or the like?

He stayed in the circle though, and methodically checked each broken pillar for movement.

They were not budging for the likes of him.

He moved out into what was once the center of the lighthouse. There were timbers small enough here for him to roll over, if not lift.

Joe chose one timber that looked dried out and relatively light and gave it a shove.

Light, my ass. He grinned.

But with a trickle of gravel, the timber creaked out of the earth, and then Joe let go, tumbling it to the side.

More rubble beneath. And an oblong piece of stone that looked almost fully intact. He brushed the dirt and stones from it, and found the edges.

Damn glad I wore gloves for this, he thought as he massaged the crumbling mud from the edges and nodded finally, his hunch proven correct.

He'd found a stone step. Probably one that had begun a long slant upward to the lighthouse's cloud-skimming loft.

"Where there are steps up, there may also be steps down," he murmured, and began rooting about the pile, looking for a likely lever to nudge.

It was kind of like playing that game Ker Plunk. He grinned, thinking back to his childhood. Pull the wrong piece of wood and the whole mess collapses and you lose. The only difference was, in this case, you wanted to lose. You wanted to pull out a stick and have the whole pile fall down.

Not on top of you, though, of course.

He shifted a small timber and suddenly had easy access to the underside of a larger beam. Its end was pinned by a number of television-size masonry shards, but he gave it a shove anyway, and things all around him began to shift.

"Heeeeeyeeeeaaah," he bellowed and pushed upward with his whole body on the old beam. There was a slow, building creak, and then a fast snap. Then a satisfying *clack* of rock banging together. The whole mess shifted to the right. As the weight suddenly disappeared, Joe lost his balance and began to fall forward with the wood, his grip still with the bottom of the now airborne beam. He let go, but his body continued its forward momentum and he tripped over debris to land heavily in the space just moments ago occupied by a twelve-foot timber.

"That may be enough of that," he murmured, and mopped a dusty glove across the sweat streaming down his forehead and into his eyes. *I don't know what I'm trying to prove here*

anyway. Anything that might have been left underground one hun-
dred years ago has long ago molded away to dust.

He lay there a moment, arm over the splintered end of a
rotted beam, catching his breath.

Something smelled, he thought.

Like the cool, wormy air of the bottom of the rock pile.

Or was it more than that? The temperature of the air
around him seemed to cool as drafts of damp air breathed by.

Joe crawled forward a foot. Then another. His head was
tucked below a person-size pillar of stone, overhung by a mass
of brick and wood. He hardly dared breathe lest he bring the
whole pile down on top of him.

But the air seemed colder here than just a couple feet above.
His hands felt their way forward beneath a low shelf of rock.

The ground dropped out from under his right hand.

With his fingers, he carefully mapped out the drop, praying
that nothing bit his hand as he blindly explored the opening.
The hole descended six inches or so, and then his hand hit
bottom. He slid his fingers forward on the flat surface another
foot or so, and then his fingers dropped into air again.

He pulled back.

There was a stairway here. Into the mountain. Into the lair
of the devil of the cliff.

Joe grinned with maniacal glee. He was going to get the
bastard where he lived.

With renewed effort, he began to widen the area around
the hole, careful not to cause a cave-in.

A half hour later, face muddied and streaming with perspiration, Joe stood back and admired the results of his labor.

A stone step. And beyond it another. And another. They
disappeared down into the blackness of the mountain.

He grabbed a flashlight from his backpack and then pulled
the pack onto his shoulders. He planted one muddy sneaker
on the first step. He turned around, looked out at his car; he
was barely able to see it from here. He swiveled again, facing
the black hole before him, and, his back to the still-towering

pile of rock above him, he descended the stairs on his hands and knees. *Like a ladder into hell,* he thought.

There were thirteen stairs. He counted. And at the bottom, he straightened and looked above him to the tiny hole of bright blue that was the sky. It seemed impossibly far away from down here.

Joe shone the flashlight around, making a careful circle of light in the underground. The base of the stairs ended in a narrow corridor that led off to the left. Not away from the cliff's edge, but parallel to it. It was a man-made hallway, with grouted stone on the floor, walls and ceiling. He felt as if he'd entered a catacomb.

That feeling intensified when he turned the corner. His steps echoed dully as he moved forward, and then went down another flight of thirteen steps. Again, thirteen.

Here the stonework vanished, and the walls reflected back a dull chiseled gray at the beam of his light. He walked forward, slower now as the comforting, familiar sounds of the mountain wind and the crying gulls disappeared completely. Here there was no sound but that of his own making. He could hear his heart beating through the stillness. It was not a comforting sound.

Something moved behind him, and he froze. He heard it again. A scuffing, like footsteps. The skittering sound of a rock falling.

Shit. One thing he hadn't brought was a weapon. He hadn't expected human interference in this little exploratory expedition, but that was stupid, wasn't it? Joe thought about what the demon had done to Angelica on the side of the road not far from here. It hadn't hurt her itself. It had used another.

"Joe?"

His heart skipped three beats.

"Joe, are you down here?"

He let out his breath in an explosion of relief. It was Cindy. It was only Cindy! But how the hell had she found him?

"Yes," he yelled back. "Stay there, I'll be right up."

He turned back and started back up the steps to the man-made part of the corridor. But she was already there.

"Hey, I saw your car and didn't see you. So I looked around a bit and saw all this stuff kicked around here at the old light-house spot. When I saw the stairs going down, I figured you must've turned archaeologist or something."

"A little investigative reporting, that's all. Let's head back up."

But she started down the stairs instead.

"No," she said. "This is great. What's down here?"

"We'll come back another time," he lied. "You're not dressed for this."

Cindy fingered her loose white cotton top and shrugged. "If this gets dirty, I'll toss it. I've had it forever."

"Actually I was thinking more of your pants," he said, giving it one last shot. She was wearing those skintight stretch pants. Light blue. Very nice around the thighs and butt, he noticed again.

"Naah." She grinned and tossed her head. "Let's go. These are comfy for walking or climbing . . . or just about anything else!"

She bounced ahead of him, and they started back down the corridor once again, deeper into the mountain.

CHAPTER SEVENTEEN

Ken heard a voice ahead of him. A woman's voice, it sounded like. But that was crazy! Who else would come this far into the bowels of the mountain? Had somebody already staked his claim?

He redoubled his pace and came to a fork in the tunnel. The path to the right sloped downward, and he chose it without even thinking. Had to go down to go out.

It wasn't even ten steps to the right and the tunnel thinned and came to a wall.

Damn.

He started to back up, and then saw a black spot to his left. He'd walked past it, thinking it was a crevice. But when he shone his light into the gap, he saw that it was larger than that. It widened in the middle and tapered at the top and bottom, as if a bomb had blasted a hole in the middle of the wall. He stepped over the bottom ridge and ducked his head below its upper teeth.

The ground here was sandy, as if the ocean had once reached here. He was close, then!

Maybe that's what the voice was. A swimmer in the bay? Could he be that near? But where was the surf? He couldn't hear it . . . or . . .

No. There it was. Distant, but audible now. He began to walk across the sandy cavern. Then he saw her.

Staked to the ground near a wall dead ahead. A raven-haired

beauty. She was in some wild-looking gold and purple getup.
Baggy pants shone metallic from the light of his flash. And
her blouse . . . three buttons were undone in front and even
in the bad light of the cave he could see a hint of boob hanging out of the gap.

"Do you want her, Ken?"

He didn't even question the voice this time. It sounded to
him like the computer in *2001: A Space Odyssey.* Or maybe a
little like that fava beans–loving cannibal psycho. But the fact
that there was nobody visible had ceased to impress him.
Maybe his brain was too addled from the fall. Or maybe he'd
already given in.

"Yes," he said. His tongue got wet with anticipation.

*"She's yours. I've saved her here for you. Introduce yourself.
You'll find her . . . most enjoyable, I think."*

"Who're you?" he asked, feeling a little strange about the
transaction, but willing to accept the prize.

"Turn out the light," she whined.

"Oh, yeah, sorry," he apologized, and turned the lamp to
face away from her eyes.

"Who are you?" he asked again.

She introduced herself, but he hardly heard. He was staring at the lacy black bra that he could see just beyond the
opening of her blouse.

"I'm Ken," he said, eyes never leaving the creamy skin of
her chest. He was growing hot all over. The chill of the river
had turned to molten fire in his veins.

"Ken Brownsell," he added, and grinned. What a sweet
prize this had turned out to be. It wasn't a cavern to be named
after him but—

*"She can make you a child that we could name after you. How
would that be, Ken?"*

He shrugged silently.

"I was hoping I'd discover a good cavern while I was
here." He couldn't keep from putting his hands on her. They
seemed to move under their own power, without direction.

He stroked her brow, and felt the sweat begin to stream down his back. He stared again at the mounds of her chest, thinking about the cave he had hoped to discover.

"This one looks like a beaut."

"Yeah," Angelica answered. "It's, um, very nice. Would you mind untying my arms?"

He moved a hand to start unbraiding the knot for her, but then the voice pierced his skull.

"No!" it yelled in his head. *"I tied her up so that you could take her here. On the floor. Against her will. It's more enjoyable that way."*

"I don't think so," he said to her.

And his hand slid from her forehead, across her chin, down her neck and down the front of her shirt, catching and then popping each button in turn.

"Please, God, no," she whispered to him. Her eyes pleaded with him to stop. And yet he could see in them a certainty that he wouldn't. He could see himself reflected in her eyes. He looked like a monster.

"That's right," the voice soothed. *"She really does want it this way. Take her. Take her now. And Ken . . . enjoy yourself for me. Let's both enjoy ourselves. . . ."*

CHAPTER EIGHTEEN

Karen couldn't shake the feeling that things were going wrong. It was indefinable, but ever present through the day. What if they had killed Angelica by tying her up the way they had? She had never wanted to kill anybody, least of all an old friend.

No, just her kid. She laughed inwardly at herself.

Thinking back on the years since they had first ventured into that secret cavern in Terrel's Peak, she realized that they had all fucked it up right from the start. They may not have gotten out of the cave alive if they hadn't agreed to the spirit's bargain, but if the deal with the devil was a given, none of them had made good use of their gains.

The paintbrush will allow you to paint the most realistic artworks you can imagine. The brush has kissed the lips of saints and copulated with the diseased cunts of hell.

So He had promised her, and the one time she had used the brush, she had made an indisputable work of art. Something that could have started her down a phenomenal career path. But instead, so afraid of the unnatural ease with which the brush allowed her to create, Karen had hidden it away.

Only Angelica had made much use of her gift, and even she had underused it. Why else was she living in a shack on the outskirts of town? Hell, with the talent the creature had given her, she should have been able to go national.

Although, even as she thought about that, she realized He

wouldn't have allowed that, would He? They had all had their incidents in trying to escape Terrel. And He hadn't let one of them leave. Trapped here by an ocean, a mountain and a jealous demon who thrived on sacrifices. The human kind. They were trapped by their choice. Trapped by their murders.

Karen shook the tear from her cheek and rubbed her eyes wearily.

Black, dead eyes stared her down, a bloody grin stretching across Bernadette's/His face. . . .

"No." She shook the image away. Not now. She closed the door behind her and walked to the van. It was a walk of finality. She wasn't sure if she'd be coming back after this trip. Despite the promises of their spirit, she had a dark foreboding about this night. Maybe the sisterhood would close the circle of death . . . or in their passing, open a new one.

Still, she started the engine and eased the van out of the driveway. Perhaps Rhonda's brutal energy would save them. Certainly Monica was of no use when it came to strength. They would look to Karen to find the answers, they always had. But she was out of answers. Her shoulders slumped as she drove the six blocks to Rhonda Canady's house and pulled into her friend's driveway with a jarring bump against the curb. She had served as pro tem leader of this little band for long enough. All her life, really. And she was ready to retire.

Rhonda came out of the house before she'd even put the van in park. She was grinning in a way that Karen found both disturbing and promising.

Maybe it was Rhonda's chance to shine.

"You ready?" Rhonda huffed as she stepped up into the passenger seat.

"Yeah," Karen answered. But she didn't sound too sure.

"Let's go find out where the damn kid is, then. She's bound to be ready to talk now. After a night in that place . . ."

"Maybe."

"What's a' matter, Kar?" Rhonda looked over and stared at her friend's face. The lines there had deepened these past couple years. The shadows beneath her eyes were as dark as bruises.

"Tonight has to be it," Karen answered. Her voice was beaten, quiet.

"Maybe it will be," Rhonda answered.

"Maybe."

Monica's house was on the far side of town, past the decaying, ironically named Terraced Gardens trailer park and the public works water tower. There were only a few houses out this far, and not one counted its years below fifty. But the trees here grew tall and heavy, and shielded Monica's sagging white-frame farmhouse from the nearby sagging 1950s trailer homes. She came out of the house a few moments after Karen's honk, carrying a bag and hustling with the jerky shuffle of an old woman.

A winning crew we are, Karen thought.

"Whatcha got?" Rhonda asked once Monica had settled herself and her bag in the backseat.

"Made some ham sandwiches." Her voice trembled slightly. "I thought Angelica might be hungry after a night down there."

Rhonda laughed—a big belly laugh that traveled through the seat to Karen, who smiled in spite of herself.

Bernadette laughed low and evil, salt water dribbling down the sides of her mouth to splatter and cool the naked, blood-smeared girls beneath. . . .

Karen blinked the image away.

"I'm betting food isn't the first thing on her mind right now," the larger woman said. "Now, don't go giving her a thing until we've gotten what we need outta her. Or we'll be leaving her there overnight again."

Monica agreed and the women fell silent, only the throb of the van's engine filling the cabin as it sped past the main drag of Terrel and up the road to the beach. The sun was setting across the water, a bloody orange globe pressed on velvet blue. Karen thought it was the most beautiful sight she'd seen in her life.

"Look at that sunset." She pointed as she pulled off the road near the ocean. The other women oohed at the sight.

Let's hope we get to see the sun again, Karen thought, and turned the key to shut off the motor.

"Let's go find us a kid to kill," Rhonda barked bitterly.

Nobody laughed.

In her mind, Karen could still hear the twisted, low voice of Him.

Let's make us a little Covenant.

CHAPTER NINETEEN

"It's chilly down here," Cindy said, clutching her arms to her chest.

"Why don't we go back up, then?"

"No." She stopped and turned back to look at Joe. His eyes were worried, and she mistook the reason.

"I'm fine. You were down here looking for something, and I want to help you find it. Just keep that flashlight pointed ahead and let's do it!"

They had been walking for more than ten minutes, the pathway leading ever downward, the air temperature dropping steadily. At first Joe had been afraid they would need to turn back because the branching tunnels might confuse them. But there had been no confusion.

There had been no branches.

The cold gray limestone passage, which was just low enough to make them walk slightly stooped, continued on and on without interruption. Their steps echoed eerily around them as they continued downward. Joe began to wonder if he had made a horrible mistake in coming here. In bringing Cindy here. What if the ceiling fell in behind them? There would be no way to go but down. And if his flashlight burned out . . .

He wrestled to squelch the growing alarm in his belly as they walked. But it was no good. Cindy skipped along ahead of him, a vision of sensual youth in her skintight pants. He had grown to care for her so quickly, it surprised him. When he left Chicago, he had sworn off women. He didn't want the responsibility. Couldn't trust himself with it. But in the past month he had somehow become responsible for not one, but two women.

Who, as it turned out, were mother and daughter. His stomach fluttered at the thought. *Shit.* What had he gotten himself into?

"Joe, look up there," Cindy cried. She pointed ahead and to the right.

The tunnel was widening, and in the distance, something glinted just at the edge of the dim reach of his flashlight beam. They quickened their pace and seconds later entered a wide cavern. Joe slowly made a circle, flashing his light in a 360-degree arc.

They both gasped.

Wherever his light touched, it set the room aglow with shimmering, reflecting light. They were standing in a kaleidoscope. Fed by the light, the colors splintered, amplified and bounced back at them in a fabulous rainbow. It was the most beautiful thing Joe had ever seen.

"It's like we're in a gigantic geode," Cindy whispered.

"Exactly," Joe breathed.

"It's incredible!"

Joe shrugged off his pack and set it in the archway of the tunnel they had just left. Three more tunnels left the glowing chamber, each spaced equal distances apart. He didn't intend to get confused about which one was the exit back to the surface. Each exited the room through gently rounded arches, each nearly identical. It would be easy to lose your bearings with just two or three turns around the room.

"They should be giving tours here," she said, moving along the walls, gently caressing pink and clear crystal outcroppings as she went. She turned back to Joe, a huge smile on her face. She was nodding vigorously, hands clenched together in a single shifting fist.

"This is where He lives," she said.

"Who?"

"Him!" she said. Her eyes grew heavy-lidded, soft. "The spirit of the cliff."

She turned and turned like a dancer, arms outstretched to the ceiling. "Are you here?" she called out.

"No, Cindy, don't!"

"It's okay," she said, ignoring him. "I've talked with Him before. He's very nice."

In Joe's chest, an avalanche began to fall.

He raced across the room, grabbed her shoulders and stopped her spinning.

"What do you mean you've *talked* with Him. You never told me!"

"I don't have to tell you *everyone* I talk to, you know," she said, lower lip bulging. "And anyway, I knew you wouldn't understand."

"Cindy, that thing *kills* people! You don't want Him to *notice* you, let alone talk to you!"

She looked around the cavern, anywhere but at Joe's face.

"He *said* you wouldn't understand. That's why I didn't tell you. That's why I've spent so much time up on the peak at night. He comes into my head and just . . . makes me feel good. He wouldn't hurt me. I know it."

Joe couldn't believe what he was hearing. All this time, he had been trying to protect her from the thing in the cliff, and here she had been communing with it. He thought about all the things he'd said to her about his investigations . . . had he given anything away?

"Okay, tell me," Joe said, pushing her down to sit on the ground. "Tell me what He said to you. What did He tell you about me?"

"He says nice things. He says I'm beautiful . . . and . . . when I lie there under the moon, He makes me feel warm all over. Loved. He wouldn't hurt me. And He doesn't ask me for anything either. Well, mostly He doesn't. The other night, when you were chasing after Angelica, He did ask me to keep you occupied, because He had business to take care of with her and didn't want you mucking it up."

"Keep me *occupied*?"

Joe pulled back in horror. "You mean, all that stuff we did in the car . . . you were just doing that to please Him?"

"No, silly! I wanted you anyway. He just gave me a little . . . push, that's all."

"The same kind of push He gives to kids at the top of the cliff?"

"Yeah, probably," she said, but there was no fear in her voice.

"Cindy, that monster killed your boyfriend! And who knows how many other people!"

"No," she said, shaking her head. "He didn't kill James—his mother did. And James isn't dead, not really."

She looked off into the dark of the cavern.

"I can feel him with me, even now."

Joe shook her by the shoulders, truly afraid now. How could he protect her if she gave herself willingly to the creature?

She looked at him then, eyes glowing bright with excitement.

"He throws away their bodies, but He saves their souls. I've talked with them. So many of them. James, Bernadette, Bob, Bill . . . kids, old people, travelers . . . They're all there, inside Him. Sometimes, in the dark on top of the cliff, He lets James come to me, talk to me. . . . I love talking with him again."

Her voice trailed off and Joe stood up.

This was crazy. She was crazy. How could she rationalize talking to a murderous spirit as if it were some kind of gentle lover?

"Because I am."

He jumped. Whirled around, peering into the dark outlines

of the tunnels leading out of this diamond palace. Cindy still sat, oblivious to his fear.

"Over there," the voice directed, and Joe felt his head drawn to stare at the tunnel farthest to the left of the one from where they had entered the cavern.

"I believe you'll find what you're looking for in there. I'll be back shortly. I'm still wrapping up my business elsewhere. Enjoy your stay."

"What is it?" Cindy asked.

Joe's heart was beating like a jackhammer.

"Did you hear Him?"

"No," she said. "I haven't talked to Him today. Did He say something to you?" She smiled. "Oh, Joe, that's great! You can hear him too!"

Joe shook his head and stepped away from her. The tunnel he'd been drawn to see led to a small side room. And there he saw what the spirit had led him here to find.

A book.

The room was really a closet carved in the gray rock, barely five feet wide by five feet deep. There was a thick wood shelf set in the wall and on it, a dark leather-bound book. The dust hadn't been disturbed in ages.

Forgetting Cindy completely for a moment, he reached out to touch it.

The cover opened with an audible creak; the pages, Joe saw, would never ripple smartly again. The cool dampness of the mountain had gummed and stuck much of the book to itself, but with trembling fingers, he gently tried to open the cover page without tearing it.

A piece of the top of the page ripped away from itself, glued by time to the page beneath. But he got the two separated, and read the blurred calligraphy beneath with wonder. And awe.

A Journal
by Broderick Terrel
Begun this 21st of April, in the year of Our Lord, 1893.

The hand had flair, a flourish that Joe found he admired. People didn't spend much time paying attention to penmanship in this age of printers and computers.

Fascinated, he coaxed open the next page and started reading the diary of the man who'd founded this town over a century before.

It began:

I write these words as a warning and an explanation for my actions. The night is a long and cold thing, even in the heavy heat of summer. It hides the life of things best thought dead. But death is not the end. And so long as men realize that, so long as they stay true to their faith and leave the seductive fangs of the darkness to their own empty ends, then they will live long and fruitful lives. Kiss the creatures of the night, though, and know your doom.

The entry ended there.

What the fuck was this moron writing about? Joe thought, shaking his head to himself.

He skipped ahead a few pages, and then carefully pried two more pages apart. The yellowed vellum separated in rippled, discolored leafs and Joe marveled again at the date. This was primary research material here! The kind of stuff they kept in the rare-book rooms at university libraries.

June 23, 1893

As I suspected, the creature will not let up. Once I revealed my intentions to the spirit, it has not ceased to taunt me with them. But how can I ignore it for long? I <u>know</u> what is to come. And what will come will kill my town. My people.

But can I make a deal with a devil to save them?

And at what price?

Joe pried again, turning the journal a few pages further.

August 1, 1893

The night is long when no ships are due. Terrel survives on ocean commerce, but still, only one or two dockings come to us per week from outside. The rest of that time, my lighthouse shines on empty ocean. Well, empty to most. But I have been below. I have walked with the sirens and the fey, feral creatures that lurk just beyond mortal sight. Why? Why was I gifted to see these things? I have written it before, but still it is hard to believe it as truth. Am I really mad? I spell it out for myself here one more time. In less than three months' time, a wind will ravage this coast. A wind like unto none that have been seen here before. The wind will break from the tombs on All Hallow's Eve, and slip like mist through the graveyards. It will drift in from the ocean like fog. And it will drip from the roofs of the highest steeple in Terrel like rain. But it won't stay silent. It will grow in colour and speed. It will smash windows and break the backs of ancient oaks that have withstood the hurricanes of ages. And in the heart of that wind, the sickly spirits of the ocean below will come out with fangs at the ready. They will suck the life of my townsfolk and leave them for dead, just as the winds whip and beat their homes down upon their heads. In the morning, Terrel will be a dead place. A graveyard of rubble and dreams. And I have the means to prevent it.

Or so the creature of the cliff claims.

Am I crazy to speak with it? Does it promise delivery from disaster that only God may guarantee? Do I damn my soul just in speaking with it?

And yet.

This is not God's battle. This is a thirst for souls by souls. An earthbound hell.

Tonight I will call him.

Tonight I will make the pledge that has troubled my heart through this heavy summer. Pray the beast will keep its part of the bargain.

Pray that I am not damned to everlasting hell for my foolishness.

Was this how it all began? Joe wondered. A town's elder making a deal with the devil to protect his people from . . . from *what* actually? A hurricane? A storm of vampires? And how did old Broderick have knowledge of what was to come in the first place? Could it have been just a plant? A ploy by the spirit to gain Broderick's trust?

He leafed through the book some more, looking for other references. Much of what he found reported only on the mundane life problems of townsfolk long dead and buried. But here and there were sprinkled hints.

August 21, 1893

The demon comes from a different time than those which would suck our lives from us, so it tells me. Thus it has the power to stop the tide—it will save us from ruin for a price; one soul sacrificed from the cliff top each year, on the anniversary of its victory. That sacrifice may be someone from outside of Terrel, but if there is not one, it will choose and call one person from the town on its own. One death per year to prevent hundreds, all at once, now. It seems a grisly price, a cruel but fair bargain. But can I live with such a bargain resting on my head?

I ask it how it came to this realm in the first place, and it says nothing. But I know that somehow, it is linked to the crystal room. And while I may be the first white man to visit that room, I doubt that I am the first <u>man</u>. Perhaps this creature was called and trapped below the earth by Indians centuries ago. It bids me worship it in the cavern and I refuse. I worship none but God I tell it, and its laughter shames me.

"Then why not beg your God to save your town?" It taunts me. I cannot answer without blasphemy on my lips. So I say nothing.

I am damned.

Joe shut the book and looked around the yellow shadows of the room. It had all begun here. Or nearby. Broderick Terrel had made a deal with the spirit to save the town from some coming blight. Real or imagined, it didn't matter anymore. It was time for the bargain to end. And time for the spirit to stop haunting the lives of a group of girls who had had the misfortune to stumble into its lair all those years ago.

Which reminded him that the daughter of one of those women was still behind him in the dark.

He grabbed the book and moved slowly back into the main chamber. The crystals twinkled like stars as his light skipped along their surfaces.

"Cindy?" he called.

He looked around the chamber, but she was nowhere to be seen.

"Cindy, where are you? Shit."

He looked back the way he'd come, but the tiny room was empty. He looked down the corridor of the center archway, and within a few feet it narrowed into a slit of a walkway big enough for a thin man to walk into sideways, if he wasn't claustrophobic. He called out to the girl again, but his voice hung in the empty air like a taunt.

The final archway led downward and stayed wide, but after stepping down it a few yards, Joe stopped. Would she have come this way or scrabbled into the corridor she knew and headed back topside?

"Ciiindy?" he called down the dark tunnel and listened. But no reply returned.

"I'm going back up," he called, and then shrugged. He hoped she was already ahead of him. It seemed like a wise course of action to *not* be underground when the voice came back from taking care of its other "business."

He practically ran back the way they'd come, covering the fifteen-minute walk in less than five. But when he stumbled up the stone stairs to the tiled room he stopped cold. There was no light coming from the final flight of stairs.

Because the final flight of stairs was obliterated in rubble. The cap had caved in, leaving him no way out but down.

"Isn't that convenient," he muttered. He dropped to the ground, still panting from the run.

Fuckin' A.

Somewhere, down in the depths of this mountain, the murderous ghost now had both Cindy and Angelica. He hoped they were still alive. But how was he going to keep them that way?

Joe trained the flashlight on the leather journal and carefully opened it once more. It might be worthwhile to know what the hell he was getting into before barreling down the passageway again.

After skipping entries from August and September of 1893, he found the one he was looking for.

October 31, 1893.

Squinting at the faded handwriting on the wavy ancient paper, he began to read.

CHAPTER TWENTY

Karen knew something was horribly wrong the moment she set foot inside the cave. He was there. In her head. And cackling with glee.

"You girls are just in time," He said. *"I didn't want you to miss the show."*

She looked at Rhonda, who nodded. "You heard Him too?"

Monica grimaced. "He's waiting for *us*? What does that mean?"

Karen ran a hand through her salt-and-pepper hair and came away with a handful of sticky strands.

"Guess there's only one way to find out."

Monica held back at the entrance. "What if she's dead?"

Rhonda reached out and took her elbow with a firm hand. "What if she's not?"

In silence, the three women continued forward.

"Do you hear something?" Monica asked, just as Rhonda, who had been leading the way, put her hand behind her and shushed them.

Karen cocked an ear toward the darkness ahead and listened. The rush of the ocean filled the background with a hiss like static, but beyond that, above it, she could hear . . . voices?

"Is it Rachel?" she whispered.

Rhonda nodded. "But I think someone else too."

They crept forward, hanging tight to the wall as it curved

into the entryway for the chamber where they had left Angelica, tied and helpless, the night before.

"Noooooo!" came a scream from ahead of them. It was an unmistakably female cry. Karen started forward, but Rhonda put a thick arm out to hold her.

"Wait," she whispered. "We can't go rushing in without knowing what's ahead. Let's find out what's going on before we go bursting into it."

Karen nodded grudgingly but motioned her friend to hurry.

Rhonda covered the head of her flashlight with a hand, which glowed bloodily in the pitch-black of the cave, but let just enough light leak out for them to see their way. They stepped faster along the stone path, and at last, Rhonda stopped, leaning forward to peer into the room ahead. The other women leaned against the larger woman, staring over her shoulder.

There was light coming from inside the cave of the Covenant. It was a weak, sickly yellow light, but it was enough to see their friend, still tied up against the far wall, but not exactly as they'd left her.

She was naked now. And a long-haired, similarly unclad man was levering himself over her struggling form.

"If she won't give me her firstborn child, I'll just take her next one," the voice said from nowhere. *"Right after I make it."* Karen started forward again, determined to stop this before it was too late—but found she couldn't move.

"Enjoy the show, my girls. Thanks for setting the stage."

Karen strained to move her arm, her leg, even a finger. But nothing worked. She was riveted to the spot, her eyes glued to the scene ahead of them. Over Rhonda's shoulder, she watched as Angelica tried to knee the rapist in the groin. He just laughed and pinned her thighs down with his own. Then he grabbed her head with both hands and lowered his mouth to hers. When he pulled back, Angelica was gasping. She spit at him, and he slapped her hard across the mouth. The sound echoed through the cave forever, but Angelica didn't struggle any longer. The man reached between their bodies, grabbed himself, and guided his way inside her, beginning His consummation.

Karen knew from her friend's stifled sobs that he wasn't gentle.

And the spirit wasn't blotting the fortune-teller's mind this time so that she'd enjoy it either.

She couldn't move a muscle, but still, a tear crept from Karen's eye and rolled down her cheek to drip unnoticed on Rhonda's back.

It had all come full circle.

CHAPTER TWENTY-ONE

"Come to me, child."

Cindy heard and obeyed.

She could see Joe's back off to the side. He was looking at something in a little alcove off the main cave chamber. It was dark now in the crystal cave, but she found she could see anyway. She rose from the floor and felt a strange yet familiar tingle stirring in her loins.

"Come to me. This way."

He guided her to the far corridor, and without pausing, she stepped through. The limestone walls seemed to glimmer with a blue-green light as she walked, the floor sloping ever downward.

"Where are we going?" she asked quietly.

"To a very special place," He said. His voice was warm in her head and heart. Her whole body felt warm. Hot, really. She could feel sweat steaming from beneath her arms, between her thighs.

"You won't be needing these," He said. And she felt her arms pulling the white shirt and bra over her head, dropping them without hesitation on the stones behind her. She stopped a few steps farther on, kicked off her shoes and shimmied out of the stretch pants.

"Now you are ready to come to me," He said. His voice was silky and low, like a blues singer. She had pleased Him and she felt happy.

"But where?" she asked again,
"To the cave," He said. *"The Cave of Covenant."*

October 31, 1893

I can feel the forces gathering. Like lightning shafts across the midnight sky. My skin prickles with their force, their gathering. I have spoken with Malachai today and he assures me that he can stem their tide, but I sensed a worry in him. The Curburide are stronger than he ever imagined they could be. But I have his promise sealed in my blood. He will preserve Terrel against these wasps of night, even if it drains his own essence to empty air.

If he wins, he gets 100 souls. By our Covenant, he will preserve Terrel for one hundred years. If he doesn't, we all perish. Long after I am gone, his invisible eyes will search the harbor from this stony lighthouse and seek the Curburide, those fey, soul-snatching beasts that gather to ride the air into our town this eve.

I pray to God to help us.

And to forgive me.

Joe looked up from the book and shook his head. Curburide? Soul snatchers? He turned the page, working his fingernails in between the sheets and slowly massaging them open. Pieces of fractured, crumbling yellow littered the ground in front of him.

What kind of fairy-tale world had this guy lived in?

The darkness suddenly felt close. The hair on the back of Joe's neck stood up, and he jerked his head from side to side, trying to see through the shadow. There was nobody here, and yet . . .

He shivered, then bit down hard on the knuckle of his right index finger.

Steady, boy, he thought. *Ease on back.*

Steeling himself against the fear, he flipped to the next

page of the book. He had to know more about what he was dealing with.

November 1, 1893

It was, perhaps, the worst storm in the history of this coast. My village lies quiet now, thankful at their hearths, thankful that they've weathered the gale. But they don't know. They have no idea how close their souls came, not to death from nature, but to damnation from the hellish attack of the Curburide. The evil wraiths rode the storm in from their hell beyond the ocean like cloud cowboys on mounts of fire. They urged it on, whipping its flanks into a whistling, crashing, destructive wind. They screamed in the night, so loud, I don't know how my people didn't die from fright just in the hearing.

But it seems that I'm the only one sensitive to the hidden breed here. Perhaps that's just as well. Nobody else need live with the voices I hear now every time I close my eyes. The inhuman laughter. The deadly threats of possession.

But Malachai was with us last night. Protected us.

Those lightning bolts the village cowered from were not made by God or nature. They were the crash and burn of a thousand Curburide souls. The ancient spirit burned and sucked up those invaders like a child sucks down a peppermint stick. They nourished him and as I watched, he grew. What I had seen as the faint haze of a saturnine man expanded and widened as he took the stature of a giant. And as he grew, his flesh became solid, so that I could no longer see the stars through him. He swung and grabbed and kicked the hazy Curburide monsters from the sky until there were no more.

His laughter was terrible. His smile pure villainy. But he saved us from certain immolation.

Now I only wonder: at what cost?
At what cost.

Joe skipped ahead a few more pages, thinking that this was the stuff of B movies and novels. But then again, he knew Malachai existed. He hadn't known its name before, but he'd heard its voice. It was impossible to believe . . . but impossible not to.

November 21, 1893
His ancestors were protectors. I have talked with him often, these past nights.

I know his story now.

How the Indian people worshipped him and his kind. How Malachai and his kind saved the souls of the red-skinned people from the periodic attacks of the devouring Curburide, who followed the Indians wherever they roamed. Who feasted on them when the storms were right. Of how the Curburide took the souls that were not protected and sentenced them to live in a limbo within the wraiths themselves. A purgatory of damnation.

Malachai's people—if people you can call them—fought the Curburide. And yet, they were much alike. They took offerings of souls from the Indians. It was done in ritual. An annual offering to the spirit that protects. And that spirit took the souls . . . and ate them. Devoured their essence and blended it with his or her own. It strengthened the spirit, but it also changed him.

Malachai has been distant and terse since All Hallow's Eve, and I'm frightened now. More so, I think than before. He is stronger than ever now. His belly is filled with so much of the dark evil of the Curburide.

What will it make of him?

Joe shut the book. So . . . the spirit *became* that which it devoured. Or took on some of its attributes, anyway. You are what you eat. That would explain how Cindy could "talk" to James and the others. But the spirits of the town hadn't been enough to tame its malevolence. Maybe Malachai needed to feast on a nunnery to neutralize its poison.

Enough.

He knew now what the beast of the cliff was and what it had become. A toying, malevolent destroyer. A spirit that enjoyed the bending of others. It feasted on their doubts, fears and weaknesses. It had become a Curburide itself.

And he had to stop it. Somehow.

He had to rescue Cindy and Angelica and all the others from its grasp.

If he only knew how.

CHAPTER TWENTY-TWO

Cindy heard Angelica's scream, but it didn't dissuade her from moving forward. The sound, a shrill, ear-piercing cry of anger and contempt, actually warmed her. She delighted in the way the scream got inside her head and moved through her spine like firewater. It was delicious in the same way as the damp, cold air brushing against the soft down of her sex as she walked through the dark passageway.

Delicious.

This was all so . . . *delicious.*

A small part of Cindy wondered why she had never felt this way before. Why the goose bumps that lined her arms and thighs didn't make her shiver. But it was only a small part. The waves of excitement rushed over her again and again, like the incoming tide.

She was engulfed in sensations. She was suspicious that perhaps the sensations were not all her own. After her nights on the cliff with the spirit, she knew, actually, that they were not all from within her. The spirit was touching her. Moving her.

But it felt so *good.* . . .

Ken thrust into the enraged woman beneath him with a violence that threatened to break his mind. The tiny piece that was still Ken cried out louder than the woman.

Screamed.

"It's not as if you haven't dreamed of this." A sinister voice chuckled inside his skull. *"I'm just giving you what you've always wanted."*

No no no no no . . . Ken cried. Whimpered, really. The woman's breasts jiggled beneath him, sloshing in time with his movements like the skin of a half-empty waterbed, their nipples engorged and dark. He imagined their dark tips were plugs, the kind of pointy caps that you could twist and pull to release the water out of a cooler. These plugs held in, not ice water, but the blood that beat through her heart.

"Why don't you pull them?" the voice asked. *"Pull the plugs and release her blood."*

No. I won't hurt her.

"But you already are. Here, try this."

Ken's right arm reached out and slapped Angelica's cheek. It flushed bloodred, but she didn't cry out. Her silence was more disturbing to Ken than her screams. But even worse than that was the way his cock seemed to grow even longer within her as a result of the violence. His body coursed with power, and that wicked kernel of Ken that made him drive out of town once or twice a year to anonymously rent films like *Tied Up and Titillated* grew stronger.

"Yes, you do like that don't you? I only give my people what they want."

Ken's hand shook, but he raised it again. This time, he slapped her breast. And then he took the thickened nipple between his thumb and forefinger. A smile grew on his face—an evil, twisted "I've got candy" kind of smile.

And then he pulled on the plug.

The pain was terrible. It flowed through her veins like acid, locked her toes in spasms of paralysis.

But it wasn't the pain that hurt her so much as the degradation. The absolute inability to lift a finger to stop what was happening to her. He pounded away at her as if she were an object, and grinned when she made any sound of distress. So she locked her jaw shut, determined to endure him without giving in to his violence.

And then he grabbed one of her nipples and yanked.

Her mouth opened involuntarily and she screamed.

"God damn you!" she cried out, and gasped as the sensation of a burning coal settled hot in her misused chest. His fist connected with her jaw at the end of her scream, and the world spun gray around her. But she didn't black out.

Not completely.

Dimly she could still feel his violation within her. Feel the tremors of pain that he caused with every unwanted stroke. But worse than all of it was the realization that even though the demon had left her completely alone, her sensations unmitigated by His own lusts, she felt tingles of pleasure through the abuse. A tiny piece of her begged for him to rip out her hair, grind her body into the dirt, slap her until she couldn't be anything but a slave of someone else's desire.

Blood dripped on her chest and face and she held out her tongue, struggling to catch its drops. Rhonda reached out a hand and smeared her tits with Bernadette's lifeblood, then lowered her head to taste it. Rhonda's big teeth brushed against one bloody nipple, and then bit down hard. An explosion of lust centered below Rachel's belly, and she reached down to touch the blood-smeared flesh of her friend's thigh. Both girls began to giggle. . . .

Angelica closed her eyes and desperately wished for it to stop. She *didn't* want this; she absolutely didn't. She didn't want to remember the bloody orgy that had happened in this very spot years before. She didn't want to enjoy this abuse, and yet, she had wished for it since that night. And since the night of her attempted escape.

Her hands encircled his neck as she straddled him, the honey between her legs thickening and creaming again, though his cum was still dripping in clear drops from her belly from their orgasm just moments before. His eyes bugged out as she felt herself cumming again, as she heard him gasping, "I loved you. . . ."

She didn't want to be raped again. She didn't.

But then she came.

And a secret voice within her, a voice that was *not* of the spirit of the cliff, laughed.

Yes you do, it whispered, and her heart tore in two.

Joe stopped at the cavern of crystal, for just a moment.

"Cindy?" he called. His voice echoed emptily through the room. The flashlight bounced with eerie fluorescence off the rainbow rocks. It was like an underground disco ball. He grinned to himself. There was something about this room, he thought. Something that stank of a connection to the spirit. But what was it? And how could he use it?

He looked around once more, noting the ruby red glow of the far corner, the emerald caste of the flat-topped outcropping in the center of the room, the open passageways ahead of him. This was the heart, he decided. The heart of the spirit.

Shaking his head, he moved on into the artery leading down, deeper into the body of the mountain.

This is an insane situation, he thought. His own mind answered him. *And how is this any more crazy than an old man enlisting one spirit to fend off an army of others?*

He grunted at himself, and then sucked in a breath. Bending over, he lifted a white cotton shirt from the ground. Just ahead of it lay a silky brassiere.

This was Cindy's!

He moved faster, and within a few feet found her discarded pants and panties as well.

What the fuck?

The gray shadows of the passageway slipped by him faster and faster. He was moving as quickly as he could without tripping or banging into walls. He could feel the air growing thicker with moisture; the ocean exit couldn't be too far ahead.

And then a bloodcurdling scream made him stop, stiffen.

"God damn you!" a voice cried.

He heard every word clearly. It was a woman—*Cindy?*—and

she wasn't far ahead, unless cave acoustics were playing him
for a fool.

He turned a bend and stopped.

Just ahead, in an open cavern, he could see Angelica's black
hair splayed out on the rocky floor, and Ken, the Cliff Comber
dweeb, plunging his white ass up and down above her like an
oil rig on a fresh strike.

But that wasn't what stopped him.

For a moment, he couldn't process what he was seeing. Cindy,
golden, buff and beautiful, was crouched over something on
the floor nearby. She didn't seem aware of him, but rummaged
around in a bag or pack of some kind. Then a smile spread
across her face and she stood again, the muscles rippling in her
flanks as she strode purposefully across the cave.

In her hand she raised a knife-size spike of steel shaped like
a long nail. A cave-climbing piton, Joe realized.

Joe watched frozen at the sight. *What the . . . ?*

She bent over the coupling Ken and Angelica, and then
began to stroke Ken's back with the steel poker.

"Cindy, *no!*" Joe cried out finally, and sprinted across the
cave to knock her away from them.

But he was too late. Cindy's arm came down with a wet
smack in the center of Ken's back. The piton was buried in
the caver's vertebrae and he flinched as the blood spurted out
from behind him. But his muscular thrusts didn't slow.

Joe tackled Cindy, who tried kicking and pushing to roll
away from him!

"Let me go!"

She jumped up and ran back to Ken. Grabbing onto the piton like a saddle horn, she pressed herself against his bloodied
backside and then threw her arms around him. Her lips touched
his shoulder and then her tongue traced a path through the
spreading stain of crimson on his shoulder blades. When she
came up for air, her lips and chin were painted in gore.

Angelica screamed again, and Joe crawled carefully closer.
He saw the reason for this yell. Ken's breath was coming in

wet, slurping gasps, and a dark slime of blood was escaping his mouth. Angelica's chest was already a smeary mess with his lifeblood, but still Ken fucked her, not seeming to notice the pain in his back or the woman suckling his wound or the death leaking in rhythmic spurts from his lips.

Joe tried to pull Cindy off from behind, but her nails raked at him, gouging his cheek.

"Noooooooo!" she wailed, and then grabbed the piton with both hands, moving it up and down like a gearshift in Ken's gory back. The blood fountained out at her and she laughed, washing her hands in the spray and then rubbing her breasts and belly with it until her beautiful tan had turned to a bloody sunburn. At last, Ken's motions began to slow, and he lay heavier upon Angelica, who had begun to retch, and cry hysterically.

But Cindy was just getting started.

She rubbed her hands on Ken's ruined back and then drew lines of blood across her cheeks, and traced thick gory trails around her breasts with a dripping finger. She washed her hands in Ken's wound and spread his blood below her belly button and across her thighs with a moan. Then she moved forward, positioning herself above the blunt shaft of the piton embedded in Ken's back.

At that moment Joe finally realized that they weren't alone in the cave. He caught the glint of eyes across the room. Abandoning Cindy's sex-death ritual for the moment, he hurried across the room in the dark and found the three women, frozen like statues. Karen Sander's face was streaming with unwiped tears, but Rhonda Canady's lips were twisted in a secret smile. Monica's eyes, however, were expressionless, strangely vacant.

"You want to give me a hand here?" he begged.

Karen saw the naked girl come strolling into the cave and inwardly winced. Wasn't that the girlfriend of Rhonda's boy? The bastard had gotten her too?

She struggled to call out a warning, something, but she still couldn't move. Then the reporter came stumbling into the cave and she felt a surge of hope. How many minds could the creature control at once? Maybe if they all tried to break free at the same time . . .

She closed her eyes a moment and poured all her will into moving her foot. Nothing. She looked ahead once more and saw the reporter tackle Cindy.

But he really only succeeded in getting himself scratched up. The girl took the fall like a linebacker and brushed him aside. She was clinging to the dying rapist like a tick. Karen strained to cry out to him, "Over here," but no sound came from her mouth. She could feel the tears coursing down her face, which felt hot with her silent efforts. She had to break free. Had to.

Maybe her silent screams did have some effect, because all at once Joe looked at her. Right at her. And then came over.

Could he break them free?

Help me, Joe, she screamed inwardly. *Help all of us.*

CHAPTER TWENTY-THREE

If he'd had to describe the sensation, it would have been difficult to find the words. The pain was excruciating, and yet, Ken's body rocked also with the antithesis of that feeling, each thrust of pleasure also a claw of agony. His breath tasted of copper; his belly squirmed in terror and lust.

No, he couldn't have named that feeling.

But he enjoyed it, this yin and yang of pleasure and pain. He thrilled to the life dripping from his body as he ripped asunder the life and psyche of another.

Still, that tiny jealous part of him wanted more. In the back of his mind, the naked body of the Gypsy woman receded and he saw the spires of stalagmites and stalactites that he'd always fantasized about even more than he had guiltily thought of taking a woman like this.

Brownsell Caverns . . .

Come One, Come All to the Fabulous Underground! the billboards in his mind barked.

"Some things are mine to give," the tar-thick voice cooed in his head. *"And others . . ."*

The weight on his back shifted then, and he felt the piton plunging deeper inside him, coming closer to piercing his blackened heart.

Laughter then. Purple stars in his soul. And he was standing up. The electricity shot through his legs and he fell to his knees. But hands gripped him beneath the armpits, hoisting

him again to a stumbling crouch. Hot warm liquid coursed
down his legs, and he wondered if he'd pissed himself. But
he couldn't bring himself to look down. Only forward past
walls of slick gray rock, as a nude, bloody body and a flash of
blonde hair whirred around him like a crazed merry-go-round,
keeping him moving, pulling him forward.

It was getting increasingly difficult to concentrate. But he
found his center. That sweet, heavy breath in his ear.

"*A little farther now,*" the breath whispered. "*Just a little
more.*"

Ken shrugged and stumbled on.

What else could he do?

Joe grabbed Karen Sander's face between his hands and shook
it from side to side. It moved without resistance in his grip.

"What's wrong with you!" he yelled.

Her eyelids blinked. But she remained mute.

He pulled her away from the fat woman's body with an
effort. She didn't resist, but her limbs didn't move either.

What should he do? He had to break *somebody* out of the
demon's spell. It occurred to him that he himself could be
paralyzed at any moment. Why *hadn't* the thing used him as
it had the others?

Or was it getting kicks just by watching him bounce
around with as much effect on his surroundings as a pin-
ball, propelled from target to target by a series of possessed
flippers?

He slapped the older woman in the face then, wincing at
the report. Her eyes blinked again, and a tear rolled down
her face. But still she made no move to speak or stop him. He
raised his hand again, and then dropped it.

What was the use? She was gone.

Her lips moved.

"Uuuh," she whispered.

Joe bent closer, putting his ear to her mouth. "Tell me," he
urged. "C'mon."

A faint hiss escaped her mouth and then a whisper. Just a hint, really. But he understood.

"Look," she'd said.

He turned around just in time to see Cindy and Ken limp out of the cave, back the way they had come in.

As they left the room, Karen suddenly came to life with a coughing wheeze and fell into his embrace.

Behind her, Rhonda also took in a great sigh of breath and Monica slumped to the ground.

"Are you okay?" he asked Karen. She nodded swiftly as a new stream of tears trickled down her face. But this time she wiped them away viciously with her hand.

Joe left Karen to gather herself together, and went back to Angelica.

She was a mess.

Her breasts were bruised and smeared with dark blood, her clothes ripped and dirtied in a pile at her feet. She trembled and cried to herself, low sniffling cries, like an animal dying in a trap.

"Angelica?" he said softly. "Angelica, it's me."

Her eyes opened slowly. Those deep brown eyes fastened on his in disbelief.

"Joe?"

He nodded.

"Not you too!"

"I'm okay," he answered. "Now let's put you back together."

He reached above her and began to undo the bindings from her arms.

When he finished, she sat up and clutched her arms across her chest. Her whole body trembled, and her lips shivered, drooling blood and spit on her thighs.

Joe took off his jacket, then his shirt.

"Here," he said, offering her the shirt. "Let me wipe you off."

Angelica shook her head and pulled away from him, curling into a ball on the floor.

"C'mon, hon," he begged, putting an arm around her. "He might come back at any time."

"What's the use?" she snuffled. "He can do whatever He wants with us. And make us like it."

She looked up at him and hissed, "I *liked* it."

Joe shook her by the shoulders, trying to rally her resistance, but Angelica began to cry again. "Joe, I liked it," she moaned.

"We have to stop it somehow," he prodded, and Angelica looked up at him, a frightening image with black trails down her cheeks crossed by smears of red blood. She laughed. Leaning back on her elbows to reveal her bloodied, bruised breasts, she taunted him.

"He knew that somehow He could make me *enjoy* this!" she said, tears streaming off her cheeks. "How can we stop that?"

Joe didn't answer, but used his shirt to wipe away the worst of her degradation. Then he offered her the discarded shirt and underwear. This time, without a word, she began to put them on.

"He let us go," Karen Sander said, walking over to them finally. "Why?"

"More important things to do?" Joe said.

"He never took you at all, did he?"

Joe shook his head.

"Why not, I wonder?"

Rhonda shambled up behind her friend, nearly dragging Monica along behind her. "Yeah, what makes him so special?"

Joe shrugged and walked over to the entrance of the cave, where Terrel's ancient journal lay abandoned on the ground. He'd dropped it when he'd tried to stop Cindy from stabbing Ken.

Behind him, a quavering voice answered.

"Maybe because he's not part of the Covenant. He's not from Terrel, you know."

Rhonda snorted, and Joe shrugged again.

"Maybe it got more of a kick watching me stumble around without being able to do anything. It feeds off our emotions, off our souls. Maybe I was more useful to it mobile. But now we've got to do something. It's taken Cindy."

Rhonda gave a deep, rumbling belly laugh, bending over to slap a thigh in the process. Joe thought she might be enjoying this whole situation just a little too much.

"What're we gonna do, champ?" she said, straightening, but still chuckling. "Go running after the little tramp until the demon turns us into statues again? Fuck that. I say we get the hell out of this cave and back to town before He notices we're gone."

This time it was Monica's reedy voice that answered. "He can reach us there too, you know."

Angelica finished with her last button, then pushed her matted, bedraggled hair from her face. "He can reach us wherever He wants. So it has to end here. Today. One way or the other."

"If you'd just tell Him where your kid is, we could all go home free," Rhonda barked.

Joe opened his mouth, then shut it again. Was there still an advantage to keeping Cindy's identity secret? He wasn't sure. But he sure wasn't going to get any help from Rhonda to save her if Rhonda knew who it was she was saving.

So yes, maybe it was still best left buried. Even if she was already possessed.

"Angelica," he said, turning away from the other women. "You've been a fortune-teller all your life, right?"

She nodded. "Mostly."

"You must have read some books about spirits and the occult, then, right?"

Again she nodded, a look of puzzlement in her shadowed eyes.

"There must be something that you've read that describes

how to get control of a spirit. How to contain it. How to make it do your bidding."

Angelica shook her head this time.

"No, Joe. Nothing that would help us with this . . . thing."

Joe held up his hand.

"No," he said. "I won't accept that. Don't say anything—just think a moment. When someone tries black magic and calls a demon, what gives the human power over the spirit? Why should any demon listen to one of us?"

Angelica slumped back to the ground, her brow furrowed in thought.

"What are the methods of power over the spirit?" he said.

"It's not something I ever really studied," she said slowly. "Once I took the demon's gift, I just sort of naturally had these premonitions. I didn't work at it much. But—"

"Hocus-pocus." Rhonda guffawed behind Joe.

He waved a hand at her. "Shush."

Angelica's eyes glazed as she stared into a distance only she could see. There was quiet in the cave for a minute. And then, slowly, she spoke.

"There is power in names . . ." she began. "I remember that much. Name the demon and you may wrap him to your will. But in the naming, you also bind the demon to yourself. His works are yours and vice versa. The calling of a demon always endangers the future of your soul."

"I've read something similar," Joe agreed.

Angelica shrugged. "Doesn't do you a whole lot of good, does it?"

"Maybe it does." Joe grinned, tapping the moldering journal in his right hand. "Old man Terrel may have left us something that will save his town once again. I don't know if it will be enough—"

Again, Rhonda laughed. "Y'all just don't get it, do you? He owns us. You can call Him fucker or prince and it doesn't matter. We're just toys that He plays with. Get used to it already."

Joe turned toward the passageway that led back to the top of the mountain. Back, eventually, to a dead end.

"It's all we've got," he said, and started walking.

CHAPTER TWENTY-FOUR

With every step, Ken's life was leaving him. A trail of crimson marked his every step, and it came home to him that it was over. He would never feel the thrill of dropping down a rope to explore the black mystery below. He would never bask in the sharp fire of the sun on an empty beach again. He would never—

"Ah, but think of what you've had. Did you ever think you could take a woman like that?" the voice asked him.

His answer was a shaky, strangely sated, "No." But was the fulfillment of his domination fantasy worth dying over?

"How about the fulfillment of Brownsell Caverns?" the voice asked. And as he stepped around the next bend, watching Cindy's pale buttocks disappear into a broadening cave, his breath sucked in with an audible gasp.

"Yes," he whispered, and fell to his knees. The hot blood streamed down his vertebrae, dripped from the crack of his ass to the rock floor. But its loss troubled him no longer. The problems of the flesh streamed away like wisps of fog from an August sun, and he gazed around him in ecstasy.

He had reached nirvana.

The cavern he'd dreamed of. Better than what he'd dreamed of. His vision was mundane—stalagmites and stalactites that protruded from the ceiling and floor. But this . . . this was a glorious underground crystal cave that he'd never even considered might exist. Hell, he hadn't believed totally that his dream cave was here, despite a lifetime of searching. And yet here he was. In the midst of an underground cavern more beautiful than any he'd ever heard of. In Terrel. Just minutes from the trails he'd blazed with the Cliff Combers.

The lights twinkled like fireworks in his eyes, electric blue and red reflecting from the dim light of his flashlight. He couldn't remember ever hearing of a more intense collection of crystal formation, especially all collected in one small room. It would draw a fortune in tourist fees, he thought, his mind jumping ahead. He'd be rich. He'd be . . .

Dead.

The strength seeped out of him in rhythmic pulses, and he suddenly couldn't hold his body erect any longer. He slumped to the ground, the lights glittering in his eyes blurring into a kaleidoscope of electric fireworks. A prism of past possibility.

"Not yet," the voice urged.

A fire lit in his groin, hotter than the one that seeped from the back of his heart. Ken started, and with painful effort, raised his head from the rocky floor.

In the center of the cavern, Cindy had positioned herself on a stone slab. Another sacrifice for him, on an altar of glittering crystal. She was the heart of the geode.

She was naked. And her legs were spread.

"Come to me," she said with the voice of the spirit. Her voice, though soft, echoed through the cavern like an explosion. Ken felt the demon's strength surge inside him and he put forward an arm. Despite the red-hot poker that stabbed and gouged through his core with every movement, he pushed himself toward her.

"Just ahead, I think," Joe called to the women behind him.

Angelica hadn't said a word after falling in step behind his lead, and Monica hadn't contributed anything since leaving the Cave of the Covenant. Behind them, her snuffling, lost-puppy whimpers continued to whine and echo through the tunnel.

Rhonda had done enough speaking for them all. If taunts were salable, Joe was, in just five minutes of vocalese, a millionaire.

"You really think you can save that little tramp?" Rhonda sneered. "You know she was fucking my son, and look what that got him? What makes you think you'll be any different? Have you ever wondered if it was even Cindy that you were fucking? Maybe the devil was already inside her then. Maybe you've been bonin' the fuckin' devil."

After a bit, Karen tiredly asked Rhonda to "just shut the fuck up."

It hadn't worked.

"Tell us, oh Great Spirit Master"—Rhonda smirked—"how will you vanquish this great evil from our town? Is there a virgin you might sacrifice? Don't look at your girlfriend. And don't look at any of us!"

Karen shot her a look and at last she quieted. In her heart, Karen felt that something was about to happen that would put an end to her lifetime of slavery. For better or worse . . .

"I don't know how much help we'll be . . ." she cautioned the reporter.

He shrugged. "Don't know what I can really do either, but we have to try."

They fell silent, the slow shuffling scrape of shoes on rock the only noise to rise above the distant rush of water sluicing from mountaintop to ocean. This, then, was the moment. *The stand,* Joe thought. *Here we make our bid for freedom*. He thought of the story of Angelica's failed escape from the spirit's control, and of its result.

They stepped into the crystal chamber.

"Yes, *yes,*" Cindy moaned as a bloody hand flopped up from the cave floor below to grasp for purchase on her chest.

The world was an electric circuit board of pleasure to her now. Every glint of light, every touch on her body, every slick massage of blood . . . it all brought her spasms of orgasmic pleasure. She yearned to have a man inside her. Any man. She needed to feel the light penetrate her. She needed Him to be inside her, bringing her to release. Bringing James inside her again.

Ken was climbing the rock pedestal with his last strength and the help of the demon and Cindy reached for him, pulling his trembling arms to her, straining to lift his shuddering, bloody form to lie with her.

In Ken's mind, the world had faded to a prism of blue and the bloody tan of the blonde girl's belly. The sight of his blood smeared across her breasts and glistening on her pubic lips excited him one last time, and he mumbled, "Yes," as she pulled him to her.

"Ease him in," the demon urged in Cindy's mind. *"Take him to your bosom as if he were myself. Take his seed and we will birth a child of our own. You will give it your beauty, and I my power. Take him. Take me. Take James."*

A smile lit her face at his name.

"James?" she whispered as the bloody caver sprawled over her. The voice of her late boyfriend seemed to echo in the cave, as if he were here and far away at the same time.

"Yes, baby, I'm here. Make love to me?"

It was his voice that spoke to her, and Cindy smiled wider, pulling at the struggling dying man, and closing her eyes to its maddened, unfocused face.

"Yes," she breathed.

CHAPTER TWENTY-FIVE

The first thing Joe noticed as they entered the crystal chamber was that the blue crystals lining the room seemed to be alive with a faint light of their own. He didn't need his flashlight. Through their unnatural light he could see Cindy spread-eagle on the rock in the center of the room. A sacrificial altar. The caver was crouched on top of her, readying himself to violate her as he had Angelica. How, Joe didn't know. The caver shouldn't be moving at all. The guy's back was a gash of ripped flesh, and blood was flowing out of him in all directions. The floor was slick with it.

"No!" Joe shouted, and dashed ahead of the women, arms poised to shove the dying rapist from the poor girl. Just before he reached them, another arm grabbed his and dragged him to a halt.

"It's His will and His right," Rhonda said through gritted teeth. Her eyes looked vacant.

He tried to shake her arm from his own, but her grip was like a vise. She was under the power of the demon; he could tell. Her lips growled something only the spirit would say: "It is the beginning of a new Covenant."

"Then we have to stop it!" he yelled again, and then turned to beseech the others for help. "Angelica, Karen," he cried. "Stop Him. Stop Him before it's too late for her. Don't let him make her suffer the way you have. Don't let Him make her one of you."

Karen darted forward, but then stopped as a voice rang out clear and powerful throughout the chamber.

"Ah, but she already is one of you, isn't she?"

The voice came from Ken's mouth, but was not his own. Joe, Karen and the others stared in shock. Cindy raised her head from the pedestal, eyes focusing with rapid blinks on Joe, and then moving to the gored man crawling over her body like a predatory lion.

She looked confused.

Ken's horrible eyes caught them all. One by one, he stared them down, and then with a chuckle, his gaze stopped on Joe.

"Tell them, Joey boy. Who is this little girl beneath me? This ripe little nugget that I'm going to impregnate with my seed, to birth a new Covenant for Terrel?"

Joe remained silent.

"Cat got your tongue, Mr. Reporter? Allow me, then."

Ken looked down at Cindy and trailed a bloodied tongue from her lips to her forehead. The red stripe glistened sickly in the light.

"The search is over, my ladies. We have found our missing child. Actually"—the possessed caver pointed a trembling finger at Joe—"he exposed her to me. Without our little reporter friend, none of us might ever have found Rachel's sweet child, raised and rocked right here in our midst. But now we have."

Joe stammered, "But how . . ."

Ken grinned, black blood staining his teeth.

"When you sleep with her, you sleep with me. I know what you know. I've never needed to forge a new Covenant to possess you because you gave me all I needed freely."

A tremor rocked the body of the caver and suddenly Ken stiffened. Cindy reached up to stroke his face and said, as if in a dream, "James."

Ken grinned and looked back at the women.

"I have your final sacrifice. Our Covenant is met. Go now while you can, or stay and begin a new one with me."

Joe was pulled backward as Rhonda yanked him toward the tunnel leading to the ocean.

"No," he said again, and held his ground against the woman and the demon. "She is not yours to take."

"Ah, but she is," Ken's grave-rough voice answered. "Ask her mother."

Without thinking, Joe glanced at Angelica, who had fallen to her knees. Tears streamed down her face.

"Yes, ask her mother," the voice continued. "Ask her how happy she is that you found her daughter. Ask her what she'll do to thank you."

Angelica's face was awash with tears, betrayal and heart-ache etched into every pore. Joe couldn't meet her eyes. How could he have been so stupid? He had brought her right to Him. He had undone the one victory Angelica had maintained over the demon.

Joe slumped in defeat. The game was won. And he had not come out on top. Once again, he had managed to undermine the woman—women—that he loved.

Ken's eyes glowed with inner sparks as Joe met his gaze.

"Time to seal the bargain," the monster said.

With that, the caver positioned his legs between Cindy's and leaned into the girl. Then he raised up, laughed aloud at Joe's open mouth and . . .

. . . collapsed on top of her.

The cave suddenly exploded with light; the blue fire in the crystals beneath Cindy's naked body glowed. Cerulean fire raced like manic Christmas lights down a strand, chasing and doubling back. Ken's limp arm hung over the edge, a dull stream of dusky red dripping from elbow to cave floor. The light illuminated his sightless eyes, and Joe felt a ray of hope. Taking advantage of Rhonda's disorientation, he leapt forward, smashing his knee against the pedestal in his haste to push Ken's lifeless body from Cindy's mesmerized form.

"Shit," he said, but the dead caver slid to the ground. Then Cindy's eyes met his own and she smiled.

"Yes, my darling," her voice rasped. Its normally girlish tone seemed deeper, harsher. "You can take his place. I need a live one for this part."

Suddenly Joe's body was not his own. His hands flew over the buttons of his shirt, ripped with clumsy haste at his belt. He could feel his erection rise, though he wanted nothing less than to make love to Cindy right now.

"Stop it," he cried silently.

"Sit back and enjoy the ride," Malachai whispered. *"You know you want it."*

He realized in horror that this was what Angelica had probably felt like the night she had seduced him. Powerless. Angry. Used. He cursed himself for not having gotten to the chapter on possession in the book George had given him. He knew of no way to fight this hold on him.

But the demon knew its business. The room seemed to fade from his view and before him, he saw Cindy as she'd been in the back of his car, innocent and sweet. As she'd been on that night in his apartment, seductive, loving. His clothes were now gone and his erection raged. Joe couldn't think of anything but lying with her. Having her.

Fucking her.

She was ready for him, her body glistening with sweat and blood, her sex engorged and open. The demon let him waste no time. The cave swam in and out of focus, a blue-green wash of light and sound. He could hear voices, distantly. A scream? Below him Cindy's eyes danced with light, her mouth whispering over and over, "Yes, James, yes."

And then he heard the laughter.

It began deep in the back of his brain and spread with his impending orgasm to shiver through every muscle.

"Say g'night, Gracie." The laughter mocked him as he slipped and slammed in the blood covering Cindy's body and came deep inside her. As his orgasm rocked him, Cindy's mouth opened in an O of pleasure. She yelped a series of short, sharp cries, and then moaned with contentment beneath him.

"Oh, James," she whispered, still not seeing the world around her.

Joe could see Rhonda to one side of their rock altar, her large teeth gritting, hands above her head. The piton that had spelled Ken's end was now in her hands.

The demon had used him and now was throwing him away. And he was helpless to stop Him. His hips shivered in the last throes of ecstasy and he watched, in slow motion, as the steel spike completed its upward arc behind Rhonda's head and then began its descent toward his spine.

Then there was another sound, another "no," and something hit him, hard, jarring his awareness closer to reality. A weight slapped his body down harder onto Cindy, whose "whoof" of surprise blew spit onto Joe's frozen face.

There was a scream, and another impact, this one less intense than the first.

Karen threw herself face-first over the top of Joe and Cindy, protecting them from Rhonda's attack with her body. Monica screamed as Rhonda brought the steel down to stab Karen instead of Joe.

Something snapped in Monica at that moment. All her life she'd been the one bossed around. The one who'd meekly said "okay" and done whatever the group wanted. The one who the demon had told to kiss the lips of her dead friend Bernadette, and who had. She had been bossed by Rhonda, had sacrificed her child to a demon and married a man who would just as soon beat her as kiss her. But one woman had helped her keep her sanity through it all. One woman had sat with her night after night at her kitchen table, soothing her fears. Karen had saved her.

And as Monica saw Rhonda bring the steel spike down to stab her—their—friend, Monica felt the anger of a lifetime surge at Him, at Rhonda, at herself for her entire wasted life. It coursed through her in a white-hot angry instant filling her with a power she'd never felt before. Every hesitation she'd ever known was washed away. Monica sprang to action, throwing her thin arms around her friend's beefy neck and holding on for all she was worth.

Get up, Karen's lips mouthed to Joe. Her brow creased in violent tremors of pain, and she closed her eyes and collapsed to the stone altar half on top of him.

Joe didn't waste the time she'd bought him. He slid from between Karen, who was gasping for air, and Cindy, who seemed oblivious to everything, and stood, naked and trembling, to stare at the scene behind him.

Monica was screaming at the top of her lungs, her ear-piercing cries echoing through the cavern like the sound track to a horror movie. Rhonda twisted and struggled, battering behind her clumsily to remove the other woman from her neck. For a moment, Monica held her off balance, but with her own natural strength and the urging of the demon, Rhonda quickly recovered, and threw the woman to the ground. Not content with freeing herself, Rhonda stomped over to Monica, who was already turning to fight again. But this time, Rhonda had the upper hand. She held the smaller woman's shoulders and pushed her back to the ground. As Joe watched in horror, Rhonda grabbed the other woman by the hair and began methodically bashing her old friend's face into the rock of the cavern floor. Joe could hear each wet, thudding impact.

"Spirit," he screamed. "I invoke your name, Malachai, and command you to stop."

"Don't do this," a cold, familiar voice whispered in his skull.

But at Joe's command, Rhonda did stop, her face suddenly gone blank.

"Malachai, if you wish to remain any longer in this realm, I insist that you release them all," he continued. Behind him, Angelica coughed and cried. And then he heard footsteps slap the rock. They faded as she ran from the chamber.

"You have damned her," the voice mocked. *"She can never live with the knowledge she has gained of herself. She runs toward the depths of the water now."*

Joe looked back and forth between a bloodied, confusedly blinking Cindy lying on the dais and the now-empty corridor that led to the ocean.

"Who will you save?"

"Stop her," Joe commanded, and the spirit laughed.

"There's only so much you can command using only my name," He said. *"I'm under Covenant to another."*

"That other is dead and buried," Joe answered. "And that hundred-year Covenant has been done for years now. Your pledge to Broderick Terrel is over. You have no right to remain here any longer."

"Ah, but I have extended it," the spirit taunted. *"Just ask the women around you."*

"An unfair bargain," Joe complained. "They had no choice in the matter."

"Nobody forced them to my cavern," the spirit said. *"Nobody forced them to push their children from the top of the cliff."*

"I don't believe that," Joe countered. "But it doesn't matter. You yourself said moments ago that this Covenant with these women was over. You are free and not bound on this plane to anyone . . . and so I name you—"

"Yeeeaaaiiii," Rhonda screamed, and charged at Joe, mouth drooling long dribbles of saliva, sausage fingers clenched in rakelike claws.

Joe sidestepped her attack and screamed, "Malachai, I command you—"

"You don't know what you're doing."

"Stop this instant. You—"

"Don't!"

"—are mine to bind."

From an achingly long distance came a sudden shriek. And next to him Joe felt rather than saw Rhonda slump to the ground as the demon released her.

He was surrounded by bodies. The blue crystals electrified the room again, just as it had when Ken's body had finally expired. Did that mean the demon had claimed another soul? Was the light a signal that someone had been "absorbed"?

He knew without question that Angelica had just died. And now her spirit was locked inside the crystals. Locked in the dungeon of the demon, Malachai.

Sliding the piton slowly from the wound Rhonda had carved with it in Karen's bloody shoulder, he twisted around and smashed its needle point into the glowing crystals in the center of the cavern, those that supported the sacrificial dais.

A hurricane exploded in his head.

"AAAHHhhhheeeiiiiii!"

A shriek of unearthly power . . . and peril.

But Joe stabbed again and again, chipping away blue electric sparks and bits of crystal as clear as rock candy from the pedestal. An unseen force lifted him, and he flew backward through the air. He crashed with a shattering impact into a wall, and slid with a painful scrape to the corner of the cavern.

But he didn't stop. Instead, arm over arm, knees grinding the grit of the floor into his flesh, Joe advanced again on the speeding phosphorescent trails of power, and hammered at the seat of the demon's strength.

"Demon, I release you and command that you—"

"Covenant!" screamed the voice in his mind, and behind its desperation he could hear a thousand keening wails of grief and bliss. The voices of all its captured souls. Would they be free upon the earth if Malachai was killed? Or would they dissipate to silent air? Joe couldn't stop to wonder as he was once more propelled backward. This time his head hit the cave floor with a blinding smear of heat.

"Let us come to terms, and I will spare your girlfriend, and the souls," Malachai begged.

"You will be mine to command?" Joe asked, hardly knowing what he was saying.

"Name your terms," the demon barked back. The whirl-
wind in Joe's head grew louder. He could hardly think. The
demon's voice wheezed aloud through the silent tension of
the cave, its power bleeding visibly like poison across not only
the damaged crystal center, but chiming away through the
cave walls as well. The room was aglow with deadly blue
power, but parts of it seemed to be fading, blacking out completely. Joe had struck the nerve in hammering at the center.
He considered ignoring the demon's request and finishing
the job, hammering at the crystal until no light lit the cavern
at all. But he had no assurance that that would stop the demon from killing and possessing again. Would the removal
of its seat of power kill it, or only send it in search of new
victims to replenish itself?

*"You have called me by name and I cannot possess you until a
bargain has been agreed upon. Name your terms."*

"You will not hurt the people of Terrel anymore," Joe
called. He tried to think but couldn't focus. What else should
he require?

"You will do as I say, whenever, whatever I tell you."

"Those are your terms?"

"Yes."

"Then I accept, and a new Covenant is struck," the demon
answered, and the din behind His voice lessened somewhat.
The blue glow began to fade from the cave walls, but still
swirled and twisted amid the broken stones of the altar.

"I am yours to command," Malachai said. *"And you are mine to
follow. Until your death, since you did not state another end time.
Guard yourself."*

With that, the last bright glow of blue light winked out,
an implosion of contentious energy, and Joe looked around
shakily. The room still glittered faintly with an LED blue
glow, but now its power seemed at rest, its light faint. A
moan from the dim altar made him look to Cindy, but her
eyes were closed and the sound wasn't hers. It came from the
ground.

"Joe," Karen Sander croaked. Her eyes fluttered, then focused hard on his own. "Joe . . . did we win?"

"Yes," he said, crouching beside her to put a hand behind her back, and carefully ease her up.

"It's over," he said. *"I hope."*

EPILOGUE

There is nothing quite like a summer's day near the ocean. The breath of salt mingled with the lilac-rich scent of budding flowers, the buzz of soaring insects, and an unclouded golden sun could make life taste like . . . honey. Or something. Joe looked away from the piercing blue of the sky to focus again on the casket beneath the red and white canopy.

Reality check. People were dead.

Cindy held his arm with both hands, but said little through the service. She'd said little for the past three days, asking only that Joe hold her tightly. He'd complied without question.

Rhonda stood at the back of the small gathering at the cemetery. She looked as if she wasn't sure whether she should come forward or go home. Her grief was palpable. Joe would never say it to another soul, but it was her hands, possessed or not, that had caused this ceremony.

The minister stood before a wooden lectern and gave a speech suspiciously similar to the one Joe remembered from the funeral for Rhonda Canady's son just weeks before.

There really wasn't much you could add to the experience, he supposed.

"As she was in life, so she is in death," the minister said. Joe thought it sounded like a threat.

Angelica leaned over and whispered in Joe's ear. "What kind of a thing is that to say?" she complained, and Joe shook his head, stalling her, wondering where the holy man was going.

The blue-green bruises from Ken's abuse had turned to yellow near Angelica's eyes, and her arm hung in a sling, heavy in its white cast. She'd broken it in her fall into the cold water of the underground river. The blue light of the chamber hadn't signaled her death, as Joe had believed. It had been Monica's soul that fed the demon that last time, not Angelica's.

But how much of Angelica really remains alive? Joe thought. She cast odd, veiled glances at her daughter and drummed her fingers absently on the heavy plaster on her arm. She hadn't laughed or cried since leaving the hospital. Her eyes looked perpetually shell-shocked. Joe wondered if she would ever speak with a Gypsy accent again.

"Monica was a quiet soul, a woman always concerned with the good of others," the minister continued. "She will watch over us all now, from where she is above."

"She's not above, not really," Malachai whispered in Joe's head. *"She's with us now. Right here. Anything you'd like us to do, master? Raise the corpse up in the casket, perhaps, give 'em all a little scare?"*

"No," Joe said aloud, and shook his head. Cindy looked sharply at him, then turned away. She knew who he was talking to. Was she jealous now that Malachai had claimed him as master? He had forbidden the demon from talking with her. Would she still want to see him, after the death and dust settled? He didn't know how to ask. Could she live with the fact that he'd made love to both her and her mother?

Could he?

He wondered if he should ask Malachai to heal Angelica's soul. Could he use the monster to achieve a good end, as Terrell had? And if so, at what price?

"I am yours to command," the demon reminded. A sadistic hint of glee colored its tone.

Its voice hung like an anchor from Joe's soul.

"Yes, I know," he mumbled, looking at the broken mother on his left, the silent daughter on his right. The women he had unwittingly hurt, and now pledged himself to protect. Somehow, to heal. *At what price?*

"I know."

Turn the page for an advance look at John
Everson's next terrifying novel...

SACRIFICE

Coming in June 2009

PROLOGUE

Goose bumps peppered Ted's skin. The temperature dropped every step forward. The air swam with palpable presence, as if he was walking through a liquid current of clammy spiderwebs. Ted shivered, but kept moving.

It had all happened down here. His sister Cindy had finally told him the story after he'd badgered her enough. A spirit had lived inside this cliff, a spirit that had killed and killed and killed again. It had demanded sacrifices from the town of Terrel for more than one hundred years. But now it was gone, along with that reporter from the *Terrel Daily Times*.

Ted had come, pressing through the dank, cobwebbed caverns, to see where it had all happened.

Once, these cold stone corridors had been the basement beneath the old lighthouse. Terrel had been a minor port, back in the day, and its lighthouse had stood high on the cliff above the town, warning errant ships away from the deadly pillars of stone gouged out of the bay like crippled fingers. The lighthouse was long gone, but the stairs leading down into the cliff remained, hidden beneath a pile of remnant boulders and rotting beams.

Ted shone his flashlight back and forth, catching the watery glint of the cool gray walls on the right and left, its light sucked away into the endless black hole ahead. His narrow beam was swallowed by that blackness, but he continued on, step by step, into the void. There was no sound besides the soft shuffle of his feet on the uneven floor, and the whisper of his jeans in motion. Ted had never felt so alone and cut off; at times, he had to remind himself to breathe.

The flashlight struggled to pry through the darkness, and then suddenly, Ted saw a reflection, an answering flicker, bounced back from the black. There was something ahead. He yearned to hurry up, to run ahead and see what was there, but forced himself to move slowly, carefully, panning the spot across the floor a few feet in front of him to make sure he didn't trip over a rock and break a leg. He didn't think he could crawl all the way back down the tunnel and up the stairs to the outside world. Even if he could, it wasn't likely he could flag anyone down for help from the top of Terrel's Peak. It was not exactly the center of town.

Heart pounding harder, Ted continued his slow, measured walk, occasionally flicking the flashlight up to eye level to look far down the path. The reflection grew with every step, a twinkling prism of blue-white light. The corridor walls narrowed. It tightened until his shoulders almost touched the rock on either side of him and he wondered if he was really just walking into a claustrophobic dead end.

And then the wall to the left disappeared, his flashlight meeting only blackness as he raised it up and down. He swung it to the right and there too the walls had disappeared. The air was even colder here, its taste on his lips salty and dead.

He brought the flashlight back to dead center and was almost blinded. The room exploded in a prism of sparkling light, reflecting off the object in the center of the cavern. The walls all around were visible now; more passages led to and away from this room.

This was it! He had found it! The chamber of crystal that his sister had described.

A pedestal—a rocky altar—of watery blue crystal rooted in the center of the room; it reflected his light in a blinding feedback loop to the azure mirrors that cut into and out of the walls all around. It was like standing in the center of a gigantic geode.

Ted walked to the center and reached out to the crystal altar with his left hand. He stopped, inches from its glassy surface. Would a jolt of blue fire scorch him for his intrusion? This had been the seat of the demon's power. Did any still remain, like a battery poised to spend its last electric jolt?

He tapped a fingernail on the cool, hard surface, but nothing happened. With his palm he traced the latticework of its surface. There were spots of darkness blotting out the window to the crystal's core. Rusted, gritty spots led away from a deep dark stain near the center of the flat surface.

Dried blood.

Sacrifice and soul-binding had occurred here.

Ted stepped away from the stone and twisted, clockwise, admiring the sparkle and flash of the room. This was nature's disco, and he the only dancer.

He grinned and moved to the edge of the room, peering into each corridor that led to places deeper inside the cliff.

His flashlight disappeared without meeting any reflection down the first two paths. They seemed endless. Then he found a side room. The corridor wound around the outside of the circular chamber, and ended in this half-hidden cubby. He walked to the end, and found a small ledge, like the surface of a desk. A look at its contents said it had been used for just that, once.

This was probably where the keepers of the old lighthouse had come to for safety during the fury of a North Atlantic storm, he thought. They would have stoked up the giant searchlight, trained its saving, warning beam toward the ocean and then crossed their fingers that any wayward ships could see it. And then, as the structure groaned and shivered in the treacherous winds, they would have fled to safety below. To here.

The shelf held a couple of old, small bottles, and what

looked like chicken feathers, in a pile to one side. In the center lay an old, rotting book. It was bound in reddish brown leather, and Ted could see without even flipping, that its pages were yellowed and mold-eaten.

The Journal of Broderick Terrel it said on the cover.

He opened the book to a random page and smiled. *This* was what he had come for. This was why he was here. The script was faded and hard to read, but its import was clear:

"I have called a demon from hell," the author had written in an early entry.

Ted set down the flashlight to shine sideways across the pages, and read on.

PART I

Leaving Home

*The rewards of a successful Calling are riches and hedonistic fulfill-
ment beyond any man's wildest dreams. But the path to union with
the Curburide is long. He who chooses this path must be committed
to the Calling in both heart and soul; there is no turning back. To
waver on the path means not only death, but eternal damnation.
Once the Calling has begun, and first blood spilled, the Caller be-
longs to the demons called Curburide. If the Calling is successfully
completed, they will also belong to the Caller—a mutual symbiotic
bond is forged. But if the Curburide detect weakness, doubt or insin-
cerity in the Caller before that bond is complete, beware . . .*
           —*Chapter One,* The Book of the Curburide

CHAPTER ONE

If the lights went any lower, the woman would have been indistinguishable from the shadows. She was dressed all in black.

All.

Even her hair was covered in a shiny skullcap ending in two pointy faux cat ears. The only skin showing was her face, but when lights flickered across the costume, her obsidian body rippled with dark reflection.

Ryan Nelson eyed the woman from heels to head and, without even realizing it, licked his lips.

Un-fuckin'-believable.

Four-inch stiletto-heeled boots merged seamlessly into glossy black bodysuit and arm-length vinyl gloves that showed every flow of flesh and muscle beneath. Not that she moved or flowed. He had been sitting next to her in the club for an hour so far, and had yet to see her do more than bat an eyelid.

The latex cat suit was not unusual. It was Sunday night—and more importantly, Halloween—in Austin, Texas, and a catwoman was the least of the odd sights he'd seen so far. Driven by the wild college crowd of the University of Texas, which nestled just blocks off the state capitol steps, the city had been forced to close off a several block stretch of Sixth Street, downtown Austin's main drag. A wild mix of college kids and locals paraded down the asphalt, in costume creations dredged from some pretty twisted and bloody imaginations. Mascara-smudged vampires leaned out of every open bar window as if this was Amsterdam's red-light district. Ragged witches French-kissed bile- and gore-streaked corpses. And when they came up for air, they all peered over second-floor balconies to watch the parade of other homemade horrors on the street below. At least three "Sons of God" pulled giant wooden crosses behind them as they trudged down the street. Ryan was quite sure that the original walk that had inspired the Stations of the Cross celebrated in Christian churches around the world had not used a cross with handy tote wheels screwed into the base.

While there certainly were many costumes of greater extravagance, Ryan's favorite so far had been an older woman. She had been dressed in ripped and mud-crusted rags. She'd walked along the crowded street with a rope tied around her waist. Hanging from that rope, with twine knotted tight around their tiny ankles, were a half dozen baby dolls. At least, he assumed they were dolls. From the smears of blood across their tortured, wrinkled faces, he wasn't sure, and he hadn't stepped close enough to confirm or deny the atrocity.

Early in the evening, he'd spent a couple hours shivering outside with the mob in the chill, unseasonable wind and laughing at the bizarre imaginations of his neighbors, until he finally left the street and slid into the comforting black confines of Elysium, an outwardly nondescript, black-walled goth club around the corner on Red River. His own facial white-paint and the pale threads in his black-and-white-striped hobo suit glowed electric blue-white in the black light of the club. As he passed through the entryway, a girl in a purple corset, torn fishnets and a bloody ax lodged in her skull caught his eye, flashed a red lipstick smile of appreciative recognition and yelled "Beetlejuice, Beetlejuice, Beetlejuice."

He grinned back and bowed, appreciating her recognition, then moved to the bar where a blood-spattered cheerleader in a gold and blue ultrashort skirt poured him a Vampire's Kiss.

The DJ was mixing ambient, ethereal Delerium as Ryan né "Beetlejuice" found a chair along the dance floor to wait for the evening's band lineup to start playing. He took an empty seat next to the young "catwoman" and silently whistled his appreciation of her getup.

Over the next few minutes, as the disco ball and a couple of red and blue spotlights worked in tandem to swirl a mind-numbing pattern across the floor, alternating from psychedelic circles to swimming neon tadpoles, Ryan snuck looks at the silent feline. He wondered if she was with anyone. She seemed to be sitting alone, and wasn't drinking. She stared straight ahead across the floor, without expression. Cat's eyes.

Over the course of an hour, she didn't uncross her legs or move the gloved hands from her lap. The black whiskers penciled on her cheeks didn't so much as twitch. She was a statue, cool dark eyes trained at some point just above the floor. There, impossibly thin men both in drag and wearing tight leather pants with fishnet shirts along with uniformly chubby women in combat boots and pink or blue hair and various shredded bits of spandex, netting and twines of chain moved in a disconnected, colorfully jerky ballet to the beats.

"Wild night, eh?" Ryan said after a while, staring straight at catwoman's face. Her expression didn't change. She didn't answer. He shrugged and sipped his blood-dyed drink, averting his eyes to the floor.

Murder Box, a local band, picked up their instruments at last, and Ryan abandoned his seat to get closer to the stage, nodding at the industrial guitar grind and bleating synthesizers as an Edward Scissorhands look-alike thumbed the bass, spiky black hair bobbing in time. A young goth girl wrapped in tantalizing curtains of gauzy black swiveled her bared hips and teased the audience as she fellated a microphone above the pounding beat.

After the set, he bought another drink and looked for a place to rest until the headliners came on, a Florida darkwave act. He slipped between a variety of ghouls and black-clad, black-eyed patrons and found himself back again at the edge of the dance floor, at the same empty seat next to the cat-woman.

He sat.

She didn't seem to have moved.

"They were pretty good, didn't you think?" he asked.

Her head tilted ever so slightly to almost meet his gaze, and then returned to face forward, still saying nothing.

Ryan drew up his death-clown charcoal-ringed mouth and sighed. Talk about ice-queens. But she was gorgeous, in an arctic way. It was one thing if she didn't want to be picked up—he'd been there. But she could at least be polite. The more he thought about it, the more it steamed him. A simple shake of the head, the barest acknowledgement of his existence, would have been enough. Purely out of spite, he leaned over her shoulder and struggled to keep a straight face as he dropped a line patently designed to piss her off as much as her silence had annoyed him.

"Do you come here often?" he asked.

No answer.

Not even a flicker of response.

Ryan sighed and presently went back to watching the goth boys and goth girls pirouetting to the gloomy self-flagellation of The Smiths. The dance floor was slowly filling, as people began to elbow their way in closer to the stage, eager to be in place for the next set.

And then she spoke.

Her voice was cool, like her eyes, but her meaning was clear.

"Do you want to take me out of here?"

Ryan turned abruptly to face her. Had she said what he just thought he heard? For the first time, her face was actually turned toward him, eyes trained fully, unblinkingly on him, awaiting his answer. Her pale lips were drawn tight.

"Huh?" he said.

"I asked if you wanted to take me out of here?" she repeated, her voice a delicate shard of deadly beautiful crystal, high-pitched and thin enough to break.

"Now?" he asked.

She moved, for the first time all night, stretching provocatively while running both black-gloved palms down the shining suit. Ryan stared as her black-gloved fingers traced the lithe ridges of her tightly visible rib cage and then reached down over the spread of her thighs. Her outfit groaned like the creasing of a tight leather couch as she stretched, catlike in her chair, and then opened both eyes wide to meet his growing interest.

"Yes," she said. "I need to go. Now."

It didn't take him long to consider. Visions of his hand unzipping that tight vinyl flooded his mind. Ryan jumped to his feet. He bent and offered his arm. Catwoman smiled and nodded, gracing his forearm lightly with a cool vinyl finger. She rose with a slow but audible crunch. In her heels, she was as tall as he was, and in mincing steps she strutted next to him through the crowd of goths and out the doorway. From behind them, Ryan heard someone again call out "Beetlejuice, Beetlejuice, Beetlejuice."

"I think someone just wished you away," she said.

"Looks like it worked."

"I'm just up the street, at the Marriott," she announced.

"Cool." He led her down the street, through the crowds of gaudy painted faces and gales of drunken laughter. Her steps clicked like sniper shots against the pavement, and she said nothing more until they had passed Stubb's and some burnt-out warehouses and turned the corner to arrive at the Waller Creek bridge near the hotel.

In five minutes, he was trailing her up the stairs of the hotel's rear courtyard, across the polished granite-tiled lobby, and up the elevator to room 618. She flipped a light switch, and Ryan saw that she had rearranged the room, piling the mattress and frame of one of the two double beds up against a wall.

A ring of what looked like pebbles littered the ground where carpet marks indicated that the deconstructed bed had stood not so long ago. Catwoman turned and pressed her face to his, drawing his breath out in a hard kiss. She stared wide into his eyes.

"I like the floor," she said, and drew her tongue from his chin to his ear, biting briefly at the lobe.

"Why don't you get out of those clothes, make yourself comfortable," she hissed. "I'll be right back."

She disappeared into the bathroom, shutting the door behind her. Ryan shed his hobo coat and tie, and kicked his shoes to the side of the bed. He sat down on the bed she hadn't dismantled and waited, grinning expectantly when he heard the run of water in the next room. He imagined her coming out of the bathroom wearing only a towel, hair let down to flow in loose curls of raven gloss over bare shoulders.

His imagination was wrong.

She returned still fully clad in vinyl, still gloved and skull-capped.

She walked over to him, and planted one leg between his feet while handing him a warm, wet cloth.

"For your face," she offered. "Can I take your shirt and pants for you?"

"Can I take your cat suit for you?" he retorted. She lifted her chin.

"Boys first," she said, looking down her whiskers at him. "I'm shy."

He laughed at that, but took the cloth and rubbed the character makeup from his face with vigorous wipes. Then he stood and unbuttoned his shirt and pants, letting them fall to the floor.

"And what do you keep in there?" she asked, nodding at the growing bulge in the pouch of his underpants.

"You don't waste time, do you?"

She grinned, and touched a pink tongue to her upper lip.

"Do you want to waste time?"

He kicked his underwear off and stood naked, hands on his hips.

"Does it pass?" he asked, confident, though starting to feel a little uneasy. This was definitely a weird one. Would she be a frigid mannequin beneath him, or would she truly become a catwoman?

She nodded. "It'll do."

Hands behind her back, she circled him, inspecting. He shivered as a cool nail scratched down from the top of his neck to the crack of his buttocks. She slid close, kissed him with her entire body, wrapping around him like a coat from behind, biting at his ear, whispering as she pinched his nipples. Her hands slipped down to move between his legs, kneading and gripping at the flesh swelling with desire.

"I need your help," she purred in his ear.

He moaned.

"I need a big, strong man to help me open the door," she purred again, and he made as if to turn around. Her hand gripped tight and held him facing forward. "I need you to give it up for me," she said, slowly withdrawing her hands. Then she wasn't there at all, and Ryan felt a chill as her voice commanded, "I need you to stay right there."

He rolled his eyes and continued to face forward, wondering if he should make a quick and apologetic exit. Catwoman really was some kind of freak.

Behind him she whispered something. Something he couldn't hear.

"What?" he asked, but her voice didn't pause.

He turned around and saw the woman had dropped in a crouch on the floor. Her forehead touched the ground and she mumbled and whispered to herself.

He felt a knot form in his belly and shook his head. In a heartbeat he'd made up his mind. Last straw.

Ryan began to step backward, noting the location of his clothes out of the corner of his eye.

Her head shot up at his silent retreat.

"Wait," she hissed. "I need your help, I'm not done."

"Well, I'm done," he said. "Thanks for the memories."

He reached for his shirt and she pounced, knocking him off balance and then pushing him to the floor on his back.

"Whoa," he said, grabbing her by the shoulders to hold her back. "I don't know what you're into, but I don't think I'm the right one for you tonight."

She slipped her arms inside his and pressed her palms to his chest. She leaned in, breath warm and sweet against his face.

"You're done when *I* say you're done," she said. Her words weren't warm and sweet at all.

He pushed against the floor with his elbows and tried to rise, but then her lips pressed wetly to his and he hesitated, involuntarily responding to the force and erotic liquid heat of her touch. A cool finger reached around his shoulder to ruffle the back of his hair. He smiled and slipped his tongue between her teeth. And then something hurt as she drew that caressing hand around his throat . . . pressing deep with cold pressure.

Something pinched his throat, and a confusing alarm of ice and fire rang inside Ryan's skull. Then the pain blossomed and he coughed at a tickle across his larynx . . . and then there *really* was pain . . . and warmth spilling out across his chest and shoulder. He tried to scream but Catwoman pressed his head to the floor and drew the second razor secreted in her palm across his neck from the other direction, severing his windpipe and vocal chords in one deep slice. A spray of blood spattered and beaded across her protective vinyl bodysuit. The pain was all-consuming and he struggled against her weight, but every movement was excruciating. The room blurred instantly. Ryan struggled to look at his killer one last time, his brain crying silently, "Why?"

She pressed him firmly to the floor and waited. His own blood dripped back down onto his lips, cascading from the jet escaping his throat to dribble impotently down the shiny black vinyl of her chest. The taste of iron from his blood slipped into his mouth and clouded his last shuddering sight as it pooled in his eye sockets.

"Beetlejuice, Beetlejuice, Beetlejuice," she said with a smile, and licked a spot of blood from her pencil-drawn, smeared whiskers.

"Now you're done."

CHAPTER TWO

"They're coming."

The voice was in his head, but that still didn't prevent Joe Kiernan from answering it out loud. He was alone in the car, and in the middle of nowhere. Nobody was likely to hear.

"What the hell are you talking about now?"

Joe didn't respond well to the occasional intrusions of Malachai, his indentured spirit. It wasn't like the invisible demon ever meant him well.

"Who's coming?" he asked. The irritation oozed from his tone.

"The Curburide. Somebody is calling them. I can hear it."

"And I should care about this because . . . ?" Joe asked, keeping his eyes on the road and his foot on the pedal.

He had miles to go before he slept. Nebraska was a long state. A long, uneventful, incredibly even-planed state. It played tricks on you, as the road unwound straight to the horizon, crossing and recrossing the damned Platte River, as if you were going in a circle, not a line. The Platte River was like the Styx—unless you were Charon, you could never escape crossing it.

"Because whoever is calling them is strong. They can hear. And they are answering."

"So?" Joe asked. "What am I supposed to do about it?"

"Nothing."

Joe watched the orange-fire tongs reaching low over the

horizon, watched the light stretch and grab one last futile time before fading into a memory of sunset's oblivion.

"Then why even bother to tell me?" Joe asked again.

"Because I thought you'd want to know."

Joe didn't say anything.

"I thought you'd want to know that you don't have very much time left to live."

The demon in his head began to laugh, louder and louder until Malachai's invisible power manifested itself physically, cracking the Hyundai's aging vinyl ceiling until it dripped dusty blood over his head.

Joe sneezed and shook his head in irritation. The demon had a penchant for the dramatic.

"They'll kill you and everybody you've ever known."

Images of Angelica and her daughter, Cindy, flashed before his eyes. He'd left them both behind in his flight from Terrel. It was Malachai's fault that he had gotten close to each of them, and Joe's fault that the two women had been brought back together, eighteen years after Angelica had given Cindy up for adoption in a vain hope to save her child from the grasp of the demon.

Thanks to Joe, Angelica's effort and estrangement had almost been in vain. But in the end, Joe had also saved both of them from Malachai's enslavement. The demon had held an entire town in thrall, thanks to a century-old covenant. The creature had holed up in Terrel's Peak, a cliff just outside of the seaport town, and demanded blood sacrifices every year to protect the townsfolk from an even worse fate—an incursion from the Curburide, a howling scourge of sadistic succubi that would have, if they'd had their way, fucked and flayed the flesh from every living being in Terrel. While Malachai had kept his bargain and protected the town from the Curburide, he had also struck a side deal to serve his own sadistic ends. A deal which would have resulted in Cindy's death, had Joe not managed to uncover the demon's real name and bind its service to him.

But in saving Cindy from the clutches of the demon Malachai, and also freeing Angelica, Joe had taken on an awful burden. The demon was now locked in servitude to him. The terms of the contract bound Malachai to Joe, and required that he do whatever Joe asked if he was to continue to have access to the earthly realm. One of Joe's first commands had been that the demon would not harm him or those he loved. But Joe had no doubt that the spiteful creature would do its best to quietly put him in harm's way, for when Joe was dead, it was unbound again. Free. It would then be able to swindle some other unwitting soul to strike a new covenant. One that would give Malachai all the advantages.

Part of him was ready to grant the demon its freedom. Part of him was ready to just lay down in the center of the road and wait for a semi to come along and cleave him in half. Let it all hang out.

Life hadn't turned out the way he'd planned. Joe had landed a plum job at the *Chicago Tribune* right out of college, and had taken to big-city reporting like a hound to a rabbit trail. He loved uncovering city hall corruption. He had broken the story about the police superintendent and his connection to the Colombian drug lord, Anabi Urubu. In a matter of months, Joe had put together a network of street kids who traded all sorts of information with him. He'd put the bust on a school principal for child pornography, and gotten a city ward boss put away for his dealings with the mob.

Joe had taken to the game with relish, never realizing that his girlfriend, the woman he intended to marry, was also in bed with the wrong crowd. And one of his exposé pieces on corruption in the district courthouse had landed her in jail for graft and forgery. She'd refused to see him after her indictment, and his fervor for turning over stones had soured. He suddenly didn't want to know what people hid in their bottom drawers and back rooms. He didn't want to know who they saw after dark, down by the alley at Eighty-third and Halsted. He didn't want to do anything but watch his own backyard. Play it safe.

Stay home.

The stories dried up, and his street network disappeared. It only took a couple missed visits to make those kids turn skittish and taciturn. One day, Joe went home from the paper, threw his clothes in a suitcase, his books and CDs and papers in a couple boxes, and got in his car and drove. He'd driven to the end of the world, the East Coast town of Terrel, right on the ocean. Ironically, in his desperation to escape the million minor sins of the big city, after only being in the tiny town of Terrel a few weeks he'd discovered a ring of murders that was bigger than any small-time crack dealer and welfare department grafter. He'd gone from mundane, selfish thievery to malevolence that transcended generations.

He'd lost a thieving girlfriend from his bed and gained a deadly demon in his head. Hardly a bargain.

The last bloody rays of sunlight faded without further conversation, and Joe's world contracted to a thin ribbon of yellow-striped asphalt. He rubbed his eyes, squinting into the headlight-burned night, and decided to call it a day when a green sign flashed by advertising OGALLALA, 2 MILES. He'd been on the road for nearly twelve hours, and it was time for a rest. He was humming a Creedence Clearwater Revival song when he pulled off the exit and headed for the center of town. The last place he'd gotten gas at hadn't been big enough to call a "town" in his estimation. It had consisted of a graying general store that seemed more a giant moldering growth on the pavement than a planned structure, a Clark service station with orange, rounded pumps from the 1960s and a tilted rusting grain silo. It was essentially a crossroads where soybean farmers met on Friday nights.

He hoped that Ogallala would prove larger. It appeared as a bold spot on his Nebraska map, which was a good sign.

He was in the "downtown" area in minutes, and pulled up to a small brick façade that boasted in simple blue neon, BRILL'S. A Budweiser sign glowed in the window.

Joe killed the engine and stepped out of the car into the crisp night air. He hadn't realized how stuffy the car had gotten until he stepped out of it with a groan of stiff joints. His stomach turned over and he realized that not only was he stiff, but he was starving. He pushed open the heavy wooden door and stepped inside.

Brill's was a good-size bar, with two pool tables off to one side, and a long bar on the other. He could see the grill behind the bar to one side, and a healthy selection of whiskies, vodkas and gins against the center wall.

"Evening."

The voice was heavy and husky, but friendly. It came from a big man behind the bar, moving out of the shadows and into the red glow of a Pabst Blue Ribbon sign.

"Hi," Joe said, pulling up a stool at the bar. Only one other stool was taken. A thin, grizzled man nursed something amber over ice at the end of the bar.

"Quiet night, eh?" Joe offered.

The big man nodded, drying his hands on a stained white towel. Joe saw he'd been washing glasses in a small sink when he'd come in.

"Not much going on here on a Tuesday night," the man said, and held out a hand.

"Frank," he said. "Frank Brill. You just off the highway?"

It was Joe's turn to nod.

"Then you'll be wanting a meal and a room, yes?"

Joe smiled. "You nailed it."

"I can handle the one; you'll find the other about two blocks down. Prescott Hotel. Not a bad place for a night."

Frank pulled a menu out from beneath the bar and set it in front of Joe.

"You can look at this if you want, and Jenny will rustle up anything from here that you want, but"——he leaned forward conspiratorially, after glancing over his shoulder at the double doors in the back of the grill area——"I'd stick with the hamburger and fries if I was you," he whispered.

"Done," Joe said, pushing the menu back. "Got anything on tap?"

"Miller, Bud, Coors," Frank said. "What can I pull you?"

"MGD," Joe said, and glanced up at the TV flickering above them in the corner. A female news commentator with overly red lips and smallish eyes was mouthing cheerily as footage of a black bodybag being carried to an ambulance played in a small window next to her sickly happy face.

"You hear about this nutjob?" Frank asked, thumbing at the screen as he pulled a beer from the tap.

Joe shook his head.

"Third stiff they've found so far, and each in a different city."

"New serial killer?" Joe asked, and took a healthy swallow from the heavy pint that Frank passed over.

"Apparently." The burly barkeep shook his head and grimaced.

"If the murders have been in different cities how do they know it's the same guy?" Joe asked. The beer slid down his throat and took the imaginary dust of a day of travel away.

"Same scenario in each place," Frank said. "Real freak show. All three bodies have been found in hotels, in rooms rented by a woman with black hair. She apparently picks 'em up at a bar, brings 'em back, strips 'em and then slices their throats. The police aren't saying what else she does, but it must be pretty twisted, because they're saying each killing was done exactly the same way. When the second one happened, they knew immediately it was done by the same person. She's cutting up more 'n just their throats, I'd guess."

Frank looked away from the TV and called to the back, "Jenny! Burger and fries up!"

"I've been on the road the past couple days," Joe said. "When did this all start?"

Frank picked up a glass near the sink and started toweling it dry with the dirty rag he'd wiped his hands on a moment before.

"San Francisco," he said. "A week or two ago. Then Phoenix. This one that they're talking about was last night. Down in Austin, Texas. Poor schmuck still had some clown makeup left on his face from Halloween."

"Creepy," Joe said, and took another swig.

"Make you think twice about who you go home with after last call, that's for sure," Frank said, turning away. "Excuse me."

The bar owner shuffled into the back with a stack of glasses, and Joe noticed the old man at the end of the bar was staring at him. The guy looked at least sixty-five, with long silver-speckled black hair matted around his ears and collar. A two-day growth of beard salt-and-peppered his wrinkled, sunken cheeks. His eyes were black in the low light of the bar, but Joe could see clearly that the man was grinning.

"They're coming," the man said, head nodding vigorously. "Oh yes," he said, getting up from his stool and moving quickly to the exit. His eyes never left Joe as his hands pushed the door open. "They're coming."

Joe's heart leapt.

"Who's coming?" he asked, but the man was already through the swinging door of the entryway. Joe jumped off his stool and went after the man, pushing through the swinging saloon-style doors and pressing his shoulder to the heavy wooden outer door that he'd come in through.

The air was cooler outside, and the handful of streetlights did nothing to blot out the velvet black sky awash with pinpricks of light. There were a couple cars parked on the Main Street, but the lights in the shop windows on either side of the bar were out, and there was no sign of the old man. The breeze tickled the hair on the back of his neck.

"Who's coming?" he murmured to himself, and stepped back inside.

In his head, he heard only laughter.

Bram Stoker Award finalist

MARY SANGIOVANNI

FOUND YOU

Those two simple words were like a death sentence to Sally. She recognized the voice, straight from her nightmares. The grotesque thing without a face, the creature that thrived on fear and guilt, had nearly killed her, like it had so many others. But it was dead...wasn't it? Sally is about to find out that your deepest secrets can prey on you, and that there's nowhere to hide...for long.

In the small town of Lakehaven something has arrived that can't see you, hear you or touch you, but it can find you just the same. And when it does, your fears will have a name.

ISBN 13: 978-0-8439-6110-2

To order a book or to request a catalog call:
1-800-481-9191
This book is also available at your local bookstore, or you can check out our Web site **www.dorchesterpub.com** where you can look up your favorite authors, read excerpts, or glance at our discussion forum to see what people have to say about your favorite books.

WATER WITCH

Dunny knew from an early age what it meant to be an outsider. Her special abilities earned her many names, like freak and water witch. So she vowed to keep her powers a secret. But now her talents may be the only hope of two missing children. A young boy and girl have vanished, feared lost in the mysterious bayous of Louisiana. But they didn't just disappear; they were taken. And amid the ghosts and spirits of the swamp, there is a danger worse than any other, one with very special plans for the children—and for anyone who dares to interfere.

DEBORAH LEBLANC

ISBN 13: 978-0-8439-6039-6

EDWARD LEE

What bloodthirsty evil lies buried in the basement of a New York City brownstone, waiting for its chance to be reborn?

When Cristina and her husband moved in, they thought they had found their dream house. But Cristina can feel something calling her, luring her, filling her dreams with unbridled lust and promises of ecstasies she'd never thought possible. The time has come for the unholy ritual performed by the...

BRIDES OF THE IMPALER

ISBN 13: 978-0-8439-5807-2